THE
BODY
IN
GRIFFITH
PARK

ALSO BY JENNIFER KINCHELOE

The Secret Life of Anna Blanc

The Woman in the Camphor Trunk

THE BODY IN GRIFFITH PARK

An Anna Blanc Mystery

JENNIFER KINCHELOE

SEVENTH
STREET
BOOKS®

Inquiries should be addressed to
Start Science Fiction
101 Hudson Street, 37th Floor, Suite 3705
Jersey City, New Jersey 07302
Phone: 212-431-5455 www.seventhstreetbooks.com

10 9 8 7 6 5 4 3 2 1

ISBN: 978-1-63388-540-0 (paperback)
ISBN: 978-1-63388-541-7 (ebook)

Printed in the United States of America

For the Camp Run-A-Muck cousins: Samara, Clyde Seamus, Ali, and Sam. And, for the little run-a-mucks: Persephone and Calliope. And for Emma, who I don't see nearly enough.

CHAPTER 1

Anna Blanc searched the officers' kitchen for her kipper tins, but her kipper tins were gone. "Biscuits," she swore under her breath. One of the cops was a thief. Now she wouldn't get breakfast. She rummaged and found a jar of honey. As no one was watching, she opened it and began to eat from it with a spoon.

The doorknob turned. Anna hid the honey jar behind her back.

Detective Joe Singer slipped in, crooning to himself. "Oh Lou Ann, make me a lucky man." He was the police chief's son and a delicious sight, especially given he was holding a dinner pail.

When Joe saw Anna, he quickly shut the door behind him. "Sherlock, I haven't seen you in days. I went to your apartment last night and you didn't answer." He crossed the room, ducked under her hat, and kissed her. "Mm. Honey sweet."

Anna pulled away. "You're going to get me evicted if my landlord sees you. He's already warned me. And someone's eaten my kippers," she said in despair, her stomach growling. "And if you want to see me, then quit the Chinatown Squad."

"I just did." He reached behind her back, took the honey jar out of her hands, and gave her a peanut butter sandwich from his dinner pail. She pulled back the wax paper and forced herself to take dainty bites.

"I threw pebbles at your bedroom window. You had to have known it was me." He took hold of her fingers. "Unless there's someone else who throws rocks at your window."

Anna slipped her hand from his and whispered, "Not here. I'll get fired. The mayor would love an excuse to get rid of me."

"Then where?"

"I don't know. I wanted to let you in. Maybe next time disguise yourself as a lady. The landlord can't object to a lady."

Joe cocked his head thoughtfully. "Hm."

The door opened again and Detective Wolf entered, looking slick and reeking of lavender aftershave. He flashed a pearly grin. "Good morning, honeybun. Young Joe."

Anna looked everywhere except at Joe, as if he wasn't there at all, as if she hadn't just been holding his hand. "Good morning Detective Wolf. I'm sorry I was late. I . . ." Anna had forgotten to make up an excuse for her tardiness, and sleeping in seemed like a paltry reason. "I . . . found some orphaned children in the street . . . I . . . instructed them in goodness and fed them Cracker Jacks. And I gave them my own clothes to wear. Even the boys." Then she kicked herself.

Wolf grinned. "I'm sure they were very grateful, Assistant Matron Blanc." Then he looked from Anna to Joe and back again. His face turned serious. "Don't let that boy get you fired. I like having you in the station."

Anna lifted her chin. "I don't know what you're talking about, Detective."

"I'm serious, Joe. If Matron Clemens or Captain Wells suspect you two are courting, honeybun is quits." Wolf poured himself a cup of coffee.

"We aren't courting. We don't have time," said Anna.

Joe shook his head. "I would never get her fired. Then I would never see her."

"Detective Snow said he saw you two spooning in the stables last summer. Told everybody. So, I told everybody Snow was just mad at Assistant Matron Blanc because she made him look like an ass. Some believed me. Some wanted to spoon with honeybun themselves. That's a precarious balance." Wolf stirred sugar into his coffee and paused before departing. "So, for heaven's sake, when you two leave, leave separately."

§

Joe and Wolf left first. Anna waited, wiping her sticky fingers. She smoothed her badly ironed skirt, shirtwaist, and mannish white tie—the hideous uniform of an LAPD police matron. She had accessorized that morning with a towering ostrich-feather hat. It barely coordinated but was the only element of her dress she could aesthetically stand behind.

She perched on the table where someone had been reading the *Los Angeles Herald*, and perused the society pages. Mrs. Hashbarger was hosting a costume ball to raise money for the opera. Several ladies she knew—ones younger than Anna's twenty years—announced their engagements. Edgar Wright, her former fiancé, was spotted at the Huntington's garden party along with the mayor, several bankers of her acquaintance, and their wives. Anna had not been invited. Of course not. She was disgraced. She frowned. The Huntingtons served the best foie gras.

Anna checked her wrist watch. Five minutes had passed, and Matron Clemens would be waiting for her. She slipped out onto the station floor. On the outside, Los Angeles Police Department's Central Station had a sort of civic grandeur. Built of heavy granite blocks, it had multiple stories to accommodate the jail, receiving hospital, quarters for the matrons and surgeons, and stables in the basement. On the inside, it smelled of men, cigarette smoke, and despair.

Anna adored it.

She clipped upstairs to the women's department. Ladies had their own steel cells and their own receiving hospital crowded on the second floor, kept separate from the men's department, juvenile department, booking desks, and interrogation rooms below.

At the top of the stairs, Matron Clemens and Captain Wells

chatted in the corridor outside the windowless storeroom where Anna had her desk.

Matron Clemens had charge of all the police matrons at Central Station, which is to say, she had charge of Anna. The two women were responsible for:

1. The well-being and reform of every derelict woman and child in the city of Los Angeles;
2. Preventing every other woman and child from going astray;
3. Preventing future hoodlums from being born, and;
4. Generally dealing with "the girl problem."

Anna's employment was somewhat provisional given that she'd taken the job under false pretenses, did not meet the hiring criteria, and her tenure had been riddled with scandal. It was a holy miracle that she still had the job. But Captain Wells gave Anna special dispensation because she had solved four major crimes—five really, if you counted the headless Chinaman. Also, Anna was exceptionally nice to look at. Even so, she wouldn't be allowed to rest on her laurels. Matron Clemens had made that perfectly clear.

The stress of it made Anna want to turn to the bottle, which she would not do because intemperance was unwise. Also, her whiskey bottle had spilled, and she lacked the funds to buy another.

Anna bobbed a curtsy to Matron Clemens and Captain Wells. Matron Clemens gave Anna a strange look, which Anna could not interpret. After entering the storeroom, she thought she might know why. A mammoth bouquet graced Anna's desk. It was the size of a watermelon and stuck out in all directions with greenery and odd combinations of flowers. It was strangely beautiful, arranged in a crystal vase, and did not have a card. Anna's stomach flipped.

She glanced up and spied Joe sauntering toward her through the storeroom door, scowling. The flowers, she deduced, were not from Joe.

Anna plopped down and began typewriting. As she wasn't much of a typewritist, she typewrote flapdoodle. Adflpwmccorejp;! She looked down, studiously consulting her ink blotter, and lowered her voice for Matron Clemens's sake. "I don't know who they're from, and I love only you."

"That's the second parade float you got this week."

"Yes, Detective Singer. It's not my fault at all. This time, I don't even know who's sending them. Men read about me in the papers and get ideas."

He looked concerned. "Do you like flowers?"

"No," she lied, and then whispered truthfully, "I like detectives."

This made him smile. He strolled around the desk, casually inspecting the flowers from all angles. "That's the weirdest bouquet I've ever seen."

"It's the thought that counts."

"What's this?" He fingered a frond of thick green leaves. "I've never seen this before."

"It's milkvetch."

"It's ugly."

"Yes, but it means something in flower language."

"What?"

"Flowers aren't just flowers. They stand for things. And milkvetch means . . ." Anna's eyes rolled to the ceiling. "Um . . . Your presence softens my pain."

"So, you soften this man's pain?"

"Not intentionally."

"What does this mean?" He touched a flower.

"That's clematis. It means mental beauty. He's very perceptive." Anna lifted a little white ball of flowers with her index finger. "And this is sweet alyssum—worth beyond beauty. He's not shallow."

"And this?"

"Cardamine. It stands for paternal error. He's got that right. This is bearded crepis, which signifies protection. I feel much safer now. Jonquil—he desires a return of affection. Not likely. Peruvian heliotrope—devotion." Anna widened her gray eyes. "That isn't easy to get. It actually comes from Peru. He must be devoted. Volkamenia—may you be happy."

"How could you possibly know all this?"

"We had a book in our library—*The Language of Flowers*. It had hundreds of flowers in it."

"And you memorized it?"

"I had nothing better to do. I wasn't allowed to do anything."

"What's this then?" He pointed to a star of dark green leaves.

Anna squinted in thought. "Woodbine? I can't recall." She crossed her arms. "Are you here to hound me about flowers?"

"Nope. There's a kid we need you to track down. He's truant for one, and he's the leader of a shoplifting ring. His name's Eliel Villalobos, and he hangs out at Chutes Park. I've heard he picks people's pockets during the Civil War reenactment. He recently pawned the mayor's watch."

This wasn't all bad news. At least Anna got to go to Chutes Park. "What does he look like?"

"Like an angel. He's ten." Joe handed Anna a mugshot.

The child did indeed look like an angel. Anna wasn't fooled by his wide eyes and rosebud lips. She took the photograph. "I always get my man."

§

Mr. Melvin, the clerk, received all deliveries at Central Station. He was a small, timid man with bad skin and a tiny mouth that made him look like a turtle. When Anna spoke to him, she never stood too close lest he retract into his shell. She liked him very much. Also, he was crucial for getting to the bottom of the flowers.

Anna approached him smiling and all but shouted so that everyone could hear. "Good morning Mr. Melvin. Who brought in the flowers for the patients in the receiving hospital? Was it the ladies of the Temperance League again?"

"Yes, Assistant Matron Blanc, the Temperance League," he said in a remarkably loud voice, given that he was Mr. Melvin.

"How kind." She softened her voice and leaned near him. "Who was it really?"

"The same man as before," he whispered, leaning away from her, looking down at his papers, never meeting her eye. "He wore diamond cufflinks."

"Hm." Anna wrinkled her forehead. "And the . . . delivery man? He wouldn't leave a name?"

"No."

"Please tell the Temperance League to stop sending me flowers." As Anna did like flowers, she added, "Unless he really feels he must." Upon further reflection, she amended, "Though, I don't like them nearly so much as whiskey."

"I will tell the ladies."

"Thank you, Mr. Melvin." Anna smiled at the top of his head. He was looking at his shoes.

Anna spent the afternoon at Chutes Park, riding the roller coaster and merry-go-round, and visiting the seal pond and monkey circus. She watched the Civil War reenactment intently, but Eliel Villalobos was nowhere to be found.

§

The next day, Anna found a bottle of very fine Canadian whiskey in her desk drawer tied with a gillyflower, which stood for "bounds of affection," and it made her heartbeat quicken. The gift bore no card. She didn't think Joe could afford such benzene; it was her father's brand. It came, of course, from the flower talker. She hadn't really thought he would give her whiskey, though she was very glad he did as whiskey was more healthful than bouquets since it could be used medicinally.

Once again, she sought out Mr. Melvin to confirm. Before she'd even said hello, he'd whispered to his typewriter, "He brought more flowers, but I told him what you said, so he took them away and brought the whiskey. I thought it best not to leave it on your desk. Should I discourage him?"

"Yes," said Anna, shaking her head "no." "As a police matron, I'm not allowed to court. And I'm certainly not allowed to drink whiskey even though I might want to very, very much."

"I'll give him the message, then."

"Thank you," said Anna.

It was Thursday. Though she had half a city to control or reform, her first priority was Eliel Villalobos and Chutes Park. She had not yet ridden the giant boat water slide. She stepped out onto First Street, which rushed like a river of people, horses, and machines. She paused to pet Bob and Dollie, two white horses hitched to a police wagon. There were a dozen LAPD bicycles parked out front, two Indian motorcycles, one ambulance, and one black-and-white police car with a gold star. None of them served her transportation purposes. Cycling was difficult in her uniform skirt, and the police chief would die of apoplexy if a woman were to drive their precious police car. The ambulance went but eight miles per hour, had no brakes, and required a passenger to help bring it to a halt.

Anna headed off to the trolley stop. The cool morning mist seeped through her sleeves, but she ignored it. She had already passed Second Street, when she decided to turn back to retrieve her coat. From one block down, she saw a man leaving through the front doors of Central Station. He was young, overtly wealthy, uncommonly handsome, and possibly Spanish or Italian. Something at his wrist caught the March sun and sparkled—a diamond cuff link.

He was, she deduced, the flower talker—her whiskey man. He'd returned.

Anna watched from across the busy street. This man had gone to great lengths to communicate with Anna—perhaps all the way to Peru. It was imperative that she immediately . . . she did not know what. She knelt and picked up a rock, reached into her purse, wrapped her fine linen handkerchief into a ball around the stone, and took aim. She threw her handkerchief across the road, thus signaling she was amenable to contact. Not because she needed another beau. No. Two beaus would cause a fist fight and Anna quite liked Joe's nose the way it was. She simply felt curious. Was he a botanist? Did he speak Spanish?

The wad caught her secret admirer square in his jaw and sent him stumbling back a step. His eyes widened in surprise. The wrapped stone bounced off and landed in the gutter. He bent to pick it up and glanced about perplexed, rubbing his jaw. Anna yelled across the street. "My stars, I must have dropped my handkerchief."

The handsome man didn't hear her. By the time Anna managed to cross the busy street, the whiskey man was gone, and her handkerchief lay trampled in the mud.

She shrugged. It didn't really matter to Anna. No matter how rich and handsome he was, her future was not with the whiskey man. After several misstarts, Anna finally had love in her life, just like a Valentine's card. Well, perhaps not *just* like a Valentine's card. There was nothing quaint or charming about the way she felt toward Joe Singer. She wanted to eat him.

She swished through the station doors, casting a sideways glance in the direction of Joe's desk, the place her eyes inevitably wandered. There he sprawled, scribbling in a notebook and sucking on a peppermint. Her pulse thump thumped.

Anna waited for Joe to look up, but when he did, he glowered, no doubt still angry about the flowers. He wasn't being fair. She had no control over admirers. She couldn't help that God had made her beautiful.

But Anna was a professional and did not glower back. She sent him her most matronly smile, which she feared only thinly veiled her true sentiments—that she wanted to know what he looked like naked. She licked her lip.

His frown vaporized, and a crooked grin stole across his face.

Anna waited five minutes in the officer's kitchen before Joe stole in and locked the door.

Anna whispered, "Don't lock the door, it's suspicious." She unlocked it.

"Why do we have to wait to get married? Marry me this afternoon. I want you now."

"Have me now."

He locked the door.

Anna unlocked it. "No. What if Snow is watching? Tonight, I'll leave my window open. But you must be prepared to move my things if my landlord catches you. I'd have to find another place to coop."

"We'd get married and I'd move you into my apartment."

"My things wouldn't fit. And besides, it's too soon. I need time. Months at least. Years maybe. I will marry you, but I've only just secured my independence. I can't simply give it up."

"I told you, Anna. I'm not going to make you do anything you don't want to do."

He looked so sincere and so delicious, she almost believed him. Almost. It wasn't that she didn't trust Joe Singer. He never deliberately lied. It's just that men were so accustomed to bossing women, they no longer even noticed.

"Oh, I want to." She took his hand and played with his fingers.

Joe leaned over and locked the door.

Anna unlocked it.

He took a deep breath. "I have an idea. You're searching for that kid, Eliel Villalobos. You've searched Chutes Park, right?"

"Right."

"Why don't you search the regular parks. I myself am going to Griffith Park. We've had a tip that the men who robbed the bank in Boyle Heights were hiding out there."

Griffith Park comprised three thousand acres of mountainous wilderness squished between Los Feliz and Glendale. It had once belonged to a wealthy rancher, Don Antonio Feliz, and should have gone to his niece, Petronilla, upon his demise, but due to some shenanigans with a false will, she got nothing. Luckily, she was able to curse the land, dropping dead on the spot, thus sealing the curse with her own blood. People had been dying ever since. The last owner, Griffith J. Griffith, had donated it to the city to get it off his hands and avoid the chain of misfortune, ruination, and death. Regrettably for Griffith, it didn't work. Cursed or no, it was a perfect place for hiking or hiding.

Anna squinted. "That robbery was weeks ago. Surely the bank robbers are gone by now."

"Yeah, but what if they've come back? I'm obliged to be thorough. Like I said, I'm going all by myself. And I was thinking, truants hang out in parks. Why don't you go search the park all by yourself? There's a particular spot I know about, very secluded, which would be a perfect spot to look, all by ourselves."

"Oh," said Anna, her heart beating faster. "Oh, yes."

"Tell Matron Clemens . . ." He locked the door, leaned in, and kissed her slow and peppermint sweet. "Tell her finding truants takes time. Tell her you'll be gone for hours."

§

Anna freshened up before leaving to hunt for truants alone with Joe Singer. When she bounded down the stairs, her mouth salty from brushing her teeth, matron Clemens intercepted her. "May I have a moment, Anna?"

Anna took a sharp, shallow breath, fearing she was in trouble for something she hadn't even done yet. Matron Clemens strode upstairs, into her office, the embodiment of authority, Anna in her wake. Anna quickly concocted a story about how she hadn't gone to Griffith Park to make love to an officer, which felt like a lie, though at present it was entirely true. Then another chilling thought crossed her mind. What if Snow had seen them going into the kitchen alone?

Matron Clemens looked stiff and cool, in contrast with her cozy office. The place resembled a grandmother's parlor. An afghan draped across the back of a blue settee. A giant needlepoint of a shepherd, which some poor woman must have gone blind producing, hung framed on the wall. Doilies melted on the furniture like snowflakes. All it lacked was a piano for singalongs.

Of course Matron Clemens's office would be homey. The lady worked most of the time. The station was her home, though she had ten children somewhere in a house on Hill Street, cared for by a relative. If one had to have ten children, it was a sensible way of dealing with the problem.

Matron Clemens closed the door, indicating for Anna to sit in a rocking chair. Anna did as commanded. The superintendent's face was unreadable, her voice matter of fact. "When you were hired, Detective Wolf somehow got the impression you were married."

Anna laughed mechanically. "Yes. Isn't that a strange misunderstanding? I don't know how he would have gotten that impression." She held her breath. She knew very well how Wolf had gotten that impression. Anna had lied.

"I suppose Wolf made a mistake," said Matron Clemens.

"An easy mistake to make. I look very married." Anna arranged her face matrimonially—that is, she tried to look grown-up, haggard, and a bit sour.

"It's preferable to have a married woman, Assistant Matron Blanc—someone who's world-wise, so to speak. Captain Wells has allowed you to stay because you've proven yourself useful. But, in response, the police commission has imposed a set of rules, which apply to unmarried police matrons."

"In other words, they apply only to me."

"That's right." Matron Clemens paced in a circle. "I opposed them, for the record, but I have no say." Her lips tilted down, and she extended a piece of paper for Anna to take.

Anna read aloud. "Do not leave town without permission. Do not keep company with men. Be home between the hours of

8 p.m. and 6 a.m." Anna glanced up, wide-eyed. "But I'm often still working . . . Do not smoke or imbibe. Do not loiter around ice cream shops, dance halls, or skating rinks? That's where the bad girls are. How can I reform them if I can't go where they go? Do not dress in bright colors? Do not dye your hair? Do not wear any dress more than two inches above the ankle? Do not get into a carriage or auto with any man except your father or brother? I don't have a brother. And you know my father has disowned me. So, am I not to ride in cars and carriages? I can't take a cab?"

"I don't have time to monitor your activities, Assistant Matron Blanc. You are primarily responsible for patrolling yourself, but the men are watching. I will trust you to do the right thing." Her superintendent looked at Anna blankly.

Anna nodded, unsure whether Matron Clemens thought the right thing was to obey the rules or ignore them. Thankfully, patrolling the more secluded corners of Griffith Park all by herself was not explicitly on the list. And matrons were allowed to keep company with officers for police purposes. And who knows. She and Joe might actually find a criminal. Or a truant.

CHAPTER 2

When Anna got off the trolley near the least popular entrance to Griffith Park, Joe was leaning up against a wooden rail looking more delicious than the man from the Arrow shirt collar ads who enticed every woman in America. He wore a pack on his back with a beer bottle peeking out the top, and held a Mexican blanket rolled up under his arm.

The marine layer was burning off in the warming winter sun. A red-tailed hawk made lazy circles in the sky. No one was around, just oak trees, hills, and, higher up, the sun-soaked chaparral—sage, cacti, yucca, and manzanita. Joe wasn't taking in the scenery. He was looking at her with a strange expression, which Anna could not read.

"Detective Singer." She used his title in case they were being observed from the bushes. "Fancy meeting you here. I'm hunting truants. And you?"

"I've scoped the place, Sherlock. We're alone."

"Except for Don Antonio Feliz and Petronilla." She called to the sky and raised her gloved hands, "We come in peace."

The hawk landed in a tree above their heads.

Joe laughed, but his smile quickly disappeared, replaced by that inscrutable expression, and he ceased to look at her, once more puzzling Anna. Was he in pain?

Anna hurried to Joe, slipped her arms around his neck, and leaned in to kiss him. He made an anguished sound and turned his head. Her kiss landed firmly on his cheek.

"What's wrong? We're here to hunt truants. You always want to . . . hunt truants."

"I do. More than anything."

"Good." Anna moved to kiss him again. Again, he dodged her lips. Anna frowned in puzzlement.

Was this Petronilla's foul hoodoo? Was Anna now cursed, repulsive in the eyes of Joe Singer? What had she ever done to Petronilla? Anna hadn't stolen her land.

"Sherlock, you know about . . . hunting truants, right? Someone has explained this to you? Your father? No, not your father. The nuns, maybe? Okay, maybe not the nuns."

"I . . ." Anna's cheeks flushed pink. "Of course," she lied, and laughed, and looked everywhere except at Joe. Despite her keen powers of deduction and extensive reading, when it came to marital matters, Anna remained just where society wanted her—in the dark. She knew some things, for example, that men had to do it, and women weren't supposed to. Men liked it. Women did not—at least that was the party line. This was clearly a mismatch and an oversight on God's part. She knew that men paid prostitutes to do it and then despised them for it. But as for knowing specifics, Anna didn't.

No one would tell Anna about the marriage bed. Not her married best friend Clara, who merely giggled and said, "You'll see." Not Madam Lulu at Canary Cottage, who stopped the prostitutes from giving Anna details. Not every bride's guidebook, *What a Young Wife Ought to Know,* which was so vague as to be useless and had no pictures. Not her mother, who passed when she was just a babe.

Joe Singer would tell her. He was the only one. It sent a warm flood of love surging through her body. She could always count on Joe. Always.

But if her innocence was part of his reticence, she dared not ask. Thus, she assumed what she hoped was a knowing expression and waited for him to show her. She felt Joe's eyes studying her, and her composure slipped. She looked down.

He made another agonized sound. "Maybe we shouldn't do this. Maybe we should wait until we're—"

"No, we shouldn't wait."

"It hurts the first time."

"I know." She hadn't known.

This sent her imagination racing. How could making love to Joe Singer possibly hurt? No doubt it was some divine booby trap. Worth it, though, she thought, if it only hurt once.

She glanced up at him. "Did it hurt you very badly?"

"Anna, it doesn't hurt men. Only girls."

Her blush deepened. Wasn't that just the way of the world.

Joe lifted his hat and ran his fingers through his hair. "If anyone found out, you'd be ruined."

"I was already ruined in the papers."

"And fired."

Anna sighed. "How could they possibly find out? Joe, you always want to—"

"I do, but . . ." He made that anguished sound again. "I don't know, Anna. Are you sure? Maybe, we should look for some bank robbers."

This was definitely Petronilla's doing. Joe Singer had always wanted to make love. Always. And he did now, too. She could see the battle behind his eyes.

"I'm sure." Though hunting bank robbers was a close second. Pain or no pain, she was wholly committed. She wanted to do whatever it was that people tried so hard to keep her from doing. And not just to spite people.

She wanted to.

Possibly, she was a man inside.

"No. I just can't ruin the girl I love."

"This isn't you. This is Petronilla talking."

He laughed. "I don't believe in ghosts or curses."

If Anna hadn't before, she did now. And she didn't like to be laughed at. "Fine. If you don't want to make love to me, I'll . . . I'll make love to myself." Anna frowned. She knew she wasn't making sense. She kicked herself.

Now Joe was staring at her with a crooked smile. He said in his lover's voice, "Really?"

Above them, Bee Rock clung to the mountain like a hive in the sun.

Joe took Anna's hand and pulled her off onto a side trail, which looked more like a coyote road than a proper path. He dragged her bushwhacking through the chaparral, around a rocky outcropping, and into a secluded haven protected by oaks, but with a view of the hills and in the distance, Glendale.

The spot was so romantic, it would make nuns feel like spooning. Joe retrieved the blanket from the pack and spread it out on the ground.

Anna smiled. She had won. She had bested a ghost.

Joe pulled her against him. "I do want to make love to you. More than anything." He lifted her chin with one finger. "What you need to know about . . . hunting truants is that I love you. I want to grow old with you. I'd do any crazy thing for you, provided it's legal. And maybe even if it isn't."

Anna nodded. She knew it was true. Joe Singer never lied.

"Me too," she said.

"The rest—it's too beautiful for words."

"Too beautiful." She closed her eyes and presented her lips.

Joe kissed her. He kissed her again. His kiss was melting fiery and burned with all the intensity of their situation, and all the passion required to overcome it—her innocence and eagerness, his experience and reticence, the danger he posed to her career, and the ghost of two dead Angelinos.

Joe drew her down onto the blanket.

CHAPTER 3

The wind rose suddenly, carrying with it an ungodly odor.

Joe lifted his head. "What is that smell?"

Anna smelled it too. She gagged a little at the scent—like rotting pork in a sweet sauce.

He groaned. "I'm finally alone with the girl of my dreams, and some creature decides to die in the most romantic spot in the park."

"It's probably a possum. Can't you find it and fling it off the hill with a stick?"

Anna slid off Joe so that he could stand. His hair poked out in odd directions from Anna's caressing fingers, but he still looked good enough to eat, and the front of his drawers was pooching out most interestingly. She was starting to see the shape of things.

Anna rose gracefully in her drawers and chemise, stuffed her feet into unhooked boots, and took his hand. She wasn't going to miss one moment of touching him, stench or no. They turned in a circle, sniffing the air.

"It must be upwind." Joe licked his finger and held it up, then tugged her toward the edge of the hillside and a panoramic view of the city below.

Anna saw a trail of ants marching in a row and followed them. There, near the edge, she saw the source of the smell.

A dead man lay on his side with a hole in his head. His hair and face were covered with ants, as if they found whatever oil his barber used particularly delectable. A revolver lay in his limp, open hand. Los Angeles spread out before him.

"Jupiter, a deado," said Anna. "It's the curse."

"Holy hell."

"You think somebody corpsed him?"

Joe moved closer, "I don't know."

Anna noted that Joe's underwear no longer pooched out so dramatically. Her own skin had grown suddenly cold. This dead man was killing the mood. Petronilla had foiled her lovemaking with Joe Singer after all, something she'd ached for since he'd first kissed her on a police sting operation last summer. She didn't know when they'd get the chance again. But while there was nothing in the world she loved more than spooning Joe Singer, there was one thing she loved just as much.

Catching killers.

She might get to help with this case.

Take that Petronilla.

Joe stood reverently. "Looks like he shot himself in the head, poor fellow."

"Are you sure?" Anna let go of Joe's hand and squatted, trying to ignore the bare, muscular legs now at eye level, and moved forward, examining the ground like an Indian tracker. She felt a breeze through the split in her two-piece drawers.

"Oh Lord," said Joe.

"Only one set of footprints, and they are clearly from the victim's own ant killers, by which I mean feet."

"Anna, not a step closer. How would I explain your little footprints near the body?"

She stood. "Say you were having a lover's tryst. They don't care what you do. Just don't say you were making love to me. Because they'd hang me."

He strolled toward the body. "Turn around and walk back."

Anna's upper lip twitched and she didn't move. He was bossing her.

"Sherlock, it's not worth it." Joe returned to her side, took a scowling Anna by the hand, and dragged her away from the death scene, back to the blanket and the pile of their clothing. He pecked her on the lips. "Anna, sweetheart, I'm sorry. We'll hunt for truants another day—"

"We'll have to find a different spot. This one's spoiled now."

"Marry me and we won't have to find a spot. We could make love every night, all night, in your great big canopy bed. Mornings too. And vacations. Mercy. Think about vacations. We could go to the courthouse tomorrow."

"Mm," said Anna, considering. It did sound like heaven.

He bent to pick up his pants and shook them out. "Now, I'm going to hike back to the trailhead and use the call box to send for the coroner's wagon. You stay here and guard the body in case vultures or a coyote or some hiker stumbles on it. Keep every living thing away from the scene. There better not be any girl footprints when I get back."

The corner of Anna's mouth twitched. He was still bossing her.

He appeared to read her thoughts and threw up one exasperated hand. "Sherlock, I outrank you."

"Just say the footprints belong to some other girl—a lost hiker or . . . or a prostitute—"

"I'm not gonna lie."

Joe and Anna somberly dressed themselves—an unhappy event, so unlike the joyful removal of their clothing. Anna sighed as she watched him button up his trousers. He smoothed her hair and straightened her tie, but she would not meet his eyes. Then, she watched Joe's wool-clad backside disappear behind the outcropping. She was alone with the corpse and the ghosts. She stared miserably in the direction of the body, which she could smell but could not see. Now she could neither hunt truants with Joe nor help determine whether the death was suspicious. As usual, Anna was denied everything good. "Curse you back, Petronilla."

She drew a picture of a gun in the dirt with her toe. She drew a picture of Joe in his underwear with a mysterious point in front. She scanned the sky for vultures, just in case, and saw a condor soaring overhead on giant wings. It was a lovely sight, but she'd rather be looking at the deado. It was a cock shame that she was a woman, because if she were a man, she could make love to Joe Singer and examine dead bodies with impunity. But as she was a woman, the two things she wanted most were denied her.

It wasn't fair, just like tight corsets, no votes, and submission to husbands.

And so, Anna did what any lady would do in her situation, faced with grave injustice, alone at a potential crime scene that was begging to be investigated.

She tiptoed to the body.

It was a gruesome sight. The man's head lay turned to the side as if watching the view down the mountain. His face teemed with ants, making it hard to discern his age or features. His thick hair, stiff with pomade, looked absent of gray. His mustache curled up just so. His suit was new and made of fine material, but the color was ugly—some kind of orangey, greenish, brownish herringbone. She checked for a label but found none. No doubt the tailor did not want to own that suit.

Anna circled the body as if she were a dancer and he were her partner of sorts—one with a propensity for vacuous staring. She wrapped her hand in a handkerchief, picked up his hand, and tried to bend his fingers. They held stiff. He remained in the peak of rigor—dead no more than thirty-six hours. Given that his hand was ambient temperature, she thought at least fourteen.

His silk tie was fiercely ugly. The man had money, but no taste—something his family should have contained. Had he no family? Were they dead, estranged, or just far away? She unbuttoned his coat and dug through his pockets. She found no wallet, no calling cards like a gentleman might carry, just a cheap, dirty handkerchief with no monogram and a salacious-looking dime novel that she wouldn't mind borrowing. In a coat pocket, she found a bottle of headache medicine with the name of a pharmacy in Oklahoma City. A small amount remained. Perhaps his family, who should be monitoring his wardrobe, was yet in Oklahoma. She put the bottle back.

She noted a depression marring the ground beneath his knee. Tiny pebbles stuck to the ugly wool at that knee, partly embedded in the fabric. Anna squatted again to heave the body over to its original position so that his hand once more lay near the gun.

Joe would return any moment, so Anna picked up a branch and swished it over each of her footprints until they were eradicated. Then she tossed sand, gravel, and a handful of dried leaves over the spot to hide the marks.

Then she noticed other smooth spots in the dust.

§

When Joe returned, Anna was dressed and waiting back in the place he'd left her. "Thanks Sherlock. Now, you'd better get down the mountain before the coroner comes and sees you."

"I think we should check the gun for fingerprints."

"Um hm."

"Remember, 'Every contact leaves a trace.'"

"I know Locard's Exchange Principle."

"Did you read Locard's *L'enquete criminelle*? Because it's in French, and I didn't think you read French."

"I read a translation."

"I read the original."

"That doesn't mean you shouldn't hightail it down the mountain." He treaded on soft dirt over to the body. He whipped around and glared at her. "Speaking of leaving a trace, Anna, you examined him. I can tell you wiped your footprints away. It's too smooth here."

"No. Those aren't mine."

"Don't try to deny it."

"I'm not denying anything. My wiped-away footprints are on the other side of the body, more artfully disguised and sprinkled with leaves. I'm not the first person to erase my footprints from this crime scene. I will also note that he was kneeling when he shot himself. He died backward execution style—that is, shot in the forehead." Anna lifted her skirts thigh high and dropped to one knee, knowing very well her stockings would get ruined, but figuring it would be worth it. "If you roll him over, you can see the impression from his knee and the tiny rocks embedded in his pants. His pants are dusty everywhere, but there are only rocks at his knee. Then he fell sideways like this." She fell, catching herself with her palms. She rolled over and showed Joe the resulting mark on the ground and on her stocking.

Joe considered her carefully. He moved to the body and examined the knee. "You're right, Sherlock."

"Of course I'm right. Somebody put him out of business. And I can't believe, after all we've been through, you're not letting me help."

"Anna, if they find out we were in the park together, you'd lose your job, and I would never see you. I happen to love you, so just get down the mountain and on the tram before the coroner gets here."

§

Anna returned to the station and the sharp scent of convicts and cigarette smoke, wiping her feet vigorously on the mat at the door. She took out her handkerchief and brushed dirt from the tops of her boots. She glanced up to find Wolf observing her closely.

"Where you been Assistant Matron Blanc?" he asked.

"Hunting a truant."

"You got dirt on your boots."

"So."

"What do you bet that when Joe comes through that door, he'll have dirt on his boots."

"Why would you say that?"

"I'm a detective, remember? He telephoned from the call box at Griffith Park. Honeybun, if Matron Clemens or Captain Wells suspect you've been fraternizing, you'd be fired and there's nothing I could do to protect you."

"What if I'm not the fraternizer? What if I'm the fraternizee?"

"Then they'll blame you for being a distraction. But if Detective Singer is giving you trouble, you come to me." He grinned, promising trouble of his own.

Matron Clemens clipped over, her white tie starched to perfection. Anna's tie had dirt on it.

"Good Morning, Detective Wolf. There you are, Assistant Matron Blanc. I've been looking for you. Did you accomplish your task?"

"Sure did. Didn't you, honeybun?" said Wolf.

"Why, yes. I did. Positively," Anna lied. Truthfully, she hadn't accomplished her task with the truant or with Joe Singer. "That is, I looked for Eliel Villalobos."

"Good. That's all we can do," said Matron Clemens. "I'm going to address the Friday Morning Women's Club tomorrow. They are starting an effort to find employment for girls who would like to escape a life of sin, and they've asked us to help them. Assistant Matron Blanc, you know some of the girls in the brothels. Are there any you know who might want to change their lives? If you could find someone to give her testimony, I'm sure it would help with fundraising."

"Yes ma'am."

"Very good." Matron Clemens clipped away.

Wolf leaned in close to Anna. "I know how you are. You saw the body and you're going to want to get involved."

"Of course I want to be involved. He was shot, backward execution style."

"But you can't. You've got to forget about the body and concentrate on your matron duties. Find jobs for prostitutes. Watch lost kiddies. Look out for lady prisoners."

"I can do both."

"I'll tell you what. If we need to question a female suspect, I'll ask for you in particular."

CHAPTER 4

Anna wished she could accomplish her mission—to recruit prostitutes for the Friday Morning Club meeting—without going to the parlor houses. It wasn't that she minded the girls. They had always been kind to Anna. But she had far too many bad memories. As she could not avoid going—it was a matron's duty—she would at least try to finish before dark.

Hurrying to the trolley, Anna passed a newsie hawking the *Los Angeles Herald*. He looked all of nine, but his shrill voice pierced Anna's ears. "Evelyn Nesbit Shaw Seeks Annulment from Marriage to White's Slayer. Read all about it."

Anna despised the *Herald* but bought the paper for a closer look at Mrs. Shaw's hat. The brim was small, the feathers voluminous. She wished she knew what color it was. She then noted another headline of interest. "Local banker commits suicide." Anna squeezed her eyes shut. So many bankers had fallen on hard times when the Knickerbocker Trust Company collapsed last year. So many banks had failed, including Blanc National, her father's bank. Anna could have saved the bank by marrying Edgar Wright, who had been rich enough to solve all their problems. He was handsome, pleasant, and young. He loved her. But she had chosen to go undercover in the demimonde to save women from a killer. Neither Edgar nor her father had forgiven her. Now Anna was disowned, and Mr. Blanc was ruined. She didn't know how he fared.

And so, Anna feared opening her eyes—afraid that the name of the suicide victim would be Christopher Blanc, and she would be culpable. Culpable and doubly culpable. She was, after all, on her way to the demimonde now.

She stilled her trembling hand, bravely opened one eye, and read. The banker wasn't her father. She didn't know him. She exhaled in relief.

§

Anna disembarked from the trolley on New High Street. Madam Lulu's brothel, popularly known as Canary Cottage, did not properly open until after dark. It stood three stories high and was colored like Christmas, with red bricks, green trim, and heavy scarlet drapes. It was nearly enough to put Anna off the holiday. Seven flea-bitten cats stalked and pounced in the yard, with several more strays roaming the adjacent empty field. Anna could hear ragtime piano being played and it ran circles on her insides, which twisted with anxiety. She had gone undercover in this particular brothel when hunting the New High Street Suicide Faker, the killer who targeted parlor girls. She had gambled her family, her reputation, and her fortune to dispatch that villain. She had put a stop to the murders at great personal cost. As she saw it, Madam Lulu owed her.

She knocked hard and loud on the familiar side door and waited.

A painted bird of a woman, middle-aged and thick-waisted, answered—Madam Lulu herself. She wore a red satin robe—a bad copy of a Japanese kimono—and her dyed coiffure looked slept on. Her dried lips were stained with rouge.

Anna liked the lady. Madam Lulu closed one eye as if looking through the sight of a gun. "Well if it ain't Anna Blanc."

"Aren't you pleased to see me?" asked Anna guilelessly.

"That depends on why you're here." She opened the door so that Anna could enter.

The décor was lush and vulgar, like the woman herself. The room went on forever. Scarlet carpets covered the floor; chandeliers with icicle crystals hung from the ceiling. A life-sized oil painting of a woman in a partial state of undress smiled brazenly from the wall. There was a floor for dancing and two concert grand Steinway pianos. Balconies overlooking the grand salon encircled the two upper floors. Doors on the balconies led to bedrooms. Stairs led to balconies. It smelled of cigars, spilled whiskey, and Madam Lulu's rose perfume.

A strapping man, middle-aged and Negro, pounded out ragtime piano for two young women who sat on the floor playing cards in afternoon frocks. He was, she suspected, Madam Lulu's lover. Anna smiled and offered them a little wave. The women waved back. She didn't know them. A different girl in an Arabian-style costume practiced her hoochie coochie on the dance floor, rolling her hips and belly to a sultry, imaginary tune that was nothing like the ragtime music.

Madam Lulu scratched her powdered nose. "Benzene?"

Anna considered. If she had to be here, she deserved whiskey, but wasn't sure whether Madam Lulu would charge for it. Limited by a matron's salary, Anna needed her money for other things—like to pay for the new revolver she'd bought on credit, and those two children she had tracked down and now kept in the country because she felt responsible for their mother's death. She folded her hands primly before her and perched on a velvet settee. "No thank you."

Madam Lulu waddled over to the bar and poured Anna a drink anyway. She put the whiskey in Anna's hands. "Don't be ridiculous. It's on the house."

"Thank you." Anna took the glass and tossed it back. The familiar, pleasant burn warmed her throat and soothed her nerves. It wasn't as nice as the whiskey man's whiskey, but it wasn't as bad as her own.

Madam Lulu plopped onto the couch beside Anna. "Now why are you here?"

Anna had to raise her voice above the music. "The Friday Morning Club is starting an effort to find employment for any brothel girl who wishes to reform and earn an honest living."

"So, you're trying to rob me of my girls?"

"I imagine some of your girls would rather not be treading the primrose path. Surely you wouldn't begrudge them that. Last summer, when I was undercover, Charlene mentioned she planned to quit."

"Charlene is getting old. She's twenty-five if she's a day."

"So, you see, this could be a good thing for your more senior girls. Planning is in the very early stages. Right now, I just need a girl to testify to the ladies at the club meeting tomorrow. Tell about her troubles and woe so that they will donate money to the cause. Then we can, I don't know, open a hat shop or something."

"A hat shop."

"I'm merely speculating, but yes." Anna's eyes brightened with the brilliance of her idea. "The girls could trim hats. Then we could sell them and make a bundle."

"A bundle," Madam Lulu said flatly.

"Of course, they'd need to be tasteful hats if we wished for them to sell." Anna frowned. "So, we could only really help girls with good taste." Anna brightened again. "Although girls with bad taste could make hats for customers with bad taste, so we could help everyone!"

Madam Lulu relaxed back against the settee and stretched. "I'll tell you what. You want to try to recruit my girls for your little hat shop, Princess, you be my guest."

From Madam Lulu's smile, Anna felt like there was something she didn't understand.

"I shall then. Perhaps I should speak with Charlene first. She's thought about this. She could give the speech to the ladies."

"What speech?"

"About how she planned to live a life of virtue, but things came up, etcetera. So now she's forced to live a life of sin and how she'd do anything for a chance at being an honest woman again."

"So this is what you've been up to?"

Anna's brow wrinkled. "I'm working a new case. I don't suppose you'd know anything about a man in an ugly suit murdered in Griffith Park?"

"Nope."

Anna stood. "Then I should be off."

Madam Lulu's puffy hand turned palm up. "Not so fast. That'll be fifty cents."

"For what?"

"The whiskey."

"Fifty cents is steep, and all I have is my trolley fare. And you said—

"Princess, that was before I knew why you was comin'."

§

Anna returned to Central Station late, in the dark, and sweaty from walking. Also, she'd stepped in gum. She stuck to the floor with each gummy step. But at least she'd convinced Charlene to speak to the Friday Morning Club the following day.

Anna stayed at the station long past dinner, waiting to interview a confused old lady—a witness to a robbery. It was a gift from Wolf, the most senior detective. It wasn't a murder, but it was police work.

"A beat cop is bringing her in. She'll be here any moment." Wolf flashed his teeth at Anna and held her eyes too long.

A tired Joe Singer dragged into the station, along with six cops in muddy boots and five men in handcuffs, only now back from Griffith Park. Anna's heartbeat quickened as she watched the captives. Murder suspects?

Wolf gave her a warning look. "Mind your own business, Assistant Matron Blanc."

"About what?" She blinked innocently.

From across the room, Joe began casting her smoldering glances so that she could barely concentrate on the criminals. He sauntered by and whispered, "Marry me."

It weakened Anna's resolve, and if a justice of the peace had been present, she might have succumbed. Luckily, there was no justice of the peace. She would have to avoid them at all costs.

CHAPTER 5

The meeting at the Friday Morning Club began boring, grew interesting, and then exploded. Attendance was excellent for eight in the morning. A hundred women crowded the assembly room wearing hats with brims so wide they touched.

There were forty-five minutes of gavel bangs and monotonous business before the first speaker, an elderly woman in her fifties. Her chin barely cleared the podium, yet she boomed, "Why is it that men who will protect so carefully their own women—wives, sisters, and daughters—from even an evil thought are willing to degrade other young girls, who only lack the same help and protection? Only when the sterner sex advances from their hopeless attitude of moral apathy can social regeneration begin."

The ladies clapped.

"Something is terribly wrong. Do not attach blame to fallen girls. Do we blame flowers that grow awry and force their shoots in the wrong direction through lack of proper supports? No! Women should be less concerned about protecting their sons and husbands from the vampire and more concerned about providing support to girls . . ."

The lady went on about women's responsibility to mother fallen girls and then ended with a bang. "The former reticence on matters of sex is giving way to a frankness that would startle even Paris. I hereby declare that it is sex-o-clock in America!"

Anna's ears perked up and she clapped loudly. Regrettably, that was as frank as it got.

Next, a woman of Anna's acquaintance—a Mrs. Morgan—came to the podium. The lady no longer acknowledged Anna after last summer's scandal. She was a tight-lacer with a tiny waist that made Anna's own small middle seem average at best. The tight-lacer wore a tasteful gown that pooled on the floor behind her in a silk train. Somehow, the lady found the breath to ramble on and on about fallen women and how though some had chosen a life of sin (she glared at Anna), most were hapless victims who simply required opportunity to be redeemed and elevated once again, although they couldn't be truly elevated because, once stained, virtue could never truly be unstained.

Then she said, in far too many words, that there were but two want advertisements requesting female applicants in the *Herald* that day, and that all other solicitations went through the YWCA, and that the YWCA placed women of good reputation only. Thus, there existed a need for job placement services for bad women, because, otherwise, who would hire bad women? And who would write their letters of recommendation?

Anna thought of the many respectable men who frequented the brothels and might write very nice letters of recommendation—the mayor, Detective Wolf, Edgar Wright, her father . . .

It was time for Anna to usher Charlene up to the podium. The prostitute wore bright coral ruffles on her tall, generous frame. The frock looked appropriate for vaudeville or even the circus, but not a ladies' club meeting. Her hat burst with multicolored feathers. She pivoted to face Anna and whispered anxiously, "How do I look?"

Anna squinted at the gown just so, until Charlene blurred into something perfectly lovely, though perhaps not a lady. Perhaps a life-sized balloon animal or a giant tropical flower. "You look beautiful, like a hibiscus," Anna said.

Charlene beamed.

Anna led Charlene to the podium. The tight-lacer moved aside, curling her lip at Anna in a look of disdain. Anna accidentally stepped on the lady's white silk train. It left a gum mark. The lady didn't notice. Anna accidentally did it again.

Charlene began her speech quietly, mumbling to the floor. Even Anna, standing at the side of the stage, could barely hear her.

The tight-lacer returned to the podium. "My dear, you must speak up."

Charlene began again, louder this time. She told how she had been an innocent child bride—just fifteen—and how her drunken husband beat her. Worse yet, he had whipped her baby children.

Rows and rows of decorated ladies listened attentively to Charlene's testimony, clucking in dismay at her suffering. Their sympathy and approval filled the room like perfume. Charlene bloomed under the attention of these decent ladies—glowed even. She stood up straighter and drew out her story, louder and more passionate with each moment granted her by the rapt crowd. She relayed how she had run away under the cover of a moonless night, two babes in tow, penniless and afraid, how Madam Lulu had taken them in, and how Charlene boarded her children with a family in the country. She talked about shame and humiliation, and how she would do anything for a different occupation, so she could hold her head up high again, because deep down, she was still just an innocent girl. How she longed to be respectable for the sake of her children.

Charlene absorbed their sympathy with the holy countenance of a martyr. She went on to praise the ladies for their goodness with a flowery speech that grew into a veritable garden. "I honor thee, and thee, and thee for thy beautiful mercy and thy love, plenteous like the ocean fish . . ."

Anna hung on her words, utterly mesmerized. Charlene should be in sales or religion or something.

Then, it was time for questions and gloved hands went up. The tight-lacer pointed to a lady who repeated her question three times before she could be heard. "Are you willing to work hard?"

Charlene, hands modestly folded, replied, "Yes ma'am. I do work hard."

The tight-lacer called on another woman, who bellowed, "Don't you trust our Lord for his provision?"

"I trust our Lord for *your* provision." Charlene pointed at the lady, which was rude, but effective.

The tight-lacer closed her eyes and nodded. She nodded and nodded, like a patient, knowing sage. Then, she raised her arms in a grand gesture of benevolence. "My dear, we have prepared for this moment and would like to offer you a position."

The room erupted with ladylike clapping, muted by gloves.

Charlene's eyes widened. She lifted her own arms as if to embrace the crowd and pronounced solemnly, "I accept. I hereby leave my life of sin." The ladies rewarded her with furious applause.

"Do you see what good there is to be done?" said the tight-lacer. "How simple it is. But we require your financial support. We will open a home for fallen women, guide them, train them as domestics, musicians, stenographers, and bookkeepers, and find them positions. But *you* must open your hearts and your purses—"

"What is the position?" Charlene interrupted.

The tight-lacer's brow line rose and her lips pursed, as if the question were irrelevant or Charlene ungrateful for asking it. "Selling musicale tickets at houses. A respectable occupation, and good exercise."

"Huh," said Charlene and scratched her elbow. "Selling door-to-door. How much does it pay?"

The ladies laughed as if the question were funny, but Charlene's expression was stone serious.

"Well, that depends on your work ethic. It's on commission."

"Well, what can I expect?"

"Perhaps six dollars a week, if you try hard."

The ladies clapped. Anna, who knew how much prostitutes earned, cringed.

"Six dollars a week, my ass. I can make that in an hour." Charlene snapped her proud head and marched off the platform, through the crowd, and out the door, like an angry giant hibiscus.

Anna politely swept through the dumbstruck ladies, in pursuit of Charlene, making her apologies. "Excuse us. Pardon us."

The tight-lacer tracked Anna with a hard glare, as if society's ills were all Anna's fault.

Outside, Charlene stomped up the sidewalk, her bright hat feathers shaking. Anna jogged to her side. Charlene trembled like her plumes. "I'm sorry, but six dollars a week, my ass."

"My ass," said Anna in solidarity. Who could blame Charlene? Six dollars a week wouldn't keep Anna in Cracker Jacks.

Charlene wiped an angry tear. "I've saved some money. I'm going to open a business. I just need to know how."

"A hat shop, maybe?" Anna asked.

Charlene glanced at Anna with cautious hope. "Maybe."

"Well, I'll buy a hat, and then we'll show them." Anna considered Charlene's bright feathers. She would buy a hat, but she didn't promise to wear it. But maybe other prostitutes would. Anna had an epiphany.

Charlene could start a business supplying prostitutes.

CHAPTER 6

When Anna returned to Central Station and opened her desk drawer, to her consternation and delight, there lay another bottle of Canadian whiskey, this time bound with tussilage. The flower was not native to America and must have been very hard to get. It was scraggly and looked rather like a dandelion, but it smelled like heaven, and Anna liked its meaning—justice shall be done you.

Wouldn't that be nice? To be dealt with justly. For the men to give her credit. For the unfounded rumors to subside. For her father to own her again so she wouldn't be all alone.

The dapper rich man had struck once more and very close to her heart. If it were just up to Anna, she would happily receive anonymous whiskey from him until the end of time. She couldn't see the harm in it. Clearly, he could afford it. And wasn't it more blessed to give than to receive? Anna would be blessing the man. But if Joe found out, he would get mad. If Matron Clemens found out, Anna might get fired. She suspected God wouldn't like it either. Anna scribbled a note.

Dear Unknown Man,
    Please desist in giving me whiskey. I insist, unless you absolutely must.
    Sincerely,
    Anna Blanc

Now no one could fault her, not even God. She reluctantly gave the note to Mr. Melvin to deliver to the man the next time he appeared with a bottle. "And please, get his name. I'm dying with curiosity."

He shook his head and whispered, "I've tried. He won't say."

"He's very odd." She sighed. It grieved Anna to cut off her free supply given the state of her personal finances. She hadn't had much time for whiskey, but she might need the benzene to console herself once Matron Clemens heard about the mishap at the Friday Morning Club.

It occurred to Anna that if she were the first to relate the events of that dreadful meeting to Matron Clemens, she could perhaps spin the retelling in her own favor. She looked about to assure that the coast was clear, took a swig of the whiskey, and headed for Matron Clemens's office.

§

"Hello Matron Clemens," said Anna, her neck stretched like a defensive yet beautiful ostrich, her voice tinny and tight. "There was an interesting development at the Friday Morning Club. The ladies, though well-intentioned, were previously misguided and had misconstrued the plight of the parlor girl. Luckily Charlene was able to help them see—"

Matron Clemens sat at her desk rubbing the skin above her pale, sparse eyebrows. "I heard. It's not your fault, Assistant Matron Blanc."

"I know?" Anna chirped, cocking her head. She was surprised by the verdict though she agreed wholeheartedly. Of course it wasn't her fault. Even Charlene had done nothing wrong, really, if you pardoned her French. And club ladies would do far more good teaching the prostitutes skills, like saving and accounting and how not to swear in front of ladies, so prostitutes could open their own lingerie factories or hat shops or something. But realizing this didn't make the ladies of the Friday Morning Club any better disposed toward Charlene or Anna.

Matron Clemens continued. "The clubwomen are somewhat sheltered, but they are resourceful and well-intentioned. There wouldn't be police matrons if clubwomen hadn't pushed for them. They care about girls who are unprotected. And there are fallen women who would work for six dollars a week."

"I suppose so," said Anna, feeling glad for her own position. If she were ever to lose it, she would have to marry Joe Singer right away. And they would be up all night making love. She could sleep all day, but he would have to go to work and would never get any sleep at all. And then what? He might fall asleep on the job, which might be okay, as he was the police chief's son. Likely, the captain would simply send him home to sleep, but he wouldn't sleep. Not when they could be making love. Then he would fall asleep on the job again. And what if the police chief was replaced because of a corruption scandal, which seemed to happen every six months in Los Angeles, and God knew that Joe's father was overdue. Without his protection, Joe would get fired for falling asleep on the job.

It was a quandary—one she did not have to face. Not yet. She should focus on her own job, so as not to lose it.

"Assistant Matron Blanc, are you listening?"

"Sorry. Yes. I think the club would do better to help the girls open businesses. Many of them have savings."

Matron Clemens tapped her lips three times in thought. "Very good, Assistant Matron Blanc. I'll propose it."

While Anna basked in the cool glow of her superintendent's approval, Mr. Melvin appeared in the doorframe, a young girl at his elbow. She looked about fifteen and as fair as a snow goose. Her mouth was hard-set.

Mr. Melvin stared down at a jail-made rag rug on the oak floor. "Excuse me Matron Clemens, Assistant Matron Blanc. I heard about the Friday Morning Club meeting today, and this girl is looking for employment. Can you help her?" The shy clerk slipped out of the office without making eye contact or waiting for an answer.

"Please have a seat." Matron Clemens gestured to the rocking chair.

The girl plunked herself down and began to rock—back and forth, back and forth, the wood clicking with each oscillation.

Matron Clemens seemed unperturbed by the girl's odd behavior. "And you are . . .?"

"Matilda Nilsson," said the rocking girl softly, whispering to the floor with the hint of a childish lisp. "I want honest work."

"We were just discussing that it's hard to find a job that pays well."

"I'd take anything."

"You are a prostitute?" Anna saw no need to beat around the bush.

The girl's eyes remained on the floor. "No. I mean, I was bewitched into it, and then it was too late. And I have nowhere to go." She looked up at Anna. "But if I had a position . . ."

Anna leaned closer. "Who bewitched you? Because I don't think that's legal."

"Officer Snow already told me the LAPD won't help."

Anna wrinkled her nose. Matron Clemens's face remained neutral. "So, trouble has found you, has it?"

"Yes. I met this woman, Mrs. Rosenberg, at the train station—"

Matron Clemens leaned closer. "So, you've just come to Los Angeles?"

"Yes, from Iowa. My father's wife bought me the ticket. She raised me, but I'm not her child. She has other children—a daughter my age." The girl's pale face colored. "I'm . . . illegitimate . . . It was Christian of her to raise me, but I lost a sewing needle, and that's wrong so she put me on the train to LA, so I wouldn't freeze, but so I wouldn't come back either."

And Anna had thought her father overreacted. She patted the stiff, rocking girl's shoulder. "But, of course, you have relatives here? Your father's sister, or—"

Matilda shook her head. "I don't know anybody. Mrs. Rosenberg said she would help me find work and brought me to her boarding house for professional ladies. She was very kind and invited me to dine in the café next door as her guest. I'm willing to do any kind of proper work, and I hadn't eaten since Iowa. But then she wasn't kind."

"Oh?" said Matron Clemens.

"She introduced me to men. And one man seemed very keen to know me. I tried to be polite because he was Mrs. Rosenberg's friend, and because he was a guest on our planet."

"Pardon," said Anna.

"He's from Mars."

Anna cocked her head. Matron Clemens said evenly, "Go on, Matilda."

"I didn't like him." The girl rocked some more. "He came in a space ship and wanted to see how we slept on earth. He kept waving his spindly green hands. The next thing I knew . . ." She stopped rocking abruptly and made a single, sound of despair. "I woke up with no clothes in a hotel."

"I see," said Matron Clemens.

Matilda leaned back in the chair and began to rock once more. She lisped, "He left eighteen dollars on the table, but it was Martian money, and he left a note. It said he wanted to see me again and that I should wear my hair down. After he left, Mrs. Rosenberg came to bring me home. She took the money. She said I had to split it with her, but she kept it all because half was for room and board. Of course, I left her establishment, but a gang of boys started following me, and they dragged me into an alley and ripped my frock, but some people came, and I got away.

"So, I came back to Mrs. Rosenberg and I've been staying there ever since. I ate at the café, because I have no other means of eating. The man from Mars came back and he wanted me to go with him again. He waved his spindly green hands, but I closed my eyes, so he couldn't bewitch me. He keeps leaving me notes. I can't find employment, and now I'm going to have to leave if I can't pay my rent. I'm afraid of the boys."

"Where is this apartment building?" asked Matron Clemens.

"The Jonquil Apartments. They're on South Hill Street."

Anna didn't know the place. Matilda continued to rock back and forth, back and forth. Anna's eyes followed her until she felt dizzy—or was it her story that made her dizzy? "Do you have any of the notes?"

Matilda produced one from her pocket and handed it to Anna. It was on plain stationery with no monogram and read:

Dear Matilda,
    You may as well go with me as you have no other option.
Am I really so odious?

The answer was yes. Anna felt sick. She put the note in her pocket. "Will your father take you back?"

"I won't go back there." Her pronouncement sounded final.

"Well, then," Matron Clemens said in her matter-of-fact tone. "You can stay here in the women's department tonight, if you don't mind sleeping in the jail. Then, we'll see what is to be done."

Matilda's mouth curved slightly, briefly, and her dim eyes registered . . . not hope exactly. Perhaps relief.

"Can you sew?" asked Matron Clemens.

"Yes ma'am," said the girl.

"Then you can help sew linens for the inmates. If you're quick, maybe you'll sleep on them tonight." Matron Clemens winked. It was the first time Anna had ever heard her make light conversation.

The older woman continued, "Assistant Matron Blanc, please get Miss Matilda situated."

"All right." This seemed like a rather large task. A green man from Mars? The girl clearly belonged in the giggle-giggle ward of the bat house. The question was, did the girl's insanity conjure the man from Mars, or did that bewitching man at the Jonquil, and the harm he did the girl, cause her to crack?

§

On that particular day, there were no empty cells in the women's ward or the juvenile ward. As usual, several women had sought shelter to avoid sleeping on the streets. A woman with a broken nose hid from a violent husband who she would not turn in. Others had been arrested for public drunkenness and couldn't make bail. Still more awaited trial for a variety of crimes—one for shooting her husband, one for forgery, and one for leading a shoplifting ring. Four were badly behaved socialists. Anna rather admired their verve. In total, forty ladies crowded the women's department. A few of these ladies came with children, and some children came on their own, being lost or having run away. Two women, who had failed at committing suicide, recovered in the women's ward of the receiving hospital. Any more women and they'd spill over into the men's department, which meant Anna would have to spend the night guarding them to protect them from the jailer, who was known to make advances.

The only place left for Matilda was the "cow ring," a locked steel box with barred windows where up to twenty women shared cots that had been added to accommodate the overflow. The unfortunate nickname had been coined after the "bull ring," the largest cell in the jail, which had cots for thirty-five men imprisoned for minor offenses, though it routinely housed up to fifty. Like the bull ring, the cow ring held prisoners who weren't too terribly evil. They could possibly be trusted with scissors.

Which did not preclude them from smelling.

Anna consoled herself that at least the linens were boiled weekly to keep lice at bay. "You don't have lice do you? I'd hate to shave those lovely locks. But I could wrap your head in lard."

"No."

She ushered Matilda to the cow ring and unlocked the steel

door. Thirty-eight eyes rose to meet them. Unlike male prisoners, the ladies wore street clothes—either their own shabby garments or cast offs provided by the matrons. Most lacked coats, though the station got cold at night and jail blankets were thin. Each lady shared her three-foot-wide cot with another lady inmate. Women lounged or sat on their cots with little space in between them. About half were sewing. A few shelled peas or peeled potatoes. No one tried to escape when Anna opened the box and came in with her charge.

"Good evening, ladies." Anna graciously inclined her head. "May I present Miss Matilda Nilsson of the Iowa Nilssons. Matilda, these are, well, ladies."

There were nods, mutterings of "hello," and one drunken cackle that sent shivers up Anna's spine.

A tall wicker basket overflowed with unfinished linens, and a broad, short basket held sewing things. Anna dug through the linens and found the young lady a sheet that needed hemming, a thimble, a needle, and some thread. This was the limit of Anna's sewing ability, though virtually every woman who came through the jail seemed an expert. "You know how to do this, right? Of course you do. Who wouldn't?"

The girl stared grimly at her cellmates. "Thank you." She took the sewing things from Anna, walked to the last empty space on a cot, and sat down.

It occurred to Anna that, Martian or no, the man at the Jonquil Apartments should be investigated. The girl was underage, at least on this planet, and Anna would bet her last jeweled hatpin that the girl had been wronged. Anna wanted to do the investigating, as detective work was her true vocation, but someone might need to be arrested, and matrons had no power of arrest. Still, wronged girls would not speak to male cops, at least not the savvy girls. She would ask to accompany whichever cop she could persuade to go to the Jonquil—hopefully Joe. She wished she had a twin sister, or two triplet sisters even, so one Anna could solve the murder in Griffith

Park, one could investigate at the Jonquil, and one could handle the myriad of other tasks stacking up on her desk.

Anna made a general announcement to the women in the cow ring. "Excuse me, ladies. A young man's been murdered in Griffith Park. I don't suppose any of you know anything about it?"

The ladies shook their heads, no. Of course, they didn't know, but she had to do something. She had not yet had a chance to ask Joe about the men he had collared.

Anna did a quick walk-by to check on the rest of the lady prisoners and refugees from the streets who were paired among five smaller cells. They also knew nothing of the murder. They seemed peaceable, each sitting on their cot, crowded so close together their knees almost touched. One jailbird was giving pickpocketing lessons to the others in the cell. Anna watched intently, and then practiced.

At six o'clock, a jailer would come and take the real prisoners downstairs to eat in the dining room. The room had long white tables and smelled like a jail, a hospital, vegetable peels, and an old mop, all mixed together. Certain male criminals, those deemed trustworthy, prepared the food. The cops called such helpful prisoners "trustees," and they paid for their good behavior by becoming slaves.

Jail food was slop by any measure and there was no dessert. Even so, refugees from the streets weren't invited to dine. The city paid for food for criminals and hospital patients only. Anna would have to feed Matilda and the others by some different means, or they would get air pudding. She checked the donation closet in the storeroom. There were crackers, moldy cheeses, and great, fat dill pickles. Anna thunked her forehead with her fist. She should have made a pitch at the Friday Morning Club before the debacle, but she'd missed the chance and now they'd be disinclined to give. Perhaps Matron Clemens had money left over from a previous collection. They could buy bread and lard, or something.

All this woe and Matilda's insanity weighed heavily on Anna's heart. There was no end to it, no solution, beyond offering women wages they could live upon. But even that wouldn't help the crazy women, the suicides, and the drunks. Anna said a silent prayer to Saint Dymphna, Patron Saint of the insane, that she would . . . that she would . . .

Anna didn't know what to pray for, so she simply said, "Do something!"

She hoped the saint would act fast. Drunk, dissolute, and criminal women were getting in the way of Anna's true calling—what she really wanted to be doing—solving the mystery of the kneeling man. And making love to Joe Singer. Making love to Joe Singer would make it all go away.

Anna glided down the cold stone stairs with the grace of a duchess, as was her custom when being observed. The station's veterinarian and the police surgeon were blustering in the corridor. They watched Anna closely, both coming and going. She averted her eyes and flounced to the administrative part of the building, leaving a trail of Ambre Antique perfume in the stale air.

In a room full of uniformed cops, through a haze of tobacco smoke, she saw Joe. He sat at his desk in plain clothes, filling out paperwork, pausing, tapping his pen on his delectable lips, tugging on his well-shaped ear, writing again.

The sight took her breath away.

"Detective Singer, may I speak with you?"

When he saw her, he gave her a naughty smile that turned her all to jelly. "The kitchen," he mouthed.

Anna went first. She posed seductively, draping herself across a chair, waiting for Joe, ready for a kiss.

The door swung open and Detective Wolf walked in. He quickly shut the door behind him. "Matron Blanc, will you marry me? I'm serious."

Anna straightened up. "You can't court me. I'd get fired."

"I think we could work around that."

Joe banged open the door and glared poisonously at Wolf.

"I'm going," Wolf said, grinning. And he did.

Joe locked the door behind him. "I want you."

"Have me."

"When? This is killing me. I need a distraction."

"We have a distraction—our kneeling deado. He's our number one priority. You haven't told me about your collars."

"Yeah. I took some men and did a dragnet in the park after you left. We caught some hoodlums and three bank robbers, but nobody I like for the killer."

"You actually found those bank robbers? Those idiots. That robbery was weeks ago. I thought they'd be long gone."

"And, I got a partial print off the gun. It doesn't match our deado."

"I knew it!" On the inside, Anna turned slightly green with jealousy. She wanted to do a dragnet. She wanted to catch bank robbers and like or dislike the catch for the killer. She wanted to take prints. She wanted to trap criminals.

And so, she did. "We need the deado's photograph to show to people to identify the body. I could help."

"I know, Anna. Do you think I'm right off the boat? But we can't use the ones with ants covering his head. Think about his mother. The coroner took new photographs once he'd washed the body. But the coroner's backed up, so it took him a while. They haven't been printed yet."

"We need to send the photographs to the police in Oklahoma City."

"Oklahoma City?"

"The headache medicine in the deado's pocket was from a pharmacy in Oklahoma City. He didn't have time to use it all. There was still a little left. How long does a bottle of headache medicine last? He carried it with him; he obviously used it. Not more than a few months. Our deado must be new in town. The pharmacist might recognize him."

"You are one hanging detective." He kissed her for a full minute. Anna responded with enthusiasm. Joe made a sound of frustration.

"Oh, God. I need another distraction. Something completely unromantic."

"All right." She reluctantly pulled away. "A young girl just came in, clearly underage. She said she was bewitched and seduced at the Jonquil Apartments, and that the man paid her. It sounded like she'd been drugged."

Joe's mouth turned down. "Okay."

"The landlady took the money. She said half was her cut, the rest was compensation for the girl's keep." Anna decided not to mention the part about the man being a Martian. "I thought a matron should go with a cop to investigate. I think you should be the cop."

"I think so too, because Lord knows no one else is going to do it." He pulled her close. "And afterward?"

"Come to my apartment tonight." She planted a chaste kiss on his lips. "Just, dress like a girl."

CHAPTER 7

The Jonquil Apartments looked clean, though modest, had three stories, and was nicer than Anna's own apartment building. Above the door, carved in the stone, were the words, "The Jonquil Apartments for Professional Ladies." The place stood on South Hill Street across from a pawn shop adjacent to a grander building, which, according to Matilda, had a café on the first floor and a bath house and massage parlor on the upper levels. This building had no sign, but Anna could see people dining through the window. Anna and Joe stepped off the trolley at one o'clock—she in her lovely hat and ugly matron's uniform, he in a dapper suit.

"Why wouldn't the café have a sign? Because they don't want customers." She answered herself. "Or they want particular customers, but not others, and rely on word of mouth. Perhaps it's even a private dining club."

Joe linked his arm through hers. "Let's see if they'll seat us. We can pretend we're courting."

"But I'm in uniform."

"You look like a nurse." He eyed her feather hat. "Sort of. And aren't these apartments for career girls? I'm sure some of them are nurses."

Anna unpinned her hat and held it in her hand. She smoothed her hair. "All right. Let's try."

They passed through oak doors into warm air laden with the enticing fragrance of dinner. The café had potted ferns, white tablecloths, and a quiet elegance. While Anna preferred loud elegance, as did most girls bred in the upper class, it was entirely presentable. The maître d' greeted them. He did not match the décor. Though dressed in a maître d's black tails, he was as broad as an ox and had a broken nose, like a prize fighter.

A waiter in a white jacket seated them, and when Joe looked at the menu, he said ominously, "No prices."

In Anna's experience, "no prices" meant the establishment catered to loaded people who didn't care about prices. And yet, when she glanced around, the ladies dining didn't look like they could afford "no prices." They appeared to be career girls from the apartments next door—stenographers or shop girls—in homemade frocks or dresses off the rack. Then she remembered what Matilda had said. Matilda had eaten in the café, presumably as part of her room and board. But the restaurant was clearly open to the public as well. It was both the dining room of a boarding house and a public café.

"Very curious," she said.

"If I tell them I'm a cop, we'll eat for free," said Joe.

"No. Not yet. I don't want to blow our cover. We'll just order something cheap, like coffee."

"Too late in the day. It will keep me awake."

"You're not going to sleep anyway." She winked badly and whispered, "You're coming to my apartment, remember?"

"Anna, it's all I can think about."

The waiter reappeared.

"Two coffees," said Anna cheerfully. "And I'd love a word with Mrs. Rosenberg, if she's in. I'm looking for a room."

The waiter took in Anna, top to bottom. "Mrs. Rosenberg isn't here, but I do expect her soon. Can you wait?"

"Yes," said Anna.

The waiter bowed off.

"Mrs. Rosenberg?" Joe asked.

"The evil proprietress."

"I see," he said.

As they sipped their coffee, Anna secretly touched ankles with Joe while scanning the vicinity. It was the best sort of double tasking. Though her eyes traveled the café, her mind was on the touch of Joe's wool sock and the feel of his warm leg underneath. She wanted to tangle legs with him. Bare, hairy legs. She rebuked herself— not for wanting to make love to Joe—that was natural given his deliciousness. She imagined that every girl in the world, including nuns, would want to make love to Joe Singer, if they knew him. She rebuked herself because she wasn't paying attention. She pulled her leg away, though it felt like moving an anchor. Joe shook his head and hooked her foot with his ankle.

Two men entered who looked to be of the "no prices" variety, with Homburg hats and cashmere coats. One wore an extravagant mustache. It sprouted three times thicker than any other mustache she knew. She wondered if other men were envious—his companion, for instance, whose stringy mustache barely warranted wax. She glanced at Joe, but he didn't seem to envy the mustache. He was heavy-lidded, staring at her mouth.

The bushy man and stringy man gave their hats and coats to the host and slid into a booth, close enough for eavesdropping. They seemed jolly and began to talk about an architectural project down by the shore—some fancy new hotel. Shortly, four ladies swished over and joined them at the table. One looked forty and had lines sprouting from her lips as if she often pouted.

The waiter returned and refilled their cups. "As you can see, Mrs. Rosenberg is back." He glanced toward the pouty woman.

"Yes, I see. Thank you. Two sugars, please." She sat back and let the waiter drop the cubes into her cup.

Joe helped himself to two sugars and added cream. Anna smiled at him from beneath feathered lashes.

He smoldered back.

The second lady was about Anna's age and wore her hair long, like a bohemian. Anna quickly learned her name, Claire, and that she was wild about ice cream and taught piano. The third and fourth girls were identical twins, clearly underage. They dressed with no imagination and mumbled when they spoke. They seemed rather shy but did admit they liked Parcheesi. The well-heeled men doted on the twins, whom Anna found exceedingly boring.

She leaned close to Joe and whispered, "Why do two important men want to chitchat with dull girls about Parcheesi?"

"It's fishy."

Anna frowned, worried for the girls. "Can we arrest Mrs. Rosenberg?"

"We can arrest anybody on suspicion, but the question is, do we have enough for an indictment. What did Matilda say exactly and is she willing to testify?"

"Like I told you. Mrs. Rosenberg found her at the train station and brought her back to the Jonquil Apartments pretending to be a good Samaritan. You know the routine, helping a poor girl, alone in the world. She took Matilda to the café and introduced her to . . . to . . ." Anna blushed.

"What?"

"A green man from Mars."

Joe threw his head back and squeezed his eyes shut. He made a long, slow hissing sound, like a tire losing air.

Anna lifted her chin. "He bewitched her, and she woke up with him naked and in bed."

"We got nothin'."

"Don't dismiss it. Possibly Matilda is dingbatty, but possibly the man wasn't from Mars, but just an ordinary masher who drugged her, and the shame of this has made Matilda crazy."

"Prove it, Anna."

Anna knew Joe had a point. Matilda's testimony would never stand up in court. There were no Martians evident at the Jonquil Apartments. She would have to dig deeper.

Mrs. Rosenberg stood and disappeared into the back of the café just as the waiter returned with the check. Joe examined the bill and blew out a breath. "It's triple what I normally pay for coffee."

"That's what no prices generally means." Anna stood. "Mrs. Rosenberg is getting away. Let's go after her, at least get your money's worth."

Joe took her hand. "Not so fast, Anna. Don't tip her off. Not until we have some proof."

§

Anna and Joe returned to the station, Anna somewhat downcast, Joe slightly exasperated. Mr. Melvin manned his post at the front desk behind the shiny brass rail, having just received the new City Directory. The book lay on the counter like a walrus. Each consecutive volume grew fatter than the one before, like the city it represented. Los Angeles was a magnet, attracting thousands, good and bad from all over the world, including young girls seeking their fortune, running away from something unspeakable, from emptiness, or toward some illusive dream. What were the girls dreaming about? Their choices were so limited. Love and the fruits of love—children? Anna didn't care for children. Certainly no one was dreaming of being a scullery maid or a shop girl. Maybe that is what Mrs. Rosenberg lured them with. The promise of love.

In the language of flowers, Jonquils stood for a return of affection.

Mr. Melvin cleared his throat and gave Anna a meaningful look. She paused, while Joe continued to his desk. Mr. Melvin spoke in his quiet, vanishing voice. "I have a note for you, Assistant Matron Blanc."

"Oh?" Anna's tummy rose and fell like a swing. Was it from the whiskey man, who was not Joe Singer?

Mr. Melvin slipped her a square, once-white envelope, wilted and stained brown with liquid. "I'm sorry, Assistant Matron Blanc. Officer Snow spilled coffee on it." He looked down.

Anna pursed her lips. Anything Officer Snow fouled was foul indeed. She pinched the note between two fingers, wrapped it in a handkerchief, and secreted the thing in her skirt pocket. It wouldn't do to have Joe Singer see it. "Thank you, Mr. Melvin. I'm sure it wasn't your fault. Did the . . . um the ladies' club president deliver it herself? Did she leave her name?"

"No. It was a boy. He came an hour ago."

"And you let him get away?"

Mr. Melvin spoke into his lap. "I promised him fifty cents if he'd wait for you across the street at the soda fountain."

"I don't have that kind of money," said Anna.

Mr. Melvin slid two quarters across the counter to Anna without looking up.

She pressed his hand. "Thank you. I'll pay you back."

He blushed.

Anna didn't examine the envelope until she was outside on the sidewalk. She lifted it to her wrinkled nose. It smelled of narcissus and coffee. The flap no longer stuck, and a little tear near the edge told Anna the note had been previously opened and probably read.

With two fingers, she pried the letter from the wet envelope. The elegant card swirled with embossed vines, gold leaf, and dragon-flies. A soggy Johnny jump-up was pressed inside—velvet violet and yellow, severed from the stem. Johnny jump-ups stood for nothing in the language of flowers. But, Johnny jump-ups were her favorite flower. How could he know?

Anna squinted at the note. The ink was pale, smeared, and mostly unreadable, thanks to Officer Snow's coffee. Following the rather intimate salutation, "Dear Anna," she read, "meet me," and half-way down the page, "jewelry."

At the word "jewelry," Anna's heart began to pound. She knew now that the whiskey must stop, no matter how much she liked the brand. She could read between the runny lines. This man was obsessed with her, asking for a rendezvous and threatening to give her jewelry. It would be wrong to encourage him when she was already in love with Joe Singer.

She would have to meet him. It was the only way to stop the

gifts. Notes certainly hadn't worked, and she didn't think he was dangerous. He looked perfectly respectable when she'd seen him that day on the streets. In fact, he looked rich and exceptionally handsome.

But how? She couldn't rendezvous without the details.

Anna jogged across the street to the soda fountain, hoping the boy courier still awaited his fifty cents. It was after four; school had only just gotten out. The boy must have skipped class, suggesting he was lawless and might be bribed.

Wrought iron ice cream chairs and a few little tables kept company on the sidewalk. Anna swished under the striped awning and through the door. There were potted palms, a black and white tiled floor, and a copper ceiling on which fans twirled. The brass soda fountain gleamed as shiny as a golden mirror.

Anna scanned the long, crowded counter. She noted six boys in knee pants and tall socks, who could possibly be the courier, and three ladies who might meet Anna's own description, depending on whether Mr. Melvin had said "pretty" or "gorgeous." The courier boy might be hesitant to approach given those odds. She could stand on a chair, call the room to order, and ask, but that would be rude. She saved rudeness for emergencies. She must simply deduce her way to the courier.

Two of the boys sported school uniforms, which meant parents who could pay tuition. One of the women watched them. These boys would not likely relay messages for a strange man, not while supervised. A deceptively adorable, but scruffy blond child made loud slurping sounds as he sipped his sarsaparilla—a possibility. Another boy's knee pants were two inches too short, suggesting want, but he was showing off an expensive-looking sailboat to two other boys who ate ice creams. Anna considered the candidates, peering at each in turn, and settled on the boy with the exposed knees. And because she read dime novels, she slipped beside him and said mysteriously, "Fifty cents if you are the right man."

"Miss Blanc? How did you know it was me?"

"Your patron is generous—I should know—and that sailboat is the nicest I've seen."

"Yes. He saw me eyeing it in a shop window and bought it for me. Just like that."

If she ever met the man, she would tell him to buy the child pants as well.

Anna whipped the soggy, smeared note out of her pocket. "Regrettably, there's been a mishap. The note's totally illegible. I need you to tell me who he is and where I was supposed to meet him?"

"I um . . ."

"You read the note, which was very naughty. I already know. And it was intended for me."

"It wasn't as interesting as I expected. But that information will cost you extra."

"Fine. If that's how it's going to be." Anna pocketed the fifty cents and turned to go.

"I don't remember his name. La Placita Church at eight o'clock tonight."

She gave the boy a brilliant smile and proffered his money. The urchin palmed the coins and ran off with his boat.

Anna checked her watch. She needed to leave the station early if she wanted to beat the whiskey man to their assignation. She would rebuff him in no uncertain terms, run home to bathe, change into her most beguiling nightgown, and wait for Joe Singer to come and take it off.

CHAPTER 8

Painted mandalas in rich colors decorated the ceiling of La Placita Church. Portraits of Christ, the Virgin, and the Saints glowed in towering, gilded frames above the altar. Anna wore a black lace mantilla to cover her hair. The sanctuary flickered with candlelight, each tiny flame a petition. She could taste the incense. Anna dropped a penny into the slotted box and lit two wax votives. She said silent prayers to Saint Valentine, patron saint of lovers, first, that the whiskey man would accept her rejection graciously, so she would not need her revolver, and second, that Joe would not get caught when he visited her apartment later that night, lest she be evicted.

A few scattered Catholics knelt in the pews. Ladies, heads covered in lace, sat on one side, hatless men on the other. Their lips moved, breathing the barest whispers of hope, thanksgiving, and sorrow. Anna felt her own sorrows acutely, for they were many—her newfound poverty, having no family, being a woman. Sorrow she knew. But what was Anna hoping for? Specifically, why had she come? She was curious, for certain, and the gifts must stop. Also, the man was a stranger, and Anna's father had repeatedly told her not to talk to strange men—not without a formal introduction. Crossing her father was a joy in and of itself. This whiskey man was rich and possibly knew her father. With any luck, the news of it would get back to him. Maybe he'd be angry enough to forget he'd disowned her and call.

Anna smoothed her gown, a cascade of ivory lace that emphasized her tiny waist. She moved quietly to the rail in front, turned, and checked each prayerful face, her body jumpy with nerves, her hand on the gun in her pocket for reassurance. She didn't recognize the whiskey man among the worshippers and tiptoed back into the narthex. The narthex was vacant, but for a wrought iron candelabra, a coat rack, and a basket of spare lace mantillas by the sanctuary door. She ventured to the front entrance and peered out into the darkness toward the Plaza. Was he late? How long should she wait? She moved to collect her cape from the coat rack.

A man stepped abruptly from a shadowy side door. Anna leapt backward. Her gun arm popped up. She shouted, "Reach for the roof," just as Joe Singer rushed in from outside and clocked the man in the face. Joe's fist felled him.

The man on the ground bled from his perfectly patrician nose. He wore diamond cufflinks and smelled of freesias. It was the rich young man Anna had pegged with her handkerchief on the street. He held up his manicured hands in stylish surrender. They held a mixed bouquet.

He grinned, and in a thick French accent whispered, "Anna, you came." He brought a finger to his lips. "Shh. People are praying."

Anna, still pointing her gun, leaned over for a closer look. He handed her the flowers.

She noted snapdragons. Presumption.

"Thank you." She turned on Joe and hissed quietly, "Are you spying on me?"

"Anna, I found the note on your desk. You had a rendezvous with another man." He perused the man's fine form and expensive suit. "You couldn't expect me to just stay home."

"How could you read that note?"

"I was motivated."

"You'll be comforted to know he's a total stranger."

"That doesn't comfort me."

The man rose slowly to his feet, holding his hands aloft. Anna still pointed her gun, still held the flowers, still wore her mantilla.

"Really *ma chère*, you can put the gun down."

"She's not your *chère*." Joe remained on his guard, his fists balled, his biceps tight. "Whoever the hell you are."

Joe rarely swore, not in front of ladies. It was a misdemeanor, punishable by a fine of two hundred dollars or imprisonment for ninety days. And they were in church.

Anna deduced he must be very mad. He looked so fierce, all flushed and sweaty; it made her tingle. Everywhere.

The whiskey man ignored Joe and spoke to Anna. "Anna, you have nothing to fear from me. I am—"

"She's Miss Blanc to you," said Joe. "Who do you think you are?"

Anna's eyes and mouth widened, and she made a little sound of surprise. "Jupiter. He thinks he's my brother."

CHAPTER 9

The mysterious man nodded. "Yes! I am your brother, Georges."

"She doesn't have a brother." Joe turned and looked at Anna. "You don't have a brother."

"Regrettably, no. I'm an only child—alone in the world. It's been a source of profound sadness—"

"Then why did you think—"

"Woodbine. It stands for fraternal love. I just remembered. Nothing about those floral arrangements was romantic. They symbolized protection, comfort, affection . . ."

Georges addressed Anna in French. "*Ne l'écoutez pas. Je suis ton frère. C'est assez facile de le prouver.*"

"Manners, Mr. . . . Georges," said Anna. "Joe doesn't speak French." She looked at Joe. "He says I shouldn't listen to you."

"Don't call him Georges. You don't know him."

"It would be stupid to address your own brother as Mr. and I told you who I was in the letter," said Georges.

"That part was illegible," said Joe.

"Joe's right. I thought you were another suitor. I didn't know you claimed to be my brother. I couldn't read the letter. The ink was smeared with coffee."

"But the woodbine . . ."

Anna shook her head. "There are hundreds of plants in that book. I'd forgotten the meaning of woodbine until just now."

Georges's eyes widened. "*Oh, la la.* You didn't know, and you came anyway? Anna, you shouldn't meet with strange men."

"That is the only thing he's said worth listening to," said Joe, still tense, ready to spring.

"Hah! I can take care of myself. I've had to." She cocked the gun. "Go on. Say what you have to say."

A priest appeared at the side door. His eyes widened when he saw the gun. He disappeared back the way he came. In a moment, Anna heard the door to the sanctuary lock.

"For years, I did not approach you. I thought father was right. You wouldn't be thrilled to have a bastard brother. You were untouchable, the stainless Anna Blanc."

She smiled sourly. It was no longer true. Stain stuck to her like gum.

"I wanted to do something for you after he cast you out, so I brought you the flowers. Father mentioned you had liked that flower book, so . . ."

"That strange bouquet," said Anna. "That was a clever introduction, really."

"And then you said you wanted whiskey."

Joe threw up his hands, "You asked him for whiskey?"

"Not exactly," said Anna.

"It's shameful the way father has treated you. But he does care, Anna."

Anna winced. She wished it were true. But never once had her father called to make sure she was okay, or sent her a letter, or even a check. He told people he didn't have a daughter, when everyone knew very well that he did.

Anna said softly, "Cardamine. It stands for paternal error."

Joe made a scoffing sound. "What do you want?"

Georges sighed. "A sister. That is all. And that my blood sister is not abandoned to the cruel world alone."

"She's not alone."

Anna was silent for a moment, oddly touched. But for Joe, she was alone in the world. "That's very kind, Mr. Georges." She lowered her gun.

"Father didn't want you to know because it didn't reflect well on him. But now, I think, you need me."

Anna looked at Joe, her eyes widening. "That sounds like father. It's all he cared about—his reputation."

"I reasoned that you were an experienced woman—not the naïve girl father made you out to be. You went undercover in the brothels last summer, no? I thought maybe you wouldn't be so shocked to learn that your father kept a lover. And maybe not so judgmental of your bastard brother."

Anna's eyes truly popped. "Father kept a lover?"

Joe pulled her by the arm. "Let's go. This man is up to no good."

Georges grabbed Anna's other arm. "Anna, stay."

"Let go of her!" Joe said in a tone that gave Anna the chills.

The two men tugged on Anna, which was neither mannerly nor good for her frock. She heard her uniform rip. "Biscuits!" Anna shook them both off violently. Her face felt hot, and her limbs were shaking. A breeze cooled her armpit beneath the tear. "I'm not leaving. Not yet. I want to hear him out."

"And who are you? What does this have to do with you?" Georges examined Joe, like he was merchandise that fell short of his expectations.

"I'm her fiancé."

"Really Anna? A cop?" His words dripped with sticky French disdain.

Joe's brows shot up.

"He's a very good cop," Anna said.

Georges looked him up and down. "Oh, I don't doubt it."

Anna said, "This is Detective Joe Singer. And you are Georges . . ."

"Devereaux."

"Not Blanc?" said Joe.

"I told you I was a bastard. I have my mother's name."

Joe shook his head. "Anna, I don't believe it." He leaned close and spoke low into her ear, "Don't get hoodwinked. You're missing your father and you want to have family. It makes you vulnerable. You don't know anything about him."

"I'm not saying I believe him," Anna said defensively. "But he understands my father's motivations, says 'Oh la, la' just like father, and he's well-dressed and good looking, just like me."

Joe said, "Why arrange to meet her in a church at night? That's kind of shady. Why not meet her at the police station?"

Georges addressed Anna. "You couldn't have your illegitimate brother showing up at the station. It would raise all kinds of questions. You were confirmed in this church."

She looked at Joe. "How did he know that?"

Georges smiled. He'd scored a point. "Church is respectable. Anna, would you really have met me in a restaurant or at my hotel?"

Joe narrowed his Arrow Collar Man peepers. "Why so late? Why meet at night?"

"Police matrons work late. I read it in the paper."

Anna supposed Georges would be considered good looking by any measure, but strangely, she felt nothing for him, not that familiar pull she experienced with beautiful men—especially Joe Singer whose pull was stronger than a riptide so that it threatened to sweep her out to sea.

Could Georges be her brother? Had her father taken a lover?

"Come to my hotel, Anna. We'll talk. I'll call father on the telephone. If you wish, bring your cop."

"She's not going anywhere with you, and certainly not to a hotel," said Joe.

Georges smiled cynically, and for a moment Anna saw a flash of her father.

"Yes," said Anna. "I'll go." She turned and put her hands on Joe's cheeks. "How could he know about my confirmation? About the flower book?"

"Anna. You can't just—"

"My love, you don't get to decide."

CHAPTER 10

Georges lived on the top floor of the Hotel Alexandria, on the corner of Spring and Fifth Streets—the best Los Angeles had to offer. The lavish, eight-story hotel had opened only two years before. All the furniture was fresh and new, opulent, like her father's house, but in the latest style. Everywhere was the sparkle of crystal, the glow of polished wood, and moldings climbing the apartment walls like vines. The windows framed glorious views of her city.

Anna noted cigar butts on an ash tray, and five scattered crystal glasses as if he'd had male company, and no one had cleaned up.

Georges hurried to clear the glasses. "Sorry for the mess. My man is off today. I entertained some friends."

Anna stared at the décor in reluctant admiration. She didn't want to like it too much, not before she knew. Still, she couldn't help but murmur, "It's so *à la mode*."

Georges beamed when he saw her appreciation. "My home is your home, *ma petite soeur*."

A framed picture of Anna's father graced the side table. In it, he was a much younger man. Anna had the same photograph. She supposed Georges could have bought a copy from the photographer. But he also had her father's thick French accent.

"So how are you Anna's brother?" Joe picked up the photograph as if to examine it for authenticity. He set it down. He flicked a crystal dangling from a candlestick. It sang like the real McCoy.

"Anna, you should sit," said Georges.

"And you should put a steak on that eye. It's starting to swell," she said.

Joe gave her a look, like her concern somehow betrayed him. "Let him swell."

"I'll order one." Georges glared at Joe then called the front desk to request raw meat.

Anna plopped down on the most beautiful couch she'd ever seen—all mossy velvet with curved, carved wood. To Anna it looked like a butterfly. It seemed like it could fly away. Like it could fly her away.

Joe wandered around the room, examining it like the scene of a crime that had not yet happened. He picked up a Kodak Brownie that sat on a table, raised the camera to his eyes, and pointed it at Georges. He set it down. A little gray mutt was curled up on a chair—perhaps an Affenpinscher mix. It followed Joe with its eyes, growling softly.

Georges chuckled. "Don't mind the dog. I found her in the streets—a little bastard like me. I suspect she's had a rough past."

"What's her name?" asked Anna.

"Monkey." Georges came and sat beside Anna. She scooted away from him. He smiled resignedly. "My mother was a French dancer. Your father kept her in Paris. Kept us. I'm the first crop. You are the second crop."

"What's 436 times 645?" asked Anna.

Georges eyes flitted to the ceiling. "281,220." He knit his brow. "Why?"

"What's the capital of Uruguay?"

"Montevideo."

"What has green hair, a round red head, and a long thin white beard?"

"Perhaps a radish?"

"How old are you?" said Anna.

"That one is easy. Twenty-seven." He lifted his brows hopefully. "Did I pass?"

"It doesn't mean he's your brother," said Joe.

But Georges had passed this one test. He seemed smart enough to be a Blanc, though Anna wasn't ready to admit it out loud.

Georges continued in a calming voice. "Our father used to keep my mother in Paris. When he moved to California, he brought her with him. We lived at the Fremont Hotel just down the hill from your house half the year. Half here, half in Paris. He visited three, four times a week. Then, I went to boarding school in France when I was eight. I've been back and forth ever since. Last year, I moved here permanently."

Anna took a long, deep, quivering breath and wondered if she knew anything at all about the world. This hard, fast line between the good people and the bad, the decent and the indecent, was leaving very little space for people on the good side. Anna wondered whether, in the end, anyone would remain on the right side of the line. She certainly didn't plan to. She planned to do wrong, beautiful things with Joe.

"Are you upset?" Georges asked.

"Did my father love your mother?"

"Of course. But she was a dancer."

"What about my mother?"

"I . . . I'm sure he did."

"She died when I was very young."

"I know."

"Did my mother know? It must have hurt her." Anna felt pain on her dead mother's behalf, though she was merely a fuzzy memory, like a photograph out of focus.

"I don't know. My mother knew, obviously. Having a mistress wasn't the sin. It was his marriage. But I can't regret it. Father's not the faithful type. And it gave me you."

"So, you knew about me? You always knew?"

Georges hesitated. "Not always, but for a long time."

Joe strode over. "Don't take this to heart, Anna. Not until we know for certain." His eyes fixed on Georges's diamond cufflinks. "What sort of business are you in, Georges?"

"Banking. It's the family business. Right Anna? You should know that, Detective."

"Should I?" said Joe.

Anna shook her head. "No Georges, our family bank went bust."

"Father isn't stupid. He's quite ingenious really. He saw the end coming and divested, transferring his assets to me. He may be reduced in circumstances, but I'm not. And I have other ventures, too."

"And you give him money?" said Anna.

"It's his money, I'm just sheltering it for him."

"It's not his legally. Legally you could take the money and run away to South America."

"Anna, he's my father."

"Well, he's not my father. Not anymore. He won't speak to me. He claims he never had a daughter, even though everyone knows he did. He gave me nothing. Not that I want anything from him. I don't."

"Anna, you don't need him to give you money. In my mind, what he's given me is half yours. Claim it."

"Call your father, Anna," said Joe. "Before this goes any further."

Georges strolled into the hall and plucked up a telephone from a table. "Call the hello girl." He handed the thing to Anna.

She met Joe's eyes as she spoke into the receiver. "Hello, Central. Connect me to the Blanc residence please. 64242."

The hello girl connected Anna and the phone rang. An unfamiliar voice answered—a new parlor maid perhaps. "Good evening, Blanc residence."

"Hello. This is Miss Anna. Is my father there? I wish to speak with him."

The parlor maid hesitated and then sighed. "No, I'm sorry." She sounded very sorry indeed.

"You're not just saying 'no' because he won't speak to me, are you? Because I'm sure he'd want to if he knew what I know. It really is important. I'm . . . um. . . . dying—"

"I'm sorry Miss Anna. He's out." The line went dead.

Anna melted like a candle in the sun. He was home. She just knew it. She glanced at Joe, who seemed unnaturally interested in his shoes. He knew it too.

Ending an uncomfortable silence, Georges said, "We'll call tomorrow. He's probably at his club. In the meantime, can't we celebrate? Get to know each other a little? I have a very good bottle of scotch."

"I don't think Joe would—"

"I'll drink your scotch," said Joe. It sounded like a challenge. He gestured to a cedar humidor. "And, I could use a cigar."

Anna frowned at Joe's deliberate rudeness.

Georges filled a crystal glass for Joe and one for Anna. "I could use a cigar, too, but I don't smoke in front of ladies."

"Oh, that's taffy," said Anna.

"Very well." Georges offered the cedar box to Joe, who helped himself. Joe used a cigar cutter and lighter that rested on the side table. He took a deep inhale, then sent smoke streaming through his teeth. "Good cigar."

"The best you've ever had, I'm sure."

Rude, but true, thought Anna. Joe only smirked.

The bell rang. It was the porter with a cold steak. Georges tipped him and put the steak over his swollen eye.

Anna took the cigar from Joe's fingers and placed it between her own lips. She leaned back and began blowing smoke rings. They floated up and were lost in a splendid chandelier.

Georges grinned and offered Anna the humidor. "Have your own, Anna. No, have the whole box. They've come all the way from Cuba, just for you. They are the best, and you deserve the best." He looked skeptically at Joe and lit up.

"You don't mind if I smoke? Because when Father heard I had a cigarette, there was a big hoo ha."

"No hoo ha. You do as you like. You are a grown woman."

Anna smiled incredulously. Dare she even think it? If she did have a brother. She would want him to be like Georges.

The scotch was very good, indeed, and Anna had another. And another. She kept up with the men, who seemed engaged in some manly ritual, glaring at each other, tossing back scotch.

The air was pungent with cigar smoke.

Georges asked Anna questions about her police work and listened intently as she answered them at length. Joe interjected with sordid tales of what jail was like and the penalties for running cons. Georges spoke of relatives in Paris that Anna had never met—people from a dream.

Georges's steak had made its way to the floor. The little dog hopped off the chair and dragged the meat off into a bedroom.

Anna's face felt hot, and her head began to swim like a disoriented goldfish. She dropped her cigar on the Persian carpet.

Georges got up for another bottle. Anna, whose glass was empty, tilted her head back to watch his progress. He looked like a Blanc, despite his shiner, with long lashes, bright gray eyes, and thick, wavy hair. She smiled up at Georges, who leaned over and kissed her forehead on his way back to his chair.

"Don't touch her!" Joe sprang inelegantly to his feet, knocking over an embroidered footstool. He charged over to Georges, his fists tight.

Georges slurred, "You don't mind, do you Anna?"

Anna said. "Don't sock him again, Joe darling. If he's my brother, I don't see why he can't kiss my forehead."

Joe said, "Who else would know if he's your brother, Anna?" His eyes were glassy from liquor.

Anna pulled fuzzy, scotch-soaked thoughts from her head. "Edgar Wright? They were in business when the bank was failing, when father was supposedly shoveling money to Georges. And borrowing money from Edgar."

Edgar had been Anna's fiancé, but her undercover police work had come between them—especially her undercover work with Joe.

Joe said, "He's not going to talk to either one of us."

"I think he would," said Anna. "Edgar is very decent. And he's in LA. I saw it in the paper."

"You stabbed him."

"It was an accident." Anna picked up the receiver and spoke. "Hello, Central. Get me Edgar Wright, please. 31026. Yes, I know it's very late, thank you. This is an emergency."

Edgar's butler answered and soon her groggy ex-fiancé was on the line. Anna felt suddenly shy. She hadn't spoken with Edgar since she'd burned down his farmhouse. "Hello. Edgar, dear? Are you well?"

Anna threw a glance to Joe to see how he would take this familiarity. His face screwed up.

"Yes, Edgar. You're not dreaming. It's me, Anna. I'm sorry about everything. So, so sorry. Don't hang up. It's important. Wait. Please. I need to know. Do I have a brother? Do you know a Georges Devereaux?"

Anna closed her eyes and let the telephone rest on her chest while she listened. She hooked the receiver back in its stand.

"I can't believe you did that," Joe said.

"Edgar seems fine, a little cranky. He hung up on me, but . . . I have a bastard brother." She turned to Georges and stared wondrously. "Georges Devereaux." Anna took both Georges's hands in her own, her eyes welling with inebriate tears. "I always wanted a brother."

He brought her hands to his lips, *"Ma petite soeur."*

Joe looked displeased. "It's getting late. We have to be at the station early."

Anna gazed up at Georges. "Father still won't speak to me."

"I'll work on him." He smiled, linked his arm through hers, and escorted her unsteadily toward the door. At the threshold, he turned her to face him, both hands on her shoulders. "You will always have me, Anna. I promise."

"And you will always have me," she said, effusively, her eyes tearing up.

Georges extended his hand to Joe. "It was nice to meet you, Detective Singer." As they shook, Georges leaned in close and whispered in Joe's ear, slurring his words. "If you ever hurt her, you will suffer. Believe me."

Joe whispered back, struggling to get the words out. "And if you turn out to be a fraud, I'll make sure you do time."

Anna frowned at her men. It was rude to whisper. She could hear them anyway. But they were both drunk. So was Anna.

When the door closed, Joe took Anna's arm and held it as they negotiated the hallway toward the fancy swirls of the wrought iron elevator, neither steady on their feet.

"It's late, but I don't think I'll sleep. My mind is racing. What if someone sees us leaving the hotel together? I should have worn a disguise—a false nose or something."

Joe lifted Anna's silk cape from her shoulders and draped it over her head. "There."

She giggled and readjusted the cape so she looked like the Virgin Mary.

The boy who ran the elevator paid them no mind as they rattled to the first floor. He was struggling to keep his eyes open. Anna kept her head down and thought about Georges. She couldn't stop smiling.

When they stepped out of the elevator, Anna spied a most unwelcome sight. On the sidewalk stood Mr. Tilly, one horrid newspaper reporter who was always sure to report the truth on Anna when it was most unflattering. And when the truth was flattering, he'd distort it. Luckily, he faced the other direction. She'd know the back of that ginger head anywhere. Something—no doubt a story—had kept him out after dark. She just hoped that story wasn't her. It could cost her a job. Then she'd have to move in with Joe.

Or maybe Georges because she wouldn't have to get married and he had much better furniture.

But Tilly stalked all kinds of people, hoping to uncover a scandal. She had no reason to think he stalked her tonight. Sometimes he just lurked outside hotels and brothels, gambling joints and saloons. Also, Tilly hadn't seen her. Still, Anna quickened her step, pulling Joe along until they were well around the corner. "Georges is awfully proper for a bastard."

"He's so proper because he is a bastard. He has something to prove. You came with a pedigree."

"That's right. I don't have to try." Anna lifted her chin and exaggerated her ladylike walk. She stumbled.

"I'll escort you home."

"Aren't you going to sleep with me?"

Joe's face assumed a pained expression. "Nope."

"Why not?"

"Because you're drunk."

"No, I'm not. The cold air has sobered me up."

"And because if I'm going to make love to you, I want you to myself. And right now, your mind's on Georges Devereaux."

"Of course it is. He's my brother." Anna said this with a silly grin. "I know you don't like him, but I like having a brother, Joe. I do." She squeezed his arm. "You'll grow to tolerate him. Maybe even love him, because he'll be your brother, too. Wouldn't it be delicious if we could all three hunt criminals together?"

"I don't dislike him, Anna. Maybe a little, but not if he's nice to you. I'm reserving judgment. I just don't trust him."

"How can he prove to you he's the genuine thing? He resembles my father. He has pictures of my father. He's smart and looks like a Blanc. Edgar says he's my brother."

"Edgar could be toying with you."

"No. Edgar would never. He's too good. Must you see Georges's birth certificate?"

"No, because he's rich and those things can be bought. Plus, it's going to be in French. I'll believe it when I hear it from your father's lips."

"Well, that's not going to happen. If he doesn't speak to me, he's not going to speak to you. He blames you for my career as a police matron, which he blames for my break with Edgar, which he blames for the bank failure. He would hate you if he believed you worthy of his notice. If he knew we were lovers . . . Oh my. I can't think of it."

"My pop's not crazy about you, either."

"And I don't like him."

"This conversation isn't helping."

"No, it isn't. Are you mad at me?" asked Anna.

"A little."

They walked in unsteady silence from lamppost to lamppost until they reached the side of Anna's apartment building. A two-story advertisement for an undertaker decorated the brick wall. She pulled Joe to a stop in the shadows beneath the fire escape. She heard her landlord snort in his sleep through an open window. "Don't go to bed angry, my love. Go to bed with me." She gave Joe an eighty-proof kiss, missing her mark, catching the corner of his mouth with her sweet, scotched lips.

Joe kissed her back. Anna felt her head spinning, her knees weakening, her mind drifting. She fell asleep standing, with her lips pressed against Joe Singer.

CHAPTER 11

The next morning, Anna had a headache, a vague memory of an awkward conversation with Edgar Wright, and no memory of how she got home. Still, she sang a little song in her head—one she wrote herself—about a desolate girl, alone in the world, who finally found her long lost brother. He would remember her birthday, take her side in any fight, celebrate her victories, and comfort her in dark times. They could laugh about their father and cry about him, too.

The song was absolutely true.

Two slightly disreputable Blancs, when added together, would surely equal one respectable Blanc. People might invite her to parties again. Once she and Joe were married, if misfortune befell her and she were to have children, Georges could open his wallet and provide her with an army of nannies. This would allow her to continue work as a police matron.

"Georges Devereaux," she said out loud to the mice she heard scurrying about her cupboard. She loved saying his name. She shivered with the joy of it. With the joy of having a brother, of not being alone in the world, and of having a future.

Of course, there was Joe and he counted immensely. But he wasn't blood. He might not still love her if she got old or grew carbuncles, though she would love him always. She would always want to kiss him, even if crazy old man hairs grew out of his ears. However, she would insist that he pluck them.

Anna took a double dose of headache powder and walked to the station. She passed Joe on the winding stairs as he carried a female patient up to the women's department of the receiving hospital accompanied by the surgeon, Doctor Feldheim, who was as old as the hills. The lady, too, looked a thousand years old, but perhaps the wrinkles were mere fruits of hard living. Anna had seen young female inmates robbed by life of their beauty and their teeth. The patient thrashed and dripped sweat, eyes protruding like a terrified insect.

Joe said, "Poor dear's got delirium tremors. Who knows what she's seeing." He struggled to hold her, so the doctor grabbed her feet. Anna grabbed her hand and squeezed to reassure her. The lady's hand slipped loose and smacked Anna on the cheek. She felt heat flooding the spot and her head began to throb. Anna stopped trying to help.

It was a ridiculous way to transport patients. They should have put in an elevator or had the beds on the first floor. But no one had asked Anna's advice when designing Central Station. She could have told them that this would be a problem, though she hadn't been born at the time.

Anna's eyes followed Joe, the surgeon, and the thrashing old lady into the women's department of the receiving hospital. Two beds, Matron Clemens, and the men crowded the small room. It smelled of sickness and medicine. Anna stood outside the door pretending not to wait for Joe. He came out alone and winked at her. She fell in beside him on his way down the stairs. He had dark circles beneath his beautiful eyes.

"It was the coffee, wasn't it?" said Anna. "It kept you awake. I made you drink it."

He rubbed the bridge of his nose. "It's Georges Devereaux that's keeping me awake, Anna. I should have stayed with you last night just to make sure you were safe."

Anna tossed her head. "Nonsense. Georges is no threat. You should have stayed with me for medical reasons."

"What?"

"Suppressed desire will make me hysterical. I read it in a book. You should care more about my health."

"You fell asleep standing up while I was kissing you." He whispered, "I'll stay with you tonight."

She tried to look stern, but her lips rebelled. She smiled. It was impossible for Anna to stay mad at Joe Singer because she knew that, beneath his clothes, he was naked.

Joe said, "Today is John Doe's inquest. The new coroner has selected the jury, and I've got to testify."

Anna fell quiet. She had not been asked to testify. Of course, officially, she was never at Griffith Park and had never examined the crime scene. "Have a nice time," she said, taking the high road.

"Sherlock, it's going to smell to high heaven. It's at Cunningham and O'Conner's Funeral Home, it starts at eight and will probably last past lunch. It's going to be miserable. The place is a dump."

"He died kneeling. Remember the knee."

"I will." He socked her gently on the shoulder.

Anna watched him scuttle down the stairs. When he hit the bottom step, he turned around and mouthed, "I love you." It turned Anna's legs into jelly. Then, Joe's lover face melted away and, once more, he looked practical and determined, like a heroic cop that carried drunken old ladies up the staircase. Anna realized why. Matron Clemens was looming behind her. She was holding her purse.

"Good morning, Assistant Matron Blanc, Detective Singer."

"Ma'am," said Joe, and vanished around the corner.

Anna donned a mask of saintly, sober benevolence. "Good morning Matron Clemens. Is all well?"

"It appears so. I have a meeting with the chief to discuss adding a third police matron position. I believe we'll be bringing it before the commission for a vote."

"That would be wonderful!" Indeed, it would be. Anna hadn't had a day off in three weeks, and she'd spent more than one night in the station. Matron Clemens practically lived there. Anna asked, "When will you be back?"

"Not until late. You'll have to hold the fort. The president of the Friday Morning Club and I are speaking to the Chamber of Commerce about the importance of paying shop girls a livable wage. Nothing would reduce the number of women in our jails more than decent paychecks."

Anna had to agree. Theft, fraud, and prostitution would be greatly reduced, though they would still have to contend with the drunk ones and the crazy ones.

"Take care of our new patient, Mrs. Michaelchek. The doctor is with her now. She's suffering for her sins, Lord have mercy." In a silent farewell, Matron Clemens waved her hand like a crisp handkerchief and disappeared into the jail.

Anna's mind flitted from Matron Clemens, to the old woman, and back to Joe. He had slipped away during Anna's conversation with her superintendent, and Anna never got to mouth, "I love you too." Never mind, she would tell him at the inquest. Because she *was* going to the inquest. No one had explicitly said she couldn't go and inquests were open to the public. Matron Clemens would be gone. All Anna had to do was make up some reason for her own absence, like a certain truant pickpocket.

And find someone else to hold the fort.

Anna went to check on the woman with delirium tremens in the receiving hospital. The surgeon fussed at the cabinet. The old lady jerked and trembled, handcuffed to the bed. Her sheets were damp with sweat and she smelled sour, like wine turned to vinegar.

Anna had never seen alcohol claim anyone like this. "There, there," said Anna, and gingerly patted the lady on her greasy head. It teamed with lice. Anna immediately went to the sink to wash her hand.

The surgeon took a vial from the cupboard and prepared a clean needle. "Digitalis. I'll need you to control her for me."

Anna hadn't joined the LAPD to become a nurse. Still, she held the patient's shoulders down, pressing into them with her own body weight while the doctor gave the lady an injection. The woman's tremors abated and gradually she stilled. The surgeon prepared some concoction and flushed it between her wrinkled lips. "Now I'm just giving her a purgative," he said.

"A . . . a purgative?" Anna's eyes widened slightly and then bulged. "No, Doctor!"

But it was too late. The patient had swallowed.

The doctor gave Anna a puzzled look. She sighed heavily, emptying her body of breath. It was inevitable. The lady chained to the bed was going to poop.

"There is nothing more to be done for her. She'll either get better or she won't."

There was nothing more for *him* to do. Anna would be changing the sheets.

The doctor left the bottles and vial on a tray for Anna to clean up. "Check on her every half hour or so. I'll be downstairs if she takes a turn."

Anna sagged. "Yes doctor." By that Anna meant, "I should be testifying at the inquest, because detective work is my true vocation, this isn't fair at all, and I'm feeling rather desperate right now for obvious reasons, some of which are unmentionable." How she wished someone else could watch, change, and bathe Mrs. Michaelchek. And deal with the lice.

Matilda came to mind.

"Trustee" was the name given to well-behaved prisoners or lodgers at Central Station who were tapped for special tasks like cooking and nursing. Leaving Matilda in charge wouldn't be unprecedented. The jailers did it all the time.

Anna had twenty minutes tops before Mrs. Michaelchek's purgative began to work.

When the doctor was safely down the stairs, she hurried into the cow ring to look for Matilda. The girl sat on her cot sewing tiny stitches into the hem of a pillowcase. "Hello Matilda." Anna smiled encouragingly and lifted the thing for close inspection. All four sides were sewn closed. Even Anna knew that was wrong. Anna nodded as she enunciated, "Very good."

The jailer had taken most of the herd to the dining room down below for porridge. Directly after breakfast, all the cows—prisoners or no—would be tasked with work around the jail. Some of the ladies would help with the men's dishes; others would scrub floors and empty chamber pots. The rest were scheduled to boil the linens and towels from the women's department in large vats in the basement. Anna wasn't strictly needed for that. The jailer handled that. The jailer could spare Matilda.

Anna gave Matilda a box of Anna's own personal Cracker Jacks, tar soap, a bucket, and a washrag. She led her to the bedside of Mrs. Michaelchek, who now lay unconscious. "I have a crime to solve, and this nice lady needs to be watched," said Anna. "She shouldn't be much trouble." She lifted the woman's limp arm a few inches and let it drop to the mattress. "Be kind and gentle. If she starts to thrash, tell the surgeon to give her another shot. Oh, and, shave her head please. There's a razor in the cabinet. Do you know how to use a razor?"

Anna didn't.

Matilda smiled as if watching Mrs. Michaelchek was a gift. "Yes, Assistant Matron Blanc. Thank you."

"If anyone asks for me, I'm hunting the little truant criminal, Eliel Villalobos."

"Yes, ma'am."

Mrs. Michaelchek's bowels rumbled, and Anna quickly fled the room.

CHAPTER 12

Cunningham and O'Conner's Funeral Home stood on Fifth Street, just across from a flower shop. It was a grand old pile of bricks set back from the street with a carriage house out back. A horse wandered the drive eating daisies and trailing a snapped harness. An old hearse, black paint peeling, stood in the drive mourning the loss of its horse.

Anna wore a velvet, floor-length cape to hide her uniform, and a veil attached to her hat to hide her lovely face. She stopped at the florist to buy a nosegay of narcissus in case the inquest smelled as bad as Joe Singer had said it would. She bought a second one for Joe, in case he hadn't planned. This made her hands excessively full, juggling a purse, a notebook, two nosegays, and the guilt of leaving Matilda to clean up the inevitable.

The new coroner had already arrived. His wagon had one wheel on the sidewalk, which she thought boded ill. Anna hoped he wasn't a drunk. The old coroner had gone to prison for covering up a string of murders, which Anna had uncovered, and for stealing medical books that belonged to the city—books that now rested on Anna's shelf.

Joe Singer smoked a cigarette outside the grand entrance. Anna approached him with spring in her step.

He cooed, "Hello sweetheart."

Anna stopped dead, and her heart dropped into her feet. Joe Singer was cooing at another woman like a common masher. She made an indignant noise and stuttered in a foreign accent she'd conjured on the spot. "You . . . you have nerve!"

He lowered his voice, grinning. "I know it's you, Sherlock. I recognized your shoes. Nice accent. What are you supposed to be? A Chinaman with his mouth full? No. Irish with a speech impediment?"

"Why aren't you inside yet?"

"We've got five minutes and I'm claiming every single one of them. It stinks in there."

Anna handed him a nosegay.

"Thanks." He smiled his Anna's lover smile, and her heart fluttered. "You may as well give me both of them. Wolf's going to make you go home. And aren't you supposed to be nursing Mrs. Michaelchek?"

"Inquests are open to the public. And don't worry. Matilda's holding the fort."

"Matilda belongs in the bat house."

"She'll do fine. The surgeon's there. And it's not my fault. We wouldn't be faced with this dilemma if the LAPD didn't have a double standard. I should be investigating this death with you. It's what I was born to do. As it stands, I can't even serve on the jury."

Joe said nothing. He threw his cigarette on the sidewalk and ground it out.

Anna's eyebrows kissed. "You agree, don't you? Tell me you agree."

"I agree that you're a killer detective. You've got the brains and the instincts, although your fake accents could use some work. I just don't want you to get fired. I like to see you from time to time."

She smiled beneath her veil.

He said, "Now let's go in, but not together. And I'm sorry you have to sit with the public. I'll go first so you can have an extra ten seconds to breathe."

§

The room sagged like an old man, forgotten by the people who used to patronize Cunningham and O'Conner's years ago when it was a younger, finer place. The county no doubt chose it for economy. Faded drapes drooped against dirty windows. Chairs lined up in rows as if for a lecture. The all-male jury sat, leaving most seats empty. Anna perched behind the jury in the very last row. Her chair's legs were of unequal lengths. It rocked on the dirty tile with each tiny shift of her weight simply to annoy her.

The new coroner strode solemnly down the aisle and faced his audience. He wasn't bad looking and not too old. Anna had yet to meet the man. Though he may have seen her picture in the papers, he couldn't possibly recognize her shoes. His eyes lingered on Anna's veil curiously but briefly, then he opened the proceedings. The jury took their oath, repeating his words in flat voices, vowing to inquire who the person was, and when, where, and by what means he came to his death, and into the circumstances attending his death; and to render a true verdict thereon, according to the evidence offered them, or arising from the inspection of the body, and so on.

Anna yawned. They all adjourned to the viewing room.

Besides Anna, only one citizen came to witness the stinky inquest of John Doe—a young man who smiled with inappropriate glee, showing off a bright gold tooth. He seemed to angle to make eye contact with the jurors, as if trying to draw them into his ghastly joke. Anna wondered how he'd learned about the event, as it wasn't mentioned in the papers. Maybe he came to all the inquests at Cunningham and O'Conner's. She made sure to sit as far away from him as possible.

The body lay naked with just a cloth covering his mysterious man parts. His pale skin looked slightly chewed, the work of the ants. With the insects removed, Anna could now see that he was no older than her and good looking, but for his pallor and the hole in his forehead. He smelled to high heaven.

The fifteen men comprising the jury filed past the coffin. Some studied the body intently. Others barely looked. Most plugged their noses or gagged into handkerchiefs. The creep lingered coffin-side and was hastened along with a discreet shove from the coroner. Anna

filed past, breathing through her nosegay. She only gagged a little.
Then the entire party—the coroner, the jury, Joe, the creep, and
Anna—adjourned into another room to hear testimony. The stench
followed them, having seeped into their hair and clothes.

This coroner used big words to describe the state of the body—
words Anna knew, for she had read *Legal Medicine* and a dozen
other books she had lifted from the previous coroner and planned to
sneak back into the station, one by one. The coroner went on, saying
the victim had died from a gunshot wound to the head sometime
Wednesday afternoon—likely self-inflicted.

Anna frowned.

He said that, judging from the musculature in John Doe's arms,
the man was left-handed. Ants had eaten away at his skin, and so on.

Joe, the sole witness, testified next. The afternoon he had found
the body, he had been responding to reports of a bank robbers'
encampment in Griffith Park. Which was true, though he omitted
the part where he unhooked Anna's corset. He found the body face
down, off the trail, near the side of a hill overlooking the city. He
found the gun in the dead man's left hand. Evidence suggests that
the victim had been shot in a kneeling position and then had fallen
sideways.

Anna couldn't contain herself. It was her clue and she had to
comment. Her hand shot up. She said in her Chinese-Irish accent,
"Backward execution style?"

"You could say that," said Joe. "His position was clear from the
marks on his pants, and on the ground."

The coroner checked his pocket watch. "Self-execution,
perhaps?" He smiled a little.

Anna shot him a stony glare, though he could not see it beneath
her veil. "Who commits suicide execution style? No one, surely." She
had traveled this path before, where the authorities failed to look
closely, or even swept things under the rug.

"That is what we're here to determine, ma'am," said the coroner.
"Now please, no further comments from the public." Which meant

Anna, as the creep had no comments, but simply sat flashing his gold tooth.

Joe passed photographs among the jurors. There were several images of the body at the crime scene and the disturbed soil, as well as shots of the man's pants and the imprints of his knee in the dust. Anna had seen them.

Anna stood. "I'm happy to demonstrate . . ."

Joe dropped to his knee on the dirty floor and then fell sideways, saving her the trouble. Sure enough, when he rose he had debris stuck to his knee, because the floor had not been scrubbed, maybe ever.

The testimony came to an end, and the jury voted, ruling it murder by gunshot.

As soon as the verdict was delivered, Anna rushed outside to breathe the city air, which coated her mouth like sand, gritty from exhaust and dust. It was a huge improvement over the air in the mortuary.

When Joe came out, she accosted him. "You've got your murder. That's wonderful!"

"That's one way to look at it," said Joe.

"Who is the gentleman with the gold tooth?"

"Oh, him? He comes to all the inquests."

Anna saw Wolf. He'd been lurking outside, listening to the proceedings through an open window without subjecting himself to the stench. Wolf sauntered over and took Anna by the elbow. "Assistant Matron Blanc, you're not supposed to be here."

"It was my clue. I figured it out, so I should get to say it."

"It *was* her clue," said Joe.

"Very good, honeybun. So, you admit you were at Griffith Park," said Wolf.

"Oh, let's not pretend." Anna ripped off her veil. "You knew I was there. But I was hunting for a truant, not anything so improper as . . . whatever it was you were implying," she said. "I saw everything—the crime scene, the ants. And I want to help with this case.

I cracked the case of the Boyle Heights Rape Fiend. I dispatched the New High Street Suicide Faker. I caught the Chinatown Trunk Murderer, though Joe did help a little. What do I have to do to prove myself? I can find the Griffith Park Executioner." Anna liked the sound of the name, though she had made it up on the spot. She said it again. "The Griffith Park Executioner."

"I would love to have your assistance finding the Griffith Park Executioner, honeybun, but you're up to your ears in matron's work."

"I can easily keep on top of my matron duties. That's very easy to do," she lied. "The criminal ladies practically care for themselves." In fact, if Anna spent much time on this case, they would have to.

"Okay," said Wolf. "If it's all right with Matron Clemens, you can help."

Anna clapped her hands. "I'm so happy I could k . . ."

Wolf looked hopeful. Joe's eyes narrowed.

"I could salute." Anna saluted Wolf.

He grinned.

§

The street was choked with trollies, automobiles, daring pedestrians, and horse-drawn wagons, all moving at cross purposes. Electric lines crisscrossed above their heads. Anna and Joe boarded a Red Car to ride back to the station. She dug through her purse for trolley fare. Because he was a cop, Joe rode for free. Anna didn't think of how unfair this was. She could only think of the dead man. "First off, we need to identify the victim. Then we can explore motives, which is half the battle of finding the killer, don't you think? Can't you pressure the coroner for his photographs? As soon as they're developed, we can send his picture to the police in Oklahoma City. They can ask at the pharmacy. Someone will know him. Someone is likely missing him. His mother for one. He looked barely out of his teens. We should do it right away. It's important to move quickly, don't you think?"

Joe nudged her knee with his own. "I do."

"You're so calm."

"You're the opposite of calm."

"For good reason. Can't you see? Because I'm a woman, I have to solve every murder. I have to get it right this time and every time, or they'll never let me try again. You can bumble all you want. But not me. From me they demand perfection. I've got to be smarter and work harder than anyone else. And I've got my matron duties to boot. So, don't complain to me if I don't bake you cookies or darn your socks."

"You don't bake me cookies or darn my socks. Do you hear me complaining?"

"No."

He leaned close so that their arms touched. Kissing was out of the question, but she could tell he was thinking about it. He said, "Anna, I can darn my own socks."

"Good. Can you darn silk stockings, too, because I don't know how."

§

Joe Singer puttered up the drive of the Blanc Mansion on an LAPD motorcycle from Central Station. Unexpected. Uninvited. It was the first time he'd been there since the ball celebrating Anna's engagement to a different man. Christopher Blanc didn't know that Joe was planning to marry his daughter. That secret still wasn't out. No doubt he believed Joe had recruited Anna to do dangerous sting operations with the police—though he hadn't. Anna recruited herself. And that Joe had everything to do with the breakup of Anna's engagement to Edgar Wright, Christopher Blanc's business partner—though he hadn't. Not really. That breakup resulted in a parting of ways, which in turn resulted in the collapse of Blanc National Bank.

Joe hadn't caused the wreckage of Anna's old life, or as she saw it, her liberation. He had simply still wanted her after she'd lost everything. And she had wanted him. But Christopher Blanc wouldn't see it that way.

No, Joe didn't expect to be welcomed. But maybe Mr. Blanc would still care enough about his daughter that he wouldn't want her exploited by an imposter. He should know about Georges Devereaux, just in case the dandy was a fraud. Telling Mr. Blanc could be an olive branch. Mr. Blanc might even thank him.

The Blanc estate towered grandly over the neighboring houses on Bunker Hill and its grounds spread out like a park. But the grass needed clipping and there was a pothole in the drive. Joe carefully steered around it. He turned the engine off and swung his leg over the motorcycle to the ground. Stone lions flanked the marble steps. They ignored him. The ten-foot door tried to make him feel small. He wouldn't have it.

When he knocked, a Mexican woman answered. She stood only four foot something but filled the doorway with an imposing dignity. He guessed this was Mrs. Morales, the housekeeper who had raised Anna, or at least had organized Anna's childhood.

Joe straightened his shoulders. She didn't smile. "Good evening."

"Good evening Ma'am. I'm here to see Christopher Blanc."

"Whom shall I say is calling?"

"Detective Singer. He knows me. That is, we've met. He knows my pop, Chief Singer. He's the police chief . . ."

Mrs. Morales's countenance darkened. Her tone turned sharp and staccato. "He's not home." Her eyes traveled up to Joe's hat, down to his boots, back up to his eyes.

"But, I thought you said . . ."

"Good day." Mrs. Morales shut the door in his face.

Joe stood for a moment absorbing the sting of being dismissed by the housekeeper. Mrs. Morales was formidable, like her reputation. He had to do better with Christopher Blanc, who was reputedly even worse.

Not easily dissuaded, Joe crept along the outside of the house to the back, bushwhacked through a thorny bougainvillea plant, and forced open a casement window. He pushed up onto the ledge and climbed through. It was trespassing, to be sure. But what could Mr. Blanc do? Ask Joe to arrest himself? Call his father?

Joe tiptoed across the marble tiles where Persian carpets had once cushioned Anna's footsteps. There were darker spots on the wallpaper where paintings had once hung—notably a portrait of Anna he'd admired the night of her engagement ball. Some of the furniture was missing, presumably sold. Luckily, the staff had been reduced, and the Blancs had no dog to sound the alarm. An orange cat ignored him. No one else moved in the corridor. Joe looked for an office. From what Anna had said about her father, he spent all his time there.

Joe smelled cigar smoke and followed it to its source—a door that opened onto oak paneling, red leather, and a tobacco haze. He removed his derby hat and squared his shoulders. He strode in. Anna's father loomed behind a newspaper, behind a desk that served as a wall. He glanced up glowering. He didn't seem surprised to see Joe. Mrs. Morales must have warned him.

"You broke my plant."

Joe looked down and saw a spray of scarlet petals hooked on his pant leg by a thorn. "You could say good afternoon. I'm your future son-in-law, whether you grant your permission or not."

"You're not my future son-in-law because I don't have a daughter."

"You know what? You don't deserve Anna. But you and I have still got business."

"I'm sorry, I don't have any spare change."

"I don't want your money." Joe wasn't sure whether this was true for Anna, but the point might be moot. Rumor was, Christopher Blanc no longer had any. Rumor had it, the house was mortgaged to the hilt. Maybe Georges Devereaux was holding money for Blanc, and maybe not.

"Oh, just get out." Blanc growled. "I didn't invite you here."

"I'm not leaving. Not yet. Someone is going around sending Anna gifts and claiming to be her illegitimate brother, and I don't trust him."

"So?"

"So, is it true?"

"Georges is no threat to Anna. I'm far more concerned about you." He raised his voice. "Or, I would be if I had a daughter!"

"Georges Devereaux is your son? That dandy? Really?" It wasn't what Joe had expected. He had been sure the dude was a fraud.

"Really."

Joe realized he had insulted the man. "All right." He stood, waiting. "Is that all you have to say to me?"

"Get out!"

§

Joe let himself out the grand front door, passing an empty marble pedestal, a hole in the ceiling from a missing chandelier, and Mrs. Morales on the way. He acknowledged her with a nod. "Good afternoon, Mrs. Morales."

She curled her lip in disgust.

Joe considered the visit a success. He had never had any illusions that he could be a goodwill ambassador on Anna's behalf when Christopher Blanc likely blamed him for all his current troubles. But at least Joe had his answer. Now, he would go and tell Anna the good news. She would be happy, so he would be happy for her.

And he'd have to apologize to Georges Devereaux.

Chapter 13

Anna took the stairs to the ladies' receiving hospital two at a time, as if the extra few seconds saved would make up for her three-hour absence. She found Matilda sitting serenely by the bedside of the shackled Mrs. Michaelchek. The old woman smelled a whole lot better than she had that morning, not worse as Anna had expected. Rivers of blue veins ran across the lady's newly shorn head. She appeared to be sleeping. Matilda seemed to be doing better despite her traumatic experience with the Martian, and it relieved Anna greatly.

Anna put on her crisp, authoritative voice. "Good day, Matilda. How is our patient?"

"Better, I think. I found some clothes in the cupboard and changed her gown. It was soiled. I put it in the incinerator out back along with her hair." Matilda looked tentative, crumpling her forehead. "I hope you don't mind."

"No. You've done well." Anna kept her back straight, her manner efficient and smileless, like a matron's demeanor should be. "You uncuffed her?"

"Briefly. The doctor gave me the key. Other than that, I haven't left her side. Except I did change her sheets." Matilda winced as if waiting for a reprimand. "It had to be done, I'm afraid."

Anna's demeanor softened. She couldn't help it. "Matilda, I think you are a gifted nurse." Anna meant it. Matilda seemed to give of herself effortlessly, and it suited her. Anna liked to give too, but she didn't have the stomach for this particular type of giving. For example, she was always happy to give fashion advice to strangers, solicited or no. Also, she freely gave directions.

Anna felt her face getting hot. Anna wasn't giving at all. She pinched herself beneath her cuff. She pinched herself harder. Then she took Matilda's hand. "Maybe we could talk a little later about what happened at the Jonquil Apartments. It's not just your experience. I'm sure there's something sketchy going on. But to prosecute, we'll need a witness. Matilda, you'd have to testify."

"Testify against a Martian? They can control your thoughts."

"How about against a landlady who sells girls to spacemen?" Anna said, her voice gentle. "But perhaps leave out the spaceman part."

Matilda bit her lip thoughtfully. "Is a girl ruined if she's ruined by a Martian? Does it count?"

"No. Of course not. Martians don't count."

§

Anna snuck into the prisoners' kitchen and brought a cold bowl of illicit mush to Matilda, who didn't qualify to eat jail food. She brought a licit one for bald Mrs. Michaelchek, too, in case she woke up.

Anna set the mush down by Matilda. "Matilda, please tell me again about the man who hurt you? Could it be he wasn't from Mars?"

Matilda started to rock and she wrung her pale hands. Her nails were bitten to nubs.

"I'm a detective and I'm going to catch him, but I must know all the details. For example, what did he look like?"

"His eyes were yellow and his skin was sort of green, like an olive. I don't think Martians bathe. He made the room smell like rotten eggs." She wrinkled up her face. "Afterward, I smelled of him."

The girl's obvious pain and illness shook Anna. She took a deep breath to calm herself. "I see. But you don't smell of him now. You should know that."

"Good."

"What else can you tell me about this . . . man?"

Matilda drew her legs up onto the chair and hugged herself. "Please, don't make me think of him. I don't remember anything else. I never want to speak of him again."

Anna took Matilda's hand and squeezed it. "All right. It's going to be all right."

Then she left Matilda alone with the patient, feeling determined to find this odorous Martian man and bring him to justice. She had no idea where to start, or whether, if she did catch him, Matilda would be up to taking the witness stand.

§

Anna looked in on the ladies in the cow ring and the other prisoners in the women's department. They sewed or slept or sang jailbird songs. The cells were colorless, poorly lit, and even more poorly ventilated. The walls were marred with the graffiti of incarcerated women scratched into the steel. It smelled sharply of bodies and despair. But the bed sheets had been changed. Clean, wet ones, no doubt, hung in the basement to dry. The jailer would come and take the criminal ladies to supper at six.

Other than filing; hunting for little, bad Eliel Villalobos; capturing a Martian; reforming the delinquent children of Los Angeles; and finding jobs for hundreds of prostitutes, Anna had nothing pressing to do. And so, she did what she liked best.

Detective work.

Anna snuck into the coroner's office to search for photographs of the Griffith Park Executioner's victim—the kneeling deado. Happily, the coroner was out. She rifled through the files on his desk and found the one belonging to their John Doe. Joe's photographs from the investigation had turned out well in that they represented the crime scene clearly and accurately. The victim's clothes appeared distinctly ugly—this could help when identifying the victim. But the face was blurred with insects. It would be hard for a witness to tell one ant-covered corpse from the next. There were plenty of photographs, so Anna palmed a picture that featured the man's bad suit.

She left the morgue and knocked at the darkroom. No one answered. Light filtered in from beneath the door, and so she opened it. Pictures hung on a line from clothes pins. They must be done, or the light wouldn't be on. She tested them for dryness, and they seemed fixed. She could wait and get them from Joe, who would have to get them first from the coroner, who seemed in no hurry, or she could lift one now and make today's mail.

The choice was clear. Anna pinched a close-up of the victim's poor, dead face.

Back in her storage room, she wrote a letter to the police department in Oklahoma City and enclosed it with the photograph of John Doe. The coroner had washed the ants out of his hair and cleaned him up so that he looked more like he must have before the bullet and the bugs—too young and too handsome to die. She included a list of interview questions for the Oklahoma detectives to ask any family or known associates of the man, should he be identified.

Anna would give him justice. She swore she would. Not only would it make her giving and perhaps reduce her time in purgatory, her future as a detective depended on it.

As Joe wasn't at the station where he belonged, and because justice was urgent, Anna signed Joe's name. She had enough experience with the police to know that if a woman signed a letter, no one would take it seriously. Out of habit, she spritzed it with perfume. Then she sealed the envelope and gave it to Mr. Melvin to send.

"How long will it take?" asked Anna.

"Maybe two weeks." He spoke into his necktie.

Anna ducked her head to look into his face. "Thank you, Mr. Melvin."

Anna noticed Joe hanging up his derby hat on a peg on the wall near the door. He seemed slightly out of breath and bougainvillea trailed from his pants. "Assistant Matron Blanc, when you have a moment, I've got news." He held up a copy of the *Los Angeles Herald,* his eyebrows arched high.

His very presence made her glow from the middle. "I'm available now."

Joe looked around, probably for Detective Snow, and then nodded his head in the direction of the officers' kitchen. Anna arrived first. She twinkled when he entered, ecstatic to be in his manly presence. Ecstatic to be solving crimes. "I have news, too. I've taken the liberty of writing the police in Oklahoma City to ask about our John Doe. Sooner is so much better than later when it comes to murder investigations."

"You should have let me do it. They'd pay more attention to a cop."

"Not to worry. I signed your name."

"Impersonating an officer is a felony."

"I mean, I . . ." Anna bit her lip.

Joe kissed her. "Anna, look at this article." He tilted his head and grinned. "You're gonna like it." He tapped his finger on the society pages.

Anna grabbed the paper and read. "'Miss Anna Blanc, socialite . . .' Socialite, hah!" Renowned beauty, perhaps, or *former* socialite, but no one in society invited Anna to parties now. Not since her undercover work in the brothels. Just her best friends Clara and Theo Breedlove, who had just left on a European tour. It was a sore point.

"Keep reading."

"'Anna Blanc, socialite and estranged daughter of prominent banker, Christopher Blanc, has been united with her illegitimate half-brother, Georges Devereaux. Mr. Devereaux is the product of an illicit union between Christopher Blanc and a French dancer.'"

Anna squealed, realized she might be overheard, and swallowed a second happy noise. "Oh, Joe. That's very good news. Oh, Joe."

She trembled with the joy of it, pressed her hands together as if in prayer. "My father will be horrified."

Then her smile collapsed. She put fingers to her lips. "Oh, no. What if it isn't true? The paper prints all kinds of lies about me."

Joe took her hands and squeezed. "It's true. I spoke with your father."

"He agreed to speak with you?"

"Not exactly. But I asked him point-blank. He more or less confessed to being Georges Devereaux's father."

"And then what?"

"He threw me out."

"Jupiter. I'm dingswizzled he agreed to speak with you."

"He didn't. I climbed through the window."

"Oh, my love," she said too loudly given the thinness of the door.

"Shhh." Joe lowered his voice. "He said Georges wasn't a threat. And Anna, I told him we're getting married."

"What did he say? Did he pull a gun? Does he want me to leave you?"

Joe's smile faltered. "It doesn't matter what he thinks of me. What matters is that you have a brother and that makes you happy."

"Yes," said Anna. "And look here. The article says Georges is— and I quote—'a successful businessman in his own right, winning respect despite the circumstances of his birth. He is the opposite of his sister who, despite her privileged birth, has managed to disgrace herself.'" She looked up from the paper and smiled a wide, splendid, heartfelt smile. "Isn't that wonderful?"

"I . . . Um. Nobody reads the *Herald*, baby."

"Mr. Tilly wrote the article. I'm sure of it. He must have seen us with Georges at the hotel."

"Georges probably gave him the story. I'm just glad he didn't say anything about you and me."

"But what could he say? There's nothing scandalous about me being with you in the company of . . ." She lingered on the last two words. "My brother."

"Let's call on Georges tonight and I'll apologize for doubting him."

Anna's eyebrow rose like a burning sun. "Yes, you should."

"Oh, come on, Anna. You're not mad, are you? I was just looking out for you. I'm happy for you. Really, I am. As long as he treats you well."

"He does!"

CHAPTER 14

Smiling broadly, Anna checked in on her patient in the receiving hospital. Mrs. Michaelchek snored. She sounded like a dangerous animal, though she looked safe enough. Her color wasn't good and she was still shackled to the bed. Matilda dozed in a chair at her side. Two empty bowls suggested that Matilda had eaten her illicit mush and possibly Mrs. Michaelchek's.

Anna decided to speak with the doctor to make sure he'd been checking on her. She sought him out on the first floor in the men's department of the receiving hospital. She found one insane man in a drugged stupor and a man bleeding out from a gunshot wound, crowded into a seven-by-twelve-foot room.

The surgeon had blood up to his elbows. A trustee assisted him.

Anna ventured. "Doctor, have you seen Mrs. Michaelchek? You are checking in on her?"

The surgeon shot her a dirty look. "Yes, I've been checking in on her, Assistant Matron Blanc."

Anna bobbed a curtsy and wandered onto the main floor of the station. She had a little time. That is, no one was expecting her to be anywhere at this particular moment. She racked her brain for what she could do toward solving the case of the Griffith Park Executioner. They had no leads. All they had was a body.

And pictures of the dead man in that rather remarkable suit.

She could canvass tailors. Someone had sewn that awful sac coat; it was no doubt seared into their memory.

§

Anna collected her picture of the ant-covered body wearing the bad suit, told Mr. Melvin she was out hunting Eliel Villalobos, and trekked down to the shopping district where the better tailors cut and sewed. It had, despite its color, been a well-sewn suit, and the fabric was a good weave. She called out, "Here Eliel, here Eliel" from time to time, because she didn't like lying to Mr. Melvin.

She skipped her father's tailor; he would never stoop so low. She snuck past her own seamstress's shop lest the lady see her and demand payment. The next shop appeared open. Anna went inside, jingling a string of bells on the door. "Hello. I'm an LAPD police matron investigating a murder." She smiled sweetly at the tailor, who was pinning a pair of trousers.

He was an older man, perfectly turned out. He cocked his head, "How strange."

Anna ignored the insult. "Do you know this man or this lovely suit?" She inclined her head graciously and showed him the photo. He leaned forward to look.

Horror transformed his face—at the suit or at the body, she couldn't tell. He stepped back.

Anna held the picture closer to his wrinkled face and smiled winningly. "Please, look again. Never mind the ants or the dead man. Did you make this suit? I won't tell anyone if you did."

The man put down his sewing and disappeared into the back of the shop, slamming the door.

She had apparently insulted him. Anna now saw the flaw in her strategy. No tailor would admit to knowing anything about that suit. Innocent bystanders, however, wouldn't have the same reservations.

Thus, on the way back to the station, Anna pinned the photograph to the wall in the post office along with a note stating that any citizen who recognized this man or his suit should contact Detective Joe Singer at Central Station immediately. She took the liberty of offering a large reward, leaving the amount unspecified. Large was a relative term and meant different things to different people. It didn't have to be cash at all. The reward could, for example, be the satisfaction of doing one's civic duty. It could be a horehound candy or a peppermint. Or Joe could sing a song for them on their next birthday.

§

When she returned to the station, Officer Snow was there scratching his scaly head, straining to read a letter. He grabbed Anna's sleeve as she passed. "Stop, girly."

She stopped, so as not to rip her dress, and glared at him.

He smoothed down his hair with his hand and smiled at her. His canine tooth was missing. His eyes weren't hostile. Snow's attempt at flirtation? Did he really believe his own rumors, that she would do mysterious things with cops in the stables? After how he'd treated her?

He thrust the letter in front of her face. She wrinkled her nose. His hand smelled.

"Read it," he said. "Please."

Anna noted that his smiling, scarred face had turned red. Embarrassment?

She sighed, took the letter, and perused it. The date on the letter was two weeks ago. It had likely been assigned to Snow but had been languishing on his desk because he had trouble reading words with more than three letters. If he thought his illiteracy would impress her, he was mistaken. If he thought smiling at her would make her meet him in the stables, he was an idiot.

But that was established.

She said, "It's a kidnapping complaint of sorts, lodged by one Samuel Grayson. He claims his fiancée is being held captive by her landlady. His proof includes that he is no longer allowed on the premises, and that she never writes him back. Yes, he admits, they had a fight, but believes she is definitely being held captive or, surely, she would be returning his letters. He has warned the landlady that if she doesn't free his fiancée, he will tell the girl's father where she is, etcetera. Her name is Flossie Edmands, and she resides at 807 South Hill Street."

Snow smiled at her again. He took the letter from her hand, crumpled it, and tossed it in the trash. "Thank you." He lumbered off, his face still crimson.

Did Snow have a crush on her now? She did not understand his behavior.

But she did understand why Wolf had assigned the case of the captive girlfriend to Snow—the detective who couldn't find his face in a mirror. But something about it tugged at her. She reclaimed the balled-up letter from the waste basket and reread it. The girl was allegedly being held captive. The address of the girl in question was 807 South Hill Street.

She lived at the Jonquil Apartments.

§

Anna swished over to Joe, looking perplexed. "Snow was friendly toward me."

"Uh oh."

"Any news on the Griffith Park murder?"

"Nope."

"I put the victim's picture up in the post office. Maybe someone will recognize him. It's hard to solve a murder when you don't know who the victim is."

Joe winced. "You used the cleaned-up photographs, right?"

"Yes, of course," Anna lied. "And, there's something else." She put the complaint into his hands. "Read this."

Joe's eyes perused the crumpled complaint. "What's so interesting about this? The poor sap's been kicked by his girl . . . Oh."

"You see?"

"I don't know, Anna. His claim is kind of far-fetched."

"Oh please, let's go back to the Jonquil. We have absolutely no leads on the Griffith Park murder, apart from waiting to hear from the police in Oklahoma."

"Is Matilda still here?"

"She is. She likes the mush. She's quite wonderful, actually, watching Mrs. Michaelchek. I wouldn't have been able to go to the inquest without her. She's very giving."

"I think we should talk to her again about what happened at the Jonquil Apartments."

"I have. She's holding to the Martian story."

"Anna, even if we caught her Martian, a judge wouldn't let her testify if she's mentally unwell."

Anna's shoulders sank.

Joe shrugged. "If you really want, I could go talk to Mrs. Rosenberg, but she's not going to incriminate herself."

"Maybe we should raid the place. You saw those twins."

"No judge is going to give me a warrant based on Matilda's testimony and a complaint from some poor, jilted sap."

"Then, I'll go undercover. I'll apply for an apartment. Tomorrow. They'll take me if they have an empty room. I'm pretty." Anna was more than pretty but thought it impolite to say so.

"Unless they recognize your gorgeous picture from the paper. Not to mention that you've been there before. Anna, you're sort of conspicuous."

Joe had a point. If there were shenanigans afoot—bewitching Martians, etcetera—a police matron is the last person they would want on the premises. "It's been months since my picture appeared in any paper. And I'll wear a disguise. An eye patch or a rubber nose or something."

"Fine. But no accents, and you're not moving in. Whatever you do, don't drink anything. I'll be in the café if you need me."

"Be careful. You are also very conspicuous." Anna winked badly.

§

The following afternoon, Anna returned home from the station early to prepare for her sting operation. She donned the curly black wig Joe Singer used to use when he dressed as a girl on sting operations to catch the Boyle Heights Rape Fiend. Matilda had mentioned that the man from Mars preferred girls to wear their hair down, like a child. Thus, Anna searched her wardrobe for a remnant from her younger days. She found a four-year-old gown with white ruffles and a skirt that hit midshin—one she had worn before she'd debuted in society. The dress fit so tightly that lifting her arms was out of the question. Anna would need to restrict her movements and take shallow breaths to avoid bursting the buttons. Even so, when she took her first stride, the side seam on her bodice popped open, gaping like a screaming mouth. She considered it in the mirror and liked the effect. It made her look pathetic and desperate. Anna tore a ruffle for good measure, so that it sagged conspicuously. Then she ripped the pocket.

She finished her disguise with a pair of spectacles, which she had stolen from the pocket of a man on the trolley on a separate occasion. Because she couldn't see when wearing them, she poked out the lenses.

Anna did look different—nothing like the photographs that had appeared in the paper where she either looked like a gorgeous society lady or an extremely beautiful prostitute. She just looked like an unfortunate girl—albeit a lovely one. To further distance herself from herself, she popped a piece of Juicy Fruit into her mouth and planned to chew it in public, which Anna Blanc would never do.

CHAPTER 15

Rain clouds gathered over Los Angeles threatening to drench the city and fill the river, which now only trickled to the sea. Anna sashayed down the busy sidewalk toward the Jonquil Café, buzzing with excitement, like the city herself— Nuestra Señora la Reina de Los Angeles. Anna couldn't help but sneak glances at her reflection in every plate glass window along the street. She could easily pass for sixteen—her own little sister. To amplify the effect, she abandoned her graceful bearing and slouched.

Joe sauntered along behind Anna at a safe distance, smiling. He stopped at a fruit stand adjacent to the Jonquil Apartments and pretended to shop. She cast a glance at him over her shoulder and stuck out her tongue. He grinned and pegged her in the head with a cherry.

Anna squeaked.

The grocer minding the fruit stand was giving Joe an earful when Anna skipped through the doors of the Jonquil Café. Anna steeled herself, telling herself she'd be safe. It was, after all, a public café with windows to the street. Men were laughing and talking jovially.

The maître d', wearing a coat with tails, stood near a reception podium and the feathery fronds of a giant potted palm. He welcomed her, bowing his muscular body, and ushered her to a table by a window as if she were important and not a minor girl chewing gum in torn ruffles who shouldn't be unescorted in a big, bad city. He handed her a menu printed on fine paper. It felt nice to be treated with deference for a change—the way waiters, tradesmen, and shopkeepers used to always treat Anna when she was an heiress and had a running tab in every good establishment in Los Angeles.

Anna sat at the table and tried to appear forlorn, wistfully gazing out the window, because sad girls seemed most vulnerable to mashers and *macquereaux*. Inside she felt exhilarated. She always did when fighting crime. The drawn-down corners of her mouth kept flipping up into a smile. But this was serious business. Ironing out her lips, she ordered milk from the waiter and sniffled, making subtle boohoo noises and dabbing dramatically at invisible tears with one of Joe's pathetic old handkerchiefs.

She perused the menu, then glanced surreptitiously about to see if anyone watched her.

Everyone did—pretty career girls dining at tables with white cloths, and the rich-looking men scattered among them.

Anna tensed under the weight of their eyes. Could they have recognized her? Or were they just staring at the spectacle of a waif in a nice café. She saw the maître d' in conference with Mrs. Rosenberg over near the kitchen. They were considering her. The man even had the gall to point.

Anna didn't know if she was extremely successful or about to fail dangerously, blowing her cover and the case. At a loss, she boohooed louder. She looked about, snuffling. Where was Joe?

Mrs. Rosenberg glided over to Anna's table with her mouth in a pout, looking as sickly sweet as rotting fruit.

Anna braced herself to spring from the booth and run.

The pouting lady simpered, "My goodness, dear. Whatever could be the matter? You look like you haven't a friend in the world."

"I haven't," Anna said, and snorted, feeling absolutely wonderful.

"Hush now," said the landlady. She squinted at Anna. "Have we met?"

"I'm sure we have not. I'm from out of town."

"Well, I'm Mrs. Rosenberg and this is my humble café. What's your name, child?"

"Um . . ." Anna's eyes rolled to the side. Why did she always forget to pick an alias ahead of time? "Gladys," she declared. "Um . . . Sydalg," She wrinkled her nose. It was a simple palindrome, not a name at all, but she supposed it sounded Welsh.

Mrs. Rosenberg slid into the booth beside Anna. "Is there anything I can do for you Miss Gladys? Are you hungry?"

Anna nodded truthfully. She usually felt hungry now that she prepared her own meals, and the café smelled like ambrosia. "I dream of pig's feet in batter."

And she did.

"I hope you have bigger dreams than pig's feet in batter." Mrs. Rosenberg winked magnanimously and motioned to the waiter, who hovered nearby. "You aren't dreaming of your prince charming?"

"I dream of fancy ice cream," said Anna. "Two scoops."

Mrs. Rosenberg's smile tightened but she nodded to the waiter. He bowed off to the kitchen.

Anna hoped the sting operation would take a while. She truly did want pig's feet in batter and fancy ice cream. If she could stretch it out, she might get other things, too.

When the pig's feet arrived, hot and dripping with grease, Anna gobbled it up, as she imagined a desperate girl might do. She had never been allowed to gobble anything, thus gobbling delighted her. To her initial horror and then amusement, she burped. This also pleased her and enhanced her disguise. The older lady did not react with horror. Perhaps she was used to ill-mannered girls.

"Excuse me." Anna grinned sheepishly and looked around for Joe to see if he was watching. He likely did not know that ladies even could burp and would probably be fascinated. But he was nowhere to be seen. Perhaps he was watching Anna from some secret hiding place.

Or maybe the angry grocer had captured him.

"Dear, you seem familiar."

"Everyone says that. I look like . . . everyone."

Mrs. Rosenberg pressed her lips and nodded.

Not two, but three scoops of fancy ice cream arrived—diabolical and seductive in the extreme.

Mrs. Rosenberg said. "You look so very lonely. Where are your people?"

"South . . . Hill . . . ville."

"I've never heard of it."

"It's in Mexico."

"South Hillville is in Mexico?" Mrs. Rosenberg frowned, looking slightly perplexed and not a little suspicious of Anna.

Anna's heart sank. She had perhaps just blown her undercover operation. And Joe was hiding somewhere, watching her fail. She couldn't help it. Her eyes began to well for real. She sobbed, "That's why they call it *South* Hillville."

"There, there, now. I know what it's like to be on your own. But things will get better. I promise. Do you have someplace to stay tonight? Don't be afraid to tell me the truth."

"Yes."

The lady's face fell. "Oh."

"I'll sleep in a doorway covered with newspaper." Anna sobbed happily. She hadn't entirely lost her mark. "I'll get a room soon. I just got a job as a chorus girl. So, you see, I can pay for some very humble place. Or I will be able to."

Mrs. Rosenberg smiled. "Isn't that a coincidence. I own an apartment building for career girls."

Anna slumped as if the world rested on her shoulders. "That's kind, but I don't have references."

"I trust my instincts."

She really oughtn't do that, given her instincts were completely missing the fact that Anna was a cop. Or would like to be.

"You have a room available?"

At this, the smile slipped off Mrs. Rosenberg's face. Still she said, "Yes, of course. We'll make room."

"I can pay you at the end of the week."

The lady patted Anna's hand. "I know you will, dear. Eat your ice cream. I'll be right back." Mrs. Rosenberg pressed Anna's cheek and disappeared into the kitchen. She returned with a lease and pen in hand. "It's month-to-month. That way, if things change, say if you found a husband, you can go. Why don't you fill it out while I take care of some business?" She stood and disappeared back into the kitchen.

Through the window, Anna watched her appear in the yard and walk across the lawn to the Jonquil Apartments. The lady held an umbrella. It had started to rain.

Anna signed the lease and hailed the waiter. "Do you have petit fours? And cocoa?"

§

While Anna sated her sweet tooth, she watched through the window. Mrs. Rosenberg ushered a girl out the front door of the Jonquil Apartments into the rain. The girl, a beauty, dragged a trunk. She looked young—maybe sixteen—and possibly Spanish.

Anna stood up for a better look. The former tenant didn't seem to be leaving. She just sat on her trunk on the sidewalk with her arms crossed stoically.

Mrs. Rosenberg reemerged with an umbrella for the Spanish girl. It was a paltry offering, and the girl refused it. She already dripped.

Anna felt someone at her elbow and turned. A young lady stood peering out at the Spaniard and the silvery gray streets of the city.

"Why is she evicting that girl? What did she do?" Anna asked.

"It's more what she didn't do."

"Oh?" said Anna. "Tell me so I can make sure to do it. I need this apartment."

One of the girl's eyebrows rose to the ceiling as if Anna were ridiculous or something. "Mrs. Rosenberg promised you an apartment?" She looked Anna up and down. "Makes a lot of sense."

"Tell me."

"She was a bad housekeeper." The young lady smirked and swished off.

Anna was glad her landlord had no such standards. But she thought the girl might be lying. It occurred to Anna that only a highly indiscreet girl would tell a stranger her business, especially if it were nefarious. She scanned the café for someone who looked highly indiscreet. But they all appeared equally discreet, not nefarious at all—a collection of young, professional ladies, mostly in pairs or trios.

In a nearby window booth, one ashen-haired girl sat alone, her large green eyes darting hopefully to the door every time it opened. She looked bored as she sipped her soup, and possibly lonely—possibly a weak animal, separated from the herd. She might be inclined to talk, if cornered, if she truly were lonely. After all, she and Anna shared three things in common—they were both Jonquil renters, extraordinarily lovely, and about the same age. Anna pocketed the petit fours. She shed her fabricated sadness, flounced over, and blinded the girl with her teeth.

"May I sit down?" She perched in the booth beside the young lady as if it were just the normal thing to do. It wasn't—not without an introduction. "I'm Gladys Sydalg. I'm an actress and we're going to be neighbors."

"Samara . . . M . . . Mowrey."

Anna cocked her head. The girl either had a stutter, or she'd briefly forgotten her last name. Also, what kind of a name was Samara? A made-up prostitute name.

Samara smiled the kind of smile that made grown men swoon. It almost made Anna swoon. The young lady said, "If you must sit, I'll have a brandy." Once she opened her mouth, she didn't seem weak and she didn't have a stutter.

Anna deduced she was using an alias, too. "Isn't brandy included? I was hoping . . ."

"Regrettably, no. Drinking turns your nose red. Mrs. Rosenberg wouldn't want us to be inebriates. But, never fear. You'll have brandy enough. Even champagne." The girl winked at Anna and offered her hand. "How do you do?"

Anna shook. "Very well, actually. I was having trouble paying my rent, but now . . . ? Anna let her words trail off.

"You're so beautiful. I can't believe you'll have any trouble keeping a roof over your head."

"You mean if I do things with the men?"

The young lady's eyes popped. She lowered her voice. "My goodness. You're plain spoken."

"Forgive me. Sometimes I take manners for granted. You see, I have nothing to prove. I was well-born."

"You don't look well-born. I'm not complaining about your manners, mind you. I like to know where things stand. It's just . . . Mrs. Rosenberg told you everything? Or rather, what exactly did she say?"

"Everything," Anna arched her brows. "You know. About the men."

"Curious. Mrs. Rosenberg is typically not plain spoken. I had no idea until after . . . after—"

"I understand."

"You do?" She relaxed back on the bench. "Frankly, I was going to warn you, but I suppose there's no need."

Anna leaned in close. "You aren't being held prisoner, are you?"

The girl looked taken aback. "Heavens no. I'm as happy as a clam."

"Who pays your rent? A man from Mars?" Anna bent her neck backward and laughed up at the ceiling, all by herself.

The lady squinted her eyes and examined Anna. "You're a little crazy."

"I beg your pardon?"

"Don't worry, I don't mind. We had a crazy girl here, but she moved out."

"I think I met her. Matilda? She's far too young to go with men."

"Fifteen's not too young. Fifteen's marrying age. And there aren't many alternatives."

"And that Spanish girl. She wouldn't go with the men?"

"No, and look where that got her. Now she's on the streets."

Across the café, Anna noticed Joe lounging at a table and pretending not to watch them. His suit was wet. The indignant grocer must have detained him for quite some time and in the rain. Anna noted he had bought a big bag of fruit—penance for stealing the cherry no doubt. Anna caught his eye, and winked, deliberately indiscreet. "That man is watching me and he's handsome."

"He's handsome all right, but he doesn't have any money. Look at what he's eating."

It was true. Joe ate crackers with butter, which were free.

Samara said, "If you have an affair with him, Mrs. Rosenberg will likely chase him away."

"Maybe not him, then. But I am rather in a hurry." Anna lowered her voice to a whisper. "I'm paying usurious interest on a loan."

Samara winced sympathetically.

"So, how does this work? Am I to be seduced? Should I pretend to resist?" Anna asked.

The lady leaned forward conspiratorially. "Mrs. Rosenberg introduces you to a man, well, we don't use real names. You entertain him in the café and, if you like him . . ." Her voice became a whisper. "You can entertain him at the bath house or the massage parlor upstairs. Mrs. Rosenberg owns that too. He gives you money. Mrs. Rosenberg takes half. It's the same man every time, if you're suited."

"Who is he?"

"Oh, there's more than one man. It's just, I only have one man and he only has me." She lowered her voice. "I'm a mistress, not a whore. Cuts down on disease."

"You don't use real names?"

"No,"

"Then, how do you address him?"

"My man? Everyone calls him Mr. King because he has a majestic disregard for money. Or, 'The Black Pearl,' because he wears a rather large black pearl scarf pin."

"So, he's rich."

"He must be."

Anna noticed the girl wore a diamond ring—possibly a gift from her lover. It lacked symmetry and Anna didn't like it. She also noticed a fading yellow bruise on the girl's pale hand, as if she'd pinched it in a door. Or like someone had squeezed it. Did she have bruises elsewhere, covered by her clothes?

"He doesn't hurt you?"

The lady moved her hand discreetly to her lap. "Never."

Anna found this suspicious and didn't believe her. "How much money does he give you?"

"Whatever's in his pockets, but it's always more than enough. I think he'd give me whatever I asked. He's a gentleman like that. And I save every penny."

"So, he's . . . kind?"

"He gave me this necklace." She fished the pendant from beneath her décolletage and handed it to Anna. It spanned the distance between them, still hanging by Samara's neck. It was a cross, studded with red gemstones, and warm from the lady's skin. "Garnets and eighteen carat gold. He gave all the girls identical necklaces. That's why I say he's kind." She smirked. "We call it 'The cross of the legion of dishonor.'"

"So, he's a patron to all the girls?"

"No. He only sleeps with me. But he brings his friends here. He's here twice a day. Mrs. Rosenberg recruits the girls. Mrs. Rosenberg gets half of whatever we earn. I don't know what Mr. King gets for bringing the men."

Anna's smile had slipped. She tugged it back up too late.

Samara sensed her disapproval. "It's not illegal." She thought for a moment. "Tax evasion, maybe."

"It's illegal to recruit a girl if she's underage and of good reputation." Reputation—that was a sticky part of the law. If the girl was already branded a wanton, even if she were young, the law didn't much care. Joe had told her so. "And drugging a girl would be illegal."

"Who said anything about drugging a girl? We're wooed not forced. And we're all of marriageable age."

"You've never seen it happen?"

"Have you?"

Anna whispered, "Matilda."

"The Black Pearl would never drug a girl. I know him."

"What about a different man?"

"I . . . I don't know. I don't know them all. But no one drugged me."

"There were some very young girls here—two twins."

Samara glanced toward the door, then took a sip of her brandy. "What twins?"

Mrs. Rosenberg entered the café in the company of a young, blond gentleman. His clothes smacked of money, but his jaw was weak and could use a discreet powdering. His ruddy skin shone like an oil slick. Anna recognized him. How could she not? Clyde Owen had been in her confirmation class. He would see through her disguise.

"Is it warm in here?" She produced a fan and began fluttering it to hide her face, though it was a winter day and cold for Los Angeles. "Is that him? The Black Pearl?"

Samara chuckled. "Are you quite serious?"

Mrs. Rosenberg ushered the man in their direction. Anna raised the fan so that her eyes barely peeped from behind it. She fluttered it in rhythm with her rapid heartbeat.

"Miss Sydalg, Miss Mowrey, this is Mr. Smith."

"Biscuits," Anna said flatly.

Samara smirked. She leaned close and whispered, "I'd hold out."

The man slid into the booth beside Anna, leering at her. He smelled like a patchouli bush. Her fan pulsated frantically.

Mrs. Rosenberg laughed, her voice a silk flower. She put two fingers up and lowered Anna's fan. "She's got a marvelous sense of humor."

He squinted at Anna. His eyes sparked and caught fire, no doubt fueled by some perverse hope. "Anna?"

She tensed everywhere. Her eyes fluttered madly. Her ruse was unraveling. She was about to get caught. Then Mrs. Rosenberg would disappear, hide evidence, or otherwise frustrate Anna's investigation. Or maybe, she'd simply make Anna disappear.

"Gladys Sydalg," Mrs. Rosenberg repeated.

"Oh yes, Mrs. Rosenberg. Heavens, yes. She's the one I want."

Mrs. Rosenberg patiently pressed her eyes closed. "Don't be vulgar my boy. You'll spook her."

Anna's stomach turned. She wanted to flee but was hemmed in by Mr. Owen and Samara. "I don't want the room after all, Mrs. Rosenberg." She scooted so close to Samara, the girl had no choice but to get out of the way. Anna slid out of the booth.

Mrs. Rosenberg sighed. "You see?"

Mr. Owen jumped up and grabbed Anna's hand. His palm felt damp. "You know I'm not Mr. Smith. You know very well I'm Clyde, and I know you're Anna."

Mrs. Rosenberg slapped a hand over her eye.

"But it's okay. It can be our little secret. Please, make me the happiest of men . . . I mean."

Anna wriggled in disgust and pulled her hand away. Samara stepped closer. "Hey Clyde, lay off!"

The cad continued. "It's not a proposal, I'm already married, but—"

Joe's fist collided with Mr. Owen's shiny jaw. Anna hadn't seen it coming, hadn't seen him coming. She watched the man teeter and fall. His head hit the floor and bounced. His eyes closed.

The maître d' was on Joe in a flash, holding his arms from behind. He had fifty pounds on Anna's lover at least.

Anna yelped.

Mrs. Rosenberg stabbed at Joe with her finger. "Young man, you're banned from the premises." She glared at Clyde Owen, who lay on the ground with his eyes closed. She jabbed down at him. "You, too. I don't know what you were thinking."

Anna glared at Joe. "So, I smiled at you. Your reaction was

unwarranted. My actions don't need to be warranted because I signed a lease. Girls are very important, and you're just a penniless cracker eater who I've never seen before in my life. You should try the Spanish beauty sitting on her trunk outside."

"My dear, you're odd, but you have a knack for inspiring passion in men," said Mrs. Rosenberg.

"I know," said Anna.

Joe struggled against the burly maître d'. "All right. I'm sorry. I understand. My actions are unwarranted. Yours don't need to be warranted. But I don't like how he was talking to you. Tell this ape to let go of me and I'll leave."

Mrs. Rosenberg nodded, and the maître d' let Joe go. He stomped out the door onto the street.

Anna was alone in an establishment where young girls were possibly drugged and raped by Martians. Her insides fluttered. She turned to Samara, "Thank you for defending me." She smiled at Mrs. Rosenberg. "Show me to my room?"

Chapter 16

Anna and Mrs. Rosenberg trudged up the steps to the Jonquil Apartments beneath a black umbrella and the dripping branches of pepper trees. Two stone cherubs stretched their wings above the door, promising peace and protection. Joe was nowhere to be seen. Anna looked about for the Spanish beauty, but she was gone too. Anna silently wished her well.

Mrs. Rosenberg unlocked the door and took Anna's hand. Anna followed her across the threshold. The lady's hand felt cold, like her eyes. "Of course, no men are allowed."

Anna nodded. She had one goal—to find and rescue the twins and any other young girls who may be trapped by a warm bed, pig's feet in batter, and no alternatives. Then she could take them back to the cow ring where she would feed them stolen mush until the Friday Morning Club came up with a better plan, or they were sent to Whittier Reform Academy where they wouldn't be safe either, and the food was so bad they would yearn for the Jonquil. Anna squeezed her eyes shut. She had to stop thinking in hopeless circles or she would lose her gumption.

If they had witnesses, the LAPD could raid the Jonquil, she could give the story to the newspapers, and maybe some of the men who frequent the place could be prosecuted.

They tread down a colorless hallway, cold hand in trembling hand, passing apartments. Anna thought she heard the monotone drone of the twins in conversation floating through a door. One voice rose in anger. She took note of the room number. Mrs. Rosenberg paused and patted Anna to reassure her. "You'll like your room. You get one of our few singles."

She unlocked a door with a plain brass key, and then handed the key to Anna. The room was small and simple but clean. It featured no decorations and a twin bed with an old, brown, patchwork quilt—not a place to entertain men, certainly.

"I'll let you rest up. The bathroom is down the hall. And please join us for breakfast in the café. My treat." Mrs. Rosenberg exited the room backward with a puckered smile. "Good night."

When the landlady had gone, Anna stepped into the hall and flounced in torn ruffles back to where she'd heard the voices of the twins. She pushed back her fake, wavy locks, and knocked on the door without an introduction, without even knowing their names.

One of the twins answered. "Hello." She wore rouge, which she most certainly had not before.

Anna smiled and whispered, "Hello. I'm with the police."

The girl looked Anna up and down. "You don't look like you're with the police."

"I promise you, I am. There's an officer waiting outside, but he can't come in because he doesn't have a warrant."

The girl looked nervous.

Anna smiled extra hard. "I'm here to help you. Can I please come in? Pretty please?"

The girl cocked her head looking suspicious. "You're not another Mrs. Rosenberg? You know. She seems nice, but she wants things."

Anna shook her head vehemently. "I'm the opposite." Of course, she did want things. She wanted them to testify. She crossed her fingers. If this twin did not take the bait, Anna would be exposed as an LAPD police matron and could never go undercover here again. Mrs. Rosenberg and the nefarious Black Pearl would be on their guard, and Anna could never move forward with prosecution. "We want to take you somewhere safe where you don't have to do things with men."

Suddenly, the girl seemed interested. "Is there food?"

"Very good food," lied Anna. "And you'll make lots of nice friends." With Matilda, a forger, a counterfeiter, several shoplifters . . . "We're like a family there. A happy one."

The twin cocked her head.

"You can bring your sister, of course," said Anna. "But we should go now."

She heard Mrs. Rosenberg's voice somewhere down the hall. Her own voice went high with desperation. "May I please come in?"

The twin hesitated.

Mrs. Rosenberg's voice grew louder, closer. Anna blurted, "We play Parcheesi night and day."

The twin opened the door wide and Anna slipped in.

The other twin sat on the bed gaping. Anna assumed her most charming demeanor. "Hello. I'm Matron Blanc with the LAPD. I've come to take you to safety."

"I don't want to go with you. Your dress is torn and your hair is weird."

"I think we should go," said the twin who had let Anna in.

"You would. You're stupid," said the twin on the bed.

The standing twin picked up a shoe from the floor and threw it, hitting her sister. "You're stupid and ugly."

Anna winced. "You're twins."

The twin on the bed threw the shoe back at her sister. "We aren't coming."

"Then, I have no choice. You're both under arrest."

§

Anna gripped both twins by the hands and dragged them down the hall, out the door of the Jonquil, and down the street at top speed. Their squawking alerted Mrs. Rosenberg who Anna heard shouting. Joe fell into step beside them. "Are you okay?"

"Fit as a fiddle."

"Are they going to testify? Because the girl on the trunk is gone."

Anna gave him a meaningful look. "We are going to give them tasty food, a warm bed, and new friends. And they won't have to do things with men. That's as far as we've gotten."

Mrs. Rosenberg came running from behind and darted in front of Anna, causing her to stop. "Gladys Syldag, what do you think you're doing?" Her lips were puckered to a point.

"Biscuits! Joe, we're found out. We can't let her get back to the Jonquil."

Joe flashed his brass star. "Mrs. Rosenberg, you're under arrest."

§

The Henry twins had come from Minnesota on a train, virtuous yet friendless, traveling alone to the land of sunshine, fleeing a drunken father who loved the belt and had broken Sue's arm. He had pulled them out of school five years ago to replace their dead mother's labor. Anna could only tell them apart because Clementine's hair was short on one side. Sue had chopped it while her twin was sleeping. Sue was older than Clementine by ten all-important minutes. They were unloved and sixteen.

When Anna gave them a stern look, Sue clammed up, but Clementine sang like a canary. Mrs. Rosenberg had found them at the train station and offered them a place to stay. They quickly found themselves in the arms of bushy mustache man and scrawny mustache man. It had been frightening and painful, but the girls were flattered and were each briefly fifty dollars richer—more money than they had ever seen. Mrs. Rosenberg had then taken all their money, in addition to her cut, to pay room and board for the next two months. Subsequent earnings would be split down the middle. In two months, they'd owe rent again.

Anna thought this deal was rather ingenious on the part of Mrs. Rosenberg. Any girl with scruples would have to choose between the dangerous streets and excellent food. She could lie to herself and tell herself she would stay the two months and not see men, meanwhile looking for a job, but expenses would crop up, and it would be so easy to entertain just one more time—especially if it were the same man every time. It would almost be like taking a lover. Especially if all the other girls were doing it. By the end of two months, the girl would be used to the idea.

Sue and Clementine had only been at the Jonquil Apartments for a week. Anna promised them they could stay in the cow ring and that she would try to get them a refund.

§

The next morning, Anna and Joe interviewed Mrs. Rosenberg together in the presence of her lawyer, a Mr. W.H. Stevens. His demeanor was serious, as if he were more serious than anyone who had ever lived. Anna felt he did not take her seriously at all, but that was no surprise. His hair was perfectly controlled. He sat there frowning.

Mrs. Rosenberg folded her arms tight across her chest. "Officer, you're being absurd. I don't know any Black Pearl. My tenants are not prostitutes. They're career girls. They work in shops or in theater. Some are nurses. They certainly don't entertain men in my apartments. They have single beds, for heaven's sake."

Joe was all cop. "That's not what the twins say, and they don't agree on much. They say you lured them into sin and profited from it. They're virtuous minors Mrs. Rosenberg—or they were virtuous. Now they're broken blossoms. You're using children for immoral purposes. That's a kidnapping charge right there. Those girls are going to testify against you. Why go down alone? If you help us, the judge will go easier on you. Just give us the Black Pearl."

The woman remained resolutely silent.

Anna despised pouty Mrs. Rosenberg on the balance, but begrudgingly admired her faithfulness to the Black Pearl. Her puckered lips were sealed.

§

When they left the room, Joe said, "I think it's time for a raid—before she posts her bail. I can get a warrant. We go in, look for young girls, look for drugs."

Anna clapped her hands. "Yes! I'd love to raid."

"Captain Wells is not going to let you raid. It's too dangerous."

"A woman has to go to protect the girls."

"I've already spoken to him. He said no."

He said "no" was the story of Anna's life.

CHAPTER 17

While Joe and the other cops were out having fun raiding the Jonquil, Anna raided their lunch pails for food for the refugees. She found sandwiches of all varieties: oranges, cookies, carrots, candy, and cheese. She smuggled her loot to the cow ring in a mail bag and distributed it to the women and children who lodged there, escaping violence or the cold. "Do not tell anyone about this food," she said. "If someone comes by, hide it. Because otherwise, they might want you to share. Do you understand?"

The women and children nodded.

When Anna returned to her desk, an envelope of shimmering white lay on her desk beneath the bouquet that Georges had given her, which was now starting to wilt. She plucked up the note and held it to her nose, inhaling the scent of lavender. Inside, in fancy black script, Georges had invited Anna and Joe to his home for dinner at 8:00 o'clock that evening. It looked like an invitation from a proper gentleman, not a bastard.

It was almost as exciting as a raid. No, it was more exciting, because raids were fleeting. Brothers were forever.

Anna scribbled an acceptance, then cursed the fact she no longer had servants to deliver her note. She would have to resort to the telephone. She called the hello girl and asked for Georges's hotel.

Georges was out. She spoke to his man. "Please tell Mr. Devereaux that Detective Singer and Miss Blanc thank him for his kind invitation and are pleased to accept." Joe didn't know he would

dine with Georges, but surely he'd be happy. He looked so wonderful dressed up—like the Arrow Collar Man.

To Anna's jealous dismay, Joe had not finished raiding by 5:30
p.m., the time Anna needed to leave to get ready. She scribbled a
note to him and left it on his desk.

*My Darling. Georges has invited you to his house for dinner tonight
at 8:00. I accepted on your behalf. I look forward to seeing you dressed
for dinner.*

She hesitated before signing. After all, their liaison was a secret.
There was a chance that Officer Snow would read the note. He'd
done it before. She signed,

Your very best friend,
Helmut Melvin.

Surely the clerk wouldn't mind.

§

The Streeter apartments on First Street catered to professional ladies
of good reputation and Anna. She paid extra for the privilege. Her
small quarters were stuffed with treasure from a previous life—racks
of fine clothes filled the bedroom and spilled out into the living
room. Hatboxes balanced in towers that reached the ceiling. Her
giant oak canopy bed, which could not fit in her bedroom, sat smack
in the middle of her living room, along with a baby grand piano,
and the rest of her mother's fine antiques. This made it impossible
to walk from one end of the room to the other. Anna had to crawl
across the bed to get to the stove, which she still didn't know how
to light.

She bathed in a giant tub in the communal bathroom. Somewhere above, a pipe leaked, staining the ceiling and leaving a little
puddle on the plank floor. The situation on the home front was
dire. Rats nested in her undermuslins, and she had to throw out two
chewed pairs of drawers. Dust was a problem. Anna would need to
hire men to move the furniture, so she could beat the Persian rug.

She wondered if she might sneak back into her father's mansion to permanently borrow the vacuum cleaner. The precarious towers of hats were a problem. Twice a week, like clockwork, one toppled. Hat feathers were bent and brims dented. Even now, having to wade through the sea of gowns that overflowed her bedroom made it difficult to find the right nice thing. Looking in the full-length, gilded mirror, which balanced on a writing desk, required Anna to stand on a chair.

She had no maid to help her dress, style her hair, or launder her gowns—a definite inconvenience. After several months of trial and costly error, Anna had become marginally proficient, but it wasn't easy, and her corset was never quite tight enough.

Anna donned a sumptuous silk gown of purple chiffon and velvet, and only one scant petticoat, so that the fabric skimmed her hips and pooled at her feet. She planned to look good for Joe Singer, who, as of late, saw her in nothing but an ugly matron's uniform. She coiled and pinned her hair, then topped it with a poufy yak hairpiece for extra height and an ostrich plume clip for even more loft. She climbed onto the chair, looked in the mirror, closed her eyes, then opened them quickly, half hoping her father's mansion on Bunker Hill would materialize behind her. It didn't.

Still, she was a vision and she knew it.

She had ordered this particular gown last summer from Vionnet of the House of Doucet in Paris. It was still one year ahead of the fashions worn in Los Angeles. Her beaded slippers, too, had crossed the Atlantic, specially made by Francois Pinet. That happened back when her fiancé had paid the bills.

Anna's long white neck looked naked. Proper aristocrats wore jewels and lots of them. Jewels she lacked—the heirlooms her father had reclaimed from her when he threw her out of the house. Her fingers, too, looked long, white, and bare. She still had one fine ring—Edgar Wright's engagement ring—but it would be wrong to wear it. She had returned it to him once, and he'd sent it right back in a little brown box in the mail.

Joe did not meet Anna at her apartment to escort her to Georges's for dinner. Likely, he had never seen the note. Or, he would be late and meet her at Georges's house. Maybe he couldn't reach Anna. Maybe he called Georges.

Anna glided into the Hotel Alexandria like the queen of the ball—like she used to be. In the lobby, she passed Mr. Tilly the newspaper reporter. She smiled, a devil-may-care smile. "Jupiter. It's Mr. Tilly. Don't you wish you could write something scandalous about me tonight? But there's nothing shady about this." She twirled. "I'm merely visiting my brother." Anna lifted her chin and laughed a song, gliding past him to the elevator.

A group of five young men in lavish attire exited the elevator laughing heartily. They wore scarves and gold cufflinks, and offered her their good evenings, standing aside to let Anna in. The elevator boy levitated her eight stories to the penthouse floor. She gave him a horehound candy with a magnanimous smile.

A strapping manservant answered the door. Georges hovered behind him, waiting to greet Anna. He took her hands, stepped backward, and said, "Anna, you do credit to your brother." Georges kissed her on each cheek in the French way. She wanted to throw her arms around him and never let go. She wanted to gush and tell him how much it meant to her to have a brother who claimed her, and that she loved him second best in all the world, behind Joe Singer. Maybe the men were equally important, because Georges and Anna shared blood. His countenance reminded her of their father. The thought filled Anna with longing for her father, though the man was a veritable ass.

The manservant bustled about the suite, clearing away used glasses and emptying ashtrays. Anna deduced the young men had come from Georges's hotel suite. It made her smile. Her brother was popular.

"Come here, Anna. I have something of yours." Georges strode excitedly into the living room with Anna in tow. He opened his writing desk and handed her a box—a hinged, velvet one with satin lining. She opened it and saw the glint of jewels. Her eyes sparkled.

She knew the piece. It had belonged to her paternal grandmother. Anna had never seen another necklace with so many diamonds.

"I have others, too, in the vault at the bank."

"Father didn't want me to have them," she said.

"Father is not going to wear them. He can't sell them. They're heirlooms. I have no wife."

"You might marry."

"No, I will never marry."

"Yes, I see the allure of that. But marriage is a much better deal for men. You have all the power and you don't have to have the babies."

He steered Anna by the shoulders up to a gilt mirror cast with the shapes of ribbons and flowers. "Your neck looks bare." He took the box from her and extracted the necklace, fastening it around her neck. "Ah, that's better."

It was better. It lay against her creamy skin like a garland made of starlight.

"I'm not giving it to you. It's already yours, your birthright."

"It really should be mine . . . But I can't keep it in my apartment. It isn't safe. The rats will eat it."

"Oh *Mon Dieu*. Rats?"

"Or my landlord might steal it. I've heard him try my door handle when he thought I wasn't home. Joe installed a bolt."

"Move in here. There's a spare bedroom in the suite."

"But, we're practically strangers."

"Not strangers. Blood relatives. It would be a chance for you to get to know your brother. Soon, you'll get married and move in with that cop. You'd be much more comfortable here than in your rat trap. You'd have servants, your own bath, and could eat at the hotel." He frowned. "But perhaps you like your apartment?"

Anna may not like her apartment, but she did cherish her independence. If she lived here, under her brother's watchful eye, she couldn't make love to Joe. The servants especially tempted Anna, but the answer would have to be no.

Georges went on. "I wouldn't interfere. You could do as you please . . . Work at the police station, or not. I have a feeling you'll want to. And I support that. But know this, you never *have* to work again."

"Thank you, Georges. I'll think about it."

"So, did the rats eat your other jewelry?" He chuckled.

"Father kept my jewelry. I was only able to keep two pieces, and Detective Wolf put them on consignment for me. They haven't sold yet."

"Then, I'll get them back."

"All right."

"I wondered how you lived off that salary. What do they pay you? Ten dollars a week?"

"No Georges, I make seventy-five dollars a month. The same as a patrolman."

Georges's face lit with pride. "You don't say?"

"But my rent is high, and I owe my dressmaker and a gun shop. Also, there are two children I support in the country." She didn't mention that she was responsible for their mother Eve's death.

"You support children? They aren't your children, are they?"

"Of course not. It's just, I knew their dead mother. I don't like to talk about it."

"How very noble of you, Anna."

"Yes, I know. Don't tell Joe, because he would insist on supporting them himself and he can't afford it either. He thinks they are with relatives in Denver. The point is, my expenses are very high for a matron. Thus, I have a plan to supplement my income playing bridge. It's not actually gambling because I always win. My friend Clara is trying to get me invited to parties again. There are some loaded people who don't know me or my prowess with cards, though they mostly live in Pasadena."

"That's an interesting idea." Georges's face fell. "I regret I can't help you socially, because I'm a bastard."

"You're a highly respected bastard."

"They won't let me join the California Club."

"They're fools."

"I can't complain. I have many wonderful friends and business associates. Why don't you teach me how to play bridge? I've always wanted to learn. We can host our own party."

"It would be my pleasure."

Georges felt like home, like a brother, even if he was first crop and she was second crop, even if he was a bastard. She felt his affection without condition, and she didn't have to pledge obedience and surrender all her earthly goods, etcetera, like women had to do when they married. It was a wondrous thing. It made her realize how much she missed being part of a family.

He led her into the dining room where a table had been set with three place settings.

"Did Joe call? I couldn't find him, but I left a note."

"He did call. He won't be joining us."

"Oh." Anna said, her shoulders sinking. "I so wanted us all to be together. You will love him once you get to know him. I know he was rude, but he's wonderful, really. Did I tell you he sings and plays ragtime piano? He's hep to all the new music."

"I look forward to hearing him."

"There must be a piano at this hotel. He could play for us."

"Wonderful."

"We are solving a murder together—someone killed in Griffith Park. I've put up pictures of the victim in the post office, but I've only got one lead, and I'm waiting to hear from the police in Oklahoma City."

"Sister, you astound me."

Anna beamed. "Yes, I know."

The manservant appeared at the door to the parlor and announced, "Your father is here, sir."

Anna's face drained of color. She forgot about Joe and the murder and, for a moment, she couldn't move her tongue. "Father is here? Father . . ." Her fists tightened, and she socked the sides of her gown. "Georges, how could you?"

"Don't you think it's time he came to his senses?"

"Yes, but he's been senseless for so long. What if he can't? What if he won't forgive me?"

"Forgive you? For what? It's he that needs forgiveness."

"That's true, but I doubt he sees it that way."

"I'm sorry Anna, I thought you'd come around to the idea. I can send him away if you wish. After all, he's in the wrong."

"No . . . I don't know." Anna bit her thumbnail through her long glove, then remembering herself, dropped her hand.

"I think a grouchy, middle-aged man is no match for my brave sister."

Anna nodded.

Georges motioned to the manservant. "Show him in please, Thomas. Just be ready to show him out again if his company irks Miss Anna." Georges looked her somberly in the face. "We won't let him bully you."

Anna nodded again more vigorously and braced herself for her father's scathing eye. At least she had dressed like a queen, though inside she felt like the little match girl. Georges smiled his encouragement.

Christopher Blanc strolled into the dining room with criticism on his lips. "Georges, what do you mean by making me wait to be announced . . ."

When he saw Anna, graceful in all her beauty, he stopped talking. She stood tall, and tried to look disinterested, but the trembling of her lower lip gave her away. Christopher's jaw tightened.

"Good evening, father," said Anna.

Mr. Blanc's mouth twisted in disgust. "Oh, *mon Dieu*."

Georges's eyes hardened. "Pardon me, father, but don't you

mean, 'Good evening, Anna. It's so good to see you. I've been longing for the company of my lost daughter who I so cruelly cast aside?'"

Her father turned an angry red. "You say that as if she wasn't a whore. She's not my daughter. My daughter is dead."

Anna looked to Georges and tears began pooling in her gray eyes. She started to shake.

Georges's face flooded with color. Suddenly, he looked very much like his father. "She's not a whore! Even the papers acknowledge this. But not you! You should be proud of her. She's an LAPD police matron. She's like, she's like Sherlock Holmes."

Christopher spit right on the Hotel Alexandria's fine Persian carpet.

Georges stomped near to his father, his arm flung out toward the door. "That is it. If you won't acknowledge her, then you're not welcome here. Get out!"

Before he reached their father, Georges stopped and braced himself on a chair. He dropped to one knee, and then crumpled to the floor, convulsing. His eyes rolled back in his head and foam burbled on the edges of his lips.

Anna flew to her fallen brother and crouched beside him, careless of her dress and the fact that her father knelt at her side.

"Georges!" She took his face between her hands. Anna's eyes cut to her father, her voice a desperate squawk. "What's wrong with him?"

"Hold his head so he doesn't strike it." He sounded as shaken as Anna. He placed his hands beneath Anna's, further cushioning Georges's skull.

Anna held his head, but Georges's fit continued.

"He's not calming." Christopher called to the manservant "Thomas! His medicine. Now!"

Thomas returned with a syringe and vial. He stuck the needle into the vial and withdrew a liquid, clear and faint blue. Georges still pitched and jolted. Christopher barked, "Hold him still." Anna pinned his arms with all her might. Her father unbuttoned his shirt and yanked his shirt and jacket down. Thomas plunged the needle into Georges's shoulder.

Christopher said, "You've upset him. You shouldn't have upset him."

Anna returned to holding Georges's head, her fingers cushioning his skull as it banged against the carpet. One horrid thought crowded out all others—he was going to die before she ever got to truly know him. "I'm so sorry dearest. I'm so sorry."

When he finally stilled, her eyes went to his chest, to the rising and falling of his breath. She let out a single, hollow sob and pressed her lips to his damp forehead. "He has epilepsy."

"What do you know about epilepsy?"

"Enough. I read medical tomes. You may have tried to keep me away from books, but my friends have libraries."

He harrumphed.

"It can be fatal. It can cause memory loss. A loss of willpower." Her voice trailed off. "Insanity." She sighed. "The more frequent the attacks, the more weakened the man."

"Excuse me, Miss Blanc." Thomas knelt opposite Anna and, together with Mr. Blanc, lifted Georges—one man at his head, one at his feet. She followed as they carried him into a masculine bedroom that smelled of cologne. Anna pulled back the coverlet and top sheet on the bed, and the men lay Georges down. She undid his neck tie and collar and helped remove his jacket and shoes. She jogged to the bathroom and wet a towel.

Anna sat by his side mopping his brow with the damp cloth, whether he needed it or not. She needed it.

Christopher Blanc slumped in a chair across the room and cut the tip off a cigar. "Anna, you should go home."

"No father. I'm going to sleep here tonight. And don't you dare light that thing. He needs fresh air."

Chastened, Mr. Blanc pocketed his cigar.

Anna took her brother's hand and held it. "How often does he have fits?"

"That depends. He takes bromides to prevent them, but he says the pills make him feel dull. He doesn't like to take them. I suspect he's been skipping them. He's supposed to take them three times a day."

"Dull? He's not dull. He's interesting. He's such a fine man." Anna made a hiccupping sound. Then, she began to sob. "I can hardly believe he came from you."

"He's been a great comfort to me since you . . . broke my heart. He was living in France, but he came back."

"You don't have a heart."

"Oh, don't I?"

"No, you don't."

"You shamed me."

"*I* shamed *you*? I wasn't the one keeping a French dancer. I don't have illegitimate children. I'm not even ruined. But you. You've been ruined all along. And for no better reason than your own desires. I sacrificed my reputation to save parlor girls. That makes me a hero and you a hypocrite."

A vein stood out on Mr. Blanc's red forehead. He shouted. "It's different for men!"

"What's good for geese is good for ganders, even if they don't lay eggs. And you did lay an egg. Georges!"

"Are you calling me a goose?"

"Goose, goose, double goose." She turned her back on him and mopped Georges's brow. "And as far as I'm concerned, I don't have a father. I disown you."

§

Anna awoke with her face crushed against Georges's mattress. She raised her head. Her father was gone. She looked at her patient. His eyes were bloodshot, but open and watching her.

"Georges?"

He smiled at her. "Anna."

CHAPTER 18

Sunrise stained the sky pomegranate. Anna rode the trolley with the promise from Georges that they would dine together with Joe very soon. Even slightly wrinkled, she was the best-dressed woman on the car by a mile, though her eveningwear told tales on her. She had obviously been out all night. But she held her head up high and whistled joyfully if not tunefully. She had disowned her father and it made her feel powerful. Georges felt better, and she had a brother who was in her camp, never mind that he was defective, and she was late for work. She already felt keenly fond of her brother and could barely wait to get better acquainted.

When Joe had quit Anna several months before because she refused to marry him, she had no one—no family and no lover. It had been a frightening feeling. Now she had both Joe and Georges. Sometime soon, perhaps that evening, Joe would dine with her at Georges's hotel and they would come to know him better together. They could talk about the raid of the Jonquil.

At her apartment, Anna raced to wash and change. She flew back out to the trolley stop, forgoing her elegant yak hairpiece, opting to hide her head beneath a large feather hat. By the time she arrived at the station, the criminal ladies had already finished their mush. Matilda sat on her cot in the cow ring sewing another pillowcase shut.

When the girl saw Anna, she offered up a beatific smile. "Good morning Assistant Matron Blanc."

"Hello Matilda. How is our patient, Mrs. Michaelchek?"

"The doctor removed her shackles and she escaped in the night."
Anna beamed. "That bodes well."

Matilda looked at her shoes. "I knew, but I didn't stop her. I didn't see the sense of keeping her in jail, and she couldn't pay the fine."

Anna tut tutted. "Bad girl. That's very wrong." In fact, it's what Anna would have done. Matilda, though crazy as a loon, would make an excellent police matron.

"Yes ma'am."

Anna inspected the sewn-up pillowcase distractedly. "Are you hungry? I could sneak you some mush."

Matilda's eyes widened. "That would be lovely."

Anna felt a sudden sadness. Matilda couldn't stay forever, as much as Anna would like her to. They would have to find something to do with her. Anna cringed at the idea of the Orphan's Asylum, but it was that or a school for bad children. Unless the Friday Morning Club could find her a place. But who would hire a batty girl? She was resourceful and hardworking. Anna wondered if her friend Clara would take Matilda on as a scullery maid or something. Certainly not as a seamstress.

The fact remained, if the cow ring got full, Matilda would have to go. Lodgers were given a two-night limit, and Matilda had overstayed. Anna could take her home to her own little apartment. There was room enough in her big canopy bed, and Matilda would probably clean the place. But where would she put Joe Singer? Food would be twice as expensive. Anna would be reduced to half rations. No matter. She couldn't put Matilda out on the street. Anna could never be so cruel.

It was settled then. Matron Clemens would have to take her.

§

After securing Matilda's illicit mush, Anna resolved to visit her desk. It had piles upon it—piles of things to do: delinquents to catch, wayward girls to reform, mothers to counsel on parenting said wayward girls. Everyone blamed bad children on their mothers and gave their fathers no responsibility whatsoever. If a man committed a crime, it was his mother's fault. This made no sense to Anna, given that men had all the power.

Anna was at a loss for counseling mothers, never having had one nor been one. She had been raised by the firm hand of Mrs. Morales, the Blanc housekeeper, and the iron fist of the Sisters of the Immaculate Heart of Mary. Anna conjured advice based on columns in the newspaper. Of course no one would actually listen to advice from a mother of a wayward girl, thus none of the advice columnists had experience either.

It seemed to Anna that mothers should be gentler than they were, and that kindness was more important than pretty dresses, though pretty dresses were extremely important. She would write that down. Also, mothers should warn their daughters against passion. Anna was all in favor of passion—passion was her favorite thing—but it wasn't to be trusted. Marriage should be delayed at all costs, so that girls could become women and know their freedom. Also, daughters should be taught how much dressmakers charge before they make their order so as to avoid debt.

While Anna sat at her desk practicing wisdom, she noticed that the corpses of Georges's flowers had begun to wilt and smell. She carried the lovely, and undoubtedly expensive, vase to the bin and dumped the dead flowers into the trash. She poured the water down the bathroom sink and returned the vase to her desk. It looked beautiful with or without flowers.

Sue and Clementine, the ruined twins, wandered in.

"You're wrong *and* you're ugly," said Clementine.

Sue socked her.

"Hello," said Anna. "You slept in the cow ring last night. How was it?"

Clementine smirked. "Not as nice as the Jonquil Apartments."

"You're young. You'll have plenty of time to be prostitutes."

"It wasn't like that. Our beaus were looking for wives. They loved us."

"Your beaus were already married," said Anna. "And besides, Clementine, could you really live with that scrawny mustache?"

Sue laughed. Clementine frowned. "I . . . don't know."

"You're simply going to have to love each other."

The twins looked at each other dubiously.

Joe appeared at the doorway.

Anna's face lit up. "You're back. How was the raid?"

"The raid was a bust. We got nothing. No drugs. All the young ladies were over eighteen or at least claimed to be. I think that lawyer warned them."

"Cock biscuits," said Anna. "And no one's come forward with information on the murder?"

"Nope."

"And no word from Oklahoma City?"

"Nope."

Anna's shoulders sank. "So, we have nothing."

CHAPTER 19

Anna began to despair of ever solving the case of the Griffith Park Executioner. During the following week, she barely saw Joe, who had been recruited back to Chinatown for another case. The only development was an angry letter from the postmaster returning Anna's grizzly crime scene photo and admonishing that "Officer Singer use better judgment in the future." Luckily, Anna saw it on Joe's desk and intercepted it before he could read it.

Anna did have plenty of matron's work to do and was doing it when Joe knocked on the frame of her open storeroom door. He looked serious, but she thought he might be hiding a smile. He stepped through accompanied by a woman. "Good morning, Assistant Matron Blanc. Another witness has come forward. May I introduce Miss Allie Sutton, formerly of the Jonquil Apartments." He raised his eyebrows.

The young lady was nearly as fair as Matilda, with intelligent blue eyes, dark lashes, and glorious red hair. She was about Anna's age. Anna stood and beamed. "Hello, Miss Sutton." She turned to Joe. "Can she enlighten us about the man from Mars?"

Joe weighed the question, tilting his head. "Maybe."

Miss Sutton whirled on Joe. "Are you two making fun of me?"

"No, Miss Sutton, we're deadly serious." Now seeing the lady in profile, Anna wondered if she might have a bun in the oven. Though she went in at the sides, she popped out in the front. Another reason not to have children.

"She heard about the raid on the grapevine and she's come to bring charges against Mrs. Rosenberg and one Mr. King, a.k.a. The Black Pearl."

Anna indicated her own chair. "Do have a seat, Miss Sutton."

Miss Sutton perched nervously on the edge. "I'm not sure I should be here. In fact, I think I'll go." She rose from her seat, her gloved hands clasping each other. "I could use something to steady my nerves."

"Please stay." Anna gently pushed down on her shoulder, guiding her back into the chair. "I'd offer you a medicinal whiskey, but matrons don't ever drink whiskey."

"That's a shame," said Miss Sutton.

"But cops can drink whiskey. Officer Singer, why don't you offer her a drink?"

Joe shook his head. "I'm sorry Miss Sutton, I regret I don't have any—"

Anna opened her drawer and retrieved a bottle of Georges's fine Canadian whiskey. There was no reason not to share it. Georges was a bottomless jar. She handed it to Joe. "Here's your whiskey. Right here in this desk."

He cleared his throat. "Miss Sutton, would you like some of, uh, my whiskey?"

"If you please."

Anna handed Joe a glass and he filled it. Miss Sutton tossed it back like water.

"Better?" Anna moved Joe's hand to the bottle. He got the hint and refilled Miss Sutton's glass.

Miss Sutton sipped this time, savoring it. "Mm. My lover drank good whiskey. I got used to it."

"Oh, it's terrible to have the good stuff, and then to only have the bad stuff. So, I would guess," said Anna.

Miss Sutton nodded. "It isn't his whiskey I miss most. It's him. But I hate him too, you understand?"

Anna looked at Joe and nodded her head. "No. Matrons can't have lovers."

"Miss Sutton. The Jonquil Apartments . . ." Joe said gently.

"Oh yes. I lived there, and nefarious things were afoot. I was seventeen and acting in movies. I still do. That is, I did."

"How interesting," said Anna. "I love the movies."

"Mrs. Rosenberg owns the resort, the café, and the apartments. She introduced me to Mr. King. She introduced all the girls to someone. They took us to the resort. There are baths and a massage parlor. I don't need to tell you what happened."

"You don't need to, but I would appreciate it," said Anna. "You can't be too detailed."

Joe suppressed a smile. "Did Mrs. Rosenberg or Mr. King ever drug you?"

"Heavens no. You don't understand. If a girl didn't like the arrangement, she left. And Lori Tice even married her man."

"The Black Pearl's new lover had a bruise on her hand. I wonder if he ever hurt you."

Miss Sutton flinched at the mention of another lover. "He never hit me. It wasn't sordid. And, I'm not a prostitute. Mr. King gave me gifts, of course, but I was in love with him and he was in love with me. I'm sure of it. He was handsome and amusing. I only ever left him because he said he could never marry me."

Joe and Anna exchanged a look. Anna said, "Why?"

"Why can't a man marry the woman he loves? Because he's already married, clearly. I don't know where she is or who she is. I just know she is." She pressed her eyes with her fingertips, then looked up and cleared her throat. "So, I quit him. That was five months ago."

"When did you last see Mr. King?"

"Once more after that. He came to the Jonquil and begged to have me back. When I refused, he got angry and broke a lamp." She laughed joylessly. "He came another time when I was out. So, I left the Jonquil. I had to leave anyway or take another lover."

"Does Mr. King know you're carrying his child?" said Joe.

It was a rude question, but it had to be asked. Anna was glad Joe had done it so that she didn't have to.

"He'll find out when I testify. But I want nothing to do with a married man."

"How will you support yourself."

"I write scenarios for the movies now. I'm quite good."

"And you knew other girls at the Jonquil who were seduced by rich men?"

"Yes."

"And Mr. King brought men to the Jonquil?"

"Yes. He procures things for wealthy men. Whatever they need. Nothing too awful. Just makes introductions. Connects people. Sometimes he loans them money."

"So where do we find your Mr. King?"

"That's not his real name," said Miss Sutton. "He wouldn't give me his real name."

Joe and Anna exchanged another look.

"I'm not stupid. Deep down I knew. I suppose I didn't want to know." She wiped a tear.

"What did you call him?" asked Anna.

"Bear. I called him my Bear."

Anna turned to Joe. "How are we going to find Miss Sutton's bear? Lie in wait at the Jonquil for someone burly and covered in hair?"

"Nope, we spooked him. I doubt he'll be dining at the Jonquil Café for a while."

§

Later that afternoon, Clementine and Sue played Parcheesi on the floor in the storeroom while Anna puzzled over what to do with them. Finding the twins employment should be easier than placing Matilda as they were sane. She herself would furnish their references, attesting to their dull character and love of Parcheesi, which should keep them out of trouble, leaving the Jonquil out altogether. She wrote to every wealthy lady of her acquaintance, signing the letters "Clara Breedlove" as Anna herself was disgraced. Her best friend, Clara, was not, and probably wouldn't mind. Either way, she wouldn't find out for months, as Clara was in Europe. Anna jotted off a note to the mayor's mother, Mrs. Smucker, who she knew was ill-tempered and thus could not keep servants. She was always looking for help. Anna even wrote to the tight-lacer who ran the Friday Morning Club to see if the girls could sell musicale tickets door-to-door.

Anna heard a knock and looked up to see Joe standing in the doorway, his mouth a straight, hard line. Allie Sutton loomed beside him, slightly out of breath.

Anna said, "Hello again, Miss Sutton. Hello Detective."

Miss Sutton hurried to Anna's desk and spread the *Los Angeles Herald* out across her stack of letters. She pointed triumphantly at a photo on the front page. "There. I found this on a trolley seat, so I turned around and came back."

The newspaper was over a week old and contained the article about Anna.

Anna leaned over. "There where?"

"It's him, don't you see. The Black Pearl."

Anna leaned closer and peered at the newspaper and the picture of a man with gray eyes and thick, ebony, wavy hair. "That's not the Black Pearl or Mr. King or whatever you call him. That's Georges Devereaux."

"I'm telling you. It's my Bear," said Miss Sutton.

Joe's worried eyes met Anna's. "Miss Sutton are you absolutely sure?"

Miss Sutton's face darkened. "Oh, I'm sure."

Anna laughed. "You're mistaken. He might have some resemblance to Mr. King."

Joe said, "Miss Sue, Miss Clementine, is that Mr. King?"

Sue blinked vacuously at Joe. "We never saw Mr. King. We were only there a week."

Clementine shook her head.

Anna paced. "Of course Georges isn't Mr. King. Miss Sutton, thank you for your time. Goodbye."

Joe said, "Thank you Miss Sutton."

Miss Sutton strode to the door. She turned back before exiting. "It's him. I swear it." Then she was gone.

"Twins, you may go help Matilda with the sewing."

Sue obeyed immediately. Clementine dragged her feet.

When they'd gone, Joe said, "Anna, if he wasn't your brother, we would check this out. Mrs. Rosenberg won't talk. It's our only lead."

"If he wasn't my brother, we wouldn't already know that he's a good man."

"Being related to you doesn't make him a good man. We don't know anything about Georges."

"We know he's of good stock. And how dare you? I won't have it. I won't have you insulting Georges. You're accusing him of prostituting minor girls, and he invited you to dinner."

"I tell you what. Let's just see if Matilda recognizes him from this picture. If she doesn't, well, maybe I'll reconsider. But if she does, will you agree to let me just talk to him?"

"It's a moot point. She won't recognize him because he wasn't there!"

"Okay, Anna. He wasn't there."

Matilda wandered in from the hallway. "Matron Clemens said you might need help filing?" She looked uncertainly at the heap of paper on Anna's messy desk.

Joe handed Matilda the newspaper article. "Is this the man from Mars?"

Matilda was silent for a long moment. Her eyes grew shiny. "No."

"You see?" said Anna.

"Have you seen him before?" Joe asked.

"She doesn't know him, Detective Singer," Anna said pointedly.

Matilda frowned in recollection. "Yes. He was at the café?" Her voice lilted in a question.

The roses in Anna's cheeks lost their petals. She walked to the window and stuck her head out, breathing short, quick breaths. She heard Joe say, "Thank you, Matilda. Maybe you can file later. I need Assistant Matron Blanc's help with something important right now. Do you need me to let you back into the cow ring?"

Matilda said. "No, I'm fine. I'll go help Mr. Melvin."

The room fell quiet. Joe strode to the door and closed it. He crossed back to Anna's side and took her in his arms. She was as stiff as a corpse.

She lowered her head onto his shoulder. "He has epilepsy, you know. You could send him into a fit."

"It's probably not him," he whispered in her ear. "It's probably just someone who looks like him. But I have to check. It's my job to check."

"Let's show his picture to Samara Mowrey at the Jonquil Apartments. She's the Black Pearl's lover. You'll see how wrong you are."

§

Anna and Joe arrived at the Jonquil Café at the dinner hour. There were fewer ladies dining than before, and no men. Mrs. Rosenberg did not make an appearance, though her lawyer had arranged her bail. The maître d' glared at Joe.

Samara Mowrey was present, and once more sat at her table alone. She was eating enchiladas. Joe approached flashing his big brass star. Anna, too, flashed her little brass star.

Samara groaned. "I know by now you're with the police."

Joe sat down in the chair next to Samara and spread out the newspaper with the photo of Georges. "Good morning Miss Mowrey. See this man? A witness claims he's the Black Pearl, a.k.a. your Mr. King."

Samara glanced at the newspaper photo. "No. My lover has golden hair. And this man isn't even handsome."

"I really couldn't judge. He looks like my father," said Anna. "And, of course he's not your lover."

"Are you sure?" asked Joe.

Samara rolled her eyes. "Of course I'm sure."

Joe scooted back his chair and stood, unsmiling. "Thank you for your time Miss Mowrey."

"Yes, thank you Miss Mowrey." Anna inclined and nodded her head.

They debriefed near a palm tree in the corner of the café. Joe whispered, "Of course she'd say 'no.' I'd expected her to say 'no.' He's her lover and we're the police."

"That doesn't make Georges the Black Pearl. Now, can we go back to the station?"

"Let's ask the waitstaff." Joe swaggered over to the burly maître d'. "Do you know this man?"

The maître d' glanced at the picture. "Never saw him before in my life."

"And wouldn't tell me if you did?"

The maître d' smirked. "Of course, I am always happy to cooperate with the police."

Joe chuckled cynically. He approached the waiter. "Do you know this man?"

"No."

"Here, look again. Are you sure?"

"Yes."

"You see," said Anna. "Just let it go."

"First thing tomorrow morning, we're going to talk to Georges."

Chapter 20

Joe and Anna strode into the Hotel Alexandria in hostile silence. The elevator boy perched on a stool and welcomed Anna with a smile. "You're Mr. Devereaux's pretty sister."

"I am." Anna bent to give him a horehound candy.

"Mr. Devereaux gives me money."

Anna frowned and turned her back on the child. She nervously tucked a loose strand of hair behind her ear. "What are you going to say?"

"I'm just going to look him in the eye and ask him, straight up. Man to man. Agreed?"

"No. Not agreed. But you're going to do it anyway."

Joe's mouth flattened.

§

Georges's strapping manservant, Thomas, answered the door. Anna was glad he was so tall and muscular, so that his coat strained a little across his broad shoulders. He could carry Georges when Georges had fits.

"Good morning Miss Blanc. Please come in. Mr. Devereaux has just finished his bath. Can I get you coffee? Perhaps a slice of cold pork pie?"

"Yes," said Anna, who accepted good, free refreshment at every opportunity. "But he won't have any." She motioned to Joe.

When Thomas left, Joe shook his head. "What was that about? I wanted pork pie."

"You can't accept hospitality from a suspect."

"You're accepting hospitality from a suspect."

"I don't suspect him."

"Did you dine with Georges last week?"

"I told you I would. I had hoped that you would join us."

"I thought you deserved time alone together."

"My father was there."

"Oh." Joe fell silent a beat. "So, you two are . . . talking?"

"Not really. I disowned him. Georges had an epileptic fit, right in front of me. I thought I told you. I nursed Georges all night."

"No, you didn't tell me. So, you're worried that I'll upset him when he's ill."

"Of course."

"Anna, I don't know what else I'm supposed to do."

"Give him the benefit of the doubt."

Thomas returned with coffee for two and pork pie for one. He winced. "Do you take sugar?"

"We both take two lumps," said Joe.

Thomas's brow wrinkled. "Mr. Devereaux doesn't use sugar. We'll see what I can find." The man slunk off to the kitchen.

Anna ate her pork pie slowly, making a show of savoring it. "It really is exceptionally tasty. The cool jelly just melts on my tongue."

Joe glared. Thomas returned with a china sugar bowl and tongs. "I regret we are reduced to two sugar cubes. I will call down to the desk, but by the time we get the sugar, the coffee will be cold. If I keep it on the stove, it will be bitter."

Anna frowned. "Oh."

"I will call down now and make a second pot." Thomas put one cube on each saucer. "So sorry. Next time, I'll be prepared."

"Never mind, Thomas. We won't be staying long." Anna dropped her sugar into her cup and stirred.

"Your boot's untied," Joe said.

Anna looked down, and indeed, her lace peeked out from beneath her skirt. She bent down and tied it, then straightened up and sipped at her coffee. It tasted just as sweet as when she used two cubes. She looked suspiciously at Joe.

"What?" he said.

Anna lifted his cup. Joe reached for it. "Hey, that's mine."

She twisted away and took a sip. It wasn't sweet at all. But he was. It confused Anna.

She noticed Georges smiling from the hallway, his hair still damp, but neatly slicked back, his freshly shaved cheeks smooth and tan. "Good morning Joe. Hello, Nurse Anna."

Anna stood. "How are you. Do you feel quite yourself? You have taken your bromides, haven't you?"

Georges rolled his eyes. "Yes, Anna, I've taken my bromides."

"How are you feeling?"

"You asked me already, and I feel fine. I had a talk with father. That is to say, we had a falling out."

"Over what?"

"Over you. Now, I'm disowned too. So, we can be disowned together."

"But you have all his money."

He grinned. "Isn't it grand? He'll no doubt realize that and come to his senses. He's used to being in control. This is all new to him—relying on me."

"Oh no! I don't want to come between you, even if he is an ass."

"And he is an ass." Georges looked at Joe. "Sorry, my friend. It's just, I strongly object to his treatment of Anna."

"Me, too. But we didn't come here to talk family business. I'm afraid we've come here on police business."

Georges looked at Anna with pride in his eyes. "Go on then, sister. How can I help the LAPD today?"

"I can't say it, Georges. Because I don't believe we should be saying it. I'm against it one hundred percent."

Georges looked perplexed. "Are you . . . what? Accusing me of a crime?" He chuckled.

Joe looked as serious as a cop can look when he is fresh-faced and under twenty-five. "A young lady came to the police station this morning to give us information about a suspected white slavery ring being run from the Jonquil Café and Apartments. She identified you from a photograph. Said you went by the pseudonyms 'Mr. King' or 'The Black Pearl.' Another witness said Mr. King recruits men as clients. Some of the girls are underage."

"This lady's an actress and writes for the movies. I think she's made it all up, like a movie scenario," said Anna.

Georges wandered to the liquor cart and poured himself a drink. "Would anyone else like a drink?"

"It's 11:00 a.m.," said Joe.

"Yes." Anna took the drink Georges poured.

He dropped down on a settee and drank his brandy in one long swallow. He took out a cigar and tried to chop the end off with an ornate, silver cigar cutter but the blade was dull, and the cigar simply smashed beneath its weight. He lit the thing anyway, looking distracted. It sent up a disorganized stream of smoke.

Anna came and sat beside him. "Georges, can you ever forgive me? I don't believe it for a moment. I told him not to come."

"Well, I'm glad you don't believe it, Anna, because it's not true."

"Of course it's not true. You see, Joe. I told you. We can go now."

"Wait, Anna. It's not that simple," said Georges.

"It's not?" Joe and Anna asked in unison.

Georges sighed. "I'm being blackmailed."

"Let me get this straight," said Joe. "You've never been to the Jonquil—"

"Yes, I've been to the Jonquil. To the café. I had a series of business meetings there—I recall three. Some fellows wanted a loan."

"It's a public restaurant, Joe," said Anna.

"But not a very good one. I didn't return," said Georges.

"So, you aren't prostituting teenaged girls?" asked Joe.

"Of course he isn't!" said Anna.

"My God," said Georges. "I didn't see that on the menu."

"Isn't that what your blackmailer says you do?" asked Joe.

"My blackmailer? He was rather vague. He threatened to 'disclose my immoral behavior' to my wife and society. I didn't pay, because I am innocent. Not to mention that I have no wife and society doesn't accept me because I'm a bastard. Now you say they've gone to the police. But I assure you, there's no evidence against me."

"Do you know who your blackmailer is?" asked Anna.

"No. But I'm assuming that girl is an accomplice."

"How did he contact you? By letter?" said Joe. "Because I'd like to see it."

Georges slapped his forehead. "I burned it. I was irritated."

Joe nodded. "Would you come down to the station?" His face looked unnaturally bland.

Anna couldn't read it.

"What for? To file a report on my blackmailer?"

"We'll bring Miss Sutton back in. I thought you could face your accuser and meet Matilda, just to put it to rest," said Joe.

Georges blinked, looking stunned. "I think I'll decline."

"Listen Georges, I know you're rich, so you're probably used to getting your way. But you may not decline this time. That's not on the table. One way or another, you're coming down to the station."

Georges ignored Joe and wandered to the drink trolley. He poured himself another brandy. "Anna, will you have another?"

Joe's face turned red. He pulled out his handcuffs and charged over to Georges, his face too near Georges face. He bristled with hostility. "Put your drink down. I don't know what you've been up to, whether you're a pimp or not—"

Anna gasped.

Joe ignored her and continued. "But I'm gonna find out. You won't escape justice because you're loaded or because you're my fiancées brother. I'm taking you in whether you like it or not. So, are you coming, or am I going to have to cuff you like a pimp?"

Joe and Georges glared hard at each other, and Anna thought one of them might swing.

She thought she might swing. She narrowed her eyes at Joe and pointed to the door. "Get out."

"This isn't even your apartment," said Joe, his voice still rough with anger, never taking his eyes off Georges.

"Oh, but it is. I'm moving in. It's the family apartment. And you have deeply insulted my brother. Your evidence is flimsy flamsy at best."

"Anna you can't sway this investigation!"

Georges exhaled and stepped back from Joe. He spoke with a hopeful lilt. "Anna, you're moving in?"

"Yes, Georges. As soon as possible. Will my room be ready?"

"Of course. I'll arrange to have your things moved." He reached into his pocket and produced a pretty brass key decorated with ornate fishes. "Here. Take my key. I'll get another."

Anna took it. She saw Joe's face fall. He knew what this meant. No climbing through Anna's window. His jaw tightened. "Georges, are you coming willingly or are you going to wear the bracelets?"

Georges's gray eyes turned rock hard. "Of course. In fact, I am eager to go. Right now is a good time."

Chapter 21

Anna waited with Georges in a cold interrogation room while Joe sent someone to the address Allie Sutton had given them to ask her to return to the station. The walls were bare, the chairs hard. Anna couldn't sit still. She paced the room.

"Sit down, Anna. It will be fine. I'm flummoxed, but I have nothing to hide." He leaned back in his chair and yawned. He wore a killer blue suit and dotted tie.

"Of course you don't. Joe is being ridiculous."

"I don't know, Anna. I kind of like him. He gave you his sugar cube. And not for ulterior motives. I watched him sneak it into your cup when you tied your shoe."

Anna's brows drew together. "I know."

The door opened, and Joe entered with Matilda in tow. He looked miserable. Anna hoped he was.

"Georges, this is Miss Matilda Nilsson. She was drugged and raped at the Jonquil Apartments. She's fifteen."

At that moment, fair Matilda seemed even younger, blinking her blond eyelashes. Anna's heart ached for her.

Georges's own eyes widened and he blew out a breath. "Hello Miss Matilda. I'm very sorry you've been ill used."

"I know you. I saw you at the café," said Matilda warily. She seemed to shrink.

Georges smiled at the girl and spoke gently. "Possibly. Was I having the moules?" He made a face. "I don't recommend them. Not enough garlic. The strawberry pie was all right."

"Yes. I like the pie."

Georges's answer seemed to irritate Joe, whose lips grimly turned downward. "Miss Matilda. This is very important. Is this man the Black Pearl?"

Matilda never took her eyes off Georges. "Detective. I never met The Black Pearl. I met Mrs. Rosenberg and the green man from Mars."

Georges looked sideways at Anna, one eyebrow up, one eyebrow down. Anna shook her head. "Thank you, Miss Matilda. I will be through here in a second and I'll bring you a treat. Can you sew quietly in my office?

"Yes ma'am."

"Miss Matilda," Joe said. "Would you please send down the twins?"

Matilda nodded and hurried out. Anna felt the loss of her—a premonition of what life at the station would be without Matilda's sweet generosity.

"So now what? We wait for my accuser?" asked Georges. He seemed almost eager.

"Yes. We wait for Allie Sutton."

§

They waited together in taut silence until finally Mr. Melvin cracked open the door. Three necks snapped around to look. The clerk was alone. "Allie Sutton doesn't live at that address."

Joe said something profane under his breath.

Anna took him by the arm and pulled him into the corridor. She gave him a hard look.

Joe hissed. "Of course she didn't give us her correct address. She didn't want him to find her. She doesn't want him to know about the baby."

"Why do you even care about the Jonquil? You never gave a hoot about Madam Lulu's brothel."

"What do you mean, why do I care? Madam Lulu employs women. She doesn't lure innocent, underage girls. She doesn't drug them. Anna, you care, too. You want to catch the Black Pearl."

"He is not the Black Pearl!"

Anna caught a glimpse of movement from the corner of her eye and turned to see the backsides of Sue and Clementine, hurrying away with Matilda.

"No. Come back. I'm sorry. He made me shout," said Anna.

The girls obediently turned and tremulously came forward.

When Anna had been a child, her father had spewed red hot words. Sometimes, he spanked her. But she hadn't feared him. He never left marks. The twins fled a father who broke Sue's arm. Who knew what violence had driven poor Matilda from her family. It was no wonder hot words frightened them.

Anna smiled with all her sweetness. "He's sorry. He won't do it again."

Joe sighed. "Miss Matilda, there are peppermints on my desk. Please help yourself."

"Is the moules man still there?" She seemed wary.

"You don't need to fear him, Matilda. He's a good man. He's my brother." Anna proffered a twinkleless smile.

"He teaches Martian men our customs."

Joe leaned toward her. "Miss Matilda, what do you mean?"

Matilda looked cautiously at Anna. "How to eat."

"You saw him eating with the man from Mars?"

The girl nodded.

"Thank you, Miss Matilda." Joe smiled grimly. "Now go get some peppermints. As many as you want."

Matilda rushed off down the hall as if fleeing something. The twins watched her go, then looked cautiously at Joe. Like influenza, Matilda's nervousness was catching.

"That doesn't mean anything," said Anna.

Joe opened the door and ushered the twins inside. "Sue, Clementine, this is Georges Devereaux. I don't suppose you've met before."

Clementine scratched her thigh through her frock and said, "We run in the same circles."

Despite the situation, or because of it, Anna almost laughed.

Joe said, "Miss Clementine, what do you mean? Are you acquainted with Mr. Devereaux?"

"No." She sounded very la-dee-da. "But it was just a matter of time. I saw him at the Jonquil Café speaking with Mrs. Rosenberg. But we are friends with men like him—Mrs. Rosenberg's friends."

Joe turned to the other girl, "Miss Sue?"

"Yes. I know him. He's distinctive looking," said Sue.

"Thank you," said Georges.

Joe glared at Georges. "Don't speak."

Anna said almost pleadingly. "But you can't be sure. You didn't recognize him from the newspaper photograph." She produced the newspaper and plunked it down on the table with a smack.

Sue and Clementine flinched.

Joe said, "Girls. Help yourselves to some peppermints. Don't go anywhere. We'll talk later."

When Sue and Clementine had disappeared down the hall, Joe turned cold eyes on Georges. "Georges Devereaux, you're under arrest for the operation of a prostitution ring exploiting underage girls."

"No!" Anna forced herself between Georges and Joe. "This is bunk."

Georges took Anna by the shoulders and gently turned her to face him. "Anna, it's okay. I can fight my own battles. Tell Thomas to call my lawyer. We'll straighten this out."

"You'll be slandered in the papers."

"I didn't do it, Anna. I'll be vindicated. Just like you."

Her voice cracked. "That hasn't worked out so well."

"Go on. Cuff me." Georges held out his wrists to Joe.

Joe's face was blank, stony. The color had drained from his rosy cheeks, like a faded illustration. "That won't be necessary. Come with me." He ushered Georges to a desk to be booked.

Anna stormed over to the station's telephone exchange where a man sat behind a panel that sprouted wires like hair. "I need to place a call, please."

He handed her a receiver.

Mr. Melvin shuffled over and made eye contact with Anna's white necktie. "Is everything all right, Assistant Matron Blanc?"

"Everything is all wrong. Everything! I'm going to call my brother's man." Anna lifted the candlestick phone, put the receiver to her ear, and her hard-set lips to the transmitter. "Get me the Hotel Alexandria, please."

The front desk put Anna through to Georges's room. After fifteen rings and no Thomas, she hung up. "Mr. Melvin, if anyone asks for me, I'm going to my hotel. I need to get my brother his medicine and lunch. He'll hate the food."

Anna glanced over at Georges in booking and found Joe watching her. She looked away.

§

The doorman greeted Anna and she met his good morning with the smile she'd been trained to deliver, no matter what she felt like inside. She turned the smile on the man at the front desk. "I need someone to pack a picnic lunch for Mr. Devereaux. Can you have it for me in fifteen minutes?"

Anna didn't stay for his, "Yes, Miss." She rode the elevator to the hotel room, fumbling in her purse for sweets for the boy, and dropping horehound candies all over the floor. "Oh, just have them all," she squeaked and dashed off as soon as he'd opened the wrought iron doors.

She let herself into the suite with her fancy fish key. Anna went room by room, but Thomas was nowhere to be found. She searched Georges's desk for any indication of who his lawyer might be. She found paper, monogrammed stationery, calling cards printed with Georges's name, a variety of fountain pens, and an address book.

She flipped through the book. The man's name would not be listed under lawyer. But perhaps Georges used Anna's father's lawyer. She tapped her lip, taking a moment to recall his name—a Mr. Paxton. She found the name and number listed under P. Anna picked up the telephone. "Hello Central. Please connect me to Mr. Paxton, Esquire 41286." She waited on the line for seconds that seemed like hours, until Mr. Paxton's secretary, and finally the man himself, came on the line. "Georges Devereaux needs the best criminal defense lawyer in the city, whoever you think that might be. He's down at Central Station. He's been arrested."

Anna hung up the phone, closed her eyes, and caught her breath. She needed to get Georges's medicine, because if anyone could make someone have fits, Joe Singer could.

She found Georges's medicine kit in a marble-topped cabinet in his bath. It contained a syringe, several small bottles labeled "morphine," and a bottle of hypno-sedative containing bromides. She put the kit in her purse and flew back to the elevator to the ground floor where a picnic basket awaited her. It felt heavy, like it contained an elephant. Anna hauled it to the trolley and was back at the station in under an hour.

She lugged the picnic basket to the men's department of the city jail. A jailer unlocked the great steel door. The hallway was grated. He escorted her through to another steel door. On the other side, through a barred window, Anna could see Georges standing in the bull ring in striped pajamas, alongside embezzlers, drunkards, and automobile bandits.

Ire rose in her throat. She was going to kill Joe Singer. She approached the jailer and spoke from between clenched teeth. "Please let me into the bull ring."

He looked scandalized. "It's not safe. You don't know what those men might do. It's no place for a lady."

"And it's no place for a gentleman, and yet Georges Devereaux is there." She made a growling sound. "Detective Singer could have let him wait at my desk. Did he really think he would flee? Let me in!"

The jailer hesitated.

Anna brazenly laid hold of the key ring fastened to his belt. She tugged. "I'll let myself in." She tugged again.

His face turned bright red at her familiarity. He capitulated and unlocked the door. She entered the bull ring on tiptoes, as if to limit her exposure to the unknown substances that stained the grimy floor. But there was no way to keep oneself unstained in the bull ring. The air reeked of body odor and rotting teeth. Rat droppings collected on the cement. Fifty men, vagrants or criminals, shared space in a room crammed with half as many cots. Half of them had to stand all night or lay down on the evil-smelling floor to sleep. The tanks and the felony cells must be full.

Every eye fixed on Anna. The door closed and locked behind her. Steel walls encircled her. Anna wondered if she'd made a terrible mistake. She tried to appear collected, though inside she felt like running. The inmates seemed to lean toward her. A drunk man reached out and touched her skirt. The jailer banged a baton on the grate. "Don't touch her." With his right hand, he aimed his gun through the bars. The inmates moved back. They seemed cowed.

Georges looked up and his face registered shock. "No Anna. This is no place for you."

Anna tried to ignore the many eyes upon her, the crowd parting to let her pass. She was comforted by the jailer's gun, but not quite comforted enough. "I could say the same for you. Joe could have put you in a cell for one. They have hammocks."

"Apparently, they're full of murderers."

Anna glanced about the bull ring. "He couldn't at least get you a bunk?"

"He doesn't believe in special treatment."

"Hah. That's not going to make me forgive him." Anna held out the picnic basket. "I brought you lunch. And I brought your medicine. Three times a day, father said."

"I don't want to take it. I need my wits about me."

"You're taking your medicine. You can borrow my wits. She set the heavy picnic basket down on the grimy floor and produced a bottle of pills from her purse. She unscrewed the cap and held one to Georges's mouth. "Open."

He groaned and rolled his eyes, but obediently took his medicine. Anna held a cup to his lips and smiled. "There. I'll return this evening to make sure you take the next dose."

He swallowed. "Thomas called my lawyer?"

"No, he wasn't home. I called father's lawyer. A Mr. Paxton."

George nodded. "Then, I won't be here for my next dose. My lawyer will have me out of here in no time."

Anna opened the picnic basket. There were tarts, donuts, sardines, crackers, grapes, an orange, cut vegetables wrapped in a cloth, and five different sandwiches. Anna opened each sandwich in turn: banana and sugar, roast beef, peanut butter and jelly, egg salad, some sort of grated cheese. Lastly, there were three bottles of wine—red, white, and rosé—two Coca Colas, and four crystal glasses wrapped in linen napkins. The other inmates fixed hungry eyes upon it.

"No wonder it was so heavy." Anna said, "I don't think the hotel chef knows what you like to eat, so he simply gave you everything."

"Honestly, Anna. I don't feel like eating at all. It stinks in here."

"Oh, please eat, Georges. Please eat." She extended the banana and sugar sandwich in his direction, because it was the most scrumptious. "Just hold your nose."

He took it and smiled. "If you'll eat, I'll eat.

Anna held her nose. "I'll eat, so that you'll eat."

He laughed and pinched his nose, too. Anna bit into the roast beef sandwich and tasted horseradish, which ordinarily she loved, but today it only burned her sinuses. She finished it and tried the cheese. She finished that and had the egg salad. She drank a Coca Cola and then she had some wine.

The lawyer arrived. It was not Mr. Paxton, but an Earl Rogers, who specialized in criminal defense and who had been sent by Mr. Paxton. He had hooded eyes, and impossibly straight brown hair parted down the middle. Anna was unaware of his legal reputation.

She did know that he sometimes lodged at Madam Lulu's brothel when his wife threw him out.

The jailer let Anna and Georges out of the bull ring so that Georges could meet with his lawyer in private. A guard escorted them down the grated hallway and through the steel door. Georges carried the picnic basket. Mr. Rogers asked to speak with Georges alone.

"But I want to come," said Anna.

"It's all right, Anna. I know you have work to do." Georges held out a tart. "Here, take this. You've hardly eaten a bite." He chuckled.

Anna took the tart, squeezed Georges's hand, and departed in search of Joe Singer.

Joe strode across the station floor, saw her approaching, and veered into the little kitchen. Anna followed, and slammed and locked the door. "What have you done?" She handed him the tart.

Joe remained silent. He set the tart down on the table.

Anna perched on a chair as far from Joe as she could be in that small room. "He's my brother. He's the only family I have. And maybe, if he and I become close, father will soften and forgive me. Then I'll forgive him, and we'll be a family."

"Forgive you? For what? For catching a killer?"

"For bringing shame on him and my dead mother's memory. And now my brother, who is shameful already because he's a bastard. He didn't need any extra shame, and the situation of his birth, well that's not his fault."

"You didn't shame your family. He should be proud of you."

"Georges is proud of me!"

"So, you believe that he's innocent? That this whole Black Pearl thing is a set up?"

"Just like he believes in me. He sought me out, Joe. Regardless of what anyone in society says about me, he associates with me."

"I associate with you."

"Yes, but you can't help it. You're in love with me.

"That is my predicament."

"So, I've got to do everything I can for him, because I can't believe he's guilty. I just can't. It would be disloyal and wrong to think ill of him. And you put him in the bull ring!"

"So, what if we find out he's guilty? What if we have proof? Where's your loyalty then?"

"Don't you see? He can't be guilty. He just can't. So, you can't have proof."

"But Anna, if he's guilty, he belongs in a box."

"Let him go. I'm begging you. You once said you'd do anything for me."

Joe threw his hands in the air. "Well this particular scenario hadn't occurred to me. I thought you cared about justice."

"I love you both and it isn't fair that I have to choose between you. But he needs me and you don't."

"What are you saying?"

"I'm going to fight for him, and if it means fighting against you, so be it." She took up the tart and marched out the door.

Chapter 22

Joe sat alone in the kitchen, head in hands. Detective Wolf came in and claimed his lunch pail from the shelf. "What's up with honeybun. She looks distraught."

"I arrested her brother for using a child for immoral purposes—it's a kidnapping charge."

Wolf sat across from him. "I didn't know she had a brother."

Joe looked up. "He's her half-brother. Georges Devereaux. He's a, I don't know, banker."

"I see. So, I'm guessing you think he did it."

"He says he's being blackmailed but we have witnesses—four that place him at the Jonquil Café, and one who positively identified him as 'Mr. King,' also known as 'The Black Pearl,' which is what they call their *macquereau*. The madam won't talk. I'm bringing in a fifth person for questioning who apparently is the Black Pearl's lover."

"Young girls are your witnesses?"

"Yes."

"And this Georges Devereaux is rich?"

"Loaded. He's retained Earl Rogers."

"And his lover—is she a current lover, or a woman scorned?"

"Current lover."

"Good luck with that."

"I know, but I have a bad feeling about him. And there's a whole bunch of potential witnesses that I haven't even spoken to yet."

"And what if they surprise you—say he isn't The Black Pearl? What then?"

"They won't. It's him. I know it."

CHAPTER 23

Anna discreetly ate the tart as she headed for the stairs leading up to the women's department of the jail. She hurried, as her feelings were very likely on her sleeve, and she did not want the cops to think she had any feelings at all. They didn't appear to have feelings, except maybe irritation and whatever feeling it was that made cops leer at police matrons. It certainly wasn't love.

She passed Detective Snow, who leered on cue.

Anna slipped up into the little room used by the police matrons for sleeping when they worked overnight. She didn't stop to check on the criminal ladies in the tanks or in the cow ring. She didn't stop to talk to Matron Clemens. She locked the door and sobbed silently. She sobbed like a mute hyena. It made her throat ache. She tried to breathe deeply. She ran the faucet and splashed water on her hot face.

Georges was innocent. He would be vindicated. And she didn't want to marry Joe Singer anyway. It meant handing over the deed to her person and her things. Why would any woman want to marry any man, ever?

But she did love Joe Singer.

Still, she resolved to never speak to him again. Or at least as little as possible. She sobbed silently some more. Because without Georges and Joe, she would have no family at all, just like the old, bald woman who had escaped from the receiving hospital. No wonder she had taken up drink. Anna wouldn't even be able to afford good whiskey.

Matilda called to Anna through the door. She had been knocking, perhaps for a while.

"Just a minute." Anna splashed her face again. In the mirror, she could see that her eyes were puffy and bloodshot, her irises a searing gray. She patted her face dry with a towel and opened the door. "Hello Matilda."

Matilda looked at Anna's red-rimmed eyes and politely ignored them. "You have a letter. Detective Singer gave it to me to give to you."

Anna nodded and took the envelope. It wasn't addressed to Anna, but to Joe, and had already been opened. "Thank you, Matilda. You're a good girl. Now run along. Soon I'll get you something nice to eat."

Anna wondered what Georges had left over in his picnic basket. Otherwise it was kippers, Cracker Jacks, or cold mush for Matilda. She had to remember to get donations from the Friday Morning Club. Which reminded her, she needed to help find jobs for prostitutes. Which further reminded her of the poor dead man in Griffith Park. She had a murder to solve. Because Joe had falsely accused Georges, she had forgotten all about it. Also, she had no leads.

Except maybe she did now.

The return address on the letter in her hands was from a Sergeant Tribble of the Oklahoma City Police Department. The reply had not come to her because she had signed the letter, "Detective Joe Singer."

Her broken heart beat in two pieces. Anna tore open the letter and read:

Dear Detective Singer,

Greetings. I'm writing regarding the photograph you sent to the Oklahoma City Police Department. We have identified the victim as one Samuel Grayson, aged nineteen, of Oklahoma City. He was identified by Edward Newton at Newton and Son's Pharmacy who had supplied him with powder for a headache complaint. His father, Leonard Grayson, confirmed his identity. I questioned the father according to your request. Samuel Grayson left Oklahoma for Los Angeles. According to his father, he had no known enemies, and no one wished him harm. Leonard Grayson regrets that he cannot claim his son's remains, for he is of modest means and cannot afford to ship them.

Sincerely,

Sergeant Garry Tribble

Anna set down the letter. Why did Samuel Grayson come to Los Angeles and when? Didn't Sergeant Tribble think to ask him that? It had been on the list of questions Anna had included with her missive. She would have to write the detective yet another letter and wait another eleven days for his reply. It was sad that telephone lines didn't reach to Oklahoma City. She sat down and wrote a terse response in her elegant, feminine hand, including her list of questions once again and emphatic directions to ASK THEM. She signed the letter, "Detective Joe Singer," spritzed it with perfume, and set it with the outgoing mail.

There was nothing Anna could do for Georges at the moment, so she checked on the criminal ladies. With Clementine and Sue in residence, all the cots in the cow ring were full. The tanks in the ladies' department were bursting. Add one more lady and someone would get knocked down into the men's department, if there was space in a felony cell.

Or someone would have to go.

The jailbirds had eaten their lunch, and Matron Clemens had them sewing linens. Matilda lay on her cot with her eyes closed, lightly snoring. Anna kissed her on the forehead and left a box of Cracker Jacks by her pillow. She hoped none of the other ladies would steal it.

Anna clipped downstairs to the main floor of the station to search the new Los Angeles City Directory for Samuel Grayson's name. The Directory was published annually in February. The private census was taken each year between June and September. Then, typesetting began. People recently arrived or moved could submit their names late in hopes of making it into the back of the book—a hodgepodge of post-deadline entries. If Grayson had been in Los Angeles long enough—say at least four months—he might be in the book. If he'd arrived more recently, Anna was out of luck.

Joe Singer was not on the station floor, which was just dandy as far as Anna was concerned. Wolf sat at his desk and kept sending Anna heavy looks, no doubt laden with meaning, but a meaning that escaped her.

He sauntered over. "I released your brother, honeybun. He said he'd see you tonight."

"So, all charges have been dropped?"

"No, I regret not. He's going to be arraigned."

"Oh," said Anna.

"Assistant Matron Blanc, don't be too hard on Joe Singer. He's young and only sort of deserves it."

"You would never arrest my brother, would you?"

"Well . . . no."

"Thank you, Detective Wolf. Perhaps I will marry you."

"I think you need to give young Joe a second chance."

Anna squeezed her eyes shut and tried to think of murder. "I have a lot of work to do."

She said a silent prayer to Saint Anthony, patron saint of pigs and skin disease, that Joe Singer would get a fungus.

CHAPTER 24

Anna flipped through the hulking volume that contained Los Angeles—all of its citizens, all of its businesses, every government office. She waded through ads for everything under the sun: a Baptist church, a tamale factory, player pianos, detective agencies, and a moving company called "Big Green Vans." She checked the G's but found no Samuel Grayson. Then she checked the back of the book in the section for people who had missed the cut-off date and were added at the last minute. He was there—Samuel Grayson. Likely, he had moved to Los Angeles in October, after the census but before the final deadline. He'd been in the city five months.

Samuel Grayson lived downtown on Hill Street near the Majestic Theater. Anna rode the trolley alone through streets that teemed with vehicles, animals, and busy strangers. She passed Hamburger's Department Store where she and Joe had reconnoitered in the dressing room until the mirrors had steamed up. Anna wouldn't be here if it wasn't for that secret, crime-fighting encounter. She wouldn't have realized that she loved Joe and she would be married to Edgar. She wouldn't be an LAPD police matron. Really, the place should be a shrine. Anna bit her fist, lamenting that things weren't different, wishing that Joe and Georges were with her, all fighting crime together. But that dream was over.

§

Samuel Grayson had lived in a multi-story boarding house for single men. Anna entered the foyer where a sign read, "Women strictly prohibited." She ignored it. No one was about, likely because all the men were still at work or dead. She knocked on the door that said, "Manager."

A man answered. He had black hair and a tiny head. Anna smiled. "I am Assistant Matron Blanc with the LAPD. I regret to inform you that your tenant, Samuel Grayson, has been killed dead. I'm investigating his murder." She smiled again.

The manager looked grave. "The detective said you'd be by. He's already up there."

Anna frowned. "Oh." Of course Joe Singer would be investigating, too, but it stung that he hadn't included her. Then again, she wouldn't have sat with him on the trolley and he knew it.

§

Joe had left the door open a crack for Anna. She slipped in and found herself in a room both nicer and worse than her own. For one thing, the furniture fit. There were no leaks. It was clean. The furnishings looked brand new but were monumentally ugly. Anna had never seen a settee with such clashing colors, and the bed clothes made her gasp.

"Hello," Joe said. He looked subdued, full of regret, and very, very handsome.

Anna doubled down on her resolve. "Apology not accepted."

"I didn't apologize."

"Oh," she said.

Even if he wasn't sorry, she felt glad he was there. The fact that Joe hunted Samuel Grayson's killer meant that he was not gathering evidence against Anna's brother, which would be a futile waste of time because there was no evidence against him.

"I'll search the bed area, you stay over there. I can't bear to be near a bed with you."

Joe's eyelids lowered to an angry half-mast. "All right."

Anna checked under the bed. No dust bunnies. She ran her hand along the mattress under the sheets and lifted the mattress. No slits or tears. She found a little money. "Five dollars," she said.

"Take it. We'll send it to his father. It seems like he needs it."

At one time, Anna had needed it. But now there was Georges. He said she never need work again, which implied he would pay her frock bills. She would try to make time to go shopping.

Joe tossed the wardrobe, checking through the pockets of coats and trousers. There were several expensive, yet ugly suits that looked new. Joe held one up against himself for Anna to see. It was a ghastly rust-color—nearly orange—and busy with checks. He waggled his eyebrows.

She wrinkled her nose, and, despite everything, she smiled. Then she kicked herself and turned away.

She searched a writing desk where a metal spike speared a stack of receipts. She sorted through them. There were receipts for suits, ties, shirt collars, garters, handkerchiefs, and cufflinks—all purchased in quick succession. She found three bank receipts for deposits into the Farmers and Merchants Bank, each for one thousand dollars, and pondered whether to share the fact with Joe. It could be an important clue. But clues made her smile. She didn't want to smile at him.

Instead, she glared at him and tried to push past him, but he caught her in his arms. They were strong, hot, muscular arms. He held her carefully, and when she looked up into his face to scowl at him, he kissed her. His kiss was melting fiery, and burned with all the intensity of their situation, all the passion required to overcome it—Anna's despair, his anger and guilt, a brother facing indictment, and a dead man's tasteless apartment.

Anna pulled away. "Apology not—"

He kissed her again.

She pulled away. "Accepted," she said.

He gave her an irresistible half-smile. "I knew you'd forgive me."

"I didn't—"

He kissed her again. Anna couldn't help it. She had only doubled down on her resolve and he had kissed her three times. Had she tripled down, she would not be kissing him back. But she was. And his hands were holding her cheeks, and he was whispering, "Sherlock, you've got to forgive me." And her hands were pulling at his jacket, and he was lifting her into his arms and carrying her to the atrocious settee. And his hands were caressing her through four blessed layers of fabric, then three, then two. And she was letting him. And he was letting her.

And the doorbell rang, an obnoxious DING DONG.

It broke the spell.

Anna's mind grabbed the reins to her body and she shoved Joe off the settee. He landed with a thunk on the carpet. "Answer the door," she said coolly, though she burned like hot lava. "It could be a witness." She sat up and smoothed her skirt down over her legs.

He stood. "I can't answer that. I've got an enormous cock stand."

"Cock stand?" Anna followed Joe's gaze down to his drawers. "Oh."

There was no way a visitor would miss that. It was like a giant redwood towering on the plains.

"It's because of you," he stated.

Anna lifted her chin. "Then, I'll fix it." She reached out and pressed down on it. It popped back up. "Jupiter." She pushed down again and held it down this time with both hands.

She rather liked helping in this way. She helped some more.

"Oh God, that's not helping." He scrambled away and slipped into his pants.

The doorbell rang again. DING DONG. Joe snatched up his hat and held it over his lap. "Anna get the door."

Anna, who did not have a cock stand, but whose mussed appearance was equally damning, donned a hideous plaid overcoat pinched from a rack and answered the door. She put on her most charming hostess smile, her bun sagging to the left. "Yes?"

The visitor looked to be about Anna's age, maybe slightly older, wearing an off-the-rack suit and no hat. He needed a haircut. "I heard, um, noises. I thought Sam was back."

"Regrettably, Samuel Grayson has been executed," said Anna, tactfully.

"What?" He looked stunned.

"He's dead."

The young man stumbled back as if physically struck by her words. "He can't be. Not old Sam?"

"Never fear. We are the police, and we've come to find his killer," Anna said, aware that beneath the coat, her shirtwaist was unbuttoned, her corset cover ripped, her corset unhooked, and her uniform tie lay on the floor. She kicked it to the side.

Joe pushed through the door and grabbed the man's arm as he seemed to be tottering. It was good to keep witnesses off balance. Anna congratulated herself.

"Steady now. I'm Detective Singer with the LAPD. Why don't you come in and sit down?"

Anna noted Joe's cock stand was now less a giant redwood and more of a sort of . . . Joe caught her looking and frowned. She stopped mentally describing his man parts but tucked the image away in her mind for later.

Joe's tie and jacket were back on. He looked every bit the detective. Except that bit.

He ushered in the witness.

The man, one Lester Shepherd, sat on the edge of the settee, shaking his head. Over and over, he kept repeating, "Poor, poor Sam."

Anna didn't know if his shock was genuine, but she poured him water from a pitcher by the bed, never mind it had been sitting there for over two weeks.

Joe's tree had finally fallen, and he looked subdued—because of Anna or this Lester fellow, she didn't know. Joe asked, "How did you know Mr. Grayson?"

"I live next door," Mr. Shepherd said.

"You were good friends?" asked Joe.

He shrugged. "New friends. We ate our meals together in the dining room."

"You must have been worried. He's been gone for weeks." Anna stared him down. "Why didn't you report him missing?"

"Honestly, I thought he'd run off with Flossie. He never planned to stay here. He didn't like LA. He had talked about going down to Mexico."

This puzzled Anna. How could anyone not like Los Angeles? Especially a person from Oklahoma.

"Who's Flossie?" asked Joe.

"She was his fiancée. They eloped against her family's wishes, except they never got around to getting married."

Anna looked at Joe. "That's a motive. Her father is likely irate. Mine would kill for much less."

"As Sam told it, they left the state to escape her father's wrath. They couldn't tell anyone back home where they were living. Flossie's dad used to get violent with her. He'd been in the war, fought in the Philippines—"

"She didn't live here?"

"No, they lived separate. Like I said, they weren't married yet."

"What's Flossie's full name?"

"Edmands."

"Do you know where Miss Edmands is now?"

"I didn't keep track of her. They had a fight and she quit him. He got banned from her apartment building. She never returned his letters. He said her apartment manager was holding her captive, but I thought he just went a little crazy, you see? Couldn't accept her leaving him."

Anna squinted at Joe. "She lived at the Jonquil."

Joe's eyes flashed understanding. It was just like in the jilted man's letter to the police.

"How did you know? Sam used to work in the café there, but they fired him. I don't know what he did, but it must have been pretty bad. They wouldn't let him back on the premises. He hasn't heard from Flossie since. He was worried about her. Thought the Jonquil people were bad apples. Even thought about writing to her family, which surprised me given her father's violent nature."

"So, if he didn't have a job, where did he get his . . . um . . . nice clothes?" asked Joe.

"He inherited some money and he was investing it playing poker."

"Investing it?" Joe's manly, skeptical eyebrows arched up.

"He usually won," said Lester.

"Where did he play, do you know?" asked Anna.

"Nope." He cocked his head. "Why are you wearing Sam's coat?"

§

When Lester Shepherd had gone, Anna made Joe turn his back so she could dress, never mind he'd been the one to undress her. With his teeth. She had lost her head for a moment, but she'd found it again. Regrettably, it was full of images of his cock stand.

"I doubt he got an inheritance. The Oklahoma police said the family didn't have any money," Joe said, facing the wall.

Anna stared at his backside. "Three payments of one thousand dollars each? That's no inheritance. He's our blackmailer." She stopped. Her fingers froze midbutton. Her mouth opened wide, lips parted by invisible words too horrible to utter.

Joe turned around. "Anna."

She looked at Joe, accusing him with her eyes. "Don't say it, because I'll hate you forever and it isn't true."

"Anna—"

"Don't say it!"

§

Anna sat as far from Joe on the trolley as possible, not because of anything he'd said, but because she knew what he was thinking. This dead man, this Samuel Grayson, had been blackmailing Georges and now he'd turned up dead.

Georges was their prime suspect.

Joe stared at Anna across the cable car. He swore under his breath, got up, and moved next to her. "Anna . . ."

"You think Georges killed him," Anna said flatly.

Joe said nothing. He simply put his head in his hands.

"You think we should at least look into it. I know you. You'll jump to all kinds of conclusions, like that Georges drugged Flossie and gave her to the man from Mars. That he has all kinds of sins to hide," Anna said. "And if you convict Georges, he's dead meat. And he didn't do any of it. I know he didn't do it. If Grayson black-mailed Georges, he's blackmailed other men, too—guilty ones. And Georges never paid Grayson. So, who gave Grayson the three thousand dollars?"

Joe stayed silent.

Anna said, "I know what you're thinking. You think that just because Georges says he never paid Grayson, doesn't mean he didn't. Fine, but let me ask you this. Would a banker kill a man execution style? That's the purview of gangsters or military men."

Joe said nothing.

"So, you think he hired someone," she stated flatly.

"I didn't say that," Joe whispered dully.

"What about his gambling? And Flossie's violent father, hm? And he *is* a violent man—a military man. You know what, it was probably the man from Mars. He has the most to hide. So, don't you dare jump to irrational conclusions."

"Anna, sweetheart—"

Anna stood and got off the trolley, though it wasn't her stop.

§

Grayson had banked at Farmers and Merchants, and Anna knew the manager. He had worked at her father's bank before the gates of hell had opened and swallowed it up. If the three one-thousand-dollar deposits were made by check, she might convince the manager to tell her whom they were from.

"Hello Mr. Hale."

"Why hello Miss Blanc. How is your father?"

"Terrible, thank you," said Anna. "Impoverished. And, I'm afraid he's dying. It's the French disease, and he's in excruciating pain. They're likely going to amputate." Since her father was French, this seemed plausible.

The man looked horrified. "Oh, I'm—"

"Thank you. I confess, it's difficult. We're very, very, very close." She regretted that it wasn't true. Her father was dead to her. And now the only man she was close to was dead to her, and Georges may soon hang though he was obviously innocent. No one who loved their sister that much could kill a man. Unless, of course, that man had wronged his sister. It brought tears to her eyes.

"Please don't cry." The banker lent Anna his handkerchief.

"Mr. Hale, would you help me with something?"

"Anything, Miss Blanc."

"I'm with the police now, you see.

"Yes, I heard."

"And I'm investigating a murder." She dabbed her eyes. "The victim was your customer. A Samuel Grayson. I need to know the balance on his account. Also, he made three one-thousand-dollar deposits into your bank—four weeks ago, eight weeks ago, and one a month earlier. I need to know if those were checks. If they were checks, I need to know the names on the checks." She handed him Samuel Grayson's deposit slips.

"Are you quite certain he's dead?"

"I saw him myself. Shot in the head and eaten by ants. Did you know him? I could get you pictures."

Mr. Hale stood mute for a minute, vigorously turning a finger in his ear canal. A nervous habit? Anna tried not to show her disgust. It was hard to suppress. Disgust lingered very close to the surface.

Disgust for Joe, disgust for her father, disgust for blackmailers, murderers, and *macquereaus* everywhere.

"Right." He left the room and returned with an oversized leather ledger that he carried with both hands and heaved onto a desk. He flipped through it. "He has a zero balance, Miss Blanc. The checks were from. Hm . . ." He ran a finger down the ledger. "All three checks were from a W.H. Stevens, Esquire."

Anna gave him a gracious smile, though inside she reeled. W.H. Stevens was the name of Mrs. Rosenberg's lawyer, linking Grayson to the Jonquil Apartments. This supported Anna's blackmail theory. Which supported Joe's unspoken Georges-as-suspect theory, though he was far from proving it.

Anna wandered the two miles back to the station, deliberately taking the long way. Exercise helped her think. If she ever needed her wits about her, she needed them now. She stopped for a Coca Cola. She stopped to buy a new hat on credit, knowing Georges would pay the bill. It gave her no joy. It was Georges's brotherly companionship that gave her joy, not his money and what it could buy. His money be damned. Her father could keep it, for all Anna cared. She loved her brother.

Still, she stopped once more to buy shoes; but Anna merely went through the motions of walking, drinking, and shopping. Her mind had fixed on Samuel Grayson and how to prove Georges's innocence.

If Grayson was out of money, he couldn't be that good at poker, despite what Lester Shepherd had said about his prowess. More likely, Samuel Grayson was a braggart. As far as Anna could tell, he had five dollars to his name, plus whatever had been stolen from his corpse. Maybe he was in debt to some thug in Chinatown who had wanted to make an example of him.

Then there was W.H. Stevens, Esquire. Grayson was definitely in the blackmailing business, possibly putting the squeeze on Mrs. Rosenberg as well as Georges, and who knew how many others. Happily, Anna now had leads to follow.

But there were a hundred things on Anna's to-do list, and it was already five o'clock. She had to check on the cow ring, organize sewing projects for the criminal ladies, feed Matilda her mush, locate the little villain, Eliel Villalobos, find jobs for prostitutes, solicit donations of food and clothing, nurse any women in the receiving hospital or get Matilda to do it, and kill Joe Singer before he threw her brother in the hoosegow again. But most importantly, she needed to talk to Mrs. Rosenberg and the lawyer, W.H. Stevens. She needed to interview Grayson's fiancée, Flossie, and she needed to go to the gambling hall where Samuel Grayson played poker, because sometimes the best legal defense is a shadow of a doubt.

If Anna could convince the jury, that is, Joe Singer, that there were a hundred people who may have wanted Grayson dead, it would take the pressure off Georges.

§

At the station, Anna found Joe Singer writing a letter to Sergeant Tribble regarding the whereabouts and the character of Flossie Edmands's father.

"Anna, I'm trying to cover all the bases. I hope to God Flossie's father did it, but . . ."

"But what?"

"No buts. Where've you been?"

"I went to Samuel Grayson's bank. The money came from W.H. Stevens. Likely, Grayson was blackmailing Mrs. Rosenberg. Stevens is, after all, her lawyer."

"I know. I called the bank."

It was so easy to do detective work when you were an actual detective. Doors flew open. Innocent mouths talked.

"Mrs. Rosenberg probably killed Grayson. And you know Grayson was broke and likely owed money at some gambling den in Chinatown. They probably conspired with Mrs. Rosenberg and killed him, too."

Joe took her arm and looked her in the face. "Anna, are you listening to yourself?"

Anna was, and she sounded crazy. She needed to get her bearings, but she would do it on her own. "I . . . have to check on the criminal ladies." She grimaced. "Goodnight."

§

When Anna arrived back in the women's department, she found Matron Clemens to be out at yet another Friday Morning Club meeting, though it wasn't Friday morning, but rather Tuesday afternoon. She would suggest a new title for the Club. "The Various Times of the Day and Week Club" perhaps, or more aptly, "The Ladies Who Mean Well but Offend Prostitutes Club."

In the cow ring, women sat idle because Anna hadn't been there to direct them—and this when the jail was short of bedclothes. Anna heaved in a bolt of linen, a measuring tape, thimbles, spools of thread, and needles. Sheets needed to be cut to size and hemmed. She contemplated the wisdom of giving the ladies shears, weighed against the burden of doing it herself when she had no time and didn't actually know how. She surveyed the faces of the ladies and reviewed their crimes. There were several shoplifters—part of a ring—a forger, a counterfeiter, and a lady who used tools to snip off jewelry from unsuspecting people. One dear woman had shot her husband in the thigh, having missed the bulls-eye. From what Anna could tell, he sorely deserved it. There was a battered woman seeking refuge with her children, one lady found drunk, barefoot, and without a coat in the streets, and a woman accused of marrying two different men when she was already someone else's wife. There were several lodgers who just needed a place to sleep, and there was Matilda.

Anna figured they would all make fine citizens had they been in different circumstances and she would venture to trust them. She distributed the needles, thimbles, and threads. She gave the shears to the woman with multiple husbands, figuring she had to sew for three different households and would likely have the most practice.

The more hardened criminal ladies—the ones in the felony cells—were perhaps less trustworthy. One lady could not be convinced to keep her clothes on and awaited the men from the bat house. Another had shot her husband successfully, though she swears she hadn't meant to. Mrs. Rosenberg languished here, because Anna felt it wasn't fair for Matilda to have to see her. Anna checked to make sure they were well. They appeared to be, though Mrs. Rosenberg had her head between her knees.

Matilda informed Anna that they had not washed linens that morning. Without the matrons to prod the jailer, the washing did not get done. Now, it would have to wait until tomorrow. At least Georges was home and would not need to sleep on dirty linens.

§

When the ladies were settled for the evening, Anna returned to her tiny apartment. She packed her bags, including her two spare uniforms, two nightgowns, two negligees, three dinner gowns, three tea gowns, three pairs of shoes, three hats in boxes, her toothbrush, her hairbrush, walnut stain for her lashes, a pot of Princess Pat rouge, and sufficient undermuslins to stay with Georges for a week. It wouldn't be enough, but it was all she could reasonably carry in two trips to the taxi cab, with the driver's help.

Anna took the cab to Georges's hotel, knowing he would pay the fare. Georges's man, the cab driver, and the doorman carried all her things to the penthouse on the eighth floor. She found her brother napping, so Anna made herself at home. She didn't dare disturb his rest—not to then deliver disturbing news. She would let him sleep.

Fresh gillyflowers stood for "bounds of affection" in a vase by her bed alongside a red foil box of chocolates. Anna bit into six different chocolates, looking for a flavor that would take away her pain. None did. She stripped out of her uniform and filled the large tub in her private bath. As she soaked in the warm, lavender-scented water, she thought of Joe Singer. Being naked reminded her of Joe every time. She climbed out, put her underwear on, and climbed back in. Her drawers swirled in the water.

§

Anna patted herself dry and changed into a tea gown, giving all her other clothes to the hotel maid to be properly laundered as her own efforts had been ho hum. She kept back only one glorious French lace nightgown and one uniform for the morning. As the maid rolled away a basket full of Anna's clothes, Georges appeared in the living room, looking haggard.

Anna smiled weakly and hurried to his side. "Georges, dear. Are you well? You haven't had a fit, have you?"

Georges's face fell. "Anna, please don't treat me like an invalid. It's a blow to my manhood. I'm fine."

"You are fine, then?"

"I'm as fine as can be. Though your fiancé annoys me."

"Oh, you don't know the half of it."

Georges sat down on the settee and patted the cushion beside him. "Tell me, Anna. I can take it."

"I need to warn you, dearest. A man who worked at the Jonquil has been murdered. I think he might be your blackmailer. He was receiving payments from Mrs. Rosenberg's lawyer."

Georges looked very somber. "What was his name?"

"Samuel Grayson."

"Yes, that's him."

Anna's stomach seized. She'd been right. "Obviously that woman was helping him—the one who recognized your picture in the paper."

Georges placed a hand on Anna's arm. "She might be in danger. You have told Detective Singer?"

Anna's guts unwound a bit. Georges was so good, always

thinking of others. Even blackmailers. "Perhaps we should call your defense attorney, because the LAPD could finger you for the crime. I expect Joe Singer will call on you in the morrow."

"Your fiancé thinks I did it?"

"He never said so. I just want to be cautious."

Georges began to tremble, and in a moment, he was on the floor, jerking and writhing. Anna dropped to her knees. "Thomas! Bring his medicine!"

The manservant came with the syringe and the vial.

"You're stronger. You hold him. I'll give the shot."

Thomas helped Anna pull Georges's clothes away to bare his shoulder, then held him down, while Anna filled the syringe, held her breath, and jabbed it into Georges's arm. Georges calmed.

"How often does this happen?" Anna asked.

"Once every few months. Usually, his bromides control it. But I think he's been under too much pressure, Miss."

"Indeed, he has. False accusations. And now this murder." Anna wiped spittle from the corner of Georges's mouth with her handkerchief. "Let's get him to bed."

§

Anna sat by Georges's bedside until the black sky began turning gray, holding his hand, and drinking hot cocoa, which Thomas brought her—six cups in succession. It was a world cocoa record. Finally, he convinced her to go to bed. She slept like the dead in her new bedroom in lace and on clean crisp sheets.

In the morning, she awoke to the doorbell ringing, not simply once—she could sleep through one ring—but someone laying on the doorbell as if it were a horn. Anna moaned, "Thomas! The door."

No one answered.

Anna sought her *robe de nuit* and remembered she'd given it to the maid to wash. She dragged herself in her French lace nightgown to the offending caller, growling through the door, "Who is it?"

"Detective Singer, and you're late for work."

Anna peeked through the peep hole and there he was, looking handsome and fed up.

Anna opened. "Detective Singer? Not Joe? We're no longer on a first name basis? Honestly, that suits me fine."

"I'm here in my official capacity. I'm just trying to remember that."

"Remember all you like." Anna opened the door to let him in.

"I will." Joe's eyes fixed on her décolletage. He grit his teeth. "But that nightgown isn't helping."

"Well, I hope you're discombobulated with desire."

"Where's Georges?"

"Mr. Devereaux is sleeping. He had a fit last night. I sat up with him for most of the night."

"Well, can you wake him up?"

Anna huffed and stomped to Georges's bedroom, jiggling corset-less beneath her nightgown. "He sleeps very soundly when he's had a shot." She knocked gently, then pushed the door open. "Georges?"

Georges's bed lay empty and unmade. A full glass of water rested on the night table.

Anna's voice held a lilt of surprise. "He's gone." She strode to the window and peeked through the drapes, scanning the bustling city eight floors below.

"Do you have any idea where he's gone?"

"No. A mineral springs, maybe? He was very ill last night. I'm sure he left a note. I'll just look for it."

Anna searched around the hotel room and indeed found a note at the place set for her at the breakfast table. She opened it and read,

Dearest Sister,

Thank you for nursing me last night. You are an angel. I didn't want to wake you, but I am going away to rest— maybe a few days, maybe longer. Please keep the home fires burning. Order anything you like from the hotel.

With bounds of affection,
Georges

Anna stared at Joe with bush baby eyes.

Joe pounded the door frame. "He's fled, Anna." He stormed back into Georges's bedroom and appropriated the glass on the nightstand, dumping the water in a palm plant that sat on a wrought iron stand in the corner.

"What are you doing?"

"Getting his fingerprints to see if they match the print on the gun."

Chapter 25

Mr. W.H. Stevens's law office was a dull place for waiting. It smelled joyless, like filing cabinets, piles of contracts, and envelope glue. Anna should have brought a nosegay and a copy of *Le Mode*. With nothing to occupy her mind, her thoughts ran wild. Georges had gone away to rest, but she did not know where. She knew it looked bad.

The door to the hallway opened and Joe Singer entered. He sat next to Anna on the bench. "Great minds think alike."

"Did you lift Georges's fingerprint, yet?"

"Yes. The boys are checking for a match."

"I could arrest you for stealing that glass. It's crystal."

"You don't have powers of arrest."

"I could make a citizen's arrest."

Joe took the glass out of his satchel and handed it to Anna.

"You know that if you put Georges on trial for the Griffith Park murder, and he's innocent, he'll be exonerated, and I will never forgive you."

Joe looked down. "Once upon a time, you liked the fact that I was not a crooked cop." He flashed his luscious blue Arrow Collar Man eyes at her.

Anna opened her mouth, but she had nothing to say.

The door to Mr. Stevens' office opened and a man shuffled out. He was Chinese and wearing an exceptionally nice suit. Anna recognized him as Lee Bock Dong, the new president of the Hop Sing Tong. He had chosen to overlook Joe's falling afoul of his predecessor and had spared Joe's life. She bowed to the president, though he was undoubtedly up to no good. He looked blankly at Anna, as if he didn't recognize her, like she was any other white woman. Like all white women looked the same.

"Matron Blanc." Mr. Stevens, with his air of self-importance, beckoned Anna from his office. Joe followed, uninvited.

Mr. Stevens offered them seats. His hair looked as stiff as a helmet. Joe sat, but Anna remained standing. "Let me get right to the point, Mr. Stevens. An associate of Mrs. Rosenberg's, one Samuel Grayson, has been murdered."

Something flashed across Mr. Stevens's face, an expression Anna couldn't read. She looked to Joe for a clue, but he gave her nothing.

She continued, "We know Mr. Grayson was extorting individuals who corrupted young girls at the Jonquil Resort. We know he received three one-thousand-dollar payments from you. We know you are Mrs. Rosenberg's lawyer. Were you delivering payments to Samuel Grayson on her behalf?

The lawyer looked at Joe, though it was Anna who had addressed him. "No. And please do me the kind favor of not mentioning this to her. It's none of her business."

Though he looked more important than Anna, he was, in fact, stupid. He had just revealed his vulnerability. Anna said, "Then for whom were you making the payments?"

"I won't answer that. It violates attorney–client privilege."

Joe stood and leaned on Mr. Stevens's desk. "You may as well answer, Mr. Stevens. I can get your bank records and see who's paid you. Then we'll investigate everyone on that list, including Mrs. Rosenberg. We'll go visit them late at night when we know they'll be home. Take them down to the station for questioning. So tell me, why were you making the payments?"

"I don't know." The lawyer's face had turned red, and a trickle of sweat dribbled down from his helmet of hair.

"Why don't I tell you," said Anna. "Your mystery client is a patron of the Jonquil bath house. He buys the company of minor girls, contributing to the delinquency of minors. Samuel Grayson, who used to work at the Jonquil, was extorting him. Now someone, most likely your client, has murdered Samuel Grayson. So, you had better tell us everything you know."

"I don't know anything."

"Was Samuel Grayson extorting anyone else?" asked Joe. "He had a lot of nice things . . ."

Anna made a face. "Well, not nice things, exactly."

"Not through me." The self-important lawyer wore a solemn expression.

"Not Mrs. Rosenberg?" Joe asked.

"If Grayson was blackmailing her, she paid him in cash. It wasn't going into his bank account. It would have shown up on his statements," said Anna. "But we know he had other targets. It only follows . . ."

"If Mrs. Rosenberg was being blackmailed, she didn't involve me," said Mr. Stevens.

"How many men pay for sex at the Jonquil Resort?" Joe asked.

"I don't know. Over the last two years . . . twenty or more," said Mr. Stevens.

Anna gave Joe a hard look. "So, we have twenty murder suspects. Twenty. I count, one, two—"

"I got it Anna."

§

Out on the street Joe turned Anna to face him and looked her in the eye. "Anna, you should recuse yourself from this investigation. You can't investigate your own brother."

"If I were formally on this investigation, I would most certainly recuse myself. But since my contributions are unrecognized, I don't bear that burden." She shook him off and clipped down the sidewalk.

He called after her, "Where are you going?"

She didn't turn around. "Same place you are. The Jonquil."

Chapter 26

Anna made the Jonquil Café in time for lunch. The palm in the corner was dead. No one had watered it in the wake of the raid. A few scattered girls sat among the tables. This time, Anna flashed her police matron badge at the maître d'—a different man than before. "I need to speak with Flossie. I don't know her last name."

"There is no one called Flossie here," he said, unimpressed.

No one cared if you were a matron. They only cared if you were a cop. "Fine," said Anna. "Table for one."

Anna sat in a booth and ordered albondigas because one couldn't think if one's stomach was empty, and she needed to plot her next move. Thus, she ordered a second bowl, and a third. For after, she ordered pie.

"Put this on Mr. King's tab."

"Certainly," said the waiter.

Fueled by meatballs, Anna's mind whirred. When she'd gone undercover at Canary Cottage, she'd learned that brothel girls used fake names. What if Flossie also used a fake name? She hailed a waiter. "Do you know my friend? She came here from Oklahoma with Samuel Grayson?"

"You mean Samara Mowrey?" The waiter pointed to a table.

There sat the young lady Anna had interviewed before when she had been incognito, when Joe had punched Clyde Owen, who had insulted Anna's virtue.

Mr. King's lover. Mr. King, also known as the Black Pearl.

Anna crossed the room and sat down at her table. "Should I call you Samara or Flossie? Or Samara Flossie? Or Flossie Samara?"

The girl said, "You're not a resident. You're with the police."

"Correct," said Anna. The girl was no fool. Anna took note. "You fought with your fellow, Samuel Grayson, and you broke it off with him."

"He has atrocious taste."

"Yes." Anna cocked her head from side to side, weighing whether this was justification enough. She decided it was. "I see your point."

"Besides, he's already taken up with another girl. Maybe even before we split up. I didn't think he was the cheating type, but what do I know?"

"Which girl?"

"Does it matter?"

"I would shoot him."

"Pardon."

"I would shoot him in the head, and let his body lie where it fell until it was covered with ants."

The lady blinked at Anna. "I quit him, not the other way around. Our parting was for the best. It's always for the best. Shortly after, I took up with someone else, too. I told you about him."

"I thought he was merely a client."

"He's my future husband."

Anna looked on her finger. She wore that unfortunate diamond ring. The stone was enormous, but badly cut and with flaws that made it appear cloudy.

"Congratulations. So, you've stopped speaking to him?"

"Who, Samuel? What is there to talk about? I have a new lover. Someone better able to take care of me. We're getting married. It's what every girl dreams about."

Anna knew that wasn't true. "Do you know his real name now that you're engaged?"

"Oh, not formally engaged. But it's just a matter of time."

"What is his name?"

The lady's smile faltered. "I . . ."

"You still don't know?" Anna shook her head slowly and tut tutted. "Now that's a shame."

A boy, maybe twelve, came shyly up to the table. "Miss Mowrey, where is Mr. King?"

"Why do you want to see him?" asked Anna.

"He always gives me cigarettes."

"How very kind," said Anna. "But we don't know where Mr. King is or if he's ever coming back."

Samara Flossie stood, glaring at Anna. "And to think I used to like you. Excuse me." She threw her napkin down on the table and stomped out of the café, passing Joe Singer, who was on his way in.

The boy looked guilty, as if he had upset the lady.

Anna said, "Never mind her. Can you describe Mr. King for me? What color is his hair? Or does he even have hair?"

The boy looked at her suspiciously and scampered off toward the kitchen.

"Wait!" called Anna. I'll give you cigarettes."

He disappeared through the door.

Joe spotted Anna and sauntered to her table. "We already interviewed him. He's been coached. We got nothing."

"You're running late," said Anna.

"I was interviewing Mrs. Rosenberg again. What did you learn?"

"Samara is Flossie. She believes her lover, Mr. King, is going to marry her. He's given her a truly ugly diamond ring, which is proof that Mr. King is not Georges. A Blanc would never buy a ring that ugly. What did Mrs. Rosenberg say?"

"She says Samuel Grayson used to work in the café. He had a sweetheart at the apartments—Samara Mowrey. The girl quit him, so Mrs. Rosenberg fired him."

Anna tapped her lips scanning the café, then gestured with her chin. "That girl."

"What about her?"

"Samara Flossie said he took up with another girl. I'm betting it's her."

The girl in question was a natural beauty, though it was hard to tell beneath all her ornamentation. She had clearly dyed her hair, and the color of her gown jolted the senses.

"So the evidence suggests," Anna continued.

"You think she goes with his settee," Joe said.

Anna shook her head solemnly. "Nothing goes with that settee."

"Let's talk to her."

§

Anna and Joe strolled to the garish lady's table. She was deep in conversation with a female dining companion. Joe cleared his throat and flashed his badge. "I'm Detective Singer with the LAPD and this is Assistant Matron Blanc."

"Excuse us, but we need to talk to you," said Anna.

The second young lady swallowed her words and stood up, making an obnoxious noise with her chair. Then, she fled, walking unmannerly fast across the café. Joe turned as if to pursue her, but Anna caught his arm. "No. I'm sure it's this one."

The garish young woman asked, "Why me?"

Joe said, "We need to question you regarding the murder of Samuel Grayson."

Joe looked every bit the detective, his lush mouth could be carved of stone. His dimples could be cups of justice. His mysterious cock stand slept, but she knew it was there, waiting for her to forgive him so it could rise again. But she couldn't forgive him, though Georges was only one in a field of twenty-some murder suspects. And besides, Joe hadn't apologized.

The lady screeched, "He's dead?"

It snapped Anna out of her daydream and back into the world of fighting crime.

Joe said, "Maybe you'd be more comfortable discussing this in private."

Anna looked about them. "Actually, there's no need." The other patrons, those sitting nearby, had up and left when Joe flashed his badge. No one cleared a room of the nefarious quite like the LAPD. Of course, the LAPD were their own brand of nefarious.

Now they had the waitstaff to themselves. Anna smiled, "Two Coca-Colas, please." She looked at the young lady who was struggling to compose herself. "Make that three."

"Where's Mrs. Rosenberg?" The girl demanded.

"Mrs. Rosenberg is in jail, so you had better talk," said Joe.

"Let's be civil and wait for our sodas. How are you?" said Anna, looking at Joe.

"I'm in hell."

Anna smiled tightly. "And you, Miss . . . I'm sorry, we haven't been properly introduced."

"Brown. I'm Edna Brown. What have I done to gain the attention of the police?"

The waiter appeared and slid their sodas in front of them.

"Now talk. You had an affair with Mr. Grayson," said Anna.

"No. He was handsome, sure, and we talked sometimes. But he never laid a hand on me."

"You'd have made a lovely couple."

"It was just a rumor. No substance to it at all. I have my own lover."

"What's his name?"

She shrugged. "His alias, you mean? I call him Jack. Why?"

"He's a suspect."

The girl shook her head. "Jack knows I didn't sleep with Samuel Grayson. Besides, he's not the jealous type."

"Then, how did this rumor get started?"

"Mrs. Rosenberg started the rumor, and I owed Mrs. Rosenberg a favor, so I kept quiet. I don't know why."

"Oh, Mrs. Rosenberg picked you because you matched Mr. Grayson's settee, so to speak. Of course he'd be attracted to you, which makes the rumor believable."

"All I know is that I'm sorry he's dead. He was nice to me."

§

Anna and Joe waited for the Red Car. Anna scribbled in her note-book: *Jack sleeps with Miss Brown, who has bad taste and thinks Samuel Grayson is nice. Mrs. Rosenberg started the rumor that Miss Brown slept with Grayson. Samara Flossie is practically engaged and has an ugly ring.*

Joe paced. "What did you think of her reaction to the news?"

"I don't know. She could just be a good actress."

"How did Samara, I mean Flossie react?"

Anna thought for a moment. "I never told her. I never told her he was dead."

"I have a theory."

"What?" asked Anna.

"I think Mrs. Rosenberg wanted Grayson off the property so that Samara Flossie would be all alone, so she could lure her into prostitution. That's why she started the rumor."

"So, we can add Mrs. Rosenberg to the long list of people who may have wanted Grayson dead: A loan shark, Miss Brown's lover, Samara Flossie's father, the lawyer's mystery client, and every man who's ever frequented the Jonquil Café or resort, including the man from Mars. So, you can take the heat right off my brother."

"Anna, what about the other charge? Kidnapping? Contributing to the downfall of a minor. It would help his case if you could find him."

CHAPTER 27

Anna selected an exquisite tooled leather purse with flowering vines and the image of a peacock. She chose it because it was the least expensive of all her purses—though it had been very expensive—and it was roomy enough to keep her gun. She dressed in her worst dress, which was yellow and actually quite stunning. After solving the Chinatown trunk murder, Anna was intimately acquainted with the most dangerous beat in the city, with its muddy streets tramped by men and almost no women. Most of the Chinese men wore loose-fitting tunics and pants in dark hues. She knew she would stand out like a daffodil in the mud. But stealth was not her objective. She came to exonerate Georges, wherever he might be.

She rode the trolley to the Plaza, adjacent to Chinatown and crossed to Los Angeles Street. The cheerful lanterns from Chinese New Year no longer swung from the eaves. The quarter resembled a run-down Wild West town, but instead of cowboys, there were Chinese men with long black braids. Vendors from the morning produce market were packing up, and wagons dispersed, leaving the ground littered with vegetable waste and horse manure. Being there again, Anna felt panic fluttering in her chest, a remnant from the riot, the tong war, and the deaths she had witnessed. She stopped and collected herself for a moment, simply breathing. She took the gun from her purse and secreted it away in her skirt pocket.

Mr. Jones's still operated his herbal remedy shop on the corner. She would like to see him again and peeked in the window, but a different fellow was manning the till. She wandered down Los

Angeles Street to the burned-out hull that was once the Presbyterian Mission. Its tragedy had compelled her, though it was blocks out of her way. Anna crossed herself.

She cut down to Alameda Street. The gun swished among her flounces as she walked. Most of the gambling, drinking, and whoring done in Los Angeles was done on the fifteen or so streets and alleys that made up Chinatown. The city was deliberately zoned that way, whether the Chinese liked it or not. Chances are, Samuel Grayson played cards here, on Alameda Street. Every second shop was a front for a lottery, fan tan parlor, house of ill repute, or opium den, but Anna knew Samuel's game. He played poker. Most joints offered the normal fare—poker, fan tan, lotteries—all illegal, all under the protection of the mayor, the police chief, and the Chinatown Squad, who took their cut. Ladies were not allowed, except in secret backrooms with separate entrances. She would go door-to-door until she found a gambling joint that offered poker, and where the proprietor recognized the picture of poor dead Samuel.

Anna went window to window, peering inside, her guts in a knot. The first three establishments were Chinese-only—at least she saw no other races. Each time, curious faces peered back at her, and one old proprietor shooed her away, waving his hands and speaking sharply in Chinese. Anna skedaddled. The fourth saloon had black paint over the windows. She cleared a hole in the paint with her fingernail and peeked through. Mexican, white, and black patrons were watching a woman in harem pants dance with a large white snake, her midriff bare. No gambling. Fascinated, Anna lingered to watch the dancer skillfully rolling her hips and writhing with the snake, until a man, spotting Anna's eye, covered the hole with his hand.

White and brown men played poker in the fifth establishment. Anna eschewed the back door because she didn't believe in back doors. Graciously, the man behind the bar spoke to her as he threw her out. But he didn't recognize the name Samuel Grayson, nor the photograph.

The next saloon, the Cock of the Walk, nestled between what

purported to be a barber shop and a brothel. Anna arrived at the front entrance just as an Indian was being manhandled out. She felt a camaraderie with the man. It was illegal to sell liquor to Indians, just like it was illegal to serve women in bars.

Anna swung through the door. All eyes rested on her, disapproving. She maintained her poise, chin tilted toward the tin ceiling and bellied up to the bar. She showed the bartender Samuel's photograph. "Do you recognize this man?"

"Sure." He poured whiskey into a glass and set it on a tray. "But you gotta leave. You can't drink here."

Anna took the whiskey and tossed it back.

"I just did."

"You have to pay for that."

"Why should I pay for a drink that I didn't drink because women can't drink here, so how could I possibly have—"

"Martin!"

A man emerged from the back wearing a great, drooping mustache. "What is it?"

"We have a problem." He nodded his chin toward Anna.

"Yes, we do, and it has nothing to do with the whiskey I did not drink. I need to speak with the owner."

"Let's get you out of the bar before I get fined." The man named Martin grabbed Anna by the arm and pulled her through a curtain and into a dark hallway.

Anna struggled. "Unhand me!"

He didn't. "What do you want?"

"I'm looking for my brother, Samuel Grayson. He owes me money. I know he gambled here."

"Isn't that a coincidence. He owes me money, too."

"Well you won't get it now. He's dead."

Martin's nostrils flared. He had food in his mustache. "What?"

"So, he owed you a lot of money?"

"Five hundred dollars."

Anna whistled. "That's a lot of money. Are you angry about it?

Angry enough to kill him?" Joe had said that if you enrage a suspect, they are more likely to lose control of their tongue. Anna continued. "Or did you send someone to do your dirty work for you? Maybe you don't have the stomach for that sort of thing. Maybe you're not man enough. I'd guess you're as squeamish as a little—"

Martin's face contorted, and he pushed Anna roughly against the plaster wall. He needed to brush his teeth. His mustache twitched. His eye tooth was black. He ran his hand down her thigh through the layers of her gown and petticoats. "You're a pretty thing. Maybe you can pay off his debt."

Anna's own hand went into her pocket and drew out her gun. She pressed it into his belly.

He sneered. "You'd never shoot me."

She cocked her rod.

He took a step backward, but his face retained its offensive expression.

Anna backed slowly down the hall, passing the open door to the ladies' section where charity girls drank, trading favors for gifts and liquor.

"Good evening," said Anna, because manners were important.

Martin stalked after her, too proud to admit she might kill him.

A big redhead slurred, "You okay, sister?"

Anna smiled politely, keeping her eyes on Martin. "I'm fine, thank you. And you?"

"Just fine." She sounded sleepy. Or possibly doped.

Anna continued edging backward on the rugged planks in her high heeled shoes, past the ladies' lounge, toward the alley door, keeping her gun up and pointed at the bad man.

One of the ladies shouted. Martin turned his head toward the sound.

Anna's heel hit a snag in the wood. She stumbled awkwardly, jerking her arm, jolting her hand, and squeezing the trigger. The gun went off, bruising her hand with the recoil.

Martin yelped.

Half his mustache was gone. The place above his lip paused a moment before seeping blood.

Anna winced. "Ooh. That might not grow back."

Martin grabbed his mouth. Anna ran out the back door that was specifically for ladies, and through the mucky alley, soiling her shoes.

CHAPTER 28

Anna slept fitfully in Georges's empty hotel room until the birds sang and the curtains glowed. She rolled over on the feather bed and moaned, feeling vaguely hysterical, only mostly awake from a Detective Joe Singer dream. They were trapping a criminal together—a man who did unspeakable things. In the dream, the only way to catch the fiend and save their own lives was if Anna and Joe got perfect scores in ring toss. They tried and tried, but never did. Then, she woke up.

Everything was so simple in dreams. In dreams, Joe loved her. In reality, he simply didn't. Because if he loved her, he would never try to send her brother to the gallows. She knew in her gut that Georges could never do such heinous things as pimp girls and kill blackmailers. Joe should trust her. He usually did.

This was Petronilla's work. Anna and Joe had offended her, spooning on her land. Now they were cursed, and Anna didn't know how to break it.

§

Anna slunk through the door at Central Station at the changing of the shift. Patrolmen came and went or stood about in blue uniforms with brass buttons, leather helmets strapped under their chins.

Joe, dressed in plain clothes, was waiting to waylay her near the stairs.

"Busy night?" he asked, unsmiling.

"No, I just had a quiet dinner, and—"

Joe grabbed Anna by the hand and spun her to face him. "Shot a guy at the Cock of the Walk. Don't lie to me Anna. He came in last night with half his mustache missing and a story about some unbelievably gorgeous girl—Samuel Grayson's sister—shooting him in the lip."

"So." Anna withdrew her hand and shook it out. He had inadvertently squeezed her bruise.

"So? So?" He threw up his hands. "So, don't go to Chinatown alone. Don't interview murder suspects alone. Take me with you." His cheeks and ears were flushed with anger.

"Don't read me the riot act, Detective Singer. You don't get to be huffy with me. You've lost the right. And if you want to fight crime with me, you have to be better company."

"Why did you shoot him? Never mind. I know it was an accident. You're not that good of a shot."

Anna stepped closer and poked him in his manly chest. She growled. "Believe you me, it was no accident. He raised my ire, so if I were you, I'd watch your step."

Joe's angry blue eyes burrowed down into her gray ones. They were unmannerly close—too close for a detective and a police matron.

A patrolman strolled by and cleared his throat, smirking.

Joe took a step back. "Assistant Matron Blanc, meet me in the kitchen. That's an order."

Anna stormed to the kitchen. Joe followed, shutting and locking the door.

Joe pulled her into his arms and kissed her until she was weak-kneed and breathless. "I'll come to you tonight."

"Yes. Come to me, Joe. Come make love to me where I live now—in Georges's hotel room."

Joe swore and let her go. He paced to the wall and back again.

"Question the man with half a mustache. He's the bookie that Samuel owed money to. And for the record, he tried to dishonor me, so I shot him."

Joe made a loud anguished sound in the back of his throat that the cops could probably hear out on the floor. "Are you all right? Tell me you're all right."

"I'm fine."

He didn't look all right. He looked a little wild. "I'll kill him."

"I don't need you to rescue me. I rescued myself. Besides, I don't want him dead. Let him suffer forever with his silly half mustache because it's not going to grow back. I scalped him." She proffered a fleeting smile. "But let's question him first."

§

Martin, the owner of Cock of the Walk, also had a last name. "Mr. Rooster?" Joe said skeptically.

"Is he serious?" Anna made a chicken noise, then laughed for a full minute. It relieved her stress a little, so she did it again. Joe laughed at Anna laughing.

Mr. Rooster didn't laugh. His asymmetrical moustache made his frown ridiculous.

"You should learn to laugh at yourself," said Anna.

"Shut up you little . . ." The man stopped midsentence when he saw Joe's murderous expression.

Anna had been waiting for Joe's anger, and here it was, splendid and violent red, contorting his face. He was moving slowly and steadily closer to Mr. Rooster.

The man gulped and quickly backtracked. "I beg your pardon, Miss."

Anna wasn't about to help him.

Joe grabbed Mr. Rooster by the lapels and sat him up in his chair. "Where were you two weeks ago last Wednesday?"

Mr. Rooster's eyes rolled to the ceiling. Finally, he said. "In the county jail."

"Biscuits!" said Anna.

Joe narrowed his eyes. "What was the charge?"

"I got in a fight."

"A cockfight?" Joe deadpanned.

Anna bent over at the waist and giggled.

"Whatever got done, I couldn't have done it," said Mr. Rooster.

"He could have hired someone to kill Samuel Grayson," said Anna. "In fact, he probably did."

"Why would I want him dead if he owes me money? I wanted him to pay me back."

Anna tapped her lip and looked heavenward. "To punish him? To make an example of him?"

"Grayson always paid me before."

§

Anna and Joe went into the hallway to confer.

"I believe him," said Joe. "Only a fool would loan a gambler five hundred dollars unless he had excellent credit."

"Regrettably, I believe him, too."

"But we can try him for attempted rape."

"No. The defense attorney would tear me apart, given the things that have been written about me in the papers. They made me out to be a . . . bad woman."

"Those newspaper stories were discredited, and other newspaper stories vindicated you. You were investigating a murder undercover in the brothels. Not a whore."

"You don't understand. Once a woman is tainted, it never goes away."

"So, what do I do?"

Anna sighed a deep sigh of resignation. "Just let him go."

"All right. If you say so. But I've got my eye on him." His face went flat. "There's something else we need to talk about."

"What?"

"Georges."

Anna remained stony silent.

Joe said, "Well, where is he? Any word?"

"No."

"Are you looking for him?"

"No. I'm sure he's just . . . convalescing."

"He's got a court date and a fifty-five-thousand-dollar bond. If he's innocent, he'd be better off here defending his name. They'll issue a warrant. He'll be in contempt of court."

"How long does he have?"

"A month."

"All right. I'll find him."

"There's something you should know . . . My pop has added five patrolmen to help Wolf and me with the investigation into the Jonquil Apartments. Not just Georges. All the men we can identify. Mrs. Rosenberg. Everybody. He's serious about addressing the girl problem. This morning patrolmen went out to the Jonquil Café, the Jonquil Apartments, and the resort to get a list of the girls' names to testify. And a list of the male patrons."

"Wolf is helping too?"

"He doesn't have a choice."

"But you do."

"Anna, I'm on your side. I'm always on your side."

"Hah!" Anna turned her back to him.

"I'm just trying to protect you. If he's guilty, I don't want him anywhere near you. If he's innocent, I'll find the real Black Pearl. I promise."

CHAPTER 29

Anna searched Georges's desk for his address book, but it seemed like he'd taken it away with him. She couldn't call his friends because she didn't know his friends. She didn't know anyone who knew Georges except perhaps her ex-fiancé, Edgar Wright, who she would never call upon unless she was thoroughly drunk or desperate. She called Georges's lawyer, Earl Rogers. A little girl answered the phone. Mr. Rogers wasn't in, but the girl said she would take a message.

Anna set down the phone and pressed her forehead with the heel of her hand, thinking. Where could Georges be? She wondered if her father knew.

There was only one way to find out.

She took the trolley to Angel's Flight, then took the funicular up to the top of Bunker Hill and walked the rest of the way to the Blanc Mansion. Though in need of maintenance, it remained one of the grandest houses in Los Angeles—an architectural gem, surrounded by gardens, and with views of the city all the way out to the sea.

Anna knocked on the enormous door, coming for the first time as a visitor. The butler answered and gawked at her like an incredulous hillbilly.

"Do close your mouth, Robin," said Anna.

"I'm sorry miss. I didn't expect you."

"Is my father at home?"

"No, he's out."

Her father's servants claimed he was out every time Anna called on the telephone. They were, no doubt, under orders. But she didn't think Robin was lying. Her father's auto was not in the drive, and she couldn't smell his telltale cigar.

She thanked the butler and began trudging down the drive toward Angel's Flight. As she rode the funicular down the hill she noted the Fremont Hotel where Georges had said he and his mother used to live when he was in Los Angeles six months of every year. Where was his mother staying now? Maybe in France, or maybe not. Maybe she was staying at the Fremont Hotel.

§

The Fremont Hotel had been stylish years ago when Georges and his mother had first moved in. It still had a faded glory, but Anna could understand why Georges had sought greener pastures. The question was, had his mother?

"Is there a Miss Devereaux in residence," she asked the clerk at the front desk.

"Mrs. Jeanne Devereaux?" he asked.

Anna blushed. "Yes, I meant, 'Mrs.'"

The Mrs. must be a ruse to cover the shame of unwed motherhood. If she had married, she would bear a new name, and she wouldn't live here in this hotel, supported by Anna's faithless father and now, no doubt, Georges. Was she still beautiful? She must be well past forty. Had she stayed for the money or for love? Georges had said their father had loved his mother. What about her. Had she loved the volatile, brilliant, unfaithful Christopher Blanc? Did she still?

"She just left," said the clerk.

Anna's shoulders sagged.

"She's never here in the evenings."

"Why not?" said Anna.

"She goes to church. I know because she's always inviting everyone."

Anna perked up. It was an odd pastime for a French mistress, but it could work in Anna's favor. If Anna were lucky, she could perhaps arrange an introduction through the priest, who would surely be on her side. "Which church?"

"The Azusa Street Mission."

Anna borrowed the clerk's City Directory and found the address of the church to be 312 Azusa Street, not far from City Hall. She took a cab, because she could, and she could because of Georges—Georges who she must find.

The church was a dump, like a big, white, plank box in terrible need of painting. Like something you'd store fish in. Except, the box lived. It veritably shook with sound, like the fish were still flopping, and they were giant sea bass. Anna disembarked. "That can't be a church." She looked quizzically back at her cabby, but he was already clip-clopping off in his hansom.

Music flowed from the box's windows. She heard no instruments, just voices joined in a rousing chorus. "Blessed assurance, Jesus is mine . . ."

Anna thought the lyrics rather presumptuous, but she resolved to keep an open mind.

She moved toward the building with a funny feeling in her stomach. This fish box wasn't like a church at all. The doors opened at her tug, and instead of fishes, strange noises swam out. It was crowded and stank of sweat, breath, and roses.

Negros and whites mingled together. She noted a few Mexicans and even Chinamen. They swayed together with their hands in the air, singing at the top of their lungs, whether they could hold a tune or not. Tears streamed down a grown white man's face, and he wasn't the only one crying. A strapping Negro in a bow tie stood up front and preached, barely audible over the music.

Then Anna realized why she couldn't understand him.

He wasn't speaking English.

She had never known anything like it, not in stories, not in her dreams. The song ended, but not the noises. People prayed out loud, all at the same time, in that same mysterious language that was not English, French, Spanish, Chinese, or Latin, all of which were familiar to Anna. Esperanto perhaps? Or maybe it wasn't one same language.

It was holy chaos, so vibrant, she felt it rattling her bones. Could this be Petronilla's doing? Anna crossed herself and leaned against a wall. She said a silent prayer to Saint Gotteschalk, patron saint of linguists, that he would grant her understanding. He didn't.

Every man, woman, and child held a Bible in their hands or had one in their lap. One man waved his in the air, but no one read them. Then all the people hushed, except for the crying man who sobbed into the silence. He looked very ordinary—like someone from a regular church, only blubbering. People swarmed him, put their hands on him, and began to pray in the burbling mystery language, rudely talking over one another. It disconcerted Anna, and she was tempted to turn around and wait back at Jeanne Devereaux's hotel. But Anna couldn't risk letting her father's mistress slip through her fingers. She needed to find Georges, and she needed to find him soon, before he missed his day in court. Joe said so, and Joe Singer never lied.

A Negro child in a white ruffled dress stood on a chair, shouting out with an authority uncommon for a child her age. She had to be twelve. "Someone here is under the conviction. Someone needs to repent. God sees you. God is calling you." She turned and, with burning brown eyes, looked straight at Anna.

Anna glanced behind her, but there was no one behind her. She froze. She wasn't interested in repenting. Not yet.

Then a woman made her way forward and hovered near the podium, head bowed in shame. Anna's shoulders rose and fell as she breathed in relief. Luckily, she was not the only one under conviction.

The preacher man touched the woman, who must have been very sorry indeed. She collapsed. Anna gasped. She waited for someone to help the lady, but no one did. They just left the woman to lie on the carpet.

Anna tapped the shoulder of a man next to her. "Excuse me. A Christian is down."

His face registered what looked like euphoria. "Hallelujah."

Anna looked around her. "Could someone please call a doctor?" No one responded. Anna began wading through the crowd toward the lady on the rug. Across the room, another member of the congregation collapsed, and was similarly ignored. Two more dropped. Anna turned in circles. She changed her mind and began wading away from the stricken as the disease seemed quite virulent and she didn't want to catch it.

The girl in the white dress burst into song, unintroduced, and without accompaniment. No embarrassed family member stopped her. People swayed with their hands in the air, like grass on the hills in the wind. Anna felt exceptionally hot and confused. The room was flooded with sound and high-strung emotion, as if wrung from a dirty sponge.

Four men carried in a writhing, hissing man, each holding an arm or a foot. He reminded Anna of Mrs. Michaelchek. They were quickly surrounded, and Anna could barely see the man through the bodies. She heard the preacher shout. "In the name of Jesus, come out of him!"

She heard a soul-chilling scream. Then the people lay the man on the carpet. He was limp and possibly dead.

"Jesus!" someone shouted. "Jesus, Jesus, Jeeeeeeesus."

Anna took stock of her situation. She could run, and she wanted to. Or she could help Georges. But how would she find his mother in this confusion? She closed her eyes and steeled herself. Then, she went forward, farther from the safety of the door. Since shouting out seemed to be something they did here, she shouted herself, to the best of her corseted ability. She shouted until she felt breathless and slightly faint. "Jeanne Devereaux! Jeanne Devereaux! Jeeeeanne Devereaux!"

The people still swayed like grass, reaching for the sun. Some craned their necks toward Anna as she pushed her way to the front begging everyone's pardon and shouting, "Jeanne Devereaux!" A mulatto woman waded through the crowd after Anna, possibly to exorcise her. She moved gracefully and wore bohemian clothes. Anna grimaced and held up her hands defensively, backing away. "No, thank you. I'm not possessed."

"I'm Jeanne Devereaux." Her accent was French.

The preacher put his hand on Anna's shoulder. She swooned, defeated by shock, heat, her corset, and the overwhelming scent of too many Protestants.

§

Anna had the vague impression of being touched by a dozen hands. Her eyelids fluttered. "Stop it. Please stop it." She began swatting at them ineffectually.

A man scooped her up and carried her away, holding her against his suit jacket. He lugged her up a flight of stairs and laid her on an itchy horsehair couch.

"I think I know this girl. It's Anna Blanc," said a woman.

"She's been slain in the Spirit," said a man.

"I'm not dead," murmured Anna.

Jeanne Devereaux knelt beside her. She smelled nice, like Anna's own Ambre Antique perfume, and Anna wondered if she knew anything at all about the world.

CHAPTER 30

The lady's eyes were like amber with fire trapped inside—this woman, Christopher Blanc's mistress. "Do you have a prophecy for me?"

Anna squinted at her. If God was playing telephone, Anna was certainly not in the loop. "I rather think not. God never tells me anything."

"Of course he does, but you have to listen." Jeanne Devereaux looked to the man who had carried Anna.

He had glistening ebony skin, round wire spectacles, and smelled of eucalyptus. He assured Anna firmly. "You have a message."

Anna blinked. Asking Anna for a prophecy was like asking a poodle for legal advice. God didn't favor her. God didn't talk to her. God never helped her, although sometimes the saints came through, but even that was spotty. Anna's head swam. "I'll pray to the Magdalene." She was, after all, the patron saint of bad women, and Anna had been very, very bad.

Mrs. Devereaux and the man exchanged a knowing glance as if Anna needed instruction.

It dawned on Anna that she did have a message, though it wasn't from God. Still, she could borrow his credibility. She struggled to sit up. "God says Georges is in trouble. He says tell me where Georges is."

"Trouble? What is his trouble?"

"God says, 'Don't talk here.' He says, 'Talk in your hotel.'"

§

Anna and Mrs. Devereaux rode in silence, though, behind them, the cabby spoke incessantly in what Anna took to be a thick Scottish accent. Like the people in the church, she couldn't understand him. All the while, Mrs. Devereaux stared at Anna, almost pleading for information with her eyes. Luckily, the woman was trying to obey God, because Anna couldn't bear to speak of Georges's troubles in a cab. Anna could hardly bear to speak of them at all.

Anna snuck peeks at the lady. She had the nose of a European aristocrat, an enviably long neck, and wavy black hair swept up beneath a simple but striking hat. This elegant mulatto woman was her father's lover and Georges's mother. This meant Georges was passing as white, but any children he had may look black. His children's children might look white, and their children might look black, and so on.

Her family was a veritable checkerboard.

Georges had a hard road as a bastard. If people knew he was a white black man, it could make things worse for him. A jury wouldn't sympathize. No wonder Georges said he'd never marry.

His children could give him away.

Anna didn't care if Georges was part Negro any more than she cared about the color of his eyes. Except for this; she knew the fates of people who came from mixed unions. If Georges were found out, he would be ostracized by whites and Negros alike. He would fit nowhere. He would have to go back to France where people weren't so hateful, and Anna would lose him—the only family she had.

The cabby stopped in front of the Fremont Hotel. Anna and Mrs. Devereaux took the elevator in awkward silence.

Anna didn't know how she should feel about this woman who had possessed Anna's father first—who Georges said her father had loved, maybe still loved if old people still had feelings. Mrs. Devereaux hadn't betrayed Anna. Rather, Anna was incarnate proof of her father's betrayal of Mrs. Devereaux. By all rights, Mrs. Devereaux should hate Anna.

Anna cast down her eyes. "Are you a forgiving woman?"

"I've seen a man with no arm grow an arm right in front of me. I know a blind man who can now see. I know a dumb woman who now prophesies. I've known God's power."

It wasn't quite what Anna had asked.

"I am called to forgive, just as He forgives. He gives me the power, and He has power, indeed."

Anna inclined her head and nodded, unsure of what to say. She didn't speak Protestant. She wanted to ask the woman everything— had Mrs. Devereaux loved her father? Did she love him still? Were she and Anna related? Why didn't she take Georges to see Anna? Why wasn't she Catholic? Would she please invite Anna to church the next time men were growing arms?

She didn't feel like she had the right to ask.

Mrs. Devereaux let her into a simple, well-appointed suite and shut the door. Her amber eyes burned, and she commanded Anna, "Now, Anna Blanc, prophesy. What's wrong with my son?"

"He's going to be indicted for kidnapping and contributing to the downfall of minor girls, and he's a suspect in the murder of a man who tried to blackmail him. He's fled and it's going to make things worse for him. God says you must tell me where he is."

"What do you want with Georges?"

"To prove his innocence, of course. He's my brother. Naturally, I love him."

Mrs. Devereaux stared at Anna long and hard. "Yuma. He's in Yuma." Then, she fell into prayer.

CHAPTER 31

The next morning, a line of Chinamen stood at the booking desk, no doubt victims of a fan-tan raid in the wee hours that would result in payoffs—the LAPD extorting the Chinese. Anna found Joe working at his desk. "Hello, Detective Singer. How are you?"

He glanced over toward the booking desk. "I'm disgusted, and you, Assistant Matron Blanc? How's your day?"

"Interesting."

"I think that's good. I have news about the case. You're not going to like it. Sit down."

Anna sat.

"Georges's fingerprints were inconclusive."

"What do you mean?"

"We couldn't rule him out. The partial from the gun is kind of smudged, but it could be a match."

Anna said, "Or not."

"Or not."

"They aren't his fingerprints anyway."

"What?"

"The fingerprints you took from the glass obviously belong to Thomas, his man. The glass was full when you took it from the nightstand. Georges doesn't get his own water. Thomas brought him the water glass. Georges never touched it."

"Whether the prints were Georges's or Thomas's, it ties Georges to the murder."

"Or it would if the test wasn't *inconclusive*."

"There's a guy coming to visit from New York. He's the NYPD's fingerprint expert. He'll be able to tell."

"Thank you for going the extra mile to hang my brother."

"Anna, I have a cousin, Jeremiah, and he's really charming, but he's not a good man. He's a card sharp and he cheats, and he's mixed up with all kinds of bad people in Chicago. Well his little brother, Luke, was the opposite—honest, hardworking. And he was a musician, like me. Played the harmonica and the fiddle. My favorite cousin. We would play together. Jeremiah and Luke were also close, and people knew it. That was Luke's downfall. Jeremiah crossed the wrong people, and Luke was found shot through the heart. They killed him Anna. We lost him. They punished Jeremiah through Luke. So, if Georges is a bad seed or he has nefarious associates, I don't want him anywhere near you because you might get hurt."

"Why do men always think they know what's best for women? Aren't men the ones causing all the trouble? Joe, I'm a grown woman."

"And, Sherlock, I'm a cop."

"But what if he's innocent? He *is* innocent."

"If Georges is innocent, I've still got to find him and bring him in. It's my job. Then, he can defend himself. It's much worse for him when he's on the lam. So, if you know anything—"

"Georges is in Yuma."

Joe gaped. "Yuma? There's nothin' in Yuma. It's just a place on the way to somewhere else."

"It's the desert, and that's good for your health."

"Anna, he's hiding. It's one place I'd never think to look. How did you find out?"

She tapped her lip. Joe might not believe the word of her father's mistress given the lady's stakes in the game. "The hotel clerk told me. I just had to ask. See, nothing to hide."

Joe looked skeptical. "Unless he paid the clerk to lie to us."

"Unlikely. Georges could have left us misleading information in his note if he was in the habit of misleading sisters, which he is not."

"Well, we don't have any other leads. All right. I'm going to Yuma."

"We're going to Yuma. Wolf said I could help."

§

Anna and Joe planned to meet at La Grande Station to catch the afternoon train. Joe returned to his apartment and Anna to Georges's hotel room to pack. By necessity, they would stay two nights, maybe three. It was unfortunate that Anna could no longer stand him. She piled three hat boxes on top of her steamer trunk and dragged the thing backward, bump bumping it down the steps to the curb where she flagged down a hansom.

The dome of La Grande Station towered over the corner of Second Street and Santa Fe like an Arabian palace, its golden turrets gleaming in the sun. Anna's hansom driver hopped down and handed her out onto the wide, dusty street. She reached into her purse to pay the man and found a monogrammed handkerchief, Princess Pat rouge, and a tiny silk purse for coins, which, regrettably, was empty. She had forgotten to plan for her fare.

She should have gone through the pockets of Georges's cashmere coats and checked beneath his cushions for change. She bit her lip, looked up at the cabby, and offered him her lace handkerchief and a hopeful smile. He twisted his ruddy face into a sneer and spit near her shoe. The man climbed up onto the top of his hansom and drove off, leaving her trunk and hat boxes in the dirty street. Anna gaped after him. There was no reason to be so rude, simply because she had forgotten to plan for her fare. She would have paid him someday, but now she had no inclination to do so. She piled the three hat boxes on top of her trunk, bent over and pushed the trunk along the concrete. She hit a bump and the hat boxes rolled like coins into the gutter. "Biscuits!"

Joe Singer appeared and scooped them up one by one. "I would have come by with a wagon, Sherlock, if I'd known you'd be bringing the kitchen sink."

"Pardon me if I like to change my drawers."

Joe's eyes widened and he laughed. "Matron Blanc, you shock me." He grasped the three hat boxes by the strings, setting his own small carpet bag on top of the trunk. It had a floral pattern, and Anna wondered if it had belonged to his mother. He pulled the trunk by the handle, dragging it up the steps, onto the wooden platform. Anna tried not to appreciate it.

He said, "I got our tickets. I'm afraid we're traveling third class."

"Maybe you are." She approached the ticket counter. "Hello. I'm Anna Blanc. Can you attach the Blanc car to the train please?"

"Which train? The one to San Francisco?"

"No, the one to Yuma."

"But ma'am, that train is scheduled to leave in . . ." He checked his watch. "Fifteen minutes."

"Surely you can attach one little railcar. It won't make us too late, will it? We can make up the time on the tracks. How long is it to Yuma?"

"Fourteen hours." The man at the ticket counter looked dubious. "Let me ask the station master, Miss."

"You have your own railcar?" said Joe.

"My father did, so I assume that Georges has it now. And he would want me to travel in comfort when I capture him. You, however, he would want in third class."

"If he has the railcar, wouldn't he take it to Yuma?"

"It's a very conspicuous car. I don't think he wants to be found. Not when he's convalescing."

"Uh huh," said Joe. "Don't you think your father would have told them not to let you take the railcar?"

"Only if he thought of it."

The ticket taker returned with another man in a long coat and an official looking hat. He had a great bulbous nose and short, flipper arms. He resembled an elephant seal. He introduced himself as the station master. "Good evening, Miss Blanc." He cleared his throat. "How do I know you are Anna Blanc?"

Anna beamed at Joe. "He didn't think of it."

"Don't you recognize her?" asked Joe. "She's only the most beautiful woman in Los Angeles."

"I'm impervious to flattery," said Anna.

"It's only flattery if it isn't true," Joe said.

"You can't ride in my railcar."

Joe reached into his suit jacket pocket and pulled out his badge. "I'll vouch for her. Detective Singer, LAPD. But just ask any of your men. Her picture's been in the *Herald* a dozen times."

The ticket taker examined Anna's face. "That is Anna Blanc, Georges Blanc's half-sister," said the ticket taker.

"His favorite sister," said Anna.

The station master looked to Joe. "Why would she want to go to Yuma? It's nothing but desert. You're not going on further east? Maybe New Orleans? Oklahoma City?"

"No. I hear Yuma has a very nice prison," said Anna.

"We're on official police business," said Joe.

The station master wagged his big nose back and forth. "Watch out for rattlesnakes and Gila monsters."

"Monsters?" said Anna.

"Gila monsters. They're big lizards, big as dogs. Nasty creatures. They leap through the air to attack and can spit venom ten yards. And their breath is poisonous. They'll kill a grown man with their fetid breath alone. My cousin knew a man who was bitten by a Gila monster. He died slowly."

Anna looked at Joe. "It would be a shame if a Gila monster got you."

Joe smirked.

"We are definitely going to Yuma," said Anna. "Add it to the Blanc tab."

The station master frowned. "We don't have men to staff your car, Miss. This train is mostly carrying freight."

"I don't need staff. Much," said Anna. "There must be men on the train. Trains don't drive themselves. Somebody shovels the coal."

"I beg your pardon Miss Blanc. If they stop shoveling, the train stops."

Anna tapped a finger on her lip. "Well then. If I truly need assistance—if there are plumbing problems for example . . ." She lifted her chin and looked at Joe. "I'll simply call the police."

The station master turned to Joe for confirmation. Joe frowned but nodded.

Anna smiled. "It's settled then."

§

The Pacific Fruit Express rolled into La Grande Station. It was a mixed train with three passenger cars and a string of refrigerator cars carrying lemons, oranges, grapefruit, artichokes, and strawberries for the people in the East. Attaching the Blanc car to the middle of the train took an hour, delaying departure. Anna waited on a bench, hoping that the other passengers milling about impatiently didn't realize it was her fault. Rather, she hoped they thought Joe was to blame. She stared at him reproachfully to make it seem so. Also, she thought that if she stared at his face long enough, he would no longer seem so handsome, like when you say the word "the" so many times in a row that it begins to sound wrong.

"What?" he said, still handsome.

"Nothing." She stared harder.

Two men in black bow ties and tails passed by carrying large baskets covered in white cloths. They boarded the lonely Blanc railcar. Ten minutes later, the men disembarked empty-handed. At last, the station master snuffled over. He offered Anna his flipper and escorted her to the train while Joe followed dragging Anna's trunk, three striped hat boxes grasped by the cords, and his small carpet bag tucked under one arm. Her hat boxes banged against his shins as he walked.

Anna had only ridden in her father's railcar twice, on pleasure trips to Santa Barbara where they had stayed at the Arlington Hotel. They had visited the old mission and played on the beach, watching the seals and dolphins swim, and getting tar on their feet. Her father mainly used the train for his own business travel. Who knows what Georges used it for, or if he used it at all.

The station master unlocked the door. "If you need anything . . . I guess you ask him." He tipped his nose toward Joe.

"Thank you, kindly." Anna inclined her head, then mounted the steps to the private car.

Joe followed, struggling to get through with his heavy load. Once inside, his eyes expanded to wagon wheels. "Holy smoke." He set the luggage down. The Blanc car resembled the interior of a plush hotel suite, sumptuous and grand. A log burned in a great tile fireplace before a polar bearskin rug with a taxidermy head. There was a tufted velvet settee. An ornate carved table held crystal goblets and decanters, and a phonograph. A large arrangement of fresh calla lilies had been waiting on the off chance that a Blanc would come for a ride. The baskets, which contained an array of foods, chocolates, and wine, graced a small dining table. The bed was large enough for two. Heavy damask drapes hung over the windows. Anna pushed them aside letting in the sunlight. She turned and gave Joe a saccharine smile. "I should be comfortable enough."

He wandered into the private bath where there were more calla lilies, bath oils, and soaps shaped like flowers. "Holy smoke."

"You said that."

"Sherlock, you could fit a baseball team in your bathtub."

"Don't be silly. I don't want to bathe with baseball players."

He smirked and strolled back into the living area. "Are you going to be okay in here all alone? Are you sure you don't want a bodyguard? Someone might break in and steal, I don't know, this." He picked up a bronze table lamp shaped like a lady. He set it down. "Or this." He lifted a crystal decanter full of spirits. He replaced it and sauntered to the door leading to the other cars. "Is the lock secure?"

"Yes, it's secure." Anna plopped down on the settee and stretched. "We couldn't have third-class passengers trying to get in."

He opened the portal, flipped the lock, and tried the handle. It refused to turn with the lock engaged. "All right. I'll leave you in peace. Don't feel guilty."

"Oh, I won't."

"We could be discussing the case."

Anna tilted her head back and forth as she weighed this. "No."

Joe carried his carpet bag out through the portal, into the next car, and presumably through another car and into third class.

The train began to roll, chugging through the city, down through the center of Chinatown, tooting its horn. Anna watched out the window. The whores on Alameda Street stood in doorways making obscene gestures at the train, lifting their skirts to show off their frillies. Anna waved back, looking closely to see if she knew anyone, but they were girls from the cribs, not the better parlor houses, and looked unfamiliar. The train flew past warehouses, greenhouses, breweries, and tall buildings. They passed fields of strawberries and asparagus where Chinese men in shabby hats tilled the soil to feed the city that oppressed them.

Anna removed her hat and plopped down on the bed. She needed to think about the Griffith Park Executioner, so she could catch him and exonerate Georges. Who was he and why did he kill? Was he an Angeleno, or someone from Grayson's past, from Oklahoma City? She lay back and stared at the vines and flowers painted on the vaulted ceiling, tracing them with her eyes. She pictured Samuel Grayson lying in the dust, covered in ants. She pictured the Jonquil Café, the girls there, Lester Shepherd. But her mind kept drifting to Oklahoma City.

Anna fell asleep.

§

Anna awoke in pitch darkness, on top of the coverlet, still wearing her traveling ensemble. She sat up, refreshed, having slept through most of the night. It was unusual for Anna to sleep through dinner when someone else had cooked. She rose and stretched. She flipped on the light. The night was frigid. She heaped more coals into the fireplace and splashed them with brandy. With a match, she set a piece of her father's fine stationary aflame and tossed it onto the coals, crossing her fingers. They caught.

She moved to the gramophone and put on a recording of Enrique Caruso singing *La Donna È Mobile*. She took off her shoes and tucked her feet beneath her on the settee, poured herself a goblet of wine, and nibbled on grapes and cheese.

The car grew toasty warm. She decided to remove her wool travel ensemble so as to be even more comfortable. She drew the drapes, unbuttoned her skirt and jacket, and slipped out of them. She shed her corset cover and unhooked her corset. She peeled off her chemise and dropped her petticoats and drawers. She rolled down her stockings and slid her garters down her legs.

She liked being naked.

She lay down on the white bear-skin rug in front of the fireplace, her head on the bear's head like a pillow. The fur felt delicious on her naked skin, silky and soft. Caruso crooned. She thought of Joe. She pictured him in his underwear.

She thought of moving into the railcar permanently and just traveling up and down the state naked. She thought of Joe's cock stand. She massaged her aching muscles.

Someone knocked on the door.

Anna froze. "Who is it?"

"It's your estranged fiancé. I'm really sorry to wake you."

"What could you possibly want at this hour?"

"There's no food in third class, the guy next to me is whistling, and I'm right by the toilets. I haven't slept a wink."

"I'll bet there's no wine, either, and no gramophone."

"And it's cold."

Anna rolled over onto her belly and ate a grape. "That's too bad. My fire is toasty warm."

"Anna." Joe rattled the doorknob. "Please, let me in."

"You should be nicer to my—"

The lock clicked, and the door flew open. Joe stood in his derby hat, shivering in the space between cars.

Anna froze, grape halfway to her mouth, naked on the bearskin rug.

Chapter 32

Joe's perfect mouth dropped open. "I . . . I . . . Oh Lord." He turned his back. He turned around again. "Oh Lord." He turned his back again and stepped outside, closing the door.

Anna heard him making strangled, anguished, animal sounds in the space between cars.

She wasn't sure what to do. On the one hand, Joe was what she wanted. On the very important other hand . . .

Anna couldn't remember the other hand. She wanted him back. "Help! Police!"

The door opened. Joe stepped inside and closed it behind him. He was breathing hard.

Anna was now wrapped in the rug like an Eskimo, the polar bear's head beside her own, her heart thumping. "We're fine now, thank you."

"What?"

She cleared her throat. "I was in the bath, you see . . . but . . . I tripped and rolled across the floor, and then . . . I flipped over the chair onto the rug and—"

"I'm trying to picture that."

"It happens all the time."

"Oh God, I hope that's true." Joe tossed his derby hat and stripped out of his coat while crossing the railcar in two long strides. He leaned down and kissed Anna on the mouth. He kissed her again. His kiss was melting fiery and burned with all the intensity of their situation, and all the passion required to overcome it—his threat to her kin, her familial fidelity, the fierce gaze of a taxidermied bear, and a door that did not lock.

He kissed her like he was starving and she was a very delicious liverwurst sandwich.

She liked it intensely.

With great effort, Anna turned her head away. "You and I are fighting, and you can't fight naked."

"I don't know. The Greeks used to do it." He moved his kisses lower, thrilling her skin.

She gasped. "You'll get a cock stand, and everyone in third class will realize—"

"I have a plan for that."

It was too late, anyway. He already had a cock stand.

Joe's logic made perfect sense, and his body was exceedingly interesting. So, Anna did what any girl would do in her situation, being covered in kisses by a delicious policeman while wearing only polar bear fur. She arched up against him, letting her head fall back.

"Oh, cutie," Joe whispered passionately.

There was a bang, and a man's loud voice. "You villain!"

Joe whirled about, dropping Anna on her bottom. She clutched the rug to her chest. A sleepy, disheveled conductor loomed with two blackened railroad men who very likely should have been shoveling coal but were now staring at Anna with googly eyes. The conductor swooped up the bronze lamp shaped like a lady and clobbered Joe over the head, denting the velum shade. Joe's blue eyes lost focus and he fell backward, collapsing flat on his spine, though everything was not flat.

Anna shrieked. The conductor threw his arm toward the door. "Go on. Get him out of here!"

She screamed again and kept screaming as the men yanked Joe Singer up by his armpits. He struggled and kicked as they dragged him out of the car.

§

After the railroad workers had tossed Joe off the train, Anna sat on the couch wrapped in a robe, sipping a brandy.

She furrowed her brow. "Are we almost in Yuma? I mean, you left Detective Singer alone in the desert. He could have broken his . . . something."

"He deserved it, the cad. And anyway, we were summiting the hill. The train wasn't going very fast."

"Yes, but he hasn't any water." Anna stood, crossed to the liquor cabinet, rummaged for a sterling silver flask and filled it from the sink. She went out the car door and peered down into the gap between cars, the cold wind whipping her hair. She carefully dropped the flask onto the tracks. It disappeared with a clank, sucked into darkness.

"Do you think he'd like some grapes?" Anna strode to the picnic basket, retrieved a bunch of grapes, and dropped them down, too.

The conductor shook his head with feeling. "You truly are an angel."

"Yes, I know." She tossed Joe some cheese.

"Please. I know it's delicate, but if you could just tell me exactly what happened.

Anna did. That is to say, she relayed as much truth as she could possibly spare, because women were judged more harshly than men.

She cleared her throat. "I had just gotten out of the bath . . . I sometimes bathe without my clothes . . . and then . . . " She tapped her lips and looked heavenward. "I slipped on a banana peel. Then the door flew open. It was the wind because my robe blew off. Detective Singer was guarding my car. I wrapped myself up in the rug . . . I must have swooned because I don't remember anything else until, well, right now.

It wasn't a good story, but kissing Joe Singer always made Anna feel a little undone.

The conductor made a growling sound and proclaimed grandly. "He was guarding you? Who was guarding him?"

"Did he misbehave? I don't recall."

"You are fortunate the other passengers heard your cries for help and summoned me."

Anna nodded yes and no at the same time, moving her head in a circle. In truth, she wasn't sure whether it had been a good thing or not. Could Joe and Anna fight naked? Anna wasn't Greek.

The man puffed out his chest and lifted his wattle. "You realize that if I hadn't rescued you, things would have been dire indeed."

Anna weighed this, as well. Would it have been dire to fight Joe in the Grecian style? Or had Anna missed something wonderful, an opportunity she would never get back? She cursed the conductor. And blessed him. Then she cursed him again.

Principles were important. But principles weren't everything. In principle, Joe was her enemy. But his behavior had been friendly and pleasant in the extreme.

Chapter 33

Half an hour after the conductor had Joe tossed from the train, the locomotive rolled into Yuma station. Darkness still clung to the desert. Anna quickly dressed. She stripped a fine linen pillowcase from her pillow and filled it with supplies from the picnic basket—chocolate, pate and crackers, and two bottles of champagne. She added the decanter of brandy, though it was crystal, thus heavy and easy to break.

Anna donned an enormous new hat decorated with artificial fruit and wrapped herself in a cloak. She collected Joe's discarded coat, put his hat into her pillowcase, and joined the flood of rumpled passengers disembarking from the train. On the platform, she perched on a bench, staring down the tracks, waiting for Joe. He would be walking for hours. She felt a pang of guilt. The winter desert was frigid in the wee hours, and he was unprepared. He could be hurt, having been tossed from a moving train. For all she knew, he was now being eaten by a Gila monster.

So, Anna did what any girl would do in her position, with her estranged love in danger. She headed down the moonlit tracks, past railcar after railcar filled with produce, in the direction from which the train had come, the pillowcase and Joe's coat slung over her shoulder.

The conductor called after Anna. "Miss Blanc! Where are you going? Where do we take your things?"

"Please leave them on board. I've decided to go on to Oklahoma City. Do hold the train for me." She hollered back without turning around. "I'm just stretching my legs."

"You can't walk out into the desert alone. It's still dark. Come back!"

Anna broke into an awkward run, leaping from railroad tie to railroad tie, which spread out before her like an endless ladder. For all his heroic posturing, the conductor wasn't very persistent. When she cast a glance behind her, he wasn't following.

She slowed to a walk when she could no longer hear him calling her, carefully watching each footfall to avoid the dangerous desert creatures she had been warned about. Away from the noise of the station, she could hear coyotes yipping in the darkness—the darkness into which she was venturing. It raised her hackles. She thought she could fight a single coyote if she kicked it or came at it with windmill arms, but it sounded like a whole pack singing. If Joe were being eaten by a pack of coyotes, he would certainly need her. Anna doubled her resolve.

Her enormous hat weighed on her neck, shifting with every stride, tugging on her scalp. From time to time, she tilted back her head to see past the brim to the glowing horizon. She became aware of a coyote that periodically moved in the scrub ahead or behind her. She could see his silhouette. Anna knew how coyotes worked. Joe had told her. A single coyote lured their prey while the rest of the pack hid. Then the whole pack attacked. They attacked dogs sometimes, or children, or a small woman crawling on hands and knees through the desert.

Her neck began to ache. She ripped the heavy artificial fruits off her lovely new hat and threw them at the coyote, apple by pear, angry at yet another *chapeau* ruined. She hit the coyote on the nose with a pomegranate. It yelped and ran away, only to double back and resume its slinking.

She watched the sun rise on the Sonora desert. Dawn revealed a severe landscape and an orange sky. Saguaro cacti stood like men, waving their arms at her as if warning her to turn back. There were twisting Joshua trees and spiky yucca with pale flowers on towering stalks that loomed like ghosts.

The sun chased away the coyote, who was no doubt now seeking out his den. But other creatures were about—scorpions likely, snakes to be sure, colonies of fire ants, and whatever a Gila monster was. She heard rattling in the brush—an insect, or maybe a snake.

Anna would have to keep to the tracks and watch her step.

She worried for Joe, who had no large hat to protect his complexion from the rising sun. Also, he had no pate and no champagne, but she would soon remedy that. She could only hope he had found the flask, grapes, and cheese.

The day quickly grew warm unlocking the scents of sand and heat. The pillowcase became heavier with each step. She shed the coat she wore and the one she carried, tossing them over the low arm of an exceptionally tall saguaro cactus beside the tracks. They fell slack in the windless day. She would have to remember to pick them up on the way back.

The cold night had succumbed to the March sun. It shone down with a tepid brilliance. Anna had tired of walking and despaired of ever saving Joe Singer when, to her relief, she encountered a miracle—a handcar on a turnout from the main track. It had a teeter-totter handle—the kind you pumped with. A dirt road ended where the handcar rested. It must be someone's personal handcar. God obviously wouldn't mind if she borrowed it, or He would not have provided it. With both hands she pulled the switch so that the little car could access the main track. She set her pillowcase on the platform and hoisted herself up, which wasn't easy in a corset and skirts. From her new vantage point, she could see farther. Her spirit sank. She could see dirt, cacti, rocks, and yucca. She saw false water like mercury sparkling in the sun. She saw tracks disappearing over the horizon. She could not see Joe Singer. Anna pushed the teeter-totter lever down, leaning with her whole desperate body, causing the handcar to lurch forward. She was thrust off balance and fell onto her backside, pricking her hand on a nail. She picked herself up, sucked the blood from her finger, and pulled the lever back up. She forced it down again, propelling the handcar onto the track.

Slowly, she developed a rhythm—up and down, up and down, pushing forward with each cycle. Periodically, she stopped to drink champagne.

It was gone noon when Anna finally spied a lone figure limping down the tracks in the distance amid the watery illusion of a mirage. For the first time in hours, she could breathe again. She felt grimy, tipsy, had blisters on her hands and feet, and her arms burned with exercise, but she didn't care. Joe Singer was alive, upright, and walking. She let the push car coast up to Joe, then pulled on the brake. His pants were ripped, his white shirt had dirt stains. He carried his carpetbag hoisted over one shoulder. He was singing under his breath, "She's my little Eskimo."

The heat, exhaustion, and champagne were having their way with Anna. She felt she might not look her best. She tucked a stray lock of hair behind her ear and lifted her chin. She began to descend from the handcar, caught her Louis heel on a ladder rung, and felt herself falling gracelessly forward into the air, flailing her limbs. Joe caught her in his arms. She buried her face in his salty neck and began to sob. "I'm sorry they tossed you from the train, but it wasn't my fault, and I'm of two minds about you."

"I know." Joe held her against him and she didn't resist. "Where did you get the handcar?"

"If I told you I stole it, would you arrest me?"

"No, I'm planning on becoming an accomplice. You got any water?"

"I gave you water."

"I drank it." He pulled the silver flask from his pocket. It was dented nearly in half.

"There's champagne on the handcar." Anna hiccupped.

Joe smiled. "That explains a lot." He climbed the steps to the platform with leaden boots, favoring his right leg. The champagne bottle lay propped up between a wooden box and Anna's pillowcase. Joe grabbed it, tilted back his head, and swigged, finishing the last few sips.

Anna looked back down the tracks toward Yuma. They had a long journey ahead of them, and it would only get hotter. They had been walking or pumping for hours.

A feathery mesquite tree near a large rock formation cast shade onto the desert not fifteen feet from the tracks. "Maybe you should rest in the shade. I brought food and your hat." Anna rummaged in the pillowcase for Joe's derby hat, which now had a dent, and set it on his bare head. "I was so worried that you'd been injured falling from the train. I feared you'd been eaten by a pack of coyotes. Even though you don't deserve my sympathy." She touched a red mark on his cheek. "Are you hurt?"

"I'm bruised and I've got cactus spines in my—"

"I can get them out," she said quickly. Even if they were fighting, she should not withhold treatment.

"Thanks. But we are miles away from any tweezers."

Anna took his hand. "Come and rest in the shade, then." She led him to the shadow of the rock formation, his hand warm and comforting in hers after the horror of fearing for his safety. The second champagne bottle felt hot to the touch. She popped the cork. Warm bubbles overflowed the top. She rescued them with her mouth, then handed the bottle to Joe. He tipped his head back and drank.

Anna lowered herself onto the ground with her legs out in front of her, her back against a rock. Joe took off his hat and lay down with his head in her lap.

She stroked his hair. "Are you hungry?"

"Starving."

She began to feed him from the pillowcase. Having forgone the heavy silverware, she resorted to dipping crackers in the pate and raising them to his curved, sunburnt lips.

Joe chewed and swallowed. "How far is it to Georges?" He intercepted the next cracker and guided it to Anna's mouth.

She swallowed. "You mean how far to Yuma?"

"Same thing. Georges is in Yuma."

"Yes . . . Well, maybe."

Joe tilted his head back to look up at her. "What do you mean, maybe?"

She folded her arms across her breasts and looked away.

"We took the train to Yuma because Georges is in Yuma. You told me the hotel clerk said Georges went to Yuma."

If Anna's judgment hadn't been compromised by champagne, if she hadn't been thoroughly exhausted, she may have remained quiet. But as her mind was muddled by the heat and the bubbles, and she was especially susceptible to Joe Singer when he'd been thrown from trains, and as he had cactus spines in his bottom, she confessed. "I may have misspoken."

"I don't understand."

"It might not have been the hotel clerk that told me Georges was in Yuma. It might have been someone else."

"Who?"

"A . . . um . . . a French dancer."

Joe sat up, turned his face to her, and frowned. "Georges's mother told you?"

"Yes. And at the time . . . well . . . I believed her. She's a woman of faith. But now I'm thinking . . . would a mother, no matter how religious, really tell her lover's wife's spawn—the wife who replaced her—would she tell her rival's spawn how to capture her blood son so they could arrest him? And if I were feeling spiteful, I might send someone on a wild goose chase to Yuma."

"And you just decided that now?"

"Actually, I wondered about it from the beginning, and decided she was definitely lying while we waited for the train."

Joe ran his hands through his hair. "You lied to me."

Anna crossed her arms. "I'm sorry. It's just . . . You are trying to hang my brother."

"It's my job."

"You should have recused yourself and given the case to Detective Snow."

"Detective Snow? You know he couldn't solve a murder if it happened right in front of him. Anna, a man is dead."

"Yes, I know. It's a tragedy. It really is. He's never going to laugh or sing or buy ugly suits again. But persecuting my brother won't change any of that. He didn't do it."

"If he didn't do it, you don't want Detective Snow on the case. He might plant evidence. You want someone honest."

"Wolf then."

"Wolf's in love with you!"

"You're supposed to be in love with me too!"

"It's because I love you that I'm staying on the case! Luckily, Captain Wells doesn't know I'm in love with you, so he's not going to take me off the case. Why did you have to drag me all the way out into the desert? You just wanted Georges to get away."

"That's not true," she said without conviction. Even Anna wasn't sure what was true. That was a danger when one lied. She put her head in her hands. Torn ribbon that had previously adorned false fruits dangled from her hat.

"Why did you bring me out here, Anna?" He swept his hand across the forbidding desert horizon and rippling mirages. "I thought you wanted to be a detective."

Anna wiped her brow with her sleeve. "Georges didn't do it. I wanted to find the real killer. I thought we could carry on to Oklahoma City, and I didn't think you'd go because you were too busy chasing Georges. We have to interview Samara's father or rather Flossie's father. I suppose his name would be Edmands."

"And the Oklahoma City cops couldn't interview him or at least establish an alibi before we trek all the way out there?"

"Like they interviewed Samuel Grayson's father? I've tried with them. They didn't ask him any of the questions on my list. We need to interview him all over again. By the time we get back, maybe Georges will be home."

"I can't believe you lied to me. And I'm not riding on your ding-busted handcar." He made a loud, agonized growling sound. "And all I can think about is you naked." He narrowed his eyes at her, rose painfully to his feet, turned his back, and limped down the tracks toward Yuma.

Anna sat dumbly against the rock and watched him go. She shouldn't have lied. She shifted against the rock. She was a bad estranged fiancée. She had known that story was taffy all along. She just hadn't admitted it at first because deep down, she had wanted to lead Joe astray—the man she loved. She wasn't foolish. Foolish could be excused. She was duplicitous. She pinched herself hard. She did it again.

Anna loved her brother, too, and loyalty was a virtue. Pursuing him as a suspect was an unspeakable betrayal of kin.

But did she truly know her brother? What if he was guilty? For the first time, Anna allowed her mind to visit that possibility. What if he had drugged Matilda and killed Samuel Grayson? Shouldn't she want him to hang? She pictured his beloved face and tried to imagine him as a killer. Then, Anna pinched herself for disloyalty.

"Why do you have to be so hard on my brother when I love you so much?" she yelled after the tiny speck on the horizon that was Joe.

As she watched him leave her, she became aware of a bad smell, a horrible smell, like Lucifer himself had indigestion, as if hell was opening up to swallow all liars. She hadn't done it; it wasn't a lady's smell. Joe couldn't have done it. She reached down beside her to grab her pillowcase and flee the ungodly odor. She felt something smooth and fat, like a large snakeskin purse bursting with money. It was laying on top of her pillowcase.

Anna had no snakeskin purse, and if she had, it would not have been bursting with money.

Before she could react, something clamped down hard on her finger. A sizzling pain shot up her arm. She tried to retract it, but the grip was like a vise. Anna bent to face her attacker and looked down into lizard eyes and the face of a beast of mythic proportions. He stretched as long as a baseball bat, wider than her thigh, with a coral-colored pattern on his sin-black skin.

Anna tried to stand and couldn't; the heavy monster still dangled by its jaws from her finger. She collapsed onto rocky soil and cacti that pricked her such that Joe would need tweezers. The giant lizard clung. The pain worsened, blinding her. She felt dizzy, like spinning sunlight. She picked up a rock and struck at the beast again and again.

Everything went black.

CHAPTER 34

Anna briefly regained consciousness lying on her back on the handcar. Joe had made a tent to shade her face with his shirt, her hat, and two champagne bottles. She was touched that, even when her very life was threatened, he cared about preventing freckles. She looked up to see him in relief against the dazzling sun. He wore his derby hat and undershirt, his bare arms muscular and sun-reddened, laboring to push the lever down and up with a keen ferocity. His lips were moving, singing only silently with the rhythm of the handcar. She wanted to say something to him, such as to offer again to take the spines out of his biscuits, but her tongue felt heavy and she didn't feel she could spare the breath. Her dress was wet with perspiration, and she shivered. Her finger burned. She lifted her head to assess her injury. The monster was gone, but her digit had swollen up like a sausage at the end of a log that must be her arm. Anna turned her head and vomited. This horrified her and she swooned.

CHAPTER 35

The snorting sounds of her own snores awakened her. Joe sat beside her, mopping her brow with a wet cloth. He was as red as a devil. Out the window, she saw an impossibly green tree, its trunk and branches the color of winter grass. A sheet draped the vanity mirror, covering the glass. Her brow crinkled in confusion. She lisped thickly. "I'm dead, aren't I? He ate me." An even more terrible thought struck her. Her lispy voice sounded panicked. "I'm in hell!"

Joe put a calming hand on her shoulder. "No baby. We're in Yuma. You've just had a bad lizard bite."

"He was a bad, bad lizard." The words sounded wrong, like "He was a ba ba liza."

"Yeah, but you showed him."

"I did?" She glanced at her bandaged sausage finger at the end of her log arm.

"You did." His mouth smiled. His eyes did not.

Anna tried to close her mouth, but her tongue seemed to be propping it open. "Where's my railcar?"

"It went on to Oklahoma City. You've been asleep since yesterday."

"Biscuits."

There was a knock, and a man let himself into the room as if he'd been there before. He was tall with dark eyes, nearly black hair, and a doctor's bag. "Good. She's awake."

"Anna, say hello to Doctor Helmer."

The doctor was young and nice looking, though he wore spectacles. Anna worried that she had not fixed her bun. She proffered her most winning smile to make up for her disheveled appearance, glancing up from beneath feathered lashes. "Hello." She tried to clear her throat but could only make a rasping sound as desiccated as the desert.

The doctor leaned over her with his stethoscope. She saw a strange reflection in his eyeglasses—a monkey man with a face swollen up, lips and tongue protruding many times their natural size, worse than an orangutan—a hellish vision for a lady still in the fog of sleep. Anna recoiled in horror, yet at the same time felt a morbid fascination. The poor soul's tongue was inflamed so that his mouth could not close, his eyes mere puffy slits, his skin red and welted. A rat's nest of messy hair sprung from edges of his grotesque face. She looked around to locate the unfortunate creature, then realized the reflection was her own.

She was the monkey man. She bellowed like an ape in distress.

"Anna, it's okay."

The doctor's opinion of her hair no longer mattered. She was a monkey face, and Joe Singer had witnessed it. She may be angry with her fiancé, but the point was moot. He'd saved her life—he was heroic that way. But, he'd never want her now.

Anna was ugly.

The doctor felt Anna's forehead and took her pulse. "She's very lucky to be alive." He poured a tincture from a bottle into a spoon and pushed it past her swollen tongue into her mouth. The laudanum tasted as bitter as her fate.

The doctor set the bottle on the dresser. "The danger now is infection, in which case, she could lose her finger." He lowered his voice ominously. "Or worse."

Worse? What could be worse? With her trigger finger amputated, she could never use her rod again. She could never be stealthy if she looked like an orangutan, and stealth was important for detective work. Now everyone would stare and point and recognize her as the orangutan lady who looked like a man— the least fair lady in the land.

"Just let me die."

Joe leaned close and whispered, "I'm not going to let you die."

"Yes, but I'm ugly now."

"You've looked better."

Doctor Helmer unwound her dressing revealing a deep, angry furrow down her pointer. The Gila monster had filleted her finger with his teeth. The gore fascinated Anna but would have been far more interesting on someone else's hand. The doctor gave her medicine to swallow, then washed her wound in a basin. He began to stitch it together with thread. It hurt. She closed her eyes so that she could no longer see her reflection in his glasses. "The nuns said I shouldn't rely on my beauty, that I must develop character." She scrunched up her swollen face. "But I didn't."

Joe took her good hand. "Yes, you did. Now go to sleep."

§

When she next awoke, her finger throbbed. Joe was sleeping in the bed next to her with one arm and one leg draped over her body. He wore only his undershirt and drawers and smelled heavenly—like soap and man. He must have bathed. His bare, hairy leg touched her bare fuzzy leg.

She liked it intensely.

She herself felt sticky and stale. Also, she resembled an orangutan. How could he sleep next to her when she looked like something from a nightmare? She turned her face away self-consciously. "They are going to throw you out of the hotel, just like they threw you off the train."

"The proprietor thinks we're married," he mumbled, half asleep.

"You lied?"

Joe Singer never lied. It was part of his code. She turned to look at him. He had sleepy eyes and needed a haircut. Nonetheless, he looked good enough to eat.

"I carried you over the threshold. That's got to count for something."

"You lied."

"No. I didn't correct them. Someone had to nurse you."

"You would do anything for me?"

"Near enough."

"Because you feel sorry for me because I'm ugly now."

Joe yawned and stretched. "Anna, my cousin's face swelled up when he got stung by a bee. In a week he was right back to normal."

"Yes, but that's not going to happen for me. This is Petronilla's work. I wasn't stung by a bee. I was bitten by a dragon. And I will probably lose my finger."

"Maybe, but you don't really need it."

Anna furrowed her brow and thought about this for a moment. How important was a pointer finger? Needed for pointing, surely, but pointing was rude and thus prohibited. Important for pulling triggers, but couldn't Anna pull a trigger with her middle finger if she practiced? Pointer fingers were necessary for good manicures and filling out gloves, but one could stuff gloves, and with a face as morbidly fascinating as Anna's, no one would ever look at her manicure. They would stare at her face as they backed slowly out of the room.

Joe was right. She didn't need it. Perhaps she could survive an amputation.

"Anna, you're going to be okay. I promise."

Anna nodded dumbly. He was being kind, even after they'd fought. It stirred her conscience. She said in a half sob, "I'm gullible and duplicitous, and I dragged you all the way to Yuma."

Joe sat up on one elbow and caressed her swollen face. "You make good sense when you take laudanum." He reached for the laudanum bottle from the nightstand, filled the spoon, and slipped it between her lips. He began to sing a catchy tune in his beautiful tenor voice.

"She's on the case again.
Got me tossed off the train

The desert could not stop her
She slayed the Gila monster."

"I didn't get you tossed off the train."

"Sweetheart, it was worth it."

§

Anna slept all day and through the next night, with Joe periodically waking her to give her laudanum or to feed her sips of broth with a spoon. Grief for her lost beauty and threatened finger filled her stomach so that she couldn't take food. She would turn her ugly face away, refusing it. In her foggy state, she heard the afternoon train whistle.

When she awoke the following morning, Doctor Helmer was unwrapping her dressing. She felt sluggish from the laudanum and her finger ached. Talking was still difficult—like wielding a club instead of a rapier. She yawned her monkey mouth, then lisped, "Doctor, are you going to amputate?" She sounded like "Docta, ah you goin a amputay?"

"Well, good morning, Mrs. Singer. No, not today. Perhaps tomorrow if it shows signs of infection." He extended his hand to Joe to shake. "She should try to walk a little today."

§

After the doctor left, Anna drifted up and down the hotel hallways on doctor's orders and Joe's arm. People averted their eyes instead of looking upon her with admiration the way they normally did. No matter that Joe had covered the mirrors; the strangers were her mirrors. This, Anna feared, was to be her new life as a monstrously ugly, fingerless woman. Without her beauty to rely upon, she must concentrate on developing character, like the nuns had always said. And, she should develop her detective skills.

Anna took note of the calico curtains, which, oddly, hung drawn in the middle of a warm winter morning. Through a one-inch gap, she could see through the window that a crowd of people filled the street. She could hear their voices. She leaned on Joe to steer him. "To the window, please."

Joe steered her away. "I don't want you to look out the window."

"All right, I trust you." She fluttered ape lashes.

"I'm skeptical but touched."

Anna tried to pull him in the direction of the window. Joe dropped anchor. In her weakened state, she couldn't budge his manly and determined frame.

Now Anna could hear the crowd jeering. She let go of Joe and lurched toward the window.

He caught her around the waist. "Anna, don't."

"It's not your decision."

He let go. "No Anna. It's a—'

She hobbled forward and threw back the curtains.

"Hanging." Joe put his arms around her from behind.

In the street, two men stood on gallows. One wore a noose. He looked up and locked eyes with the ape in the window adding horror to horror. His face twisted. Before she could take in the scene, before she could steel herself, the trap door opened, and the man swung.

The morbid cheers of the crowd drowned Anna's cry of dismay. The man convulsed on the end of the rope, like Georges in a fit, and then stilled. He had been alive and now he was dead. He had been someone's brother perhaps, and now he was nothing.

Anna's knees went weak and she collapsed against Joe. She turned, hiding her face in his shirt.

The image of the dying man seared itself into her mind, and though she no longer saw him with her eyes, she saw him. She saw his face clearly, a handsome face with tanned skin, a patrician nose, and gray eyes. Georges face.

Joe swept her up into his arms and carried her back to their room. He laid her on the bed, where she wept until she fell asleep.

§

In the morning, Joe brought Anna coffee in bed. "The hotel owner asked around for me. Georges isn't in Yuma. But we knew that."

She said, "How long have we been here? Five days?"

"Six."

"We have to leave. We have to exonerate him."

"Your brother has got the best lawyer in Los Angeles—arguably the country. Even if he's guilty, the prosecution has a hard road. He's just got to show up to court in three weeks."

"When is the next train to Oklahoma City. I have to be ready."

"There are fruit trains almost every afternoon. But you aren't going to Oklahoma City. You aren't going anywhere. Not until you're better."

"Are you bossing me again?"

"Anna, this is police business, and I outrank you."

Anna chose to ignore this. In the LAPD, she could never have any rank at all. She had long since decided that the LAPD ranking system failed to honor her, thus she would not honor it, though she would give the appearance of honoring it when expedient or necessary to avoid punishment.

"Sherlock, you know that if rank were based on ability or dedication or bravery, you'd outrank us all."

She sat up in bed, smiled sweetly, and lisped, "Thank you, Detective. I feel much, much better. As good as new. And time is of the essence as my brother's very life is on the line. His court date is approaching. He could hang."

"Sherlock, your life is on the line. Take your laudanum."

It became clear to Anna that Joe might be more of a barrier than a help, and she needed a plan. He gave her a spoonful of laudanum, and when he turned his back, she spit it out on the floor. It didn't matter how extreme her pain, she must be ready to seize any opportunity to get to Oklahoma City. This required a clear mind and supernatural reinforcements.

Anna prayed to Saint Dismas, patron saint of condemned men, that Georges would not hang like the man in the street, dying to the jeers of a bloodthirsty crowd, and that Anna would be good if that's what it took to save him.

And so, Anna concentrated. She repeated to herself over and over, "I will not tell fibs. I will be giving, like Matilda. I will not steal spectacles from men on trollies." With sadness she repeated, "I will not make love to Joe Singer." This virtue should be easy as he would no longer want her, nor would anyone else. Also, he had thrown her brother in the bull ring.

She said a prayer to Saint Drogo of Sebourg, patron saint of ugly women, that she would be able to keep her vows, and that exceptions could be made in special circumstances such as emergencies or when her need was very great.

§

Anna spent the morning, wandering the halls frightening guests because the doctor said it was important for regaining strength. When Joe slipped his arm through hers, she said, "I don't need to lean on you. I told you, I'm better now."

"Maybe I like holding your arm."

Anna let him help her but said nothing. What was there to say? She was ugly. He was scrumptious and trying to hang her brother.

She passed time beating Joe at poker as her new face had only one expression—orangutan—thus she had no tell. She could think of one thing only. Saving Georges from the noose.

Joe tried to distract her, reading aloud to her from the proprietor's collection of pulpy dime novels.

A group of female figures was discernable on the quarter deck. At the sight, a thrill of anguish ran through our breasts. We would have laid down our lives to save them from their inevitable doom, and yet what could we do in the face of such a tempest. As I thought of the impossibility of rendering succor to those shrinking females, as I dwelt on their lingering agonies—

Anna, who normally loved lingering agonies in dime novels, was plotting in her head. She had to get Joe out of the way so she could take the train to Oklahoma City. She interrupted him. "You should take a bath?"

"Are you saying I smell?"

"I would never." But he did smell. Intoxicating.

"Baths cost money and I just took a bath last night. Fourteen hours ago."

"I'm just saying you should take another one." She wrinkled her nose.

Joe sniffed his armpit, looking puzzled. "All right. But we were just getting to the good part. You know he's going to rescue those shrinking females. I'll bet you a Coca Cola he hooks up with one by the end."

"I'll bet you two to one the shrinking females all die a horrible death."

"I'll take that bet. It's a dime novel; you know they're going to survive."

"Not always." Anna stared at him pointedly and waved her hand in front of her nose.

"All right!" Joe sighed, set the book on the nightstand, and stomped to the bathroom down the hall. Anna could hear him running the cold bath water. She heard him tramp down the stairs to get kettles from the kitchen. It was not the Hotel Alexandria. This was Yuma.

Anna went to the mirror, closed her eyes, and tugged off the sheet that had shrouded her reflection for so many days. She counted to three and then opened, stifling a gasp. Her complexion remained ruddy instead of its normal milky white, making her gray eyes glow unnaturally by contrast—like two silver coins in the sun. Her ears appeared abnormally small, mere warts upon her swollen head. Her mouth and tongue protruded, though less than before. The effect was distinctly masculine. A face perhaps only a brother could love.

She steeled herself against tears. Today she would begin life as an ugly, lonely man-woman.

It occurred to Anna that manly clothes could be a better thing. Even a boy orangutan outranked a human girl in the eyes of the LAPD. If she looked male, ape or no, Sergeant Tribble might take her seriously. She just needed to steal Joe's clothes, slip away, and take the train, provided one came this afternoon. Then she could proceed with her investigation to exonerate Georges with clout. She tried to remember what time she heard the whistles? Four o'clock? Five o'clock?

Anna dressed in Joe's extra set of clothes from his carpet bag. What she didn't put on, she threw out the window. She gathered up all the bedclothes and the sheets from the mirror and heaved them over the sill, watching them crash into the bushes below. She collected his brass LAPD badge in the shape of a star and stowed it in her pocket.

Out in the hall, she heard Joe's footsteps and the bathroom door clicking open and closed. She waited until she thought he was good and naked, grabbed a hatpin, and slunk out. She could hear him singing in the bath.

> *I'm goin' get right up and put on all my*
> *clothes.*
> *I'm goin' to go right out and take in all the*
> *shows.*
> *I'm goin' drive around in an open carriage.*
> *If I meet my girl there's goin' be a marriage.*

Anna checked her wrist watch. It was 4:00 p.m. and she hadn't yet heard the train whistle. This was a good sign. She quietly picked the bathroom lock with the hatpin and opened the door. Joe Singer sat in a big porcelain bathtub, surrounded by bubbles to his waist, singing and scrubbing his head. His eyes were closed, his broad chest interesting and bare. Regrettably, she didn't have time to look. He slipped down under the water to rinse.

Anna gathered up his clothes from the floor and his skinny leather wallet. She scooped up his towel and bath mat. His head broke the surface of the water. He rubbed his face, slicked back his hair, and opened his eyes. They popped. "Sherlock!" He leapt to his feet.

Joe stood there naked, glorious, and sparkling wet. His body was like a marble statue, but with no discrete fig leaf, just a few unfortunate clumps of bubbles. His blue eyes burned with some unknown emotion.

Her feet stuck to the planks. With her whole being, Anna wanted to stay. She wanted to stay and watch the bubbles pop and watch him air dry, or better yet, to dry him herself. She had his towel.

In the distance, a train whistle blew.

She remembered that she was an ape and her brother might hang. Joe lunged for her. Anna leapt backward, out of his grasp. It took all her strength to turn and run, closing the door behind her.

CHAPTER 36

Anna ran toward the sound of the whistle. When she reached the station, the train had started to roll. She tried her best to run for it. Behind her, she heard Joe's voice calling. "Anna!"

He was as resourceful as he was delicious.

His sweet yelling voice cut her. She knew she was choosing Georges over Joe. She didn't turn around, though she was curious to see what he was wearing. She grabbed the rail of the rolling caboose and hauled herself up the steps. Only then did she turn to look for Joe. She could hear him but did not see him. Then, he flew through the depot onto the platform, leapt off the platform onto the tracks, streaking along like he himself was a steaming locomotive. He was wearing someone else's overcoat, his churning legs bare beneath it.

A cop pursued him, blowing a whistle.

The train had not reached full speed. Joe was gaining on her. The cop was gaining on him. Anna gripped the rails.

He was running right behind the caboose, glowing with exertion. Anna dripped with sweat, because, if Joe caught the train, he would surely make her get off, and she would have to face what she'd just done. He lifted his determined eyes to the rail and leapt. Anna watched him fly, his hands grasping for the rail. His fingers made contact. For a moment he hung there, his toes on the train, his fingertips on the rail. Their eyes met.

She didn't think he would forgive her for this. "Goodbye my love."

He slipped off, landing briefly on his feet, then falling back onto his biscuits, his coat flying up, exposing his manly legs. Joe grew smaller. "Sherlock!"

Anna waved and watched until he was just a dot on the tracks being arrested for indecent exposure and theft of an overcoat. She felt stunned at what she had sacrificed. She blew her love one final kiss and slowly, sadly made her way through the caboose into the passenger section of the train.

Anna lowered herself onto the hard, wooden bench in third class, the only seat left, right outside the closet containing the toilet. She hadn't yet bought her ticket, but she had Joe's wallet. She could buy it on the train.

Guilt poked at her heart. Joe wouldn't be able to pay the hotel bill, and they'd likely throw him in jail. She thought of Georges in jail because of Joe, and the guilt went away. She could always bail him out on her way back through Yuma.

A woman sold meat sandwiches from a little cart, but when Anna pulled the bread apart to look at the filling, it looked green and had a bad odor, so she tossed it out the window. It would be a hungry two-day journey and she didn't feel well.

No one on the train spoke to Anna. In fact, they scooched away from her, no doubt because of her face. For so many years she'd been beautiful—the most beautiful woman in the room, perhaps in all of California. She hadn't realized the privileges her loveliness had bestowed. She hadn't considered them or noticed until they were gone. Now ugly and dressed as a man, no one smiled at her or engaged her in charming conversation. No one offered to buy her food or wine or upgrade her seat to first class for free.

How inconvenient to be ugly. How sad to be alone. But the swelling did impart one gift—coarse, manly features—a manly countenance to wield in this a man's world. Full personhood and masculine authority for fighting crimes.

Take that Petronilla.

Anna spread out in her seat, her knees comfortably apart, and openly read *Dark Secrets,* one of the hotel proprietor's seamy pulp magazines for men, which she had borrowed because it was an emergency.

§

As they neared Oklahoma City, Anna watched the open landscape from the window. Everything looked flat and white with snow. Anna had only seen snow once before when her father had taken her to Mount Wilson. It had been magical, though she hadn't been allowed to make snow angels or have a snowball fight. She had been treated to a new fur coat, hat, and muff, which she had only worn once. It was a shame she didn't have it with her now.

When Anna disembarked from the train, the porter did not offer to hand her down, but stood idly nearby. She jumped down the last big step—a challenge in Louis heels and rolled-up pant hems—and scowled at him. No one opened the door for her as she crossed the threshold of the depot. Everyone gave her a wide berth.

Her finger hurt.

She moved out onto the unpaved streets of Oklahoma City with its dirty snow, busy sidewalks, and new brick buildings with turrets and awnings. There were horse-drawn buggies and trolley tracks, but apparently no cars. Los Angeles, it was not. It had, until the previous year, been Indian Country. Most people were white, but she did pass Indians on the streets. They wore wool suits and broad brimmed hats with no feathers at all. Their dark skin and high cheekbones made them unmistakable. Instead of coats, some draped themselves with blankets, which they accessorized with brightly colored beads. Anna approved of their aesthetic. She felt sorry they had lost their land. She would like to tell them so, but they spoke their own language, or perhaps many languages. Anna couldn't tell, and none of them spoke to her as she was very, very ugly.

Anna asked a woman the location of the police station, but the lady hurried off without answering. Anna wanted to say, "Wait, I'm beautiful on the inside," but she'd stolen Joe Singer's wallet and it wasn't true. She didn't want to add this lie to her long list of sins.

Anna decided to walk the length of Broadway. If she didn't find the station itself, she would surely find a cop. Cops earned their livings helping even ugly people. As she trudged on paths of packed snow and ice, she blew into the air to watch the cloud of frozen breath coming from her mouth. The cold numbed the pain in her finger.

She had two goals for her visit to Oklahoma City: First, to more thoroughly interrogate Samuel Grayson's father to find out why his son had gone to Los Angeles in the first place; and second, to find out more about Samara Flossie's father, rule him out if he were innocent, and to capture him if he were guilty. She decided to start with Sergeant Tribble. Though he was incompetent as a detective, he knew where to find Samuel Grayson's father.

The police station did indeed stand on Broadway. She brought her ugly self up the steps, into the warmth, and stood at the shiny wooden counter waiting for the clerk. When it was her turn, she lowered her voice several octaves. "Good afternoon."

At the sight of her distorted face, the clerk recoiled. She soldiered on. "I'm Detective Singer with the Los Angeles Police Department. Please tell Sergeant Tribble I'm here."

"He's out."

"I'll wait." Anna lowered herself gracefully into a chair. She crossed her arms, not in anger, but to hold herself, for she needed comforting. She almost forgot to spread her knees like a man.

Some cops came into the station through the backdoor. The clerk hurried to them as if he had a tale to tell. Shortly, he returned and ushered Anna into a small, smoky office. Sergeant Tribble balanced his cigarillo on the side of a broken china plate and stood, his gawking eyes fixed on Anna. He extended his hand. "Detective Singer, it's a pleasure to meet you. Forgive my surprise, but that is some face."

Anna was aghast at his candor. "I'm not that ugly."

"I've got to be honest," he said. "Yours is the ugliest face I've ever seen." He laughed as if what he had said was funny. "I don't know how you do your work. I'll bet witnesses run screaming." He ho-ho-hoed.

Anna frowned, not at his rudeness but at the implications for her investigation. If witnesses were to run screaming, her whole trip, her whole deception, the loss of her beauty, the loss of Joe was for naught. It made her feel like she had nothing left to lose.

She peered into his face. "You're ugly, too."

And he was. "But compared to you . . . You know what I mean—"

"You're also too wide in the hips, like a woman, and your breath is bad."

The sergeant's mouth dropped open.

"It's nothing personal." Anna bobbed a curtsey. "What a pleasure to finally meet you."

He cocked his head and stared at Anna. She remembered that men did not bob curtsies, so she stuck out her left hand to shake as her right hand was bandaged. "You know why I'm here?"

"The Grayson case? I've told you—"

"Why did Samuel Grayson go to Los Angeles?"

He took Anna's hand and looked down at it, drawing his brows together. She snatched it back, knowing it was suspiciously soft.

He said, "I didn't think it was important."

"What have you found out about Flossie Edmands?"

"Um."

"What about her father? Does he have an alibi?"

"Her father? I . . . um . . ."

Anna let his answer dangle. She could see that further questioning would take her nowhere and huffed in exasperation. "Can you at least give me their addresses so I can find Mr. Edmands and Mr. Grayson to question them?" She wanted to add "properly" but didn't as this would be rude.

§

Anna pushed the door of the police station open into stinging cold. She bought fried pork rinds from a shop and tried to hail a cab. A hansom stopped for her, but when the driver saw her face, he urged his horse on.

She growled under her breath, "Biscuits."

Eating, walking, and shivering, Anna started the journey in her Louis heels, in the snow, in the dusk. Joe's coat was made for Los Angeles winters, not biting Oklahoma winds. Mr. Grayson, Sergeant Tribble had informed her, lived five miles down Tenth Street on a farm outside of town. She hailed each passing hansom. They slowed for her, but when they saw her face, they urged their horses on. Soon there were no more hansoms and no more buildings. She walked precariously in the tracks of sleighs where the snow had packed down to ice.

CHAPTER 37

S amuel Grayson's father lived in a small, sod house surrounded by snowy fields with a sod stable. Light gleamed from a window. The hinged top half of the stable door stood open, and a mule watched the twilight. Anna arrived exhausted, her feet raw. She knocked on Mr. Grayson's door, bracing herself for the resident's inevitable revulsion. A lady answered. She had chewing tobacco on her teeth and looked too old to be Samuel's mother. Her eyes perused Anna, bulging only a little.

"Good afternoon." Anna spoke in her low, gravelly, man's voice, and smiled sweetly with her grotesque, swollen lips. "I'm Detective Singer with the Los Angeles Police Department and I'm here to speak with Mr. Grayson." She bobbed a curtsy and flashed Joe's stolen badge. "I don't actually look like this. I was cursed by Petronilla. Thus, I was bitten by a Gila monster."

The woman nodded. "I'm Mrs. Grayson, his mother. Come in." The woman stepped backward, opening the door wide so that Anna could pass.

Anna had expected more suspicion, more resistance to her ugly face. After all, she was a stranger, her explanation bizarre, and night was coming. But grief did strange things to people. Perhaps the lady simply didn't care anymore. It caught Anna off guard and she said in her own voice, "Thank you." Then, to cover up, she fabricated a violent coughing fit.

Anna passed under the low threshold into a small room with the artifacts of both a kitchen and a parlor. Bundles of dried herbs hung from the ceiling like mistletoe. The table and chairs looked home-hewn. The air smelled faintly of bad meat.

An empty hook poked from the wall waiting for a hat. Anna looked at it and hesitated. She was faced with a quandary. Any gentleman would remove his hat when entering a home. If Anna removed Joe's hat, her pretty coiffure would give her away. If she retained her hat, it would reflect badly on Joe.

She happily retained her hat.

The lady said, "Sit."

Anna sat.

The lady said, "Tea?"

"No, thank you."

"One lump or two?"

"Is Mr. Grayson at home?"

"He's in the other room." The woman set the kettle to boil. "You'll take two."

"May I please speak to him?"

The lady made a sweeping gesture with her hand toward a curtain-covered doorway. "Be my guest." Then she called out, "Percy!"

It was an odd sort of introduction. Anna stood uncertainly for a moment, then moved to the curtained doorway, which was only three steps distant in the small room. She pushed the curtain aside. Two beds dominated the space. Mr. Grayson, as Anna assumed him to be, slumped in a chair, as pale as chalk. A plate of fried chicken balanced on his lap. Flies settled on the chicken and on his open, staring eyes. He did not swat them away.

Anna yelped.

The woman rushed in from the parlor. "What is it?"

"He's dead," said Anna.

"No, he's sleeping."

"I don't mean to be rude, but he doesn't smell sleeping."

The woman tiptoed closer. She looked at the corpse, then she looked at Anna. She put a finger to her lips. "Shh."

Anna tiptoed quickly into the living room. If she hadn't

needed information to save her brother, she would have tiptoed right outside, into the cold, and away from this house of horrors. Instead, she bravely backed up against the door and plugged her nose. Her low, gravelly voice now also sounded congested. "I'm the detective investigating your grandson's death. I wanted to ask Mr. Grayson why Samuel went to Los Angeles, but he's sleeping. You must know."

The lady emerged from the death room holding the plate of chicken, sniffing at it. "Samuel's not dead. He's away." She walked close, reached out, and touched Anna's misshapen face. "I'm a medicine woman. I treat everyone in town. I can help you with that swelling."

It occurred to Anna that if this woman's son lay dead, her skills as a medicine woman were suspect. Also, she was crazy. "No, thank you."

The woman appeared offended. "You obviously need my help."

What Anna needed, besides a new face, was information. She did not want to offend her witness. Maybe the lady wouldn't charge much. "Wash your hands first?"

The woman made a cynical, hissing sound. "Have some chicken." She pushed the plate into Anna's hands and bustled over to a pot belly stove where the kettle steamed. Anna, though in need of sustenance, would not eat this. While the lady's back was turned, she threw it out the window. She set the plate on a side table.

The lady fussed in the cupboard with jars of herbal things, mixing them up into a tea. "Sam left because Flossie's father would have killed him if he stayed. Sam was taking Flossie to start a new life. I don't know where they went. Wasn't safe to know."

Anna leaned forward with interest. "So, Flossie's father is violent and perhaps murderous?"

"He killed his wife, but they never proved it. Never found the body. Just a smear of blood on the cabin floor."

Anna brightened. This was excellent news.

Mrs. Grayson pushed the tea cup in Anna's face. "Drink."

Anna pushed back against the door. The lady raised the cup to Anna's swollen lips. "Drink," she growled.

For Georges, Anna drank. The medicine tasted bitter, like the skins of walnuts. She let it run down her throat as her hostess tipped the tea cup.

The lady nodded her approval.

When Anna had swallowed the whole nasty draft, she took a gasping breath. "Why would he kill Sam?"

"No doubt he caught Flossie in a compromising position with Sam." She looked proud of this.

Anna tried to picture various compromising positions. She thought of being naked on the polar bear rug, and Joe being thrown from the train. Those men hadn't even known Anna, yet they had defended her honor. She thought it very likely that a father might shoot the man who ruined his daughter, backward execution style, face-to-face. That way, he could look him in the eye. "Would you happen to know where Flossie's father lives?"

"He has a farm about five miles out of town. He makes moonshine. It's pretty good."

"I could use some moonshine." Anna lifted her pant leg and considered her aching feet. Broken blisters lined the edges of her feminine shoes. She'd already walked five miles today. Another five seemed insurmountable in the snow, and the sun had set. She didn't care to face violent Mr. Edmands alone at night. She would have to go tomorrow. "Is there a hotel nearby?"

"No. You can sleep with us. I'll just go get the bed ready." She disappeared into the death room.

Anna's shoulders slumped. She needed a place to shelter, but there was no way she would bunk with Mr. Grayson. She should have known there would be no hotels five miles from the center of town. This wasn't Los Angeles. She stared out the window. The mule poked his head over the gate. She could barely see his eyes glowing in the dark.

"May I please sleep with your mule?" Anna called.

The lady in the other room didn't seem to hear, but neither did she object. This, Anna reasoned, was tantamount to consent. She said in a low, plugged-nose voice. "Thank you. And please tell Mr. Grayson I said goodnight."

§

Anna trudged through the snow to the sod stable, her nose too gloriously frozen to smell anything. Joe hadn't dressed for a winter in Oklahoma. He had packed for the Sonora Desert. Thus, Anna had no scarf, no muff, no long underwear, no wooly hat, and no fur coat. But if she had to hop up and down all night to stay warm, she would do it in the service of saving her brother.

The white plain spread out before her. She passed the chicken lying in the snow.

As she approached the stable, she heard animal sounds. When she opened the door, a baby goat escaped. "Biscuits!" She hurriedly closed the door and chased the goat in circles until, at last, she was able to tackle it in the snow. She wrapped her arms around the struggling beast until it stilled, then carried it back to the stable through fresh snow that now rose past her ankles. This time, she opened the door with one hand, one hip, and greater care. She slipped in with the baby goat and dropped it. It skittered away mewling. The stable air felt less frigid, heated by animal bodies, and had a faint animal smell to her frozen nose, like fur, hay, and manure.

Five goats and the mule inhabited the small stable, making it hard for Anna to find space to lie down. She scooped the poop using a tin cup someone had left there, and piled the poo into the corner. She covered herself with a scratchy horse blanket and shivered herself to sleep.

Chapter 38

When Anna awoke, three goats were curled up against her body. A fourth stood over her eating the back of Joe's coat, and the mule's backside hovered dangerously close to her head.

She disentangled herself from the herd and peeked her head outside the stable. The sun was rising.

If it was all the same to Mr. Grayson, and Anna felt sure that it was, she would borrow the mule for her trip to visit Flossie's father and simply return it later. As it was early, and it would be rude to wake Mrs. Grayson to ask for permission, and as Mr. Grayson was dead, Anna would simply leave a note. She had no paper or pen, thus she wrote the note with her foot in the snow. "Borrowed mule. Thanks ever so much."

Anna found the bridle, but no saddle. Despite being an excellent horsewoman, she had never bridled anything, always having relied on stable boys. Still, she managed it and threw the blanket over the mule's back. She led the reluctant mule out into winter, bid the goats adieu, and mounted from a watering trough half-buried in the snowy field.

§

Riding a mule through snow was more difficult than riding in a private railcar. The mule's feet sank deep into powder now up past its knees, if mules can be said to have knees. The snow was coming down hard, blowing into her face, making it difficult to see. She blinked the snowflakes out of her eyelashes. They were quickly replaced by new ones.

Her fingers, those not bandaged, quickly lost color. Her cheeks stung by cold wind. She hadn't known the weather could be so fierce while daffodils poked up their heads in Los Angeles.

Beyond the first mile, she encountered no farmhouses and wondered whether all this land, these vast fields, belonged to the Edmands farm. The snow grew deeper on the ground and thicker in the air. The brim of Joe's hat filled up with snowflakes. Her colorless hands burned. Her toes lacked feeling even as she flexed them to keep her shoes from falling off. Each step the mule took seemed a labor. It walked slower and more slowly still. At last the mule stopped.

Anna knew how to urge on mules from reading adventure magazines. "Yaw!"

The mule didn't move. Anna kicked it with her heels, three times hard. "Yaw, yaw, yaw!"

The mule himself kicked back violently. Anna slid off his back onto her biscuits in the snow. The horse blanket slipped into a drift, and the mule ran off onto the white plain.

This was Petronilla's doing.

Anna picked herself up and brushed off her trousers. She was cold, muleless, and alone. There were no trees where she could shelter. Her nose ran, and it froze in a tiny icicle. Her face covered with snow faster than she could wipe it off, blown by the wind beneath her derby hat. She felt miserable, oddly warm, and sleepy. She recovered the blanket and spread it out like a picnic blanket. She lay down on it, vaguely aware of what was happening to her. She'd seen Joe crazy with cold. This was worse. Dying here anonymous and alone would be stupid. No one would claim her body. Georges would hang. She prayed a silent prayer to Saint Medard, patron saint of snowstorms, that he would smite the ghost of Petronilla. He did not.

A man trotted down the road on a horse, his face wrapped in a scarf against the bitter wind. When he saw Anna, a mere smudge on the white landscape, he pulled his horse up. He wore a wool blanket and a broad-brimmed hat—an Indian.

Anna lifted her face to him. She regretted that she looked like an ugly, frozen man, and not like the beautiful young woman she actually was on the inside, because that would be handy. She closed her eyes and lay back down. She expected him to ride away and leave her to die.

Instead, he dismounted. Without saying a word, likely because he did not speak English and Anna did not speak Indian, he scooped her up in his arms. Anna tried to protest this familiarity, but her lips seemed frozen in place. He carried her to his horse and put her in the saddle. He swung up behind her, holding the reins with his arms around her. She sagged into him.

They rode for half an hour before two sod houses came into view. He stopped the horse in front of the first house. She supposed he had things to do and planned to drop her off with white people. Her spirits lifted when she saw a sign that declared, "Whiskey."

The man dismounted and reached his arms up for Anna. She slid into them. He carried her like a bride. "You're a woman."

His English surprised Anna, and her pale cheeks filled with color at his meaning. She stuttered with cold. "Y . . . .y . . . yes. An ugly woman. I'm M . . .M . . . Miss Blanc. How do you do?"

"I'm Mr. Colbert."

He carried her to the door of the little sod house and called out, "Hello? Mr. Edmands?" There was no answer. He called again to no avail. The stranger leaned on the door with his shoulder, pushing it open, and carried Anna across the threshold.

The house possessed but one small room with the usual furnishings, two beds, and a stack of crates filled with whiskey bottles. It felt little warmer on the inside. Anna missed the body heat of the goats, but at least she was sheltered from the wind. The stranger set Anna down and pulled back a quilt on a bed. He turned his back and faced the wall.

Anna knew what he meant. She needed to get out of her wet

clothes. She removed her wet Francois Pinet shoes and Joe's overcoat, tossing the latter on a chair. She stripped off her wool suit
jacket dropped her pants, which were wet to the knee, and peeled
off her silk stockings. She laid down and pulled the quilt to her chin,
trying not to think of who might have laid there before and how
hard it would be to comb nits out of her hair, and how disgusting it
would be to need to.

She curled up to save heat. "You can turn around now."

The man did. He'd taken off his scarf. Black, straight hair
cascaded down past his shoulders. Anna could see now that he
was both young and handsome. He had great poise, like a gentleman.

Mr. Colbert removed Joe's crushed derby hat from her head,
revealing her smashed, feminine coiffure. He cocked his head, and
his eyes lingered on her hair and ugly face. He removed his own
damp blanket coat, took off his dry vest, and tucked it around her
hair, presumably to keep her head warm or to shield his eyes from
her badly mangled bun. He took off his shirt and handed it to Anna.
He wore only a thin undershirt, and Anna could see the lean shape
of him. His neck was brown and thick with muscles.

She put his shirt on and curled back up under the quilt.

Anna watched him as he went about filling the stove with coal,
splashing it with whiskey from a bottle, and lighting it. He went
outside with the kettle and came back having filled it with snow,
setting it to boil.

Anna trembled under the covers. "W . . . w . . . whiskey?"

He brought her the bottle. She took it with her soggy, bandaged
hand. After she had swigged, he sat on the edge of the bed, pushed
up her sleeves, and unwrapped the dressing. It pleased her to see
that the swelling in her arm had subsided, and the bite seemed to be
knitting. It wasn't so ugly anymore. He took her hands in his hands
and blew hot breath onto them, holding them close to his lips. He
blew again.

The man gazed at her with intensity; so much so that she

wondered whether he especially preferred women who looked like ugly men. And since she did not know Indian customs and did not wish to be rude, Anna gazed back. He had such wonderful cheekbones.

The kettle whistled. He went to retrieve it, pouring the water into a basin, mixing it with snow, testing it with his hands. He brought the basin to the bedside and knelt beside the bed. "Give me your feet."

Anna still felt little in her white toes. She swung her legs over the side of the bed, keeping them mostly covered with the blanket, but not so covered that the blanket would get wet. In fact, she was very careful not to get the blanket wet.

He took her feet in his hands and placed them in the bucket, massaging them under the warm water. Her toes began to hurt as they warmed. It was all she could do not to cry out.

The front door swung open with a blast of cold air. Joe Singer stood on the other side. He was mussed and hatless, icicles in his hair. His expression gave her heart frostbite.

Mr. Colbert dropped her feet.

"J . . . J . . . Jupiter."

Joe simply stared at her. She was wearing a vest as a turban. She winced at the thought.

Her teeth chattered. "D . . . d . . . detective S . . . S . . . Singer, this is M . . . M . . . Mr. Colbert. He s . . . s . . . saved my life, although I probably w . . . w . . . would have been fine."

Joe squinted at Mr. Colbert. He did not smile. He did not extend his hand. He shimmied out of his wet coat, unbuttoned his shirt, crossed the room, and wrapped the shirt around Anna's shoulders. Now there were two men in their underwear. At least there was that.

"What happened?" said Joe.

"W . . . well, I met with Mr. Grayson, but he was d . . . dead. Then Mrs. Grayson made me drink a nasty p . . . potion. I got away, but it was dark and cold, so I hid in their stable and slept with the goats. Then, I borrowed their mule, but it bucked me off in the snow and ran away. I was just crawling the rest of the way, when Mr. Colbert came along and kindly offered me a ride on his horse." Anna smiled at Mr. Colbert.

He smiled back.

Joe rubbed his face. "You could have died."

"Yes, but that's not my fault."

The room had warmed from the fire, and Anna started to thaw. Her trembling subsided.

Joe sighed and looked up. "Mr. Colbert, thank you for saving my strange fiancée—"

"He means estranged," said Anna.

"Anna, why don't you give him his clothes back. I'm sure Mr. Colbert wants to be on his way. We owe you a debt of gratitude." He didn't look grateful.

Anna unwound her turban. She knew what she must look like— an orangutan in a bad wig. The men turned their backs, probably because of her face. A sob welled up, surprising her. She bit her lip to hold it down as she undressed beneath the covers. She took off both men's shirts, then put Joe's shirt back on. She took a deep breath. "Mr. Colbert, here are your shirt and vest. Can you stay for dinner? There must be food here somewhere. Joe can boil eggs and make rice. And I can't do anything."

"Mr. Edmands could come home any minute. He won't like finding us here, but he might shoot Mr. Colbert because he's an Indian." Joe turned to Mr. Colbert. "We don't want to trouble you any further."

Mr. Colbert looked at Anna with probing eyes. He must have sensed Joe's anger. "My home is one hour's ride from here. I can take you with me."

"She stays with me."

"Thank you, Mr. Colbert," said Anna. "But I have to interview Mr. Edmands. I've come all the way from Los Angeles to do it."

"Will you be safe? I won't leave if—"

"I'll keep her safe," said Joe. "I'm a cop."

Mr. Colbert looked unimpressed.

Anna winced as she stood in the basin on her thawing feet and extended her hand. "Mr. Colbert please keep in touch. You can reach me at the Los Angeles Police Department. And can I send your Christmas card general delivery? Are there many Mr. Colberts in town?

"I am Miko. Miko Colbert." He took her hand.

"And I'm Miss Anna Blanc. A N N A B L A N C."

Joe looked impatient.

"Thank you for everything." She shook, then let Mr. Colbert's hand drop.

Miko walked to the door and opened it. He cast a backward glance at Anna.

"I'll write," she said.

And then Miko Colbert was gone.

"You're mad."

"You think so?"

"How did you find this place?"

"Anna, I wouldn't bring up Sergeant Tribble. Did you eat?" Joe took a summer sausage out of his bag and hacked off a piece with his knife.

"Of course. I had pork chops, lamb chops, chop suey—"

He strode over and popped the sausage into Anna's mouth, silencing her. She devoured it, then opened her mouth like a baby bird. He fed her another chunk.

She chewed and swallowed. "I'm sorry—"

"It's not enough."

"I'm sorry, but my brother's neck is on the line, and as far as I can tell, it's up to me to save it. How did you get away?"

"I don't keep all my money in one place. And now, thanks to you, I'm considerably poorer."

"Oooh. Joe Singer paid off a cop. I didn't think that was in your repertoire." She hobbled to the window on sore feet and peeked out after Mr. Colbert. He was riding off on his magnificent black horse.

"I'd never met an Indian before. It's strange but I almost think Mr. Colbert liked me."

"Have you looked at yourself lately?"

Joe had a right to be angry, but his words were a punch to her gut. "I just thought . . ." Her voice trembled. "It's not like you to be cruel."

A shaving mirror hung on the wall. Joe unhooked it and brought it to Anna. She averted her gaze. He moved the mirror so that it was in front of her face. She closed her eyes.

"Anna, look."

"No."

"Look."

She opened one eye. The mirror needed resilvering. She opened two eyes and saw her reflection, speckled with gray. Her mouth was not distended. Her face had returned to its original heart shape. Her rash had faded from angry red to a delicate shell pink. Dark moons encircled each eye, but her eyes were large and wide again.

Anna no longer resembled an orangutan. Mrs. Grayson's potion had worked.

"I'm beautiful."

"I told you."

"Would you still love me if I had stayed ugly?"

"I don't know. In that scenario did you rob me, steal my clothes, and run off to Oklahoma?"

It had been a stupid, irrelevant question. Anna regretted it.

Joe stared out the window while she dressed in her own clothes, which he had brought from Yuma. She didn't ask to borrow his comb, but carelessly arranged her hair without one. Anna needed to focus on the crime or her heart would explode. She tried to think of Georges and not Joe.

"I interviewed Mrs. Grayson."

"Poor Mrs. Grayson."

"You have no idea." Anna wandered over to a dresser where a wedding photograph stood in a wooden frame—likely Mr. and Mrs.

Edmands. The fashion was from the right time period. She picked it up and pocketed it. "It was very important. You see, Mr. Edmands is notoriously violent. People believe he killed his wife. And he threatened to kill Samuel. He's a suspect."

"Good work, Sherlock. We'll find him and interview him." He withheld his customary smile.

"Yes, but Mr. Edmands isn't here. At least he hasn't been here all day. His stove was cold when we arrived."

"There are animals in the barn."

"There's no perishable food in the kitchen. It's dusty." She ran a finger along the table and showed him her dirty fingertip.

"All right. There's a house nearby. Let's talk to the neighbor and find out where he's gone and when he's coming back. But first . . ."

"What?"

He gave her a hard look. "Give me back my badge."

§

Mrs. Cindy Snyder lived in the adjacent farmhouse. She opened the door when Joe knocked. When he flashed his badge, she invited them in for coffee. The woman was weathered, and had few teeth and fewer visitors, Anna guessed. Patches covered both of her elbows yet, she gave them the last of her sugar. The coffee tasted weak, as if she were trying to stretch it. Anna felt guilty for drinking it and for everything else she'd ever done or said in her life. She pinched herself. She dropped two coins of penance on the floor, although the money was Joe's or maybe the LAPD's, she didn't know. Anna added a bill.

While Anna explained their mission, Mrs. Snyder worked her jaw the way toothless people sometimes did, like a cow chewing Juicy Fruit. "Mr. Edmands is gone."

"When did he leave?" asked Joe.

"In January."

Anna turned to Joe and raised her eyebrows. "He's violent, has motive, and Oklahoma City is no longer his alibi."

"That's a long time to be away from his farm," said Joe.

"My husband and son have been tending to his durned animals."

Anna and Joe exchanged a shocked look. The lady had sworn in front of a cop. Anna smiled sweetly. "Do you know where he went?"

"No. But he was looking for Flossie, asking everybody in the whole durned town. He must have gotten a lead and followed it. I told my husband *not* to watch his animals so that Edmands couldn't go. Durned fopdoodle didn't listen."

Joe spun a quarter on the table. "How could Edmands track them down if even Samuel's family didn't know where they'd gone?"

Anna said, "Maybe Samuel Grayson told Edmands where to find Samara Flossie. He was a man scorned. Maybe it was revenge. Or maybe it was love. Maybe he thought Edmands would rescue her from the Jonquil."

"That's kind of risky given the dad wanted him dead," said Joe.

"It's a small town. Everyone knows everyone. Everyone's in everybody's business, right?"

"Right," Mrs. Snyder chimed in.

"They couldn't just sneak away. Someone would have seen something. Edmands just had to find that someone." Anna leaned back in her chair. "And who would have seen something?"

"Those durned railroad men."

§

They spoke little as they rode double on the back of Joe's rented horse. They were silent as they returned the horse to the stable and walked to the train station.

"I know what you're thinking," said Anna. "You think that even if Georges didn't kill Samuel Grayson, that he still might be the Black Pearl. You think that's why he went to convalesce."

Joe closed his eyes and sighed. "I was thinking I got a headache. I was thinking it hurts too much to think."

Joe quietly lounged against a pole while Anna inquired whether Mr. Edmands had come to ask about his daughter and Samuel Grayson, and whether the Blanc railcar was ready for the next train west.

The ticket seller looked nervous. "I didn't tell him anything. But he bought a ticket to Los Angeles."

Anna smiled and made I-told-you-so eyes at Joe.

The ticket man called the station master who regretted to inform Anna that her railcar was on its way back to La Grande Station, as they did not know where she had gone and so had telegrammed her father for instructions.

"Biscuits!" said Anna.

Anna and Joe ate silently in a café adjacent to the station. She ordered chicken and dumplings, Indian fry bread, meatloaf, and apple pie. She ate her own food, and Joe let her eat half of his head-cheese sandwich. Afterward, they returned to the station in time to board. They rode third class, next to the toilets.

Anna lifted her chin. "Georges will be home by now."

"I really don't think so."

CHAPTER 39

When the train arrived in Los Angeles, Joe escorted Anna back to Georges's hotel without comment. They had been gone for nearly two weeks. Anna felt dirty, exhausted, and ruined—out of place in a hotel with such a large chandelier. The dangling crystals cast rainbows onto the marble floor. She collected her pretty fish key from the front desk. "Did the Southern Pacific send my trunk and hats? I left them on Mr. Devereaux's railcar."

"Yes ma'am. They're in your room. A maid has unpacked and laundered your clothes."

At least she had her clothes back. At least something was right in the world.

It was early evening, and a different boy manned the elevator. He politely stared at his shoes. She wondered where the other insulting boy had gone. Joe walked her to her door. She put her key into the lock and then stopped. She turned to face Joe. "I don't want you to come in. In fact, maybe you should go."

Joe blew out a breath. "All right." He took a few steps backward, his eyes on Anna. "Good night, Sherlock. Whatever happens, you know I love you."

Anna didn't answer. He swore, turned his back, and disappeared into the elevator along with half her heart.

His love for her, her love for him, and her love for Georges, exhausted Anna. She had no idea what came next, or where Georges was. Home, she hoped, and well after a good rest in some therapeutic location. Still, she braced herself in case the apartment was indeed unoccupied. Joe was so convinced Georges was on the lam, he didn't even stay to check.

Anna opened the door and Thomas came striding to meet her. "Miss Anna, good evening."

Anna smiled. "I didn't expect you. I mean I did."

Georges came from his study, saw her, and grinned. "Well hello!" He seemed exceedingly cheerful for a man accused—like someone walking on clouds.

"Hello!" she beamed at him. If Joe could see Georges now, surely it would dispel his suspicions.

Georges took Anna's hand. "Where have you been?"

Anna thought it best not to say she had gone to hunt Georges, especially as he had come home. "I went to Oklahoma City to investigate a suspect in the Samuel Grayson murder. Where have you been? Are you well?"

"Another suspect. That's a relief." He grinned. "And Joe went with you?"

"Yes, but I didn't let him ride in your railcar."

He chuckled. "You mean our railcar."

She smiled despite everything, because his cheer was infectious. "Georges, I met your dear mother."

Georges blinked. His smile melted. His brows drew together, then relaxed, then drew together again. "Why? She's not your mother."

This stung Anna, though it was true. Georges had never been cross with her before, and he had just been so happy.

"I was looking for you. I didn't know where you'd gone, and Joe said it would harm your case if you missed your court date."

"Well, I didn't, did I?"

"I'm sorry."

He collapsed into a chair and put his head in his hands. "No, I'm sorry." His words sounded stiff with anxiety. "Anna, I can't see inside your mind. What are you thinking?"

"That this shouldn't come between us!"

"If it ever came out, it would."

"It wouldn't."

"You see now why I can never marry?"

"Because if your children came out with dark skin, they wouldn't be accepted. You wouldn't be accepted."

"I'd probably just go back to France. But I don't want to."

Anna came over and knelt by his chair. She put her hand on his shoulder. "Marry or don't marry. But don't leave me again. I didn't know where you'd gone. Joe thought you'd fled. Your mother said you'd gone to Yuma."

Georges smirked. "Yuma? Really? Well, that's funny."

"Why?"

"She lied. You know she's a very religious woman."

"Where did you go?"

"I went to Santa Barbara. There's a quite comfortable hotel there. The Arlington. It's beautiful. I'll take you sometime."

"Yes, I know it! I would love to go. And I get ten days off a year."

"You don't say?"

CHAPTER 40

Anna clipped into the station, happy because she had a viable murder suspect who was not her brother, and dreading the pile of work she would undoubtedly face. There were prostitutes to employ, truants to find, Friday Morning Clubs to appease, children to re-form, and refugees to feed. Then, of course, there was the problem of Matilda. Anna only hoped the women's department had not been too busy, and that Matilda was still in the jail to help her.

Detective Wolf followed Anna up the stairs to her storage closet. "Assistant Matron Blanc, welcome back. Where have you been, and have you found Eliel Villalobos?"

"I've been . . . um . . . following a lead. A very promising lead. In fact, Eliel Villalobos has been spotted several days journey outside of the city. Naturally, since he is a very important crim-inal, I had to investigate, with Matron Clemens' permission, of course."

"Yes. That must have slipped her mind because she was asking me where you were."

Anna shook her head and tut tutted. "It must be hard being old."

"Assistant Matron Blanc, she's only forty. But never mind. I told her you were looking into something for me."

"And I was. The truant. I am very close to cracking the case."

"That's good, Assistant Matron Blanc."

"I'm sure I'll have your truant found by the end of the week. I have people working on it."

"People?"

"Yes, you know."

"I don't know, but I'm afraid to ask. And I noticed Detective Singer was also away on a case."

"I couldn't care less."

"You have a nice day, Assistant Matron Blanc." Detective Wolf winked.

Anna winked back badly to be polite. He grinned and departed. She heard his footsteps moving down the stairs. Matron Clemens entered the small storeroom where Anna sat at her desk. "Assistant Matron Blanc, you disappeared."

"No. I mean, yes. Detective Wolf sent me on a very important secret mission that I can't speak about. It was urgent, and I left under the cover of night with no chance to tell you where I'd gone."

"I see," said Matron Clemens.

"How are Matilda and all the ladies in the cow ring." Anna braced herself for a hard truth.

"Matilda has been a great help in your absence."

Anna's shoulders relaxed. "So, she's still lodging with us?"

Matron Clemens looked serious. "For now."

"Did you get more money for food from the Friday Morning Club?"

"Yes, I did."

"Have they found prostitutes to work their bad jobs?"

"I'm afraid not. The endeavor has been a failure."

Anna kicked herself. If only she could have found a prostitute willing to work for low wages. But with wages that low, the woman would need to supplement her income, which would only lead to more prostitution. It was a vicious cycle.

Matron Clemens continued. "But, all's well that ends well. We are planning a special school for fallen women to teach them how to start their own businesses."

"Hat shops! Or maybe they could sew frillies. They know so much about them."

"I commend you on your idea, Assistant Matron Blanc. I've given you the credit and Captain Wells is very pleased."

Anna flushed with pleasure. Praise from Matron Clemens was sparse, and her male colleagues stole the credit for Anna's detective work themselves or wrongly attributed her successes to Joe. In fact, Anna was rarely praised by anyone, except Joe, who always gave her due credit.

This thought made her sad because she was estranged from Joe and he sorely deserved it.

Matron Clemens put on her gloves. "I'm off to an appointment with the Friday Morning Club president and the president of the Chamber of Commerce. We are looking for seed money as well as volunteer instructors."

"Wonderful. I'm sure they'll help. Many fine, upstanding men from the Chamber of Commerce are well acquainted with the girls from the demimonde. I should know."

Matron Clemens was silent for a moment. "Indeed."

"I hope Charlene can attend the school for fallen women."

"Of course." She looked at Anna's desk. "You have much work to do. You must not fall behind, Assistant Matron Blanc."

"No ma'am.

When Matron Clemens had departed, Anna settled in to prioritize her work, which was indeed plentiful. She sifted through the files on her desk—mostly arrest records for bad children whom Anna was expected to reform. She began to formulate a lecture in her mind to enlighten them about how rules were made to be followed and if one broke the rules, one must always be discreet.

She got no further. Anna could not concentrate on bad children when her own brother faced the risk of the noose. She sat back in her chair. Her matron work would have to wait until Georges was safe. The most important thing was to locate Samara Flossie's father. But how could she find him? How could he have found Samuel Grayson? She dug in her purse for the photograph of the Edmands' wedding and set it on her desk.

Anna imagined that if she were Samara Flossie's father, she would go to the City Directory, just like Anna had done, and look up Samuel Grayson. But Samuel wasn't listed in the regular section of the directory. Edmands would only find him if he knew to look in the back where people who had missed the deadline were listed. This was unlikely. Only locals would know. If someone had told him to look in the back, that would have led him to Samuel's apartment building. Samuel's neighbor had mentioned Mr. Edmands but had not reported seeing him. Perhaps he hadn't known that Mr. Edmands had come for Samuel and lured him to Griffith Park. Had Mr. Edmands found Samuel's apartment? She would start with a visit to the apartment manager to show him the photograph of Edmands.

Anna draped a blue cape with a fox fur collar around her shoulders, covering her ugly uniform. She stashed her rod in her tooled leather purse, retrieved the Edmands's wedding photograph, and descended the stairs like a queen. Joe was at his desk with the City Directory open in front of him, scratching on a sheet of paper. Anna tiptoed quietly over. She didn't know why she tiptoed, except she didn't feel like she had the right to be near him. But business was business. "Good afternoon. Georges is back in town. He was relaxing at home when I arrived last night."

"Where did he go?"

"Santa Barbara. You know. Fresh sea air. Convalescence."

"Santa Barbara." He got this distant, thinking look on his face. "What's in Santa Barbara? What was I reading?"

"It's a vacation spot with sunny beaches. And there's a Catholic mission. Plus, oil wells in Summerland and a bunch of spooky spiritualists. It's where I recuperated after dispatching the New High Street Suicide Faker."

Joe snapped his fingers. "There's a new movie studio. Flying something."

"A movie studio?" Anna's face fell. "Oh. Are you still busy trying to hang my brother?"

"The Griffith Park murder is my top priority. I'm canvassing movie studios looking for Allie Sutton, and I'm making a list of all the hotels within a mile of the train station to see if Mr. Edmands ever checked in. If he did kill Samuel Grayson, Flossie is in danger."

"Fine." Anna turned her back.

"Where are you going?"

Anna knew if she told the truth, he'd want to come, and she couldn't quite stand him right now. "I'm hunting a truant."

CHAPTER 41

Anna took the trolley to the apartment building formerly inhabited by Samuel Grayson and knocked on the manager's door. Having a rich and powerful father had been useful when soliciting help from the community, but she hadn't realized the extent of its utility until it was gone. She did, however, have a brass star, and at least she no longer resembled an orangutan. When the door opened, the apartment manager loomed on the threshold. He had inky black hair and a tiny head. Anna smiled her most charming smile. "Good afternoon." She carefully enunciated, "I am police matron Anna Blanc from the LAPD." She bobbed a curtsy.

He cocked his tiny head and looked at Anna. "So, what's that then?"

"I'm basically a detective. I have authority. That's why they gave me this badge." She puffed out her chest and pointed to the matron's badge pinned to it. She cocked an eyebrow.

The man stared at her chest.

Anna quickly unpuffed her chest and frowned. "I'm here to investigate the murder of Samuel Grayson and I need to ask you a few questions."

He directed his words to her bosoms. "Why don't you come in and sit down."

Anna hesitated. The pin-headed manager made her feel ill at ease and slightly queasy. Still, she had an important job to do and Georges's life depended on it. Thus, when he opened the door wider, Anna entered his apartment. He closed the door behind her.

The apartment had a similar layout to Samuel Grayson's abode, but the furniture was neither as new nor as dramatically ugly, though it was ugly enough. It smelled of stale cigarette smoke and cat urine. The manager motioned for Anna to sit on a love seat. She sat, and he sat rather too closely beside her. Anna popped back up again. "I prefer to stand. It helps me think." She began to pace. "Did anyone ever come to visit Samuel Grayson or inquire after him? Anyone? Anyone at all?"

"Well, let me think."

Anna paced to the end of the room and turned around to find the man standing right behind her, like her own shadow. Anna tried to move around him, but he cornered her between the wall and a large chair. He leered.

His face reminded her of a stinkbug.

She wished to stomp on his foot but now was not the time. Instead, she leered back, trying to make a stinkbug face of her own so that he would see her as his equal. It seemed to do the trick.

He stepped back and his mouth dropped open.

She pushed the wedding photograph in his face. "Did this man come here?"

"Uh. No. A lady came. I saw her knocking on his door and I threw her out. No ladies allowed. That's my policy. He wasn't home so she slid a letter under his door."

"Are you sure this man never came inquiring?"

"If he did, I never saw him."

This answer displeased Anna, even if it were true. But Mr. Edmands could have tracked Samuel down, lured him to a meeting in the park, and the stinkbug manager simply didn't see him. The stinkbug could have been sleeping or petting his cat. He never would have seen Anna if she hadn't banged on the door. Maybe Mr. Edmands had engaged a lady to draw Samuel out.

"What did the lady look like? Old? Young?"

"Young."

"Plain? Pretty? Beautiful?"

"A peach."

Anna sighed. "Did she have golden hair or raven locks?"

"Her hair was brown."

Samara Flossie was quite peachy, her hair was light brown, and she had said she'd written Samuel a letter telling him to leave her alone. But Samara Flossie would never draw Samuel out on behalf of her homicidal father. She was hiding from him. He had to have found Samuel another way. Perhaps Samuel Grayson did write Samara Flossie's family. Anna tapped her lip. "When was this?"

"Five, six weeks ago."

"About the time Samuel Grayson disappeared."

"Yeah. Just before. Because I saw him that night and wondered what a girl like her wanted with a guy like him. I suppose he had fancy clothes."

Anna grimaced. "You can probably have his clothes. The police don't want them."

"Yeah, looks don't mean anything. Take me for instance. Guys without money don't get girls. He had money and he didn't. You know what I mean."

"No."

"Well, he lived here." He was speaking to her bosoms again and edging closer with that stinkbug leer.

Anna had all she needed and all she could take from the lecherous and inarticulate manager. "I think a female bug might like you." She slipped past him, flung open the door, and ran.

CHAPTER 42

Whuen Anna returned to Central Station, she was stopped in her tracks by the shrill voice of a lady who clearly had feelings to spare. It was the tight-lacer from the Friday Morning Club, and she was completely unhinged. She hurled loud, angry words in the general vicinity of Matron Clemens—but perhaps not at her—something about fools and retribution. Her feather hat shot two feet into the air, quivering like the mad lady attached to it.

Matron Clemens stood tall, her face placid, and spoke in a cool, soothing voice. "Yes. I see. Mm hm. A detective is just the thing."

It was a matron's duty to soothe lady victims, gain the trust of female suspects, and cope with all feminine disasters. While Matron Clemens was up to any challenge, Anna thought she should come to her aid on principle—especially since Anna had dealt with more than one irate lady of means. She had, for example, dyed the hair of Mrs. Masterson's formerly white poodle a shocking blue black. It was an experiment that needed to happen, and spared Anna from a similar fate. She had been eight.

Anna assumed a pleasant smile and glided over, making gentle hushing sounds and gesturing gracefully that the lady should keep it down.

The tight-lacer turned on her. "Don't wave your hands at me, Anna Blanc!"

Anna frowned.

Mr. Melvin shuffled over with a steaming cup of tea, which Matron Clemens had no doubt ordered. He extended the tea cup to the quivering lady with both hands, his eyes averted, like a man from China.

The lady stopped midquiver and took the tea. "Thank you." She sipped. Anna couldn't help but wonder if her sudden silence was merely the eye of the storm.

Matron Clemens smiled. "Now could I trouble you to start over? Why don't you sit down and tell us more?" She ushered the lady into an interview room and over to a chair. Anna followed. The tight-lacer sat. Her abdomen bulged beneath her tiny waist.

Matron Clemens continued. "Then, I'll better know which detective is needed. Have you been robbed, or—"

"My husband's being blackmailed!" The lady assumed a sarcastic tone. "He's as innocent as a baby but thought it a better idea to pay out three thousand dollars to a criminal than to stand up for himself. The only thing he's guilty of is weakness."

"Have you considered a cure for manly weakness. I see them advertised in the paper all the time," Anna said helpfully.

The lady stared dumbly at Anna.

"I'm sure they are extraordinarily useful. They would never make them for ladies, though, lest we dose ourselves up and take over the world." Anna chuckled.

Silence followed this comment.

Matron Clemens, with her usual blank expression, spoke. "Indeed." She turned to the tremulous lady. "Mrs. Morgan, I assume you and Assistant Matron Blanc have met."

"We're slightly acquainted," said Anna. "Mrs. Morgan is the vice president of the Friday Morning Club."

"I'm Mrs. *Octavius* Morgan." The tight-lacer said as if this should impress them.

Anna hated it that women couldn't simply use their own names but instead had to wear the brand of their husband's name. If married people had to have the same name, they should simply choose a new one together. Her mind wandered to new last names that would suit Joe Singer, like Arrow and Delicious.

The lady continued. "My husband has been making payments to . . ." She threw up her hands. "Oh, I don't know. Someone. He—the black-hearted blackmailer—claims that my husband . . ." She snorted.

"Do go on," said Anna, interested.

"That snake accused him of consorting with bad women at the Jonquil Resort, and said he would reveal everything, but it's just an attempt to extort money."

Anna beamed. "That's wonderful news!"

The lady frowned. Matron Clemens looked blank.

"You don't believe he would do such a thing?" asked Matron Clemens. "Some men do."

The woman set her chin. "I don't doubt my husband for a moment."

Anna tapped her lip. "He's stopped, no doubt. The blackmailer has stopped." Dead men did not extort.

"Well, yes. But I want the money back."

"I'm afraid that won't be possible, unless you want payment in ugly suits and atrocious settees. Your blackmailer is dead, and I will need to question your husband regarding his demise." She covered her mouth with her hands and looked at Matron Clemens. "Did I say, 'I?' That's silly. I meant Detective Singer. I'll just go get him."

Anna flounced off to find Joe. She arrived at his desk slightly breathless with excitement. He sat writing a report and singing softly to himself. *"Virginie baby, you make me crazy."* He scowled at her.

Anna lowered her voice and hissed. "Virginie is my middle name. You can't sing about Virginie here. People will guess."

"I can't not sing about you."

"Then give me a pseudonym."

He held her eyes and crooned. *"Sherlock baby, you make me crazy."*

He was making her crazy and she tingled everywhere. Anna closed her eyes to break the spell, opened them, and lifted her chin. "I have happy news."

"Oh yeah?" He sipped coffee from a tin cup.

"Samuel Grayson—I'm almost positive it was him—was black-mailing a different innocent man." She frowned. "One Octavius Morgan. But this victim suffered from manly weakness. His wife is here complaining about it."

"I think you mean something else."

"I know what I mean. Unlike George, this weakly victim paid. Don't you see? Grayson was in the habit of blackmailing innocent men."

"Oh, I see." His chair scraped the floor as he stood. "I want Georges to be innocent. I really do."

"Then we'll both be happy."

"Lead the way to the dissatisfied woman." He flashed her a grin, looking, unfortunately, irresistible.

Anna clapped her hands. "She's the one screeching in the interview room."

When they arrived, the lady was sitting quietly alone. Joe sobered his expression.

"Where is Matron Clemens?" Anna asked.

"She and an officer are summoning my husband. His office is just around the corner. She said the police would need to speak with him. Is this the detective?"

Joe extended his hand. "Mrs. Morgan, I'm Detective Singer. I'm sorry for your troubles."

"I'll be assisting Detective Singer with this investigation and asking you questions," said Anna. "For example, if Mr. Morgan is innocent, why did he pay? I mean, besides manly weakness."

A violent coughing fit overtook Joe.

Anna gave him a reproachful look.

"Because he's in discussions with the Episcopal church to design their cathedral. Even a whiff of scandal could sink the deal."

Joe had recomposed himself, though his face was still red from his coughing fit. "Mrs. Morgan, when did you discover your husband was paying a blackmailer?"

"I noticed the money was missing from our bank account. I asked him directly and he explained the situation. He'd never lie to me. I told you he was an honorable man."

Anna had heard that before. "Are you sure?"

"Of course. He's an architect. Quite renowned."

"Oh." Anna wrinkled her brow. "Your husband's an architect. Is he by chance designing a hotel on the waterfront?"

"Why, yes."

It pained Anna, but she forced herself to say, "He doesn't have a scrawny mustache, nor a very magnificent mustache? He has an ordinary mustache? Or none at all?"

"Why, he has a famously luxuriant mustache."

"Jupiter." Anna's posture sagged. She gave Joe a meaningful look.

He squinted at her. "Mrs. Morgan, will you excuse us for a moment?" Joe linked his arm through Anna's and drew her out of the room. When they stood safely in the hall, separated from Mrs. Morgan by a thick oak door, he lowered his voice. "Sherlock, what was that look?"

"I had thought that if Mr. Morgan were another innocent victim of blackmail . . ." Anna squeezed her eyes shut and shook her head. "I was wrong. Octavius Morgan is guilty of more than just manly weakness. Remember at the Jonquil? The magnificently mustachioed man talking with his friend with the scrawny mustache about plans for a new hotel? Sue and Clementine's lovers? You know, the twins?"

Joe blew out a breath. "Oh."

"If Mr. Morgan is magnificent mustache man, we know for a fact he's broken at least one blossom. This makes him our number one suspect in the murder and perhaps he is our man from Mars or the real Black Pearl."

"Okay. Let's talk to him."

§

Five minutes after Matron Clemens escorted Mrs. Morgan out the door, a patrolman escorted Octavius Morgan in. Anna recognized him immediately as Sue's lover—the magnificent mustachioed man from the Jonquil Café. His eyes roamed the station wildly as Matron Clemens escorted him past Anna and Joe and into an interrogation room. His mustache gleamed, turning up at the ends in perfect curls.

"Yep, that's him." Joe turned to Anna, "Why don't you question him?"

Her face lit up. "Really?"

"Really. I'll just sit next to you and look menacing. You know. You charm him. I'll be the threat."

"All right." Anna beamed at him like a ray of sunshine. "You be the threat. I'll question him first for as long as I can, and when he clams up, we'll bring in Matilda. He might be our man from Mars."

"Agreed."

She was still beaming as they entered the interrogation room. Beside her, Joe's face hardened into stone.

Anna led. "Good afternoon Mr. Morgan. I am Assistant Matron Blanc, and this is Detective Singer. My, what a luxurious mustache you have."

Mr. Morgan's hand reached up and touched his upper lip. He grunted unintelligibly and shifted in his seat. "Why am I here?"

"We just want to question you," Anna smiled sweetly. "Your wife has accused you of manly weakness, but I don't believe it for a moment."

A hint of a smile flitted across Joe's stony face.

Mr. Morgan looked confused. "She accused me of what?"

"Don't worry Mr. Morgan. It's not a crime." She tossed her head dismissively. "And, like I said, I don't believe it. Rather, I'm accusing you of bad timing, among other things."

"Bad timing?" Little specks of sweat beaded on Mr. Morgan's forehead. A rivulet trickled down his nose and disappeared into his mustache. Was it guilt?

"Case in point—if you were going to kill your blackmailer, you shouldn't have paid him first. He only gambled the money away and spent it on ugly suits. His suits are criminal, and now you are an accomplice."

The suspect paled. His collar was soaked from sweat; his breathing had become quick and shallow. He loosened his necktie leaving it slightly askew.

Joe leaned forward. "Would you like a cup of water?"

"No, that's my line." She frowned. "But I don't want to get him water."

"All right. Let's switch," said Joe. He went to the door and poked his head out, whispering to someone in the hall. "Could you please bring Matilda here. I think she's upstairs. Oh, and a cup of water please."

Anna's mouth hardened. She stood and paced behind Mr. Morgan, lowering her voice. "We know you contributed to the delinquency of Miss Sue Henry, exchanging money for her attentions. I saw you together and she will testify. And for this you will pay. Do you deny it?"

"It's not illegal. She's a whore."

Anna slammed her fist down on the table, causing him to jump. "It *is* illegal. She's a child, and you ruined her. And she's not a whore. She thought you were courting her."

"I didn't know how old she was. You can't prove that I did."

"And when Samuel Grayson blackmailed you, threatening to tell your wife and the whole world, you killed him. But stupidly, you paid him first. Bad timing."

"I didn't kill Samuel Grayson."

"Where were you four weeks ago Tuesday?"

He rolled his eyes up in thought. "I was in Fresno visiting my aunt."

"Can you prove it?"

"Yes. I can provide half a dozen witnesses."

"Are you loaded? Do you buy garnet cross necklaces for girls at the Jonquil? Are you the Black Pearl?"

His eyes flashed. Helmut Melvin opened the door carrying a cup of water and accompanying a quivering Matilda who seemed to be holding her breath. When she saw Mr. Morgan, she exhaled.

"Miss Matilda, is this the man from Mars?"

She blinked her blond lashes. "No."

Mr. Morgan leapt to his feet. "I won't be made fun of by a woman."

Joe put a hand on his shoulder and pushed him back down into his chair. "Sit down and answer Matron Blanc's questions." He loomed with menace.

Anna drew her brows together and looked at Joe. "Now no one is being nice."

"He doesn't inspire kindness. Let's put him in a cell," said Joe.

§

When Octavius Morgan was settled in the bull ring, Joe walked Anna upstairs to her storage closet. Her face registered disappointment.

"Good work, Sherlock. You caught him."

"Not yet, I didn't."

"We arrested him for contributing to the delinquency of a minor. That's not nothing."

"Agreed. It's just I was hoping he was the killer, I mean, if Edmands isn't the killer, which he probably is."

"Morgan might have done it. We haven't checked his alibi. I'll ask his wife before she finds out we arrested him. Then, I'll follow up with whoever it was he allegedly visited in Fresno."

"It's just . . . when I accused him of corrupting Sue, he sweat. He didn't seem worried enough about the murder."

He put his hand on her shoulder. "I'll look into it thoroughly. If he did it, he'll pay for it."

CHAPTER 43

In life, the odds always seemed stacked against Anna, mostly because she was female, but partly because she had the worst imagin-
able luck. In her present circumstances, she desperately needed luck.
If she couldn't crack the case of the Griffith Park Executioner, her
own dear brother, Georges, might hang. She wouldn't be able to
look at Joe, much less make love to him, because it would be his
failure, too, his betrayal, his deadly mistake. She would be alone.

Anna didn't trust herself to save Georges on her own. She needed
supernatural help, and she needed it soon. God was powerful, but
unreliable, and not always on her side. The saints were a better bet,
but how could she assure they'd be in her camp when she'd been so
naughty as of late? They might not always understand when something was an emergency.

A little repentance might be just the thing. Anna opened her
bottom desk drawer and removed a stack of rubber diapers and
inside diaper squares that she kept for refugee babies. They covered
a treasure beneath—a manual stolen from the coroner for Anna's
education—his brand-new copy of *Legal Medicine*. It had all kinds
of wonderful insights on worms, scavengers, and how to best collect
clues from dead bodies—even rotting and dismembered ones. She
had read it seven times already, having stolen the previous coroner's
copy as well, though that copy had burned. She felt this particular
repentance would be a sacrifice she could manage. Georges could
always buy her a new one.

Anna carried the book, hidden by a fur muff, downstairs into the coroner's office. He wasn't there, though a cup of coffee steamed on his desk. She left him a note asking him to please visit Anna in her own office.

She returned to her desk and sat on the edge of it, as she sometimes did when she was alone, her legs swinging. She picked up the Edmands's wedding picture and was staring at their unsmiling faces when the coroner entered. Anna leapt to her feet. He wasn't wearing his white coat, just a fine suit, his hair neatly cut and combed, his tie well-coordinated. Anna noted that he had luminous brown eyes and a thorough knowledge of legal medicine—the kind that might make other police matrons—those who were not in love with Joe Singer—swoon.

He came over to her desk. "Assistant Matron Blanc, we've never been properly introduced." He stuck out his hand. "I'm Dr. Haar, the coroner."

Anna took his hand and shook it. "I'm very pleased to meet you."

"Likewise. Now, how can I help you?"

Anna handed him the book. "I recovered this tome from a thief. You don't know who it might belong to?"

"A thief? How odd."

"I thought so. The thief didn't explain, although he said he was very sorry."

He opened the book and read the book plate. "Yes, this is my book. Thank you for recovering it."

"It's my duty."

"If you ever need anything from me . . . I don't know, if you'd like me to give advice to a troubled boy or—"

"Attending an autopsy would be wonderful. One for a murder victim, or perhaps a decomposing body. Practical experience is everything. I feel it will help me in my work."

"Your work? Right." He laughed. "Anything you wish. Your reputation precedes you." He colored. "I mean, your professional reputation. Not your . . . You solved two murder cases."

"More than that, actually. I dispatched the New High Street Suicide Faker and the Trunk Murderess of Chinatown. I also solved the case of the Head Chopper Offer and the Hatchet Thrower, also of Chinatown."

"I am impressed." He looked impressed.

"They mostly give Joe Singer the credit, but you can ask him. I solved the cases. Detective Singer always tells the truth. He's *too* good, if you know what I mean."

"I'm not sure that I do."

An awkward silence followed. The coroner picked up the framed wedding photograph of Mr. and Mrs. Edmands. "Are these your parents?" He glanced at the photo, which depicted a young couple dressed in clothes that had clearly been sewn at home. "My mistake, these aren't your people. You come from wealth."

"Yes, they're not. It's a murder suspect and his late bride. He probably killed her. His name is Mr. Edmands. He came to Los Angeles two months ago. He's violent, drunken, and I'm looking for him."

The coroner examined the photograph more closely, this time focusing on the man. "Two months ago, you say?"

"Yes."

"I've met him."

Anna's pulse quickened with excitement. "You met him? Where?"

"Unfortunately for him, I met him on a slab. He died in a bar fight in Chinatown, late January, right before Chinese New Year. He was a drinker. Red nose. Enlarged liver. Even dead he smelled like a still."

Anna frowned hard. "That can't be right. You met someone else. What was his name?"

He rolled his eyes to the ceiling and rubbed his chin dramatically. "Let me see . . . John something."

"You see—"

"Oh yes, John Doe." He quirked a smile.

Anna's mouth curved down. "No, it can't be the same man. How could you possibly remember him after two months when you meet so many dead men?"

"He had a strawberry birthmark on his forehead. Look." The coroner pointed to the photograph and a shadow on Mr. Edmands's brow."

"That could be dirt."

"A dirty face in a formal wedding photo? I think not, Assistant Matron Blanc."

Anna had known her explanation to be false, even as she uttered it. But there could be more than one man with a strawberry birthmark. "You could be mistaken."

"Maybe. I can tell you one thing about him. The label in his shirt was from a shop in . . ." He wrinkled his brow, thinking. He snapped his fingers. "Oklahoma City."

Anna's good mood vaporized. Her key suspect, the man that could lift suspicion from Georges, was already dead when the crime had been committed. He had likely never found Samuel Grayson at all.

Anna's eyes lost focus and she no longer paid attention to the coroner. She was thinking.

"Assistant Matron Blanc?"

Anna only vaguely heard him over the sound of her hopes crumbling.

"Have a good night, Assistant Matron Blanc."

When Anna raised her eyes to answer him, he had already gone. She'd been rude. She kicked herself. Then, she kicked herself for kicking herself because what did rudeness matter when her brother's very life was on the line. She kicked herself again because she didn't know how to exonerate him, and because she was mixed up, as if she'd lost her compass and her way.

Chapter 44

Awash in anguish, Anna's stomach rumbled. She hadn't eaten since breakfast. It reminded her that Matilda would have to be fed. She strode to the cabinet where the matrons kept charity food for the refugees. She knew Matron Clemens had secured new funds, but had she stocked the cupboard? Anna opened the cupboard door and found a tub of lard, a bunch of carrots, pickled herring, six loaves of stale bread, and a stalk of brussels sprouts with roots and dirt still attached.

She made a sandwich of lard, herring, and bread. Joe walked in and found her chewing. "Anna, come sit down. I have something to tell you." He looked somber.

Holding her sandwich, she followed him back into her storage closet and sat at her desk. He closed the door. Anna set down the sandwich, which no longer seemed so tasty. Her stomach now churned with dread. "What is it, then? Is it Georges? Has he had a seizure?"

Joe took Anna's hand. "No. I mean, I don't know. Anna, that's Georges's fingerprint on the gun."

Anna snatched her hand away. "Suddenly you're sure. Before you said it was inconclusive."

"The guy from New York—the NYPD fingerprint expert—he says it's Georges's. No question about it."

"Then that's Thomas's fingerprint on the gun. Remember? Georges didn't drink the water. Thomas obviously filled the glass."

"You were right about that. The partial fingerprint on the gun doesn't match the fingerprints on the glass. Those prints probably are Thomas's. But I got Georges's fingerprints from this." He picked up the crystal vase on Anna's desk, the one that had contained the strange floral arrangement that Georges had used to introduce himself to his sister.

"There must have been lots of fingerprints on that vase."

"Presumably belonging to you, Mr. Melvin, Georges, and whatever florist made that weird arrangement. One of them matched the print on the gun. So, unless the florist did it . . ." Joe sighed. "I wanted to tell you before we bring him in."

Anna felt dizzy and slumped in her seat. She could come up with no more convincing explanation than that Georges had pulled the trigger. And even if she could, it wouldn't help if Georges were guilty. Joe would test Georges's fingerprints from the man himself.

But Georges was kin.

It occurred to Anna that Samuel Grayson had kin, too—a batty grandmother—and that Anna needed to find the truth to bring justice to Samuel, though his grandmother thought he was just out of town.

Anna could not flinch. Who would she be if she flinched? She would be a flincher. Maybe she was a flincher.

She realized that Joe was kneeling beside her, that his arms were around her. "Anna, I'm so sorry."

Anna twisted free from his embrace and stood up. She did not feel like cuddling. She wanted to hit something. She punched Joe on the shoulder and ran.

§

It was 5:00 p.m. when Anna let herself into Georges's hotel room. The place felt ominously empty. Still, she called out, "Georges? Thomas?"

No one answered. She threw her purse, coat, and hat onto the settee. She wandered through the suite, finding no one, except the pampered little dog who slept on a cushion. She needed to speak with Georges, to ask for an explanation, because she couldn't think of one. She opened the door to his study. It smelled like her father's study, of cigar smoke, wood polish, and leather. And, another scent—something faint but recognizable—the spicy scent of a Blanc man—a male body wearing Old Bay Rum. The scent evoked a jumble of feelings Anna couldn't even name. Her whole life, her family had consisted of one man—a father whom she had loved and who had, at last, abandoned her for bringing shame upon him. And then Georges came along. Now, against his will, Georges would abandon her too. He would leave her for the gallows.

Anna ran her fingers along the books in the oak bookcase: *The Commercial and Financial Chronical*; novels in French by Flaubert, Victor Hugo, and Dumas; and *The Language of Flowers*. He must have taken it from her father's house. She moved to his desk looking for a clue, anything that might give her direction. She found nothing but a sense of guilt. She was a bad sister. She pinched herself. And a bad detective. Even though she wasn't a cop at all. She pinched herself twice.

Anna stripped off her matron's uniform and frillies. She donned a nightgown and *robe de nuit* that she'd bought with Georges's money. She flopped onto her bed that was Georges's bed in Georges's hotel room and cried until her head ached.

The clock chimed 5:30. She felt the mattress sink under the weight of someone's body as he sat beside her on the bed. A hand stroked her hair. "*Ma douce sœur.* Is it Joe Singer? What has he done? Should I have a talk with him?"

Anna growled, "Your fingerprint is on the murder weapon."

Georges was silent for a moment. "That's impossible. And how can he know that? He doesn't have my fingerprint."

"He got it from that beautiful vase of interesting flowers you gave me."

"It must be a mistake."

"A fingerprint expert from New York made the match."

Georges sighed. "What was the murder weapon? A knife? A revolver? A bottle of poison?"

"A revolver."

He thought for a moment. "I owned a revolver. I kept it in my automobile. But it was stolen weeks ago along with my umbrella and a blanket."

"Why did you have a revolver?"

"Rich men are sometimes held up on the road, Anna. Highway men."

"Did you report the gun stolen?"

"What's the point? I'll never see those things again."

Anna rolled over and looked up at him trying to see if he was lying—if he lied as easily as she did. Her father, too, was a liar with his second family and hidden fortune.

Georges's dark eyes seemed sincere, but she could rarely tell when someone was lying.

"There was one print on that gun and it was yours." She glared. "Aren't you scared? They could hang you!" Anna buried her face in her arms. "And then where will I be?"

"Anna, I didn't do it. I didn't kill that man. I never met that man. You have to believe me. Why would I kill him? I didn't give him money. I was innocent. I had nothing to lose. No wife. No one to be angry with me. Possibly father, but he would be one to talk, that hypocrite. Only you. I only have you."

A knock sounded at the door. "Police. Open up." The voice sounded stiff and determined. It was Joe, come to toss Georges back in the hoosegow. Joe was right, it had been a mistake for Georges to leave town to convalesce. Now they thought he was a flight risk. Joe would haul him off to the bull ring and his lawyer would not be able to get him out. Not this time when the charge was murder.

Anna buried her face again. "Don't open it. Tell Thomas not to open it."

"Thomas is off tonight. I have to open it, *ma chère*. He'll break down the door." Georges stood and left her bedroom.

Anna could hear his footsteps cross the hotel suite and the front door latch click open. This time, it was Wolf's voice she heard. "Georges Devereaux. I hate to trouble you. But you are under arrest for the murder of Samuel Grayson."

Chapter 45

Anna rose, her eyes puffy and swollen, and followed Georges into the living room, wearing her flowing, lacy *robe de nuit*. Joe was cuffing him. He had puffy eyes too. He looked bereft. Wolf stood by looking pained. He wandered over to Anna. "Hello, honeybun."

Anna tried to speak, but only made a sad little squeaking sound.

Joe wouldn't look at her at all.

Georges said, "Good night Anna. I'll see you tomorrow. Don't you worry. I'll be all right."

Anna's jaw trembled. "Where were you four weeks ago on Tuesday? The day Samuel Grayson was killed?"

"I don't know."

"I'm coming with you."

"Honeybun, you might want to get dressed first."

Anna looked down at her *robe de nuit*. "Oh."

Wolf said, "I'll take Mr. Devereaux. Joe, you stay and wait for honeybun to get dressed. She'll need an escort to the station."

"I won't go with him."

"We'll all wait," said Joe.

Anna strode back into her bedroom and began to undress. She cursed her buttons, her hands trembling. It took her half an hour to don her frillies and change into a clean matron's uniform. When she reemerged and saw Georges seated on the butterfly settee with his hands in cuffs, she ran to the bathroom and leaned over the sink. She thought she might vomit.

Joe came to the bathroom door. "Anna. Are you all right? Sweetheart, I'm sorry."

She was horrified that he might hear her throw up, and she was horrified in general. Her words dripped with Gila monster venom. "Go away."

He did.

Her stomach settled a little. She brushed her teeth, washed her face, and steeled herself. She retrieved Georges's medicine from the medicine cabinet, because if anything would give him a fit, this would. Then, she strode into the living room with her head held high. "I'm ready."

Joe put his hand softly on Georges's shoulder. "Let's go."

§

Anna slept sitting upright in a chair outside Georges's felony cell—that is to say, she didn't sleep at all. Georges tossed and turned in his hammock, accompanied by three foul-smelling, criminal louts who swung in a row like worms in their cocoons. A fourth slept on a mat on the floor beneath the hammocks. They weren't mere hoisters and hoodlums. They were murderers. Anna wanted to talk with Georges, but she didn't know what to say and they had no privacy.

The following morning, the newspaper circus began. Georges's picture and details of his arrest were plastered on the front page of both the *Los Angeles Times* and the *Los Angeles Herald*. Anna wasn't sure which patrolman had leaked the information to the press, but she said a silent prayer to Saint Roch, patron saint of the accused, that their lives would be forever devoid of love—like Anna's would be if Georges were to hang.

The *Herald* especially was cruel in an article written by Mr. Tilly.

Would we really be surprised if the Blanc line proved to have criminal blood? Scores of Angelinos lost their savings when Blanc Bank failed. Why, then, is Georges Devereaux so rich? From prostitution? Or did Christopher Blanc hide assets with his son? Daughter Anna has certainly lived a dubious life, and it's taken its toll. Many agree, she is losing her bloom . . .

It continued to excoriate for half a page. Worst of all, it included an unflattering picture of Anna dressed in her ugly matron's uniform, her face still not fully recovered from her Gila monster bite. Her father would be livid.

The next week was a blur. Everyone at the station stayed hushed around Anna, who spent her days at the station learning to sew pillowcases with Matilda. Anna also sewed hers shut. She went downstairs to sit outside Georges's cell and to make sure he took his medicine; but men were constantly having to use the chamber pots, driving Anna away. Thomas had meals delivered from the hotel, as well as clean clothes for Anna, who now slept upstairs in the matron's quarters. Thomas took her dirty clothes away to be laundered.

Though Georges smiled and thanked Anna when she brought him his food, he wouldn't eat or otherwise speak to anyone except his attorneys. His lead attorney, Earl Rogers, had brought in reinforcements in the form of seven more attorneys—Davis and Rush, Dunn and Crutcher, Norman Sterry, Oscar Lawler, and Samuel Hawkins. Mr. Rogers came daily, alone or with all or some of Georges's counsel. They had private conversations with Georges in one of the station's interview rooms. Anna wanted to be part of their conspiring, but Georges said no.

It didn't matter. She couldn't help. Her brilliant brain felt numb. If Georges were innocent, she couldn't find the logical path to that conclusion. Neither could she believe him capable of first-degree murder.

She closed her eyes and tried to visualize what had happened that day in Griffith Park—what she had seen. She and Joe had gone there to make love, he with the pretense of hunting bank robbers, she with the pretense of hunting a truant.

He later did hunt bank robbers—bank robbers who had killed a bank teller. Murderers.

Anna took the defense attorney aside. "Mr. Rogers, the day Samuel Grayson was killed, Detective Singer was hunting for some bank robbers who were camping there. Later, he caught the bank robbers. They were in Griffith Park. Perhaps Samuel Grayson stumbled upon their encampment. Maybe he saw them counting money or heard them talking about robbing banks, so they shot him. At least one of them is a known killer."

Earl Rogers raised his eyebrows with interest. "Really? Thank you, Miss Blanc. I'll look into it."

§

While Georges waited for his own hearing, Mrs. Rosenberg was indicted by the Grand Jury. Some thirty girls and women, ladies rounded up by LAPD patrolmen, testified against her. She pled guilty to having led girls astray, was sentenced to twelve months in county jail, and was fined a thousand dollars. The district attorney decided not to allow her to testify against any of the implicated men, as it would have given her immunity. He wanted her to pay for her crimes. Clearly punishing bad women was more important than punishing bad men.

The wealthy, weakly architect, Octavius Morgan, managed to elude indictment altogether when the Henry twins, the prosecution's star witnesses against him, slipped out of the station one afternoon and were never seen or heard from again. In fact, the entire Jonquil Apartments had emptied. The girls—those who had testified against Mrs. Rosenberg—had scattered to other cities without a trace. W.H. Stevens was in Mexico and could not be reached to testify that he had paid Samuel Grayson on Morgan's behalf. In a final blow to Georges, Joe verified that Morgan had indeed been in Fresno at the time of Samuel Grayson's murder.

Georges went before the Grand Jury. Though no girls testified, he was indicted and would stand trial on three counts—kidnapping, degenerate practices with minor girls, and murder in the first degree. Earl Rogers assured Anna that Georges could escape the Black Pearl rap with the twins gone and the Jonquil empty, providing Allie Sutton didn't crawl back out of the woodwork. Thus far, Joe had been unable to find her. Matilda was the only one to place Georges at the Jonquil Café, and she was not right in the head. She would never be allowed on the stand, and even if she were, she could only say she saw him there, and that was not a crime.

The murder rap, Earl Rogers said, would be difficult to beat because Samuel Grayson had tried to blackmail Georges, and Georges's fingerprint was on the gun.

The mayor hated Georges because Anna's father had lost the mayor's money. He found the meanest judge in Los Angeles to preside over the trial, and the most cunning prosecutor. Deputy District Attorney Keyes was to prosecute Georges's case. Anna knew Keyes by reputation. The detectives rejoiced whenever the district attorney assigned Keyes a case they had investigated. He almost always won. This time, the detective did not rejoice. In fact, the detective—Joe Singer—had lost weight. He never smiled or swapped stories with the other men, which wasn't like him at all. A cloud hung over everyone at Central Station. All the men looked at Anna with pity in their eyes, except for Detective Snow, who sneered. Matron Clemens left cupcakes on Anna's desk, possibly baked by one of her over-abundant children. Anna ate only four, then selflessly gave the rest to the ladies in the cow ring.

Weeks passed, and Anna suffered. She returned to the street that was full of tailor shops and canvassed again with a photograph. "Please, do you know this man or why anyone would want to kill him?"

No one did.

She visited the Cock in the Walk, armed of course, and hung about the ladies' lounge with the charity girls, hoping to hear something, some clue, that could lead to Georges's exoneration.

She returned to the scene of the crime searching for some piece of evidence she had overlooked, but spring rains had washed the scene clean. Anna was out of ideas. She simply wished the trial would happen and be done with.

§

The evening before his trial, Anna sat outside Georges's cell, simply turning her head and covering her ears when the men used the chamber pot. She stayed with him into the night, though Georges had little to say. He just sat, unshaven, in the dark, on the edge of his hammock in his striped jailbird clothes and rocked. The other men in the cell whispered stories about crimes their friends had committed and gotten away with—a bank robbery, a counterfeiting operation, a revenge killing. Anna suspected they were telling their own stories, thinly veiled for her benefit. They were men without conscience. Georges did not belong among them. Finally, the jailer came and ordered the men to be quiet.

At midnight, Georges stood. "Go to bed. You'll need your sleep."

She had become bored in their silent sorrow and agreed. She rose. He took her hand through the bars and squeezed it. "I've left everything to you, of course. All father's wealth will be yours." He smiled weakly. "He will be at your mercy. You won't be too hard on him, will you?"

"You didn't do it, did you, Georges?"

Georges face turned red and his voice betrayed anger. "Not you, too, Anna. Of course I didn't kill Samuel Grayson."

"Then father will never be at my mercy because you won't hang!" Anna spoke with desperation. She pictured the man in Yuma swinging from the gallows, the crowd jeering. Her memory mated with fear, and then the man wore Georges's face. He was Georges, now swinging, struggling at the end of a rope.

CHAPTER 46

The morning of the trial, Wolf snuck Anna a bottle of good whiskey, as Anna's bottle from Georges had long been drained. It wasn't the same quality, but it had the same effect, and Anna was grateful.

Wolf sat with Anna in her closet with the door closed. He clinked her glass. "To Georges."

"To Georges." Anna tossed back two glasses in succession.

"Captain Wells gave you unpaid leave for the trial?"

"Yes."

"You need to borrow some money?"

"No. I have Georges. It's not fair that Octavius Morgan doesn't have to stand trial and Georges does. So what if he has an alibi for the murder. He's obviously contributed to the twins' downfall. I saw him eating with them."

Wolf said, "Eating with twins is not illegal."

"They as good as told me he ruined them. It was understood. One can't speak explicitly about these things although I'd like to."

"It's hearsay."

"Octavius Morgan, with his manly weakness. He disgusts me."

"Matron Blanc, I'm speechless."

"It's true. He must have given the twins money and spirited them away to who knows where. They would never have just left on their own. They had nothing." She sighed. "I'm worried about them. They'll kill each other."

"We'll watch him. We'll get him on something else."

329

"I'm sure he's cozying up to the mayor right now, to make sure that doesn't happen."

"There's uh, something you should know."

"What is it?"

"The mayor sent private detectives to look for Jonquil girls, especially Allie Sutton. I'm afraid he hasn't forgiven your father. Joe sent them up to a movie studio in Santa Barbara with a subpoena."

The news hit Anna like a wrecking ball. "Of course he did."

"Honeybun, have another drink."

§

The Los Angeles County Courthouse sat up on a rise above the corner of New High Street and Temple. It reigned majestic in red stone with a jutting clock tower and giant palm trees standing guard in relief against the blue sky.

At the top of the steps, a woman stood delivering a speech through a megaphone. Anna recognized her as the elderly speaker from the Friday Morning Club. The lady called out, "Years have taught us that men will not assume the work of being our sisters' keepers. Women, it is up to us. So long as there is an 'unprotected' woman in the world there are no truly protected women."

It occurred to Anna that for once, the Friday Morning Club was not on her side. The lady was here to support any girls testifying against Georges. Anna doubted herself. And then she kicked herself for disloyalty.

Wolf escorted Anna up the crowded stone steps, which stretched up the side of the hill. Inside the marble atrium, Anna was elbow to elbow with men pushing to get into the courtroom to see the trial of the fallen millionaire, Georges Devereaux. She was blinded by flashbulbs, her ears assaulted by their deafening reports as Mr. Tilly and other newsmen snapped her picture. She held a hand up to block her face. Wolf wore his badge and his authoritative face. "Police. Let us pass." He ushered Anna through the crowd to the elevator, pushing to the front. When the doors opened, he led Anna inside the wrought iron cage and blocked anyone else from joining them. As the doors closed, the reporters ran for the stairs.

Anna felt untethered, like she was floating above her own nightmare looking down at her beleaguered self and this tragedy. Wolf's boots looked very shiny. She could almost see her face in them. She wondered how he got his boots so shiny, if he did them himself or had a boy do it. She looked at her own less shiny shoes. She should have given them to the maid.

When the doors opened on the fourth floor, Wolf escorted her to the courtroom where the trial would soon begin. She heard the reporters' footfalls as they charged down the hall after her. She did not turn but glided on Wolf's arm into the courtroom. The photographers followed, flashing away.

The judge's grand mahogany bench rose above the room like the throne of God. The jury was seated below in their box. There were tables for the defense and the prosecution. Spectators, like Anna, were relegated to pews set behind a wooden railing.

Jeanne Devereaux already sat in the back in a sea of men. Her eyes were closed, her mouth moving in prayer. Anna tensed, hoping she remained discreet. If Jeanne Devereaux were revealed to be Georges mother, he was doomed. On the wall above her, the motto of the superior court was painted in black, "Gently to hear, kindly to judge." Anna hoped it were true. She hoped the judge was more merciful than God.

The woman from the Friday Morning Club entered the courtroom carrying a sign that read "Fair play." She would not meet Anna's eyes.

The pews were filling up. Wolf flashed his badge and made two men move to give Anna a seat near the front. He sat beside her and stayed with her, leaning close to whisper in her ear, "Don't you worry, honeybun." His breath smelled like whiskey. She must, too. She wondered if that sordid detail would make the papers.

Everything about the courtroom felt ominous. The jury of

twelve men were clearly in a sour mood. The judge looked dyspeptic. The prosecution looked cheerful. The great Earl Rogers appeared nervous and kept sweeping back the cowlick that threatened to escape his straight, brilliantined hair. The seven other members of Georges's legal defense couldn't all fit at the table and had to form a ridiculous second row of chairs, crammed too close to the first wooden pew. Two of the men were whispering to each other. They began to laugh.

Anna wanted to scream, "This is my brother's life and you're toying with it!"

An officer led Georges into the courtroom in handcuffs, setting off another frenzy of noisy flashbulbs. He squinted at the brightness of the cameras, bringing his arm up to block the glare. He wore his finest suit and stood tall, like a Blanc. Anna prayed he wouldn't have a fit.

The dyspeptic judge, the meanest in Los Angeles, banged the gavel and called the courtroom to order. Anna's head spun. She was only vaguely aware as the charges were read and the judge admonished the jury to be impartial. The deputy district attorney made his opening statements. "The Jonquil Café, Resort, and Apartments, where many young girls gathered from department stores, restaurants, and other places of employment were alleged to have been lured to meet wealthy men, plied with alcohol, and ruined . . ."

Etcetera. Etcetera.

Joe took the stand for the prosecution. He told about finding Samuel Grayson's body in Griffith Park. For the first time, Anna was glad she hadn't been officially on the case. She would have to testify. The prosecution gave the jury pictures of Samuel's body, covered with ants, just as they had found him, with the gun lying in his open hand. They passed them around.

Joe told how Samuel had been kneeling, and how he knew that from the marks on his pants and in the dust. If Anna hadn't deduced his position, there's a chance that Joe wouldn't have noticed, and the death would have gone down as a suicide. Maybe Anna herself had sealed Georges fate. She began to tremble.

Or maybe Georges had sealed his own fate. Anna pinched herself hard for thinking it.

Earl Rogers stood and paced as he cross-examined Joe. "What were you doing in Griffith Park?"

Joe's face turned crimson. "It's not relevant to the case."

He was thinking of Anna. In his quest for honesty, would he throw Anna to the wolves, too?

Earl Rogers smiled. "I think it is."

"Well, some bank robbers had been spotted in Griffith Park." Misleading, but true.

"Did you catch the bank robbers?"

"We caught three of them later that day."

"Would you say they were dangerous men?"

"They shot a bank teller. So, yes, I would say they were dangerous."

"And they were in Griffith Park when Samuel Grayson was killed—also shot?"

"Yes."

"Did it occur to you that those bank robbers might have killed Samuel Grayson when he stumbled upon their secret encampment? Maybe he overheard them speaking about their crime. Maybe he saw bags of money."

"I didn't like them for the murder."

Earl Rogers smiled. "You didn't *like* them for the murder? Why not? They were present. They had a potential motive."

Joe spoke with confidence. "Instinct."

"You disregarded them as suspects because of instinct? Even though they were present, dangerous, and had motive? Isn't that a little cavalier? I mean, what if your instincts were wrong, Detective?"

"They weren't wrong."

"How do you know?"

"I questioned them thoroughly. I don't believe they ever saw Samuel Grayson. They acted surprised."

"Could they not have been good actors, Detective Singer? Con men often are."

"I'm a good judge of—"

Earl Rogers waived his hand. "No more questions."

Joe's face turned red as he left the stand, and Anna almost felt sorry for him.

The coroner testified. The fingerprint expert testified. W.H. Stevens, now back from Mexico, testified in exchange for immunity that Samuel Grayson had demanded money from Octavius Morgan, and that Morgan had paid through Stevens himself. Allie Sutton did not testify, and Anna began to relax. The private detectives had not found her in Santa Barbara.

The trial veered into the dull as the defense brought the first of fifty different character witnesses to the stand to testify in Georges's defense—bankers, businessmen, the president of the Chamber of Commerce, chairmen of boards, a priest. Anna wondered if the strategy was to drown the jury. The judge adjourned the court after ten such testimonies, to resume the remaining forty on the following day. Each witness had said roughly the same thing—that Georges was upright, generous, civic-minded, godly, and that they've never known him to have anything to do with loose women or, in fact, ladies at all. He was a confirmed bachelor.

The following day the jury would hear testimony from the remaining character witnesses. It promised to be more of the same— more boredom, more confusion, more horror.

CHAPTER 47

The next morning, Anna waited for the trolley in front of the Hotel Alexandria. She planned to take the trolley to a stop three blocks from the Courthouse where Wolf had said he'd meet her to escort her to the trial. This would avoid any scandal of being seen together in the morning at her hotel should the press be lurking. The weather was gray and cold, and mist clung to her hair. She stuck her hands into her pockets to warm them, fingering a coin and a button left there from another day. Probing the far corners of her pocket, she found a folded piece of paper. Anna unfolded it and read silently:

Dear Matilda,
    You may as well go with me as you have no other option.
Am I really so odious?

Her lip curled. It was the note from the man from Mars, the man who had drugged and violated Matilda, the man who had driven her mad. Anna hadn't thought enough about Matilda because she'd been so caught up in Georges's troubles. She wanted to exonerate Georges because he was her brother, but Matilda had no one. Matilda needed Anna too.

Anna examined the note, letting the ink words prod at her numb, mixed-up brain. Surely her mind was only dormant, not gone entirely. Surely need could arouse it. She rubbed the note between her fingers. The stationery was thin and plain. Anna would have thought it too plain for the kind of men Mrs. Rosenberg catered to. Rich men always used a better quality of paper. This was paper for the masses. She held it up to the light looking for the watermark.

It was stamped, "Mars Paper Co."

Anna's brain began to whir. Mars paper. Was it the paper, and not the man, that was from Mars? Or was the man from Mars, too? Why would a wealthy man use such plebeian paper? He couldn't use proper personalized stationery to leave notes for wronged girls—not if he were to remain anonymous. Still, why use such bad paper when he could afford a finer grade? Why would he even have it in his office?

Perhaps if he owned the company. It was thin, but the paper company was her only lead.

Anna strode back to the hotel and took the rumbling elevator up to Georges's suite. "Thomas! Where is Georges's Brownie?"

§

The Mars Paper Company stood on Eleventh Street, not far from the tracks. Anna arrived by hansom with Georges's Brownie loaded with film. The brick factory stood three stories tall, with airy windows on the second and third floors. She dismounted near the factory loading dock where two men heaved bundles of paper onto a wagon. The paper looked dingy, like newspaper without the ink. Anna swung through the front door, making bells jingle, and found herself in a wholesale paper shop. A clerk presided over the bulk sale of envelopes, cheap sheet paper, low-grade stationery, and butcher paper. Anna saw no high-end stationery. Anna's own writing paper was whiter, a heavier weight, and monogrammed. It was a shame her stationery now had the wrong address—the address to a life she no longer lived. She would have to get new and charge it to Georges.

The Jonquil Apartments did not cater to clerks, so she flounced right past this one. "Don't mind me. I'm just looking for a . . . you know." She moved behind the counter and toward a door labeled "Employees Only," looking for a bigger fish.

The clerk called out, "Hey!"

Anna ignored him. As he moved to follow her, the bells jingled again, and a customer entered the building, splitting the clerk's attention and he hesitated. Anna slipped through the door into a hallway that smelled like new books. She bolted the door behind her. Light streamed in from a row of high windows that caught the morning sun. She moved down the hall until she came to an office with a name placard, "Mr. Elmer Clark, Proprietor."

Anna knocked. No one answered so she let herself in. The office ceilings rose fourteen feet, and she could see the exposed steel beams. The office was modestly furnished, but a rather good portrait hung on the wall. It showed a lanky man in his prime, healthy, but not handsome. His suit and facial hair placed him in the 1880s. Was that the man from Mars? If so, he must be old now.

Anna noted a second door inside the office, which she planned to explore next. She shuffled through papers on the desk. Bills, mostly, for papery things like pulp and glue, and one from a physician. A full brandy decanter rested on the desk by two crystal snifters. Anna picked up the decanter, removed the stopper, and sipped from the top. She sipped again, because she was thirsty. She opened a drawer in his desk. She found coins and a five-dollar bill, which she pocketed. She found a good pen and a silver matchbox, which she also took. In the next drawer she discovered three medicine bottles— bimeconate of morphine, solution of podophyllin—described on the label as a liver tonic.

And a bottle of chloral hydrate.

Chloral hydrate. It's what M.M. Martinez, the proprietor of the Esmeralda Club, had slipped into a young girl's drink before he and his friends had their way with her. He was caught and fined one hundred dollars. The girl had been sent to reform school.

Anna took the chloral hydrate and emptied it into the brandy decanter.

She heard a toilet flush and spun about just as the second door opened. A tall, spindly man with a jaundiced complexion and yellow eyes emerged from it in a cloud of stink. His fingers were so long as to be grotesque, but his suit was very nice. Anna's eyes widened. "Jupiter."

He smiled at her the way men sometimes did; that is to say, there was something obscene about it. "Well, good afternoon, young lady. What are you doing in my office?" He crept closer.

Anna wanted to spit. Instead, she collected herself. "Good afternoon." She smiled and bobbed a curtsey. "This is a lovely paper company. The paper is so . . . white." She fluttered her eyelashes and backed toward the door.

"Why, thank you."

He took ownership of the paper; thus, he must be the owner—the proprietor, as the door plaque said. Anna grimaced. "You probably use it for writing notes and such, even though it's plebian."

He frowned. "Well, I do, but . . . Why are you here?"

Anna opened her purse and retrieved the Brownie. She raised the camera and snapped his picture.

"Wait a minute. Who are you?" He looked mad.

"Josephine Singer, I'm with the *Herald*."

He gave her a look of disdain. "You're not with the *Herald*. You're a woman."

"I'm actually a man in disguise."

His face registered confusion.

"We're doing an article on the Jonquil Apartments, on the men who drug and deflower young girls. Are you one of them?"

His eyes bulged.

"I'll take that as a yes."

Before he could stop her, Anna turned tail and ran.

§

Anna took the Brownie back to Central Station to the LAPD

darkroom and added the film to the queue to be developed. There was no way Mr. Clark could be Samara Flossie's Black Pearl. He was simply too old and ugly. But he was very likely Matilda's man from Mars.

CHAPTER 48

Holding Wolf's arm, Anna attended Georges's trial the following day. She had missed a parade of character witnesses, as well as the testimony of an officer of Georges's bank who said no checks signed by Georges had been written to anyone named Samara or Flossie. There were no telltale check stubs. No financial trail supported the accusation that Georges was the Black Pearl.

Samara Flossie took the stand for the defense in a frilly frock meant for a girl, not a woman. Her hair flowed down her back, ornamented with a large bow, like a child. She looked younger, but ridiculous. Anna's neck prickled at her bad taste, or something. Samara Flossie swore on the Bible to tell the truth, then perched in the witness box. The lawyer, Earl Rogers, glanced at Georges and frowned.

He addressed her. "Miss Edmands, are you acquainted with the man known as The Black Pearl?"

"I am," she said.

"How do you know him?"

"He was my lover."

Earl Rogers paused. This was not what she had said before, not what they had practiced. "He *was* your lover? I had come to understand that you were engaged."

Samara Flossie shook her head no.

Anna looked to see if she still wore that ugly ring, but Samara Flossie's hands were folded in her lap and Anna's view was blocked by the rail.

"Is he in this courtroom?"

"Yes."

A hush fell over the crowded courtroom; Anna could hear the whir of electric fans. Earl Rogers' shoulders tensed. He swept back his cowlick. Anna knew for certain this was not what Samara Flossie had told Earl Rogers before.

Mr. Rogers ambled closer to the witness stand and smiled. "You were engaged to be married to this 'Black Pearl'?"

"Practically engaged."

Her hand came up and touched her face. Anna noted that she still wore the ugly ring, but on her right hand, not on her left ring finger.

"What is his real name, this 'Black Pearl'?"

"Georges Devereaux."

Anna heard a feminine gasp—likely Jeanne Devereaux. People were mumbling.

"How do you know that? Did he introduce himself?"

"No. It was in the papers."

"You're engaged to be married and you didn't know his name?"

"Practically engaged."

"No further questions, your honor."

Anna's eyes flitted to Georges. She couldn't read his face. She wished she could read people, like Joe could, and like them for this and that. Anna began to sweat profusely. Samara Flossie had switched teams. Someone had paid her to lie on the stand. Perhaps the real Black Pearl.

Deputy District Attorney Keyes rubbed his hands together in rude delight. It was his turn to cross examine Samara Flossie, and there was nothing Anna could do to stop him. "Miss Edmands, when Georges Devereaux went before the Grand Jury, the court served you a subpoena, but you did not appear. Neither were you found at home."

"Yes. I was out of town."

"Where did you go?"

"San Diego."

"Why would you go to San Diego when the court had served you a subpoena. That's breaking the law. You could be fined."

"I was paid one thousand dollars if I would leave the city and not testify against the Black Pearl. That would more than cover any fine."

"Who gave you this bribe?"

"I don't know. A private detective. He didn't tell me his name." She bent down and dug into her purse, bringing out a stack of bills and setting them on the stand. "Here's the money. You see? Proof."

"Why did you come back?"

"The LAPD hired private detectives, too. They found me and brought me back. I was kept under guard until today, when I was brought to court."

She hadn't been kept in Anna's jail, which was probably deliberate on Joe's part.

"I see. You say the Black Pearl is in this courtroom?"

"Yes, he is."

"Are you sure?" The prosecutor walked over to where Georges sat. "This man? Georges Devereaux. He is the Black Pearl?"

"Yes."

Georges looked at Samara Flossie. She dropped her eyes.

"But the Black Pearl is just a name. It's not against the law to be called 'the Black Pearl.' Tell the jury what he did."

Her voice rippled with emotion. "He seduced me when I was just fifteen and unspoiled—lured me with gifts and money. I had nowhere to turn."

Anna knew that was taffy. Samara Flossie had already confessed to being Grayson's lover, and she was nineteen when she came to the Jonquil. And she'd already said Georges was not her lover.

"What about his temperament. How would you describe him? Is he even-tempered?"

"No! He's jealous. He's violent. And he threatened poor Sam. He said he would kill him if he ever came near me."

As she spoke, she carefully avoided looking in Georges's direction.

"And did you go near Sam?"

"No. I never did. I was too afraid."

Also taffy. She'd delivered a letter to Samuel Grayson's apartment.

It was Earl Rogers's turn to cross-examine the witness. He ran his hands through his straight-slicked, brilliantined hair and paced before the witness. "Miss Edmands, how old are you?"

"Sixteen."

"You look nineteen or twenty."

Samara Flossie frowned. No woman wanted to hear this. It was an insult.

He continued. "In fact, you were nineteen when you came from Oklahoma City with your lover, Samuel Grayson. Isn't that right?"

"I know how old I am."

"So do I, Miss Edmands. So do the police. May I remind you that it is a crime to lie under oath."

"I—"

"Back to Samuel Grayson. You were lovers. Then what happened?"

"We were not lovers."

Earl Rogers smiled. "You told Detective Singer that Georges Devereaux was not the Black Pearl. Now you are saying that he is. Did someone pay you to change your story? Perhaps the real Black Pearl? Is that where you got that thousand dollars?"

"No!"

"No further questions."

§

Anna's hopes rose when the defense called Joe Singer to the stand. He knew Samara Flossie was lying, and Joe always told the truth.

Samara Flossie stepped down from the witness stand passing Joe Singer on the way up. He gave her a hard look. She cast her eyes to the tile floor and strode quickly down the aisle, sliding into a pew in the back.

Joe took his seat on the stand.

Earl Rogers cleared his throat. "In the course of your police investigation, you've questioned Miss Edmands before, is that not right Detective?"

"That is correct."

"Did you show Miss Edmands a photograph of Georges Devereaux?"

"Yes, I did."

"Would you say it was a good likeness, Detective Singer?"

"Yes."

"A clear likeness."

"Yes."

"Is this the same photograph?" He held up the newspaper page with Georges's picture.

"Yes. It's from the same issue."

He walked to the jury box and handed a juror the picture to examine and pass around.

"What did Miss Edmands say about the photograph? Did she say Georges Devereaux was the Black Pearl?"

"Quite the contrary. She said Georges Devereaux was not the Black Pearl. She was certain. She said the Black Pearl had blond hair. No. She said golden hair."

Anna couldn't help it. When Joe glanced down at Anna, she smiled at him.

§

When the court adjourned for lunch, Joe sought Anna out, fighting the crowd until he reached her side. "Sherlock, can we talk?" He gave Wolf a look, the meaning of which eluded Anna. "Wolf, would you excuse us?"

Wolf raised his hands in tacit permission. Joe grabbed Anna's arm, leading her out into the corridor and deeper into the building, away from the crowd. He opened the door of a broom closet and pulled her inside. It was dark and small.

He faced her. "You smiled at me. You know how long it's been since you smiled at me?"

She put her arms around his neck and kissed him, long and sweet. She kissed him again. She felt like she was in the Sonora desert, once more outside of Yuma, thirsting in the sun, and Joe was the champagne she needed to sustain her.

When she paused for breath, he asked her, "What was that for?"

"You destroyed Samara Flossie's testimony."

"I was telling the truth."

"She wasn't."

"Anna, something's happened between Samara Flossie and the Black Pearl. They're no longer almost engaged. It's why Samara Flossie flipped her testimony. She was protecting him before. Now, she's a woman scorned. She wants revenge."

Anna stepped away from him. "So, you're saying her pack of lies is proof that Georges is the Black Pearl? Hah! That he tried to pay her off?"

"Anna. I know he's your brother and you love him, but you have to face the facts. Otherwise, you're in danger. What if he killed Samuel? What if he's bringing rich men to the Jonquil to ruin young girls? He's bad news, Anna. I want you away from him."

"I'm not afraid to face the facts. Because I know in my heart that Georges isn't capable of murder. Just like you know I didn't do it, and I know you couldn't do it because, although you're being a complete ass right now, you're too good. And there's such a thing as being too good, Joe Singer. Throw any fact at me, I'm not afraid."

"Georges had a motive. He has no alibi. His print is on the gun."

"I'm taking my kiss back." Anna tried to kiss him backward, to suck back her kiss, but it didn't work. It seemed very much like she was kissing him again. She tried it once more.

Joe Singer was kissing her, taking nothing back. He held her to him with a sort of desperation. Anna rubbed against him to wipe his touch back off. And there it was. His cock stand, and his hand on her bottom through three blessed layers of fabric.

"Yes," she whispered. "No. Yes."

"I love you, Anna. I've never loved anyone like I love you."

"No, yes, yes, yes."

He dropped to his knees in the dark.

§

Anna emerged from the closet glowing and confused, with Joe Singer on her lips, wondering if she knew anything at all about the world. They returned to their separate seats, Wolf scooting to make room for her on the pew. She felt Wolf's curious gaze on her. Anna turned around to look at Joe with wide-eyed wonderment.

He stared at her with longing across the courtroom.

A man entered and hurried down the aisle, passing a note to the deputy district attorney. The prosecutor seemed pleased, and Anna's thoughts snapped from Joe's dreamy, suffering eyes, back to the trial. The deputy district attorney stood and asked permission to approach the bench. Earl Rogers followed him, and they whispered with the judge. Anna, who had completely unwound in the closet, wound tight again.

Earl Rogers shrugged to his legal team as he returned to his seat. He whispered to one and began a game of telephone; the message passed from lawyer to lawyer along the chain.

The prosecutor stood. "I call Allie Sutton to the stand."

Anna paled and wound tighter. They'd found her. They'd found Allie Sutton. Anna looked at Wolf, wide-eyed. "It's not his turn. The prosecution is done bringing witnesses."

"She's on the witness list, but they couldn't find her. Apparently, she's just now been found. The judge is going to allow it."

"Can't we stop it? She was in league with Samuel Grayson. She's a blackmailer."

Wolf's lips flattened. "No, honeybun. I don't believe we can."

Allie Sutton waddled from the back of the courtroom, obviously pregnant. She swore on the Bible and took the stand.

The deputy district attorney began. "Miss Sutton, did you live at the Jonquil Apartments?"

"Yes, I did."

"What did you do there?"

"I slept and ate mostly." She turned to the judge. "That's a silly question."

"Were you gainfully employed at the time?"

"Yes. I'm an actress. And I write scenarios for the movies."

"Did you have a relationship with the Black Pearl?"

She looked down. "Yes, I did."

"And how old were you when this liaison began?"

"Sixteen."

"Sixteen." He paced. He was trying to be dramatic. "Sixteen and unspoiled."

"I didn't say that."

Tittering erupted in the courtroom. The prosecutor coughed uncomfortably. "Sixteen nonetheless." He paced some more. "What was the nature of your relationship?"

"We were lovers. He wooed me, like any other suitor. Flowers. Gifts."

"Money?"

Allie Sutton colored. "Yes. But it wasn't like that. We were in love, he and I."

"Maybe you were in love, Miss Sutton, but I doubt Georges Devereaux was in love. He eats little girls for breakfast, doesn't he?"

Earl Rogers jumped to his feet. "Objection, Your Honor."

The dyspeptic judge scowled. "Sustained."

"Who else was Georges Devereaux in love with. How many girls did he ruin at the Jonquil Resort?"

Allie Sutton asked. "If you please, who is Georges Devereaux?"

"The Black Pearl. Your lover." The deputy district attorney seemed put out.

"I was his only lover. Where is the Black Pearl?"

"He's the defendant, sitting right here." He gestured to Georges.

"That's not the Black Pearl. The Black Pearl has golden hair."

A low rumble of voices shook the courtroom like a trembler.

"But that's not what you told police."

"From a picture in the newspaper. The ink was badly smeared. It's true, this man here is like the Black Pearl. He's got the same cleft chin, similar shoulders. But I assure you, the Black Pearl has golden hair. This man has black hair. Besides, I know the father of my baby. It isn't him."

"It isn't who?"

"The defendant—Georges Devereaux did you say? He is not the Black Pearl."

Anna squeezed Wolf's arm and whispered. "See. He's not him."

The deputy district attorney scrunched his eyebrows together. "Are you still lovers?"

"No. I left the Jonquil Apartments and hid from the Black Pearl."

"Why?"

"I found out he was married. I want nothing to do with a married man."

§

Joe, unsmiling, was recalled to the witness stand. He would surely tell the truth and discredit the one witness who spoke in Georges's favor. It was the right thing to do. He would do the right thing. He always did.

The deputy district attorney mopped his forehead with a handkerchief. "Detective Singer, did you bring Allie Sutton in for questioning?"

"No. She brought herself in."

"Did you show her a picture of Georges Devereaux from the newspaper?"

"No. She brought in the newspaper and showed Assistant Matron Blanc and me. She said she was sure he was the Black Pearl."

"Was the ink on that photograph smeared?"

"Not that I recall."

"No more questions." The deputy district attorney returned to his chair.

Joe remained in the stand, and Earl Rogers stood. "You say you don't recall if the ink was smeared." He said it like a statement, not a question.

"I didn't say that."

"Yes, you did. No further questions, your honor."

Joe's ears turned red. He came down from the witness stand and took his seat. Anna's stomach flipped. Earl Rogers had just taken another bite out of Joe Singer. She wanted to sit with him and cheer him up. With her lips. She kicked herself for thinking it. Then she kicked herself for kicking herself. She thought about the very lovely broom closet, then pushed it out of her mind.

The defense called Georges. He rose with dignity, like a Blanc, and took his oath. His black hair was perfect. Anna sat up straighter in her seat.

Earl Rogers began. "Georges Devereaux, are you the so-called Black Pearl?"

"No. Of course not."

"Did you know a man named Samuel Grayson?"

"No, I did not."

"But didn't he write you a letter threatening to tell the world you were the Black Pearl unless you gave him large sums of money?

"He threatened to tell my wife that I slept with girls at the Jonquil Café."

Earl Rogers leaned up against the stand. "Mr. Devereaux, are you married?"

"No."

"Have you ever been married?"

"No."

"The victim didn't know much about you, did he?"

"We had never met."

"Had you corresponded?"

"He sent me one letter. I never responded."

"Did you sleep with girls from the Jonquil Café?"

"Absolutely not."

"Then, why would Mr. Grayson think you did?"

"I ate at the Jonquil Café for lunch."

"You were a regular customer?"

"No. Just three times. I had a series of business meetings there. When my business was concluded, I never returned." Georges made a face. "I wouldn't recommend it."

There was tittering in the courtroom.

"I should say not. How did Mr. Grayson know where to send the letter?"

"It is my belief that he followed me home and asked the doorman for my name. The note was left at the front desk of my hotel. My name was spelled wrong."

Georges continued to answer Earl Rogers's questions to great advantage. Until Mr. Rogers asked about the gun. Then Anna noted that Georges was gripping the wooden edges of the witness stand, his knuckles whitening. He began to tremble.

Anna stood up, frowning at the front of the room. "Excuse me." She began forging her way between knees and pews.

"Honeybun, where you going?" Wolf stood. He nodded to the man on his left. "Excuse me."

Georges fell face first onto the witness stand. Anna cried out. She ran forward as he began to convulse and slipped off his chair onto the floor behind the stand.

"Help!" Anna ran to him, knelt, and tried to hold his head.

The room became noisy with voices. Someone shouted, "He's an epileptic."

Christopher Blanc appeared at Anna's side, along with Joe, Wolf, the bailiff, Thomas, who had brought a syringe, and Mr. Tilly. Joe helped Anna cushion Georges's head, which smacked hard against their fingers. Mr. Blanc squatted and peeled down Georges's clothes to bare his shoulder. Anna made a sound of distress and frustration. She looked up to see Jeanne Devereaux hovering on the margins. She saw Samara Flossie out of the corner of her eye. The girl looked smug. "Adios."

Flashbulbs went off with noisy clicks, blinding Anna.

As the men held Georges's limbs, Anna's father looked up at Mrs. Devereaux with soft eyes. "Sit down."

She disappeared from Anna's view. More flashbulbs and noisy voices. The judge banged the gavel. "No photographs in the courtroom! You are out of order."

Thomas forced the needle into Georges's arm, and, at last, he stilled.

Chapter 49

Anna sat by Georges's bed as he slept a morphine sleep, under house arrest. Wolf wandered the apartment drinking Georges's good whiskey and touching things. He came in and out of the bedroom. She heard him drop something in the living room. Joe stood in the bedroom doorway looking defeated. "That was pure genius, even if it wasn't on purpose."

"You think he had a fit for sympathy? I take offense at that. He's sick."

"I know. But since epileptics are more susceptible to moral failure, they'll go easier on him."

"You still think he's the killer."

"I don't know. I just know you aren't seeing straight."

"I'm not seeing straight? You're not seeing straight. You're wrong about my brother."

"Sherlock, prove me wrong. And don't start with your conclusion—that Georges is innocent—and build your case backward."

Anna made a sound of objection, her mouth open like a cave in a mountain of confusion. Had Anna done that? It wasn't very detectively, and it didn't show faith in her brother.

She closed her mouth. "Fine. I resolve to be brave. I'll face any hard truth about Georges or about you, Joe Singer. I will see straight. That's how I will catch the real killer."

"Okay," he said softly and put his hand on Anna's shoulder. "And I'll be fair. As fair as I can be. I'll be your sounding board."

Anna closed her eyes and concentrated, trying to be brave, trying to think like a cold-hearted cop and not like a sister. She arranged the facts in her mind, rearranging, turning them around to consider them. She pictured the park, the trail, Joe's cock stand. "I'm being heartless like you and it still doesn't add up. Tell me this, detective—how would Georges lure Samuel Grayson to Griffith Park? Not to the park entrance, mind you, but halfway up the mountain. To go for a hike? Clearly the answer is no. You don't hike with your blackmailer." Anna paused.

"Keep going."

"I'm thinking . . ."

"Think out loud, Sherlock."

"Who would go hiking with Samuel Grayson or who would Samuel Grayson go hiking with? Not Georges. Maybe his neighbor, Lester Shepherd. They were friends. Except Samuel Grayson wasn't there to hike. He wasn't wearing hiking clothes, even though, I'm sure, they make orange ones. He was wearing that awful, expensive, rust-colored suit. He had dressed his best—which wasn't too well because he had awful taste."

"I'll give you all of that. Samuel Grayson wasn't there to hike."

"Why was he there?" Anna paced to the dresser, paced back to Joe, standing in the doorway.

"To meet someone who he was blackmailing."

"He could have done that at the trailhead. It's isolated enough. There was no one around the day we found the body."

"So why was he there?"

"Why were we there?" Anna asked.

Joe whispered in Anna's ear in case Georges could hear. "To make love? That's why I was there. It's the most romantic spot in Griffith Park."

His breath on her neck made Anna tingle. It made her angry at her body. "Then, tell me this, how did Georges lure Samuel Grayson up to the most romantic spot in Griffith Park? Was he wooing him? Or being wooed? Is that how he got him to kneel? Did Samuel propose to Georges?"

"You're being facetious, right?"

Anna put her hands to her cheeks. "Jupiter. I had a brain wave."
"What?"

Anna crossed to the bed, leaned down and kissed Georges on the
forehead. "I'll be back." She grabbed her purse and called, "Thomas,
I have to step out. Joe, I need a cop."

Anna flew out the bedroom door, passing Wolf in the living
room, who fumbled the expensive vase he'd been examining. He
barely caught it. "Honeybun, where are you going?"

"To catch the real killer."

Joe followed Anna as she strode to the elevator. The elevator boy
did his job, ignoring them.

"It was Samara Flossie, Joe. She was wearing that ugly diamond
ring, that ugly, ugly ring. It wasn't from the Black Pearl. It was from
Samuel Grayson—the only man in the world who could choose a
ring that ugly."

Joe buried his face in his hands and groaned.

"Her hand was bruised, remember, I told you? Like mine after
I shot Mr. Rooster's mustache off in Chinatown. Her bruise was
from the revolver, because she didn't know how to handle a gun.
Samuel Grayson proposed, on one knee, and Samara Flossie shot
him, reverse execution style."

"Okay. What's her motive?"

"Because she wanted to marry the Black Pearl and Samuel was
in the way. He had threatened to write her father to tell him where
Samara Flossie was. Her father would have dragged her back to
Oklahoma, or shot her, and maybe the Black Pearl, too."

"That doesn't explain Georges's print on the gun."

"It's Georges's gun all right—his *stolen* gun. Who knows where
Samara Flossie got it. Probably from that pawn shop across from the
Jonquil Apartments."

"Her prints weren't on it."

"She was out of doors, Joe. She wore gloves."

The elevator rattled as it descended. The door opened, and
Anna and Joe strode into the hotel lobby.

"She left him a note right before he died. The apartment manager saw her slide it under his door," said Anna.

"So, she arranged the meeting."

"Yes." Anna produced gloves from her purse and slipped her hands into them. "The trial is going very well. If Georges is found innocent, Samara Flossie can expect to be indicted for blackmail, though I doubt she was involved. She's going to run, if she hasn't already."

"Where is she? Not back at the Jonquil."

"No. I don't know."

They raced out onto the sidewalk and stopped, lacking direction. The morass of moving bodies, animals, and automobiles reminded Anna that they were looking for a needle in a haystack.

"She can't go to the real Black Pearl. She doesn't know his name or where to find him. He's probably married, anyway. I doubt she has an auto, but she has all that money. She'll probably take the train."

"La Grande Station then. But which train? Riverside? San Diego? San Francisco? She may have already left."

"We can take Georges's car. My old car." She flashed a brief smile.

"It will take five minutes to start it."

Joe stepped into the street to hail a hansom.

Anna closed her eyes and pictured Samara Flossie and her smug look as Georges convulsed on the floor. What did she say? Anna's eyes popped open. "Her last word to me was 'Adios.' Lester Shepherd said Samuel and Samara Flossie had planned to go to Mexico."

"She'll take the train to Yuma, then down to Mexico. If you recall, that train leaves at four o'clock. It's four now. We're going to miss it."

"Trains can be late."

A hansom stopped. Joe handed Anna in. "La Grande Station please. A dollar if you go fast."

They rode in agitated silence, jostled by the motion of the speeding hansom.

They arrived at the train station with its turrets and domes and sprang from the hansom without paying. Joe took off running in his practical man boots. Anna flew after him in her Louis heels. She turned her ankle and fell forward onto her hands. "Biscuits!" She got up and limped after him onto the platform where a stationary train began to roll. Joe was nowhere to be seen. Anna grabbed a rail and leapt on board. "Police! Stop the train! I don't want to go back to Yuma!"

She moved down the aisle of the car, checking every face. There were handsome faces and ugly faces, fat faces, thin faces, smooth faces, bearded faces—all seated. One man walked down the aisle away from Anna. He cast a glance back over his shoulder. Anna did a double take. He wore an impossibly bushy beard for a young man. It was twenty years out of style. Beneath his beard, an ugly, baggy, rust-colored suit offended Anna's senses. She abandoned her search and quickened her step to catch up to the suspicious young man. "Wait!"

The young man too, gained speed, now jogging through the aisle toward the door.

Anna could see he had the full bottom of a woman. She spoke, slightly out of breath. "It's no use running, Samara Flossie. If you leap from the train, I'll follow you. I'll hunt you like a . . . like . . . like a really good hunter."

Everyone stared at Anna. The bearded lady disappeared through the door of the railcar. Anna limped after her. The train rolled slowly out of the station. Samara Flossie stood in the doorway, contemplating a jump. Anna had always wanted to play football but had never been given permission. She took a flying leap and tackled the lady. The two fell off the train.

Anna landed on top of Samara Flossie. It knocked the wind out of her, and undoubtedly hurt. They had landed on the gravel slope that lined the tracks. The bushy beard now hung askew from Samara Flossie's lovely face.

"Flossie Edmands or Samara Mowrey—I'll call you whatever

you'd like—but you are under arrest for the murder of Samuel Grayson. Confess, you villain!" Anna captured her hand and bent back the lady's fingers.

Samara Flossie screeched. "Stop!"

"Confess!"

The lady smiled and rolled her body violently, tipping Anna off. Anna held tight and rolled back on top of Samara Flossie and down again, rolling over and over to the bottom of the slope, their bodies pressed together between the gravel and the sky. They landed in a sloppy ditch with Samara Flossie on top. Anna's head hit a rock and she felt momentarily stunned. Samara Flossie put her hands around Anna's neck and squeezed. Anna's head sunk into the muck up to her ears. The ugly engagement ring bit into her skin. The lady leveraged herself on Anna's neck and jammed her knee into Anna's diaphragm.

Anna couldn't catch a breath, couldn't expand her lungs nor open her throat. Her head felt cold from the muck. Joe Singer had gone with the train.

Suffocation was a terrible feeling. She would much rather fall off a cliff or be shot in the heart. This was not her death of choice. Thus, she collected her wits, reached up and yanked the villain's hair. The lady's hairpiece came loose in Anna's hands. Samara Flossie laughed, and only squeezed harder. Anna's strength was slipping away. She heard Flossie hiss in her ear. "I did it. I killed Samuel Grayson." Then Samara Flossie laughed.

Georges was innocent. Of course he was. This gratified Anna, and the gratification gave her strength. Anna felt with her hands for anything to use as a weapon but could feel only mud. She scraped up a handful and pushed it into Samara Flossie's face. It plopped back down into her own face. She felt dizzy and her vision began to darken. She reached out again with her hands and grasped something cool and metal, something long and steel. She struck.

The next thing Anna knew, Joe Singer was shouting her name, patting her cheeks. "Anna! Wake up!"

Her neck hurt. She spit out mud. "I'm not asleep."

Joe kissed her dirty face.

Anna pushed him away. "Don't touch me!"

§

The following day, Anna had a ring of purple bruising around her neck and a concussion of the brain. Samara Flossie lay in the receiving hospital, handcuffed to the brass bedrail and tended by Matilda. The patient's eyes rolled in her pretty head, which had a dent in the temple from the railroad spike Anna had used to biff her. The handcuffs were a formality. Wolf had already called the people from the Asylum for the Insane and Inebriate to take her away. She would never stand trial. The doctor said, shy of a miracle, she would never be mentally competent. Perhaps this fate would hurt worse than hanging.

Georges returned to court to complete his testimony with Anna supporting him from the front pew, Wolf staunchly at her side. Georges remained poised and stuck to his story, though he looked tired and pale. Then Anna testified for the defense, wearing a low collar so everyone could see her bruises.

Earl Rogers, in his closing arguments, told of Samara Flossie's murderous father, her flight with Samuel Grayson from Oklahoma City, how she quit Samuel Grayson to take up with the Black Pearl. How she killed Samuel Grayson so he could not write to her father. He recounted Samara Flossie's flight and confession and her attempt to murder Anna. The jury returned after ten minutes and found Georges innocent on every count. Anna tried to give Joe Singer an evil stare, but he was shaking his head, looking at his lap. She, too, looked at his lap one last time.

CHAPTER 50

When men in white coats had taken Samara Flossie away, Anna summoned Matilda into Matron Clemens's office and offered her the rocking chair. Matilda rocked gently, smiling up at Anna, blinking her blond lashes.

Anna held a newly developed photograph of the spindly, jaundiced man from the Mars Paper Co. She thought she would feel victorious at this moment—this moment of Matilda's vindication. She wasn't a crazy girl. She was a girl ill-used. Anna felt certain she had found the man from Mars. Maybe they could prosecute him, but Anna thought not. At least they could tell Matilda that she wasn't just batty.

But now that it was time to show Matilda the photograph, Anna didn't want to do it. Matilda would likely start rocking madly again. Maybe, she would cry, reliving the horror of it. To stall, Anna reached in her pocket and offered Matilda a horehound candy. "Candy?'

"Thank you." Matilda took the sweet and popped it in her mouth.

Anna waited a moment, smiling, and then fed her another. And then another, unwrapping them for Matilda and putting them into her mouth. Matilda, mouth full, began to look concerned.

Anna cleared her throat. "Matilda."

"Yes." She sounded garbled with her mouth full.

"I believe I've found the man from Mars."

Matilda's eyes went big.

"If I show you his photograph will you tell me yay or nay?

Matilda just stared.

"I won't make you speak to him or even see him in person. We won't be able to prosecute, but we could, perhaps, egg his house."

Matilda nodded slowly.

"And maybe I could convince Mr. Tilly to write something scandalous about him in the newspaper."

Matilda's eyes brightened.

"I do think he's gravely, terminally ill. He's not supposed to be that color. I looked it up in a medical book. Do you want to see the photograph?"

Matilda swallowed and spoke softly. "Yes."

Anna produced the picture of the spindly, jaundiced man from Mars Paper Co. "He's smelly, like you said."

Matilda winced, and her face turned red.

"Is it him?"

Matilda nodded again.

"I thought so. The Jonquil Café is no more. Mrs. Rosenberg is now in the county jail. That should make you happy."

She smiled. "Yes."

"And the man from Mars is likely dying. I myself am not all that sad about it. But you—you'll go on to live a full and wonderful life. You could, for instance, sell theater tickets door-to-door, or become a scullery maid."

"I'd like to be a police matron, like you."

Anna kissed her on the head. "You'd make a very fine police matron."

CHAPTER 51

Joe Singer appeared in the doorway of Matron Clemens's office. "Hello Miss Matilda. Assistant Matron Blanc, we gotta talk." He tossed Matilda a peppermint. She caught it and gave him a wary smile.

Anna hadn't seen Joe since Georges had been found not guilty. Her heart rushed with a flood of emotions she couldn't untangle. "Yes . . . No. I mean . . ." Anna narrowed her eyes.

Matilda leapt from the rocking chair and skittered out the door, dropping the peppermint on the chair.

"She's really afraid of arguments," said Joe. "She must have seen some bad ones."

"Yes." Anna, too, wanted to skitter out the door. And she wanted to throw herself into Joe's arms and tell him how relieved she was that Georges was safe. But he was the one who had endangered Georges in the first place. She didn't know what to do, so she picked up Matilda's peppermint and ate it.

Joe waited, looking spanking fine and faithless.

"I'm off now," said Anna.

"It's dark out. I'll walk you home."

"You can lurk at my side, I suppose. Not that I like your company or need your protection at all."

Anna clipped down the steps, strode across the station floor and out the door. She took the steps of Central Station quickly, leaving Joe behind, wanting to see him and wanting to run. He jogged to catch up with her and followed her in silence as she wandered, taking the longest route. She didn't want to go back to her hotel. She wanted to go east toward Boyle Heights and Hollenbeck Park where their love affair had begun on a sting operation months ago when a thousand obstacles stood in their way. Those obstacles paled compared to what they faced now, but Anna kept walking. She didn't want the walk to end. It would mean a greater end that she wasn't ready to face.

They ambled down Third Street. In the Third Street Tunnel, a group of young people sang in harmony, their song echoing off the walls.

You left me for another. . .

Joe began to sing along quietly. Anna loved his voice. She loved it more than any other voice in the world. More than Enrique Caruso, more than Lina Cavaliere, and more than any Vaudeville star she'd ever heard. Anna added her own voice to the harmony, but her notes sounded sour. She stopped singing.

Why had this man with his beautiful voice betrayed her? He had left her for another woman—lady justice—and then lady justice had betrayed him.

"So we're quits, I suppose," she said.

"I suppose so."

"I can't ever forgive you. You probably should just marry that piano girl—the one you almost married before."

"Nah. She wouldn't have me now. I threw her off for you."

"Yes, I'm sorry, but I didn't know you would try to send my brother to the gallows."

He looked down and smiled. It was the unhappy smile of a man defeated, a wistful smile of surrender. "What about you? What are you going to do? Since you won't have me."

"I'll never marry." She raised her chin. "I suppose I'll take a lover. Wolf maybe."

Joe flinched. "I suppose so."

"I'll probably just take a lover, and fall in love, and make love all the time. I won't miss you at all."

"I suppose not."

"I'll stay in Georges's hotel suite while he's away. They won't mind if I have a regular male visitor in the evenings, and they'll be discreet. We pay far too much rent."

"Oh." Joe was silent. "Where's Georges going?"

"He's going to Nice for a year to convalesce—away from the gossip and the newspapers. The trial took a lot out of him, you know, and his health is fragile."

Joe spoke softly. "I know."

"I'll keep working at the station, of course."

"Of course."

"And you? You're going to move to San Diego or something? It might be just the thing."

"Nope. I'm not moving for you." She saw anger in his eyes. "I'm staying right where I am—Central Station. Somebody's got to catch the Black Pearl."

Anna's heart lifted at this, though she didn't want it to.

They fell silent again until they neared the awning of the Hotel Alexandria.

In the shadows on the street, Anna chirped with false cheer. "Good night, Joe."

"Good night, Assistant Matron Blanc."

For a moment, she thought he might kiss her, but it was anger not passion that burned in his eyes. Anna hurried to the elevator, her own eyes glassy, her lip trembling. The new elevator boy stared at her rudely. She croaked, "The penthouse please." When the elevator door rattled open again, she ran to her hotel suite and flung its door open. She flew to the window to look out and watch Joe walk away, but he was already gone.

Chapter 52

Anna drove Georges, Thomas, and the little dog, Monkey, to La Grande Station in the bumblebee-yellow Rolls Royce convertible, which used to be hers, and then became Georges's, and now was hers again. She wore a new black velvet cape with a fox fur collar, and a matching fur hat, even though it wasn't that cold. She felt cold on the inside. The station's turrets towered over them like an Arabian palace. Those turrets always made Anna feel like she was living one of Scheherazade's fairy tales—this time it was a brutal one. She waited with Georges on the platform, along the dusty tracks, while Thomas handled Georges's trunks.

Georges groaned. "Never mind. I'm not going. I can't leave you alone."

"Georges, you have to think of your health first. Besides, I'm not alone. Clara and Theo will be home any day now. I have Matron Clemens, Captain Wells, Detective Wolf, Matilda . . ."

"But not Detective Singer."

"No." Anna's lower lip trembled. "I don't think so. Not anymore."

"I've come between you."

"It's not your fault."

"He's a good man, Anna. Even I can admit that. He's not rich, but he wants to do the right thing. You shouldn't be so hard on him. He loves you. Forgive him."

"The fact that you would say that after all he's done proves how good you are."

He laughed. "Believe me, Anna. I'm not that good." He put his hands on her shoulder and looked her in the eyes. "If you need more money—"

"Even I can't spend all that money in one year. And I have my salary."

He chuckled. "Seventy-five dollars a month. You can always put things on a tab for when I return. Then *ma chère*, I'll come back rested and ready to fight another day."

"And I'll be here waiting."

The train arrived, coming south through Santa Barbara, Ventura, and Oxnard. It would take Georges east to New York where he would then board a steamer to France.

Anna embraced Georges, not wanting to let go. He smelled of tobacco, Bay Rum, and Blanc man, like her father. Like home. It was a full minute before she reluctantly pulled away, allowing him to go. She stayed on the platform with the other well-wishers after he boarded. As the train began to roll, she waved her handkerchief furiously and smiled bravely.

Georges waved back from the window of his private railcar. "Goodbye, *ma chère*."

"Take care of yourself, Georges!" She blew him a kiss.

Behind him, in the background, Anna thought she caught a glimpse of a woman.

§

Anna let herself into Georges's hotel room, which was hers now. It felt empty without him. But Georges would be back. A year would pass quickly. He would send postcards and then he'd return, and they could resume the business of being brother and sister. She could be a spinster in his home for the rest of her life. Eventually, her father would come around. He'd have to. They had all his money. She would make sure Georges never gave it back. Then, they could be a family again.

In the meantime, she could get another maid—someone to

launder her clothes and set them out. Someone to choose her jewels and arrange her hair. Someone to keep her company. She would write to an agency tomorrow.

Anna wandered into her bedroom to stash her fur hat and hang up her cape. She crawled onto the bed, rolled over, and put the pillow over her head. By her cheek, she discovered an envelope and a little box wrapped with a bow—a gift. Georges must have hidden it under the pillow for her to find.

She opened the card. It read, "Forgive him."

Presumably, Georges meant Joe. She was stunned by Georges's goodness. Now, when his own life was so tumultuous, he was thinking of Anna. He wasn't the snob that her father was. He thought Joe was a good match for her. Because Joe treated Anna well, Georges had forgiven him like a living saint.

Anna cried, biting her fist. She wanted nothing more than to forgive Joe. But what kind of sister would that make her? Why had he had to persecute her brother? He threw Georges in a cell with criminals and subjected him to public humiliation. He had endangered Georges's life.

She couldn't do it. She couldn't forgive Joe. It violated her principles.

When her head began to ache, Anna forced herself to stop crying. She turned back to Georges's gift for distraction. Perhaps it would be jewels. In her experience, jewels could be salves to the soul. Anna pulled on the ribbon until it unraveled and opened the box. There, lying on a bed of blue velvet was a necklace—a golden cross studded with garnets.

The cross of the legion of dishonor.

CHAPTER 53

Anna lifted the necklace from the jewelry box. It was the cross the Black Pearl had given to all the girls at the Jonquil Apartments. Even as her mind took this in, her body revolted, her stomach twisting like a wrung cloth. She threw the necklace down hard.

Anna strode to the living room, picked up the phone, and called the hello girl. "Please get me Earl Rogers."

The phone rang. A young girl answered. "Mr. Rogers's office, Miss Rogers speaking."

"Yes, this is Anna Blanc, Georges Devereaux's sister."

"Hello Miss Blanc."

"Georges asked me to call. He's misplaced Allie Sutton's address in Santa Barbara. Surely your father has it."

The girl was quiet for a moment. "Yes, he did have it. But Miss Sutton is not in Santa Barbara now. She's on her way to Nice."

"Of course she is." Anna disconnected, then rang the hello girl. "Hello. Get me Central Station. I have to report a criminal."

§

Two hotel maids packed Anna's things while she lay on her bed and numbly ate a chocolate cake. It was covered in chocolate roses gilded with real gold foil. She may never have such fine chocolate cake again.

Three bellhops arrived to take Anna's trunks and load them into a wagon waiting below. She took one last look around Georges's chic apartment. "Goodbye lovely suite. Goodbye nice things." She followed the men to the elevator and down to the street in a daze.

At the curb, Anna climbed into the front seat of the wagon next to the driver. The driver looked at her expectantly, then said with some exasperation, "Miss Blanc? Where to?"

"Oh," she said and gazed blankly down the street, eyes unfocused. "To the Streeter Apartments, 502 First Street, please." Her voice sounded tentative, not like a lady speaking to her driver. She felt broadly apologetic, as if she owed the whole world an apology, and that they—the world—would not accept it. Should not accept it.

Anna wondered if Joe had heard the news yet. How could she ever face him when she'd been so terribly wrong? Surely if she had been open to the truth, she would have deduced that Georges was the Black Pearl. The facts shouted it: his presence at the Jonquil Café, perhaps even dining with the man from Mars; Samuel Grayson's blackmail attempt; the flipped testimony of his two lovers; the Black Pearl's lavish generosity. Joe had sensed it all along, and she had badly abused him for it—for being a good detective.

It was no longer a question of whether Anna could forgive Joe, but whether Joe could forgive Anna. She didn't think so. She remembered the anger lighting his eyes when they parted with no kiss goodbye. That was before he knew she had violated the principles of their profession. She was no better than Joe's father, and Joe could barely stand him.

§

The driver took an hour unloading Anna's things and trying to find space for her trunks in the little crammed apartment. Finally, Anna told him to take the trunks of new hats and gowns away.

The phone in the hall rang and rang. She didn't answer it. Someone pounded on the door, sounding irritated. "Anna Blanc? Telephone!"

Anna ignored the woman. There was no one in the world that

Anna wanted to speak to. She took off her clothes, donned a night-gown, and flopped onto the bed. The phone rang again, followed by pounding. "Miss Blanc! The tube!"

Anna put the pillow over her head. It rang a third time, interminably. More pounding. Anna ignored it. Sometime later, more knocking.

Anna tried to doze. She became aware that someone was throwing rocks at her window. She crawled across her bed and pushed the heavy drapes aside. A woman stood in the dark alley wearing far too many ruffles and a floppy hat meant for daytime. A neighbor angry about the telephone ringing off its hook? Anna opened the window. "Please leave me alone!"

She moved to shut the window and the lady charged. Anna instinctively jumped back, too startled to scream. It was the murderous Flossie Edmands all over again. Fear rose in Anna. She swept up a sterling silver shoehorn from the shoe rack. The lady leapt, grabbing the sill, and hoisted her body up. Anna struck her on the head with the shoe horn. She struck again, hard.

"Ouch!" Undaunted, the intruder began slithering through on her belly. Her gown rode up exposing hairy legs, drawers, and a backside that Anna would have known anywhere. Her heart began pounding. She wasn't thinking clearly. She should have closed the window sooner because now Joe Singer was climbing through. He landed head first in the small space between her bed and shoe rack, bottom in the air.

Anna quickly drew the drapes.

Joe scrambled onto the bed and turned to face her. He had lost his hat. His wig was wild, like a Medusa. His skirt bunched around his thighs, and he was not sitting like a lady. He whispered with exasperation. "What does a man have to do to get an audience with you?"

"I'm so sorry. I'm so sorry." Anna backed away from him and into a stack of hat boxes. They fell, bounced, rolled, and opened, spilling their contents and stirring up a cloud of dust. Anna yelped in despair. Then she sneezed.

"Sherlock, you turned your brother in."

"He told me he was the Black Pearl. Not in so many words, but he did, because he wanted me to forgive you. But there was nothing to forgive."

"He told you because of me?"

"Yes, he thinks you are a good sweetheart, but he didn't know it was for naught and that you can't be my sweetheart anymore. So just go and catch the rat. He's on his way to Nice with Allie Sutton." She put her face in her hands.

"I can't arrest him. That would be double jeopardy. He can't be tried for the same crime twice and he knows it."

Anna glanced up. "But he drugs young girls."

Joe took off his wig and rubbed his head. "Sherlock, I don't think so. He's not a good man, and I want him far away from you, but I really don't think he knew about that. After the trial, I spoke with Mrs. Rosenberg again. She wasn't forthcoming, exactly, but I learned a few things. I think Georges was just a procurer, connecting rich men with young mistresses, bringing the Jonquil business. Also, he loans aristocrats money at usurious rates, and I think he might own an opium parlor."

"In Chinatown?"

"No. One for whites." Joe kicked off his skirt and began unbuttoning his shirtwaist.

He had wonderful legs, but it didn't matter now. She wanted to touch them but may not. "He's a rat, Joe, and I'm his rat sister. I crapped out." She made a sound of despair. "I'm a flincher!"

Joe stood in his underwear and waded through furniture and fallen hats to Anna. He still wore his boots. "No, baby. You're his good sister—his loyal sister."

Anna made a sobbing sound. "Really?"

He caressed her cheek. "Really."

"Maybe Petronilla wasn't against me. Maybe she was simply on the side of justice."

"Anna, I don't believe in ghosts."

"I just wanted a return of affection."

"What?"

"Jonquils, in the language of flowers, means to desire the return of affection. It's what we all wanted, I suppose—me, Allie Sutton, the girls at the Jonquil, even Georges."

"For what it's worth, I think the rat loves you." He drew her to his chest. "Even before you saved his life. Baby, you are one killer police matron."

She rested her wet cheek upon his chest. "Charlene is going to go to the new school for prostitutes. She's going to open up a frillies store."

"I'll be sure to patronize her establishment."

"Yes. And I caught the man from Mars, but he's dying."

"Oh?"

Anna looked up. "Matilda and I are going to egg his—"

Joe kissed her.

Author's Notes

Much of the story is fictionalized Los Angeles history. Petronilla really was cheated out of her father's land, which once included Griffith Park. She really did curse that land and then drop dead, so legend has it, to seal the curse with her blood. Misfortune did befall those associated with the land for generations. Look it up.

The Jonquil Apartments, café, and resort (bathhouse and massage parlor) operated at 807 South Hill Street, run by one Mrs. Rosenberg, who introduced young career girls to wealthy men to exchange sex for money. She took her cut. George Bixby, brother of police matron, Fanny Bixby, was arrested in 1913 for sleeping with two underage girls at the Jonquil. He was one of the richest men in California. He did not use his own name when visiting the Jonquil, so the girls referred to him as "The Black Pearl" because of his black pearl scarf pin, or "Mr. King" because of his majestic disregard for money. He visited twice a day, and gave all the girls at the Jonquil a gold cross, which they called "The Cross of the Legion of Dishonor."

Bixby fled but was arrested in San Diego. The architect, Octavius Morgan, testified at Bixby's trial that he himself had been blackmailed by girls from the Jonquil. George Bixby was found not guilty, and the young girls who testified against him were prosecuted for blackmail. Mrs. Rosenberg was charged with being the chief procurer for the Black Pearl and his millionaire associates and contributing to the delinquency of minors. She paid a hefty fine and spent a year in the county jail.

Was Bixby guilty? Look it up online and make your own decision. There are numerous newspaper articles available at https://chroniclingamerica.loc.gov.

The Azusa Street Mission was the birthplace of the Pentecostal movement, led by William J. Seymour, an African American preacher. It was notable for its racially integrated church body. The descriptions of the service come from eyewitness accounts.

So many little details in the book—too many to mention here—come from history. Earl Rogers was the best criminal defense attorney in Los Angeles at the time, and his daughter, Adela, did help him in his practice as a child. He really did stay at Pearl Morton's brothel whenever he got in a fight with his wife. He really did have a thing for Dolly the piano player.

The pulp novel quote comes from *The Privateer's Cruise and the Bride of Pomfret Hall*, one of Beadle's dime novels. Joe won the bet. The shrinking females do survive.

ACKNOWLEDGMENTS

My most sincere thanks to my family—immediate and extended—for their unfailing support. Many thanks to my editor Dan Mayer, and all the staff at Seventh Street Books, who waited patiently for this book. I want to acknowledge the reference department of the Denver Public Library, especially Joe, Steve, and Shelby, who dug up legislation related to "white slavery" from the 1900s. I am eternally grateful to my insightful beta readers: Joely Patten Eskens, Melissa Ford, Stephanie Manuzak, Jonathan Owen, and Liz Englehart (a.k.a. Elizabeth Bonsor). To my writer's group who provided comments all along the way: Serena Al-Darsani, Heather Bell, Sara McBride, Sarah Lurie, Rebecca Rae Parker, Cassi Clark Ward-Hunt, Michelle Ray, and Tiffany Hammond. Many thanks to Travis Miller who listened to me brainstorm. I am grateful to everyone at the Blair Partnership, especially Neil Blair, Zoe King, Josephine Hayes, and Amy Fitzgerald.

Most of all, I'd like to thank my readers. If you liked this book, please spread the word. Tell a friend. Post on Facebook. Write a review. It's the number one way readers find new authors.

ABOUT THE AUTHOR

Jennifer Kincheloe is the author of *The Secret Life of Anna Blanc*, winner of the Colorado Gold Award for mystery and the Mystery and Mayhem Award for historical mystery; and *The Woman in the Camphor Trunk*, a finalist for the Left Coast Crime Lefty Award for Best Historical Novel. She has been a block layer, a nurse's aide, a fragrance model, and on the research faculty at UCLA, where she spent eleven years conducting studies to inform health policy. Jennifer currently lives in Denver, Colorado with her husband and two teenagers, two dogs, and a cat. There she conducts research on the city's jails.